AN UNDENIABLE PASSION

Hawk leaned closer over Kayln, his breath mingling with hers. "Can you feel it, Kayln?" He whispered the words so softly she barely heard them.

The rapid beating of her heart told her she did indeed feel it. But she fought the sensations building inside her. As if saying the words aloud could make them true, she replied, "I know not what you mean, sir knight. I feel nothing."

"You lie, wench." He chuckled knowingly, his mouth so close to hers she could feel his breath on her lips. "You know precisely of what I speak."

She shook her head, trying desperately to force herself to move away from him, but she could not. A single word escaped her mouth. "Nay."

He placed one strong hand on her arm. She felt it burn her through the velvet of her sleeve and still she could not move. "Shall I show you, then?" he said.

LEISURE BOOKS NEW YORK CITY

This book is dedicated, with much love,
to my husband, Steve. Just because.

A LEISURE BOOK®

October 1997

Published by

Dorchester Publishing Co., Inc.
276 Fifth Avenue
New York, NY 10001

ISBN 0-8439-4312-2

Printed in the United States of America.

HAWK'S
LADY

Chapter One

England, 1357

The pounding of the horses' hooves drew the gazes of the peasants as they worked the ripened fields.

Kayln D'Arcy had donned a light woolen cloak, the hood thrown back over her shoulders, allowing the wind to whip her golden blond hair about her face. Unlike the contented expressions of the peasants, Kayln's visage was far from pleasant. Her gray eyes were narrowed over high cheekbones and her mouth was set in a grim line. Even the stiff angle of her slender body bespoke her anger as she bent forward, urging her roan mare to a faster pace.

The five men who rode with her, including her master-at-arms, Bertrand, were sorely tried to keep their lady's pace. Several times she felt the captain's curious gaze on her back, and there were frequent flashes of silver as spurs were set to tender flanks. But he made no comment on their haste, and for his unquestioning loyalty she was grateful.

The sun shone bright in a cloudless blue sky, heating her through the wool of her cloak. Kayln felt the perspiration pool behind her knee, which gripped the pommel of her saddle, and her fingers grew numb from holding the reins, but she barely noticed those discomforts.

Her temples ached in a tempo with the rhythmic throbbing of the horses' hooves, and she could not rid her mind of the vision of her sister Celia's white face as she told the name of the man who had fathered her child.

Philip Hawkhurst. Brother to the infamous Lord Hawkhurst, Baron of Clamdon. The baron was rumored to be a favorite of King Edward himself. Since his recent return from the war in France, she had heard the name Hawkhurst too often, mostly in connection with the man's ability to make war with a great deal of skill and enthusiasm. It seemed as if her men, including Bertrand, almost idolized Hawkhurst, even though they knew him by reputation alone.

Kayln cared little about the comings and goings of those who fought in the war. She must, of course, supply the men to fulfill her knight's fee, but the returning heroes' tales of daring did not impress her. The war had been going on for some twenty years, ever since King Edward III had declared himself King of France in 1337, and would likely continue for quite some time. There were many more pressing matters closer to home.

Celia's pregnancy numbered first among them.

Kayln dismissed the fact that Celia claimed to have been a willing partner in what had occurred. What did the child know of life? Men were little better than brutal beasts. They used women—or not—according to their will.

Clamdon was an old Roman fortress that had been built with every consideration toward its defensibility. When the Normans came, they had added further fortifications in the forms of a moat and a high outer wall that enclosed the village nestled beneath its protective and intimidating strength.

To Kayln's surprise, the guard allowed them passage through the open gate before Bertrand had even finished stating her name. They followed immediately behind a wagon loaded with fresh-mown hay. The sweet scent that drifted back to them was rich with harvest's promise, but did nothing to lighten Kayln's temperament.

When the lady and her escort approached the inner wall that enclosed the castle itself, she noted a great difference. The huge drawbridge was raised, barring visitors.

As they halted beside the moat, Bertrand called up to the guard. "Sirrah."

"Who goes there?" a voice hollered back, the owner not showing himself.

"The Lady D'Arcy," Bertrand shouted imperiously.

At the mention of a woman's name, the guard came out from behind the merlon to peer down at the small party. "State your purpose," he said, though more politely.

"I have private business with Lord Hawkhurst," Kayln called up to him before Bertrand had a chance to reply. She patted the neck of her mare as the roan danced restively, sensing its rider's agitation. She pushed her hair back from her damp forehead, then motioned from herself to her men with a gloved hand. "Surely you can see that we six are no threat to your master?"

The guard stood there a moment, scratching his head under the edge of his helmet, then nodded, obviously seeing the sense of her words. "Beware," he warned. It was only a moment later that they heard the squeaking of gears as the drawbridge was lowered and the portcullis was raised.

As her party crossed the drawbridge, their horses' hooves echoing on the dry oak, Kayln could not help but be awed. Twin towers stood over them on either side, great imposing sentinels with black arrow slits for eyes that followed them as they entered. She could see as they passed through it that the wall must be fifteen feet thick.

When the portcullis clanged shut behind them, Kayln had to repress a shudder at the feeling of being caught like a hare in a trap. Stiffening her resolve, she sat up straighter. She would not allow this place, or Hawkhurst, to frighten her.

The party found themselves at the edge of a wide green courtyard, well-cared-for outbuildings and animal pens grouped neatly about. Further back from these stood the inner keep. Kayln knew that in the event of an attack upon the castle, the women and children would be sent there for safety. The keep itself was a round structure some sixty feet high, and judging by the rows of windows, held three stories within. Unlike Aimsley, Kayln's own keep, even the top row of windows were mere arrow slits.

A groom came forward to take their horses as they dismounted. Directly upon his heels, another man approached the party. He was tall with a gray beard and hair, his eyes keen as he looked at Kayln. He reached out in greeting. "I am Harold, steward to His Lordship." As he raised his hands toward her, Kayln couldn't help seeing the ring he wore. It was a noteworthy piece made of heavy gold and bore two large emeralds. Noting her gaze, the steward smiled. "My seal of office."

He was obviously proud of the article. And well he should be, Kayln thought. Such a ring would cost nearly the earth.

Then she checked herself for allowing such a trivial matter to distract her. She was here for one reason and one reason only. To right the wrong done her sister.

Like a gale in treetops, a new wave of anger washed through her. Kayln threw her cloak back from her shoulders, staring directly into his eyes. "I have come to speak with your master."

"He will be informed of your arrival." Harold bowed respectfully. "But I must tell you Lord Hawkhurst is about the grounds at the moment and may be difficult to find."

Kayln could not repress a groan of irritation. "And just how long will it take to locate him?" Her anger burned deep, a hot flame of resentment inside her. Celia was the one person in her life whom she had allowed herself to love without reservation. And now Celia was pregnant without benefit of clergy and all because of a Hawkhurst.

"I do not know, my lady," the steward answered. "My Lord Hawkhurst answers to no one." His gray brows drew together in a frown and he looked at the ground.

For a moment, there seemed a trifle too much resentment in the servant's attitude. But when he turned to face her with clear blue eyes and a polite smile, Kayln realized she must be mistaken.

"If you would be so good as to follow me," the steward said. He motioned for her to move forward with a flourish. "I would see you made comfortable and served refreshment in the Great Hall."

Kayln D'Arcy stood firm. "I think not."

Harold appeared puzzled. He cleared his throat. "What . . . what do you mean, my lady?"

She raised dark golden brows. "I mean, sir, that I will not go with you. I will see Hawkhurst. And I will see him now."

Respectfully, Harold answered, "I assure you, Lady D'Arcy, that I will inform Lord Hawkhurst of your presence immediately."

Without deigning to reply, Kayln started off across the grounds.

Her men followed.

Harold ran to stand before her, blocking her path. "Excuse me, Lady D'Arcy. In deference to your position, I won't prevent you from doing what you will, but I must not allow your men to roam freely about the castle grounds. My master would be most annoyed. I will be forced to call the guards to detain them."

From the frantic expression in his eyes, she could see that the steward would not be moved on this subject. Turning to Bertrand, she saw that his hand rested upon the hilt of his sword. Kayln frowned. "Please do as he asks. I refuse to wait upon Hawkhurst's leisure. I wish to see this matter settled with all possible haste."

Bertrand made a grunting sound in his throat. "I do not think that would be wise, Lady Kayln," he told her, his brows furrowed in his craggy warrior's face. "We know Lord Hawkhurst by repute alone and that does not give rise to feelings of security as to your safety."

"I will be fine, Bertrand," she assured him forcefully, not wanting to discuss the matter further. "Go with his lordship's steward." She scrutinized the oppressive fortress around them. "I desire a speedy end to our visit here. This pretentious oubliette is little to my liking. I will attend you shortly."

Kayln stiffened when Bertrand looked as if he would say more.

He did not.

If there was one thing she had learned over the past six years of her widowhood, it was how to win obedience.

Kayln strode briskly through the wide green courtyard dotted with well-tended buildings and animal pens. She did not focus on any of the people working there, though she could feel their curious glances as she passed.

It was then that she heard a sound over the normal hum of activity. "You are an imbecile, boy," rumbled a deep voice with husky undertones. "Such stupidity has no right to exist. . . ." The rest of what was said became muffled by a gust of wind.

Kayln paused, horrified. She had seen too much of brutality in her childhood to be unmoved by it. Without thinking, she changed direction and hurried toward the sound.

Rounding the edge of a building, Kayln saw what looked to be the mews. The shouting was coming from inside, and now that she was closer, the deep voice was clear again. ". . . the hide flayed off of your backside for this." Thick, heavy nausea formed in her stomach and her hands grew cold and clammy at the very thought of someone beating a child. She had suffered too much at the hands of her own father to be indifferent to the misery of another.

Then she heard the sound of a boy's voice. He was sobbing uncontrollably, and Kayln winced at the pleading in his tone.

Not bothering to consider the wisdom of her actions, Kayln stepped through the open door. To her left, standing next to the bird perch, was a man. His back was turned to her and his attention was focused upon a hunched, quivering form against the far wall. Kayln had no time to take note of anything about the man except that he was tall and broad. As big as her father had been, though he was dark where Edward Chilton had been fair.

Her feet took her swiftly to the cowering boy and she leaned down to him. "Have no fear. I will protect you."

Then she swung to face his attacker. Her gaze came to rest first on the falcon perched upon the man's arm. Its golden eyes watched her intently.

Her gaze traveled upward across wide shoulders, a heavily corded neck, and a lean square jaw. The man's lips were thinned in anger under a slightly hooked nose. The straight hair that touched the collar of his white pourpoint was black as coal. Over the pourpoint he wore a black cotehardie. His legs were long and muscular in black hose. She took a deep breath and lifted her gaze. The deep molten gold of his eyes mirrored that of the bird he held. He watched her with anger, irritation, arrogance, and something that she might have believed was admiration had she not known better.

Instantly she recognized the man for who he was. Hawkhurst. He was so large and imposing she could easily believe the stories that were told about him.

The Lord of Hawkhurst exuded authority. His head almost touched the narrow beams supporting the roof of the building, his presence seeming to fill the space around him with energy.

He was decidedly the most disturbing man she had ever set her eyes upon.

The hairs prickled at the base of her neck, and Kayln forced herself to hold back a shiver that had nothing to do with fear. On a very primitive level, something about Hawkhurst made her aware of herself as the weaker female, and him as the more powerful male.

Suddenly the Lady of Aimsley realized what a dangerous situation she had placed herself in. Hawkhurst did not know of her identity as a noblewoman, and her men were back in the hall, unable to come to her aid should she have need of them. Kayln must be wary; Hawkhurst would not thank her for thwarting him. But she knew she could not walk away. Her hatred of cruelty would not allow her to.

His next words, spoken through tight lips while his gaze skewered her to where she stood, confirmed her thoughts. "What think you, madame, to interfere?"

Terror rose up inside her, swelling her pounding heart until it felt as if it were blocking her throat. She'd thought this suffocating fear long dead—put into the cold earth with her father. Not even her unpredictable husband had engendered such paralyzing emotions in her.

Fighting the heretofore buried reactions with all that was in her, Kayln raised her chin. "I seek only to make certain that an injustice is not done. Mayhap, I would take the servant as my own, rather than have him rashly punished."

"You know nothing of this fool's punishment." Hawkhurst scowled toward the boy, who was staring at Kayln with wonder.

"We will discuss this when you have gained control of yourself and remembered that we are speaking of a child," Kayln said with bravado, though she could barely hear her own voice over the frantic beating of her heart. Reaching down, she took the speechless boy by the arm and pulled him up to stand beside her. He offered no resistance, never taking his eyes from her.

To Kayln's absolute surprise, Lord Hawkhurst threw back his head and let out a loud guffaw. "And who might you be, madame, to interfere in my affairs?" It was as if he thought her puny defiance too insignificant to be bothersome.

"Kayln D'Arcy," she said through clenched teeth. What manner of man was he to toy with her so?

"My neighbor, Lady D'Arcy, Raymond D'Arcy's widow?"

"I am." She inclined her head. "And you could be none other than Lord Hawkhurst himself."

"Hawk," he instructed.

"Lord Hawkhurst," she offered stubbornly. She wanted no familiarity between herself and this barbarian.

He grinned widely, his teeth white and even. "You seek to bait me further, lady?" She was not fooled by the smile, for she could see the warning in his black lashed eyes.

Then, unexpectedly, Hawkhurst's expression changed, his features distorting in open annoyance. He reached beneath his belt, and a dagger appeared in his hand.

Having seen the same kind of abrupt mood changes in her father, she reacted without thought. Her heart leaping to a frenzied beat, Kayln threw herself in front of the boy to protect him. The knife whistled past her ear, and she realized with a quick prayer of thanks that he had missed. Taking a deep breath, she tried to slow her throbbing pulse. Kayln needed to keep her wits about her for there was no telling what might come next with this madman.

Making sure to place herself between Hawkhurst and the child, she whirled around to face the man, crying out, "You will have to kill me to reach him. And don't believe that you can do so without consequence to yourself. I am a woman of some worth and such an act would not set well with the king."

His black brows arched over the golden pools of his eyes as he asked, "You would defend the life of a rodent with your own?"

"What has this child done to make you hold him in such low regard? All men are of worth." Then, with narrowed gaze, she added daringly, "Admittedly some more than others."

Muttering an oath, Hawk strode toward them, and Kayln sucked in her breath, preparing for an assault. To her surprise, he went past them and stooped to pick up something from the floor.

It was a large rat, his knife imbedded in it. He straightened with a frown of disgust. "Have to keep rodents out of the mews," Hawk explained. "They kill the birds."

Kayln's breath came out in a rush.

The man had not been trying to kill them. Relief washed over her with cleansing sweetness.

Then, hard on the heels of this sweet weakness, a reaction set in, causing her limbs to shake. To cover her vulnerability she turned to him, her voice weak. "You could have missed and murdered either one of us."

Hawk strode to the door in two easy steps and tossed the dead animal into the courtyard. He turned and came back to her. Quirking one black brow, he leaned toward her to whisper with utter confidence, "I never miss." He wiped his knife and returned it to his belt.

Chapter Two

Kayln gaped at Hawkhurst's arrogance, unable to believe the absolute conceit of him. He stood with his feet braced wide, his free hand resting on his lean hip, totally confident of himself and his abilities with the knife. She realized there was nothing to be gained by arguing the point further. But there was another matter that she could not, in all conscience, have done with—had she a desire to do so. "The boy?"

"What of him?" Hawk asked, reaching up with his right hand to stroke the head of the falcon on his other arm.

"I beg your assurance that you will not treat him cruelly," Kayln insisted.

Hawk stiffened in mid-motion, speaking with obvious inflexibility. "That I cannot afford you, madame. The fool has come into the mews alone, when he was ordered to enter only under the supervision of the Hawk Master." He scowled with displeasure at the child's lowered head. "And loosed several of my best hawks in the process."

Though Kayln did not sanction the man's attitude, she realized this was no small matter. She asked the child firmly, "Do you realize what you have done?"

"Yes, lady." He peered up at her with watery green eyes, wiping his nose with the back of his hand.

Hawk's voice came from too close beside her, nearly causing her to start. "I take it that you see his actions as punishable?" he said.

Kayln controlled herself by focusing on the fact that though his words were polite, Hawkhurst was clearly making sport of her. It was as if he found her approval, or lack of it, amusing. "Of course," Kayln told him, then added, her tone resolute, "But I do not believe that even this warrants having the hide flayed off of a child."

Hawk blinked as if surprised, then frowned. "Why would you raise such a possibility?"

"You yourself were the source of my information," she answered, placing her hands on her hips.

His jaw hardened. "I have not yet decided on Samuel's punishment, so how came you to be privy to such knowledge?"

"I heard you as I came here. You were bellowing so that the very deafest of men could hear you."

For a moment Hawk looked puzzled. Then his expression darkened with irritation. "Look you, woman, I was but angry," he said slowly as if speaking to a lack-wit. "I must admit that my temper was sorely tried when I entered the mews and saw what had happened." He peered down at her, incredulous. "You could not possibly take such nonsense seriously."

His tone rankled, but Kayln chose to ignore it, not wishing to set off another spate of rage. The boy was still vulnerable to this man. No matter that Lord Hawkhurst said he was only speaking out of anger, she was not inclined to believe him. It was not within her realm of experience to disregard anything said by a man in a rage.

"You." Hawk turned to Samuel and made a shooing motion. "Go to your quarters. I will speak with Norton before I decide on your punishment. Mayhap you will be demoted from apprentice to the Hawk Master. It will take many hours to try to recapture those birds. If their retrieval can be accomplished at all."

When Hawk spoke of demotion, Samuel jerked around to stare at his master. To Kayln's utter amazement he ran across the room and grabbed the man's free hand. His sudden movements caused the falcon on Hawk's arm to flap its wings wildly. He began to plead, oblivious of the chaos he was causing. "Please, sir, do not set me down. I love the birds. I only came in to touch them."

Kayln watched this with marked surprise. What had happened to the child's terror?

At first, Hawk did not reply, occupied as he was in soothing the frightened falcon. Grunting with annoyance, he finally managed to calm the poor bird. "We shall see," he responded, his expression foreboding. ''If you someday hope to oversee my mews, you have much room for improvement, boy. My Hawk Master must care for my birds as if they were his own.''

For the first time Kayln thought to look about her. The mews was indeed in proper order. Fresh straw covered the floor to catch the droppings. The rests were well spaced and in good repair. The rat must have entered through the opened door, for the walls were sturdy, the holes patched. And the hawks themselves looked healthy and contented.

The child would lose much if denied the honor of such a position. But Samuel appeared only slightly chastened as he cried, ''Yes, I will learn. Oh, thank you, my Lord Hawk.''

''Now,'' Hawk ordered, ''off with you.''

Samuel turned and scuttled out.

''Why?'' Kayln shook her head slowly, unsure of the right words to use.

''Yes?'' He quirked a black brow, before turning to settle the bird on its perch.

''I don't understand.'' She rubbed her forehead. ''You were so angry a few moments ago.''

He was scowling when he looked around, eyeing her with displeasure. ''I have no need to answer to you, Lady D' Arcy, nor anyone else for that matter. But because of your concern for Samuel, I will tell you this. The birds will be found. They have been trained to the glove. It is simply a matter of locating them. Because of that I believe threatening to turn Samuel away from his apprenticeship, when his father and his grandfather before him have been Master-of-the-Hawk at Clamdon, has lessoned him well enough.'' His lips thinned as he went on. ''But should the incident be repeated, I will not be so lenient. And no one, not even you, fair lady, would sway me should I decide that punishment is required.''

She watched him, sensing the steel beneath the surface. She had no doubt that this man would mete out justice where and when he would. And no one, least of all an interfering woman, would deter him. Without thinking, she raised her chin even as she wrapped her arms around her chilled torso.

''Now.'' His tone changed to one of inquiry as he made it clear that he was the one in control. ''I am curious as to why you have graced me with your presence this day.'' He studied her with open speculation.

Suddenly, Kayln remembered her purpose in coming to Clamdon. Color rose to stain her cheeks as she realized how easily she had forgotten. Her sister's honor should have been paramount in her thoughts. Just the reminder of Celia's plight should rekindle her fury with this man.

But somehow, this incident with Samuel had drained Kayln of some of her anger, leaving her feeling limp, her arms and legs leaden. Kayln had been willing to fight if necessary to keep Hawk from harming the child, only to realize that the boy was in no danger.

Kayln looked up at Hawk, biting her lower lip, uncertain as to how to begin. As she did so, she saw that Hawk was standing much closer to her than he had been. Her eyes focused on the short stubble of dark beard that grew along his jaw. It looked wiry, and Kayln wondered if it would feel so to the touch. Raising her gaze higher, she could see his eyes, surrounded by thick black lashes, had tiny flecks of brown mixed through the gold. There was something almost hypnotic about looking into their liquid golden depths. The color swirled and deepened as their eyes locked, and she ceased being aware of anything but his nearness, the height and breadth and power of him. After a long indefinable moment, his gaze dipped to her mouth. Kayln suddenly realized that it was difficult to breathe, as if a tight band constricted her chest. Her lips parted.

Hawk leaned toward her, drawn by the unwitting temptation she offered.

The movement startled Kayln. What was happening here? If she didn't know better she would think Hawk was about to kiss her. But that was impossible.

Standing over her, Hawk suddenly seemed too large, too overwhelming. His shoulders were so wide, forcing her gaze to take in the hard expanse of his male chest.

She took an abrupt step backward, trying to think rationally. ''I believe we should talk in a more appropriate setting,'' she told him, needing desperately to leave the intimacy of this small space, with its musty scent of birds and straw. Without waiting for his reply, she turned and hurried out, taking a deep breath of air, feeling the gentle breeze cool her heated cheeks.

Unfortunately, Kayln had become so agitated that her unerring sense of direction deserted her. Now she was at a loss as to the best way to return to the hall. She looked around with consternation.

Somehow she knew she had to get control of herself. How had she allowed this man to disturb her so thoroughly? Over the years since Raymond's death Kayln had learned to hide any sign of uncertainty from those around her. It was the only way she, as a young widow, had been able to wrest control of the lands and people.

Yet in the space of a few short moments, this man had managed to expose that facade for what it was.

Hawk's husky voice came from behind her. "Allow me."

Kayln turned to see that he was offering his arm. She ignored it, gesturing to show that he should take the lead. She was not sure what had happened between them in the mews, but some inner instinct told her she should not allow Hawk to touch her.

Apparently, he did not understand her reluctance to come into contact with him, for she felt his strong fingers on her elbow. Even through the fabric of her sleeve they were warm and disturbing, sending a tingle of awareness through her that raised the fine hairs along the back of her neck.

She started away, unable to meet the puzzled gaze he turned on her. Whatever was happening to her she did not know, but she had no desire to try to fathom it out here before him. Her voice emerged a trifle breathlessly as she moved away from him, trying desperately to cover her reaction. "I thank you, my lord, but I have no need of your assistance. If you will but show the way I would be most happy to follow."

She nearly sighed her relief aloud when he started ahead with no more than a cryptic "As you will." The impression that he was amused by her persisted, and this helped her to gather her wits as her resentment toward him and his condescending manner simmered.

They met Bertrand and Hawk's steward before they reached the hall. Harold motioned toward Kayln with an elegant flourish. "Your lady, sir."

Bertrand ignored him, striding to Kayln's side. "Are you well, my lady?" It was almost as if he could sense her agitation, for he swung around to study the baron. "No harm has come to you?"

Harold tilted his chin in disdain. "As I told you, all is well. Why must you persist in these ridiculous heroics?"

To Kayln's complete surprise, Hawk's golden eyes fixed on the steward with warning. "Do not reprimand this fellow for seeing to his lady's well-being. Such loyalty from a subject is greatly to be desired. Let that be sufficient reason for you to hold your tongue." Here again was the steel, the exposed unrelenting core of the man.

Kayln watched as Harold seemed to be working hard at controlling himself, his Adam's apple bobbing with the effort. Obviously he was mortified at being chastised before them. Finally, he nodded his head and his gaze dropped to the ground. "Forgive me, my lord." He swallowed hard. "I but sought to see you sustained no insult."

Hawk swung around to study Bertrand with approval. "It is no insult to me that this man holds his lady in such high regard. You are forgiven—so long as you remember the lesson to be learned from this incident. Your own loyalty to me must be just as steadfast."

"Of course, my lord." The steward's voice was meek enough, but when he raised his eyes to his master's back, Kayln saw the burning hatred that glazed and hardened in his light blue eyes. Hawk would have need to watch himself with this one, she thought.

Then Hawk turned to bestow his full attention upon Kayln, his golden gaze capturing her own, and all thoughts of Harold were driven from her mind. "Shall we all make our way to the hall for some refreshment?"

Idiotically, Kayln felt a fluttering in her belly. Had there ever been another man born with such fascinating eyes, a man who could swing from anger to geniality in the blink of an eye? For the peace of all womankind, Kayln prayed not.

But she reminded herself that Hawk's geniality was no more than a cover to mask the dangerous emotions beneath the surface. As she followed Hawk's lead, Kayln told herself it would be disastrous to her peace of mind to allow herself to become involved with a man like Hawk. Unfortunately, the very thing that had brought her to Clamdon would likely force her into some sort of contact with the man. She bit her lip with consternation as she followed him.

As they entered the wide stone chamber, she could see two other entrances to the hall, one across from them and another at the front of the room. All opened directly into the hall, as it comprised the whole lower story of the structure. Looking about with both curiosity and trepidation, Kayln studied the home of this man called Hawk. The hall was large with a high ceiling, and the rushes underfoot were clean, though they gave off no pleasant scent as did the rushes in her own hall. At either end of the room stood huge hearths, eight feet wide and large enough for a tall man to stand in without bending. A fire was lit in one, and Hawk led them toward it. The room's one pretense at adornment hung over this hearth, a shield bearing the Hawkhurst arms, a belled hawk, rising, with wings displayed. Three great hounds were chained to one side of the fireplace. They whined and strained against their chains as their master came close to them. Hawk paused to give the nearest of them an absentminded pat, then moved to a trestle table that had been laid close by.

Kayln's men were seated at another table a short distance away, having been served their own refreshments.

Hawk turned to Kayln with a polite nod, offering her a seat. He took the place beside her.

Bertrand was still standing behind his mistress.

Hawk made a dismissive gesture. "Leave us."

Kayln felt herself stiffen. She had no wish to anger Hawkhurst now with what was still ahead, but Kayln wanted him to understand the situation. "Neither he nor any of my men will obey you. They answer to me and me alone."

Hawk swung around, his golden eyes candid as he met her gaze. She expected an angry retort, but he remained surprisingly calm, throwing her more off guard. "I beg your pardon, lady. I did not seek to usurp your authority. I fear I am too accustomed to ordering the activity in my own hall. You have leave to command your men so long as they do no harm."

Sharply she motioned for Bertrand to go to the others, but not for Hawkhurst's sake, in spite of this show of courtesy. She had no wish to discuss this delicate matter within her captain's hearing. The fewer people who knew of Celia's plight, the better.

Bertrand did her bidding. Hawkhurst watched this exchange without comment, but Kayln felt as if he were entertained by it.

Must this man always have the upper hand? Once again as he studied her, Kayln realized how alike his eyes were to the falcon's, piercing and shrewd.

A serving woman arrived with a pitcher of wine.

"Ah." Hawkhurst reached forward to take it. "I can see Harold has taken care of my comfort, as always."

Hawk filled the two cups the woman had brought and handed one to Kayln. As he did, their hands brushed. Kayln jerked away, shocked at the sensation created by that touch. It was as if a butterfly had fluttered along her arm from wrist to shoulder.

Her gaze whipped to his and away.

As he raised his own cup to his lips, his even white teeth flashed in a knowing smile. In contrast to his grin, Hawk's skin was very tanned, attesting to the fact that he spent long hours exposed to the elements. For some reason a memory of Raymond's fair skin and handsome features came to Kayln's mind. And even though the man before her was not beautiful in the way of her dead husband, Raymond suffered by comparison.

There was something overwhelmingly masculine and, at the same time, very sensual about Hawkhurst. He exuded an earthy vitality that reminded her of a cool rush of wind in a hot stuffy room. It was there in the alert angle at which he held his head and the proud set of his wide shoulders.

She looked up and found him studying her as avidly as she was him. Kayln was shocked as she saw what appeared to be appreciation in his eyes. And also confused by it. She had had suitors since Raymond's death, but the object of their affections had been her lands and moneys, not herself. She knew a strange sense of disquiet and also, in spite of the fact that she found him completely overbearing, a faint unwanted stirring. She thought of that mysterious moment in the mews when she had thought he was going to kiss her.

Somewhere inside her, a voice cried danger. The last thing

Kayln wanted was to find herself attracted to a man who was the very kind she wished to avoid. Her years of being her own mistress had shown her very clearly that she had no need of a virile, overconfident devil of a man like Hawk.

She drew herself up straighter on her seat. Often this made men pay closer attention to her because Kayln was a tall woman and could meet many men eye to eye. But this time her action did not have the desired effect.

Hawk's hooded gaze was drawn to her full bosom, which now strained against the close-fitting bodice of her maroon cotehardie, exposed by the fashionably deep neckline of her amber velvet tunic. His voice was low, intimate, and made her think of what it felt like to be in her big bed with the draperies closed. "What is it you wish to discuss with me, my lady?"

For a long moment she was held immobile by a mysterious tightness in her chest. Then a wave of determination shot through her, banishing the sensation. "I wished to discuss a matter of importance. Your family has done mine a grave misdeed and you must make restitution."

His gaze shot to her face, his eyes narrowing dangerously as he leaned back. Surely, she told herself, she had imagined that expression of appreciation, for there was no hint of it now. He spoke caustically. "Methinks, Lady D'Arcy, that you must clarify that accusation. No one speaks ill of my family without just cause."

Kayln sucked in a deep breath at the anger in his tone. Feeling the need to put some distance between herself and him, she rose and moved to stand with her back to him.

Kayln started as she felt his hand on her arm. He said quietly, "It is obvious that we should discuss this problem in more private quarters. Would you care to follow me to the antechamber?"

Realizing that she had already caused her men to stare at her with concern, Kayln nodded. Battling with Hawkhurst was not her aim. She must think of Celia.

He went to the table and fetched their glasses and the pitcher of wine, then strode across the stone floor. He led her to a small chamber just off the hall. It contained a table, a bench, and several chests, and was clearly used for keeping the records and accounts of the keep.

Hawk set their refreshments on the table, then motioned for her to take a seat on the bench. But she shook her head, preferring to remain standing.

He shrugged. "I can see that something has happened to disturb you greatly. I must, at the least, hear you out." He waited with ill-concealed restlessness.

Understanding that Hawk was indeed prepared to listen in spite of his impatience, Kayln suddenly felt the need to sit down. She sank onto the bench. Would there be another show of the blazing anger she knew lay so close to the surface, having twice viewed it this day?

Although she did not wish to admit to feeling intimidated, neither did she want to call up that rage. She must think of Celia and her future. This unpredictable man could make things very difficult for her. Kayln said carefully, "I have a younger sister, Celia. She is but fourteen and I fear she . . . finds herself in a great deal of trouble." She paused, taking a deep breath, then made herself go on. "Celia is with child and she has named your brother, Philip, as the father." She ended with a sigh of relief.

Kayln gave a start when Hawk grunted and plopped down next to her. His face was illuminated by shock and amazement. His brow puckered as he said slowly, "How can this be? Philip resides with the Earl of Norwich as his squire."

Even when he was not paying attention to Kayln directly, his nearness was overpowering. She stood once more and began to pace back and forth. She kept her gaze averted, but could not still the telltale trembling of her hands. "I assure you it is entirely possible. Celia is several months gone with child. She tells me that the . . . meetings with the young man occurred some four months ago."

Hawk's frown deepened. "It is true that Philip was visiting Clamdon at that time. But can you tell me how your sister has kept this secret for so long a time?" His eyes narrowed as he looked at Kayln, who had not ceased her pacing. "Why did she not come forward sooner?"

Kayln stopped before him, putting her hands on her hips. She cared not in the least for the suspicion she saw in his expression. "Celia had no idea that she was with child. Being only fourteen and gently reared, she knows nothing of such things. Your brother was able to overcome her natural shyness and moral upbringing by telling her that he cared for her, that he would return and marry her. In her innocence,'' Kayln said bitterly, ''she was foolish enough to believe that this would happen.''

Hawk came to his feet, towering over her, forcing her to tip her head back to look up at him.

The dark scowl on his face showed clearly that he had taken umbrage at the censure toward his brother. As his hands clenched at his sides, his chest expanded so much that it looked as if his black tunic might tear with the strain. His eyes became glowing slits and his lips thinned to a straight line of displeasure. ''Philip is but sixteen years old himself and hardly the despoiler of young women you imply. Let me make clear that he is not a boy who would speak lightly only to curry favor with a maid. If he has stated that he was planning to come back and wed your sister, then that was his intention. Though I must add that at sixteen he is foolish to have made such a pledge.'' He glared down at her, daring her to refute his brother's honor a second time.

Kayln realized she had indeed awakened the dragon as she had feared she would, but she refused to be cowed. ''No matter what your brother's intentions might have been, my sister is carrying his child. And I must add that your position does little to ease my fears for her.''

For a long moment, they stood there, neither of them willing to give the other the benefit of the doubt when it came to their siblings.

To her surprise, it was Hawk who relented first. He ran a hand over his face while taking a deep breath, which further expanded his wide chest, then let it out slowly. ''I am much aggrieved this has happened. You must believe me when I say that Philip does not make a habit of such behavior. That is why I have trouble believing he has wantonly despoiled your sister.''

It might have served as a peace offering as far as Hawkhurst was concerned, but Kayln was not quite ready to excuse him for his superior attitude. ''I pray it be truth.'' Her brows arched high. ''If not, every young woman in the countryside would soon be carrying Hawkhurst bastards.''

Kayln could tell she had gone too far when his nostrils flared and the pupils in his golden eyes became mere pinpoints. As Hawk opened his mouth to reprove her, Kayln rushed in to forestall him. "I . . . please, forgive me." She sighed. "It is only my concern for Celia and her condition that makes me speak of your brother so insultingly."

Hawk studied her for a long moment, his eyes thoughtful, as if he were taking her measure. When he spoke, it was impossible to guess what thoughts lay behind that measuring gaze. "I will send for Philip. It will be several days before he is able to reach Clamdon. Once I have met with him, I will know if he is the father of the child."

"If . . ." Kayln sputtered, shocked at his seeming doubt after all she had told him.

"He is my brother," Hawk said coolly. "I must allow him to stand in his own defense. If Philip tells me that your sister's tale is true, I will bring him directly to Aimsley. A wedding will then be arranged with all possible haste."

Kayln's back stiffened to a straight line and her jaw clenched. "How do you know your brother will freely admit to what he has done?"

Hawk's square chin jutted out. "Hawkhursts do not lie. Our motto reads, *Ubi Veritas, Ibi Jus Est.* 'In Truth Lies Right.' If Philip has lain with your sister, he will not dissemble."

Opening her mouth to tell him that neither did Chiltons lie, Kayln halted, her teeth worrying her lower lip as she thought of her father. "Nor does Celia," she amended.

For a long moment their gazes clashed like the horns of contesting bucks. Then, to her complete surprise, Kayln thought she saw an almost imperceptible glint of admiration in his eyes.

Suddenly he smiled. The hairs prickled along Kayln's arms and she felt a strange tingling along her spine. Her gaze was fixed on the whiteness of his teeth against his tanned face and she was unable to look away.

Hawk looked down at her, his golden eyes filled with irony as he smiled. "Since the two of them are of such excellent character, it will be a marriage I would have been happy to arrange myself. Although," he continued, shrugging his wide shoulders, "I would have delayed the matter for a few more years."

Even though she could see that he was not pleased by the situation, he managed to make it sound as if they would come to a reasonable arrangement. Kayln could not allow herself to be fooled by his tone nor that smile. She knew that it could disappear to be replaced by rage as quickly as it had come. She eyed him warily, feeling decidedly uncomfortable with his nearness. He was too self-confident for her peace of mind, seeming to know the answers to everything. At the same time something inside her found him inexplicably compelling.

He said nothing, only watching her with an unreadable expression. The silence stretched on, and slowly his gaze dipped to her mouth.

Kayln became aware of the change in him, and felt her own traitorous stomach quiver in response, as the air became charged with a restless feeling of anticipation. She watched breathlessly as slowly his grin narrowed and his lids came down to hood those incredible golden eyes of his.

Kayln's lips parted as her breathing quickened. She was so confused. Her insides tightened to a spring of tension and her knees felt too weak to hold her. She didn't know what had gotten into her. One moment she was angry with him and the next she wanted to . . . she wasn't sure what she wanted. Kayln couldn't move—couldn't think. A foreign kind of languor seemed to have taken over her limbs.

"Lady D'Arcy," he murmured, leaning closer to her, "has anyone ever told you that you have a beautiful mouth?" He raised one callused finger to touch her lower lip.

"I . . . oh." Kayln let out a startled gasp as he lowered his dark head, giving her no time to draw away. There was just a brush of his warm breath on her cheek before he placed his firm lips to hers.

For a brief moment she was held immobile, knowing nothing but surprise. Then Kayln's eyes closed and she felt as though her heart stopped as a bright shaft of liquid heat swept through her, weakening her limbs and pooling in her belly.

In too short a time, he was pulling away, tracing the smooth skin of her cheek as he drew back, leaving her bereft at the loss of his touch.

It was over so quickly, and yet she knew she was forever changed. Never would she have believed the press of one mouth against another could be so wondrous.

Hawk's own expression could only be termed smug as he turned to the table that held the pitcher and glasses.

Hard on the heels of her pleasure came a blinding flash of anger and shame that tightened her chest painfully. Kayln's cheeks flamed scarlet. How dare he kiss her? How dare she allow him?

When Hawk turned back to Kayln, he held a cup out toward her. She acted without thought, knocking the cup he had extended to the floor.

His eyes widened in unfeigned shock. "What do you, woman? Have you lost your senses?"

She clenched her hands at her sides. "Lost my senses! It is you who has an addled wit. What think you, my lord, to press yourself upon me?"

His dark brows arched high. "I but kissed you. No more, no less. Had you indicated in any way that you did not welcome me, I would not have done so."

"Welcome you?" She was shaking. "Methinks you mistook me, my Lord Hawkhurst." But even as she said the words, Kayln wondered if he spoke true. Had she led him to believe he might kiss her? Uncertainty stopped her from going on. She had so little experience with intimate matters, and he brought out feelings she'd never had before.

Hawk's gaze locked with hers and she could not look away. She could see the smoldering mockery in his gaze. "Forgive me, my lady. I meant no insult."

Deliberately she slowed her breathing, choosing to focus not on his attitude but his words. "I beg you remember that I will not welcome such advances in the future."

He bowed with studied care. "You have my assurances that I will not force myself upon you."

She frowned, recognizing she was completely out of her depth with this man. She wanted to be glad that he clearly felt nothing but disdain toward her, but there was a strange echo of regret somewhere inside her. She forced it away, determined to ignore it.

Kayln found her voice with difficulty. "My thanks for your

time, my lord. I will await your speedy arrival at Aimsley.''

His lips thinned. ''If my brother does admit to this.''

She stiffened, but knew she could not change his attitude by arguing, and thus kept her own council. ''So be it.''

He nodded, and she went toward the door. As he began to follow her, she held up her hand. ''Pray do not accompany me. I have already taken up much of your day. I will fetch my men and go.'' Kayln had an urgent need to be away from him and the overwhelming reality of his presence.

James Hawkhurst watched Kayln move away from him without further comment, knowing full well that she was in a great hurry to be away from him. What, he asked himself, had possessed him that he should kiss her? His wayward gaze swept one last time over the full curves of her breasts and hips, which were well defined by the close-fitting tunic she wore beneath her cote. As the door closed behind that shapely backside he had his answer.

But even her physical beauty could not completely explain what he'd done. He'd looked down at Kayln D'Arcy, seeing the uncertainty on her face, and wondered at it. She should have been glad that he had agreed to get to the bottom of this situation as she had requested. Instead her misty gray eyes had gazed up at him with all the wariness of a captive bird.

He suddenly thought of what a day this had turned out to be. If anyone had told him he would be challenged in his own mews by a golden-haired, lush-bodied goddess, then later have that very same woman accuse his brother of seducing her sister, he'd have sworn they were mad.

But that was exactly what had occurred. There was something about this Kayln D'Arcy that made him take note of her. He had admired her staunch defense of the boy in the mews, however misguided. Her determination to see justice done by her sister further called on his respect.

She was also unaccountably reserved and remote. Why, she'd even refused to take his arm when they returned to the keep.

Hawk had no need of such a prickly female in his life. He'd had enough of conflict and strife in France. He wanted to settle down, raise a family, relax in front of the fire with a sweet obedient woman who would welcome his advances at night. Or any other time he might approach her.

But all those sensible notions had flown from his mind as he looked down at her. He could not help seeing how beautiful she was, with her almond eyes, high cheekbones, and luscious mouth.

God, but she was lovely, and it had been some time since he'd been with a woman who smelled of jasmine and whose hair shone like spun gold. That full burnt-rose mouth had drawn Hawk's gaze and held it.

He remembered that Kayln D'Arcy was a widow. Did long-banked fires burn inside her as well? Did she yearn for a man's touch? The answering response he'd thought he'd seen in her eyes had told him she might.

Obviously that was not the case, judging from the reaction he had received. Hawk realized he would do well to avoid any other such contact with this unpredictable female.

What was it then that made him long to draw her back into his arms and kiss her properly—to make her admit that she had wanted him to kiss her as much as he had desired to do so? Could it be the way she had immediately rejected him? Or could it be the initial surprise he had sensed before she began to respond? It was almost as if she was innocent of such contact.

But that was impossible. She was a widow by her own admission. And no man who had the right to such bounteous fruit could deny himself the harvest. Once again Hawk allowed his memory to wander over the full swell of her breast, and felt a tightening in his lower belly.

With an inward groan of self-castigation, he forced the image away. It would be nothing short of madness to allow himself to be drawn to this woman.

Not since his parents' deaths of plague some five years ago had this castle known the sights and sounds of a family. At that time even his sister Jayne had gone to court to live with his brother Martin. For that he did not blame her. He could not imagine what it would have been like for her here without them. Even now, after he had been waiting years to return, Hawk found himself listening for the sounds of their laughter on the stairs, their playfully argumentative voices in the hall.

He acknowledged the tug of sorrow in his heart with a sigh. It was time he got his house in order and produced an heir. Now that he had finally forced himself to face the reality of his parents' deaths and return home, he was determined to live up to his responsibilities. At thirty-one, he had already wasted too many years.

The estate was not as solvent as it had once been because he had not returned to take up his duties at once as he should have. No steward, however loyal, would attend the lands like one of the Hawkhurst blood. Hawk could not repress a frown. He must make an effort not to blame Harold for the current state of his affairs. His father had trusted the steward and so would Hawk. He must simply ferret out the root of his financial problems with all possible haste.

As soon as that was accomplished he must find a wife, one who would bear his children and assure his line. Kayln D'Arcy was not the woman to fill that role. He wanted peace in his life after all the horrors of war. That was what he meant to have.

Even if the Widow D'Arcy did stir his blood as no other in his memory, he knew he must dismiss her from his mind. Though he realized that might prove difficult if what her sister had said proved to be true. They would be forced to have some contact.

Hawk drew himself up at the thought. He'd faced all manner of danger and even death in war. No slip of a woman, no matter how lovely, would get the better of him.

Chapter Three

The single gray tower at Aimsley stood tall and straight against the blue sky, like a loyal warrior. To Kayln it was a more than welcome sight, though when she compared the fortifications of her home to those at Clamdon, she found Aimsley sadly lacking.

The village, which was protectively tucked behind the castle, was not visible to her. But in her mind, she could see the neat rows of houses and the shops, baker, blacksmith, weaver, candle maker. And in the midst of it all stood the church with its peaked spire.

What she could see was the wall surrounding the keep. It was some thirty feet high and ten feet thick, with battlements along the top. The tower rose another twenty feet above that, and had a row of battlements, which were reached by a stone staircase that climbed from the top of the wall. The guard on duty there controlled the mechanism which raised and lowered the drawbridge. On seeing his mistress and her men, he opened it to admit them.

Without assistance, Kayln dismounted quickly, and turned her mount over to the serf who waited close by. Looking around herself, she felt a great relief at being back at Aimsley; in control once more and surrounded by the things that were familiar to her. Unconsciously, she lifted her chin a little higher.

In the courtyard, her people went about their daily work. Each one knew his or her specific tasks and accomplished them with a quiet efficiency. The women saw to the cooking, sewing, weaving, and preparing stores for the coming winter. The men were responsible for the care and feeding of the animals, storing the keep's share of the harvest, and as always, the security of Aimsley.

Kayln had an innate love of order. And now, like the sweet melody of a flute, her frayed senses fell into accord. She had been foolish to allow Hawkhurst to unsettle her.

Dismissing her men, she quickly made her way to the kitchens. From there she was able to access the passage to the Great Hall. There she met Alice.

Raymond had hired Alice to act as a nurse to her when Kayln had come to Aimsley as his bride ten years ago. He'd had no understanding that a fourteen-year-old had no need of a nursemaid.

Alice was a slight woman and very thin. Everything about her was narrow, her nose, her lips, her view of her surroundings and those abiding in them. She plucked nervously at the bodice of her gray cotehardie, her wimpled head bobbing.

Kayln's brow creased in anxiety. "My sister?"

Alice rushed to reassure her mistress. "Lady Celia is resting quietly. I gave her one of my potions to help her sleep. She'll likely not awaken till morning."

The nurse paused for breath, then, as if she could not prevent herself, asked, "What did Hawkhurst say? Will he see that right is done?"

Kayln felt decidedly uncomfortable talking about Hawk. For that brief moment when he had kissed her, Kayln had felt more vulnerable than ever in her life. And she needed to make sure that emotion was fully conquered in order to keep from exposing it to anyone, especially Alice.

If Kayln didn't miss her mark, Alice already knew more of her private life than she would wish. She suspected that Alice was aware that after a five-year marriage, Kayln was still as much a maid as any nun.

She gave herself a mental shake, not knowing why she would think of that now. "Hawkhurst has said he will contact his brother."

"The boy will marry her?" Alice prodded.

"Hawkhurst assured me that Philip will do what is right, should he feel that he is the one responsible."

"Should he feel . . ." Alice sputtered, her head jerking upward. "As if our darling girl would tell a falsehood about such a thing."

Kayln did not know herself what would happen now. But

she did not wish for the elderly nurse to become upset. "Now." She held up a cautioning finger. "Do not get yourself in a dither. We have no reason to believe the boy will lie."

Despite these soothing words, Alice scowled.

When it appeared as if the nurse were about to say more, Kayln went on. "We both know Celia would not lie. All will be well." Determinedly Kayln repressed her own doubts.

Alice did not cease frowning, but she did restrict her comments to a simple "We shall see." Her thin brows raised so high they disappeared under her wimple.

Kayln said nothing. The time she had spent with Hawkhurst had stretched her nerves and patience to the breaking point. Wearily Kayln turned away. "I will attend Celia."

"She may not wake easily," Alice told her quickly. "As I said, I have given her a potion and she is sleeping. Women in her condition need rest as much as anything."

Kayln stopped, her stomach fluttering. Alice had referred to her sister, who was little more than a child, as a woman. She could not suppress a sense of inadequacy at knowing her child-like sister was indeed more a woman than she.

Unconsciously she moved her hand down to cover her empty womb. How many times had she longed for a babe of her own? But that was not to be. She was determined to live her life under her own direction and no man's.

Alice seemed completely unaware of how her words had affected her mistress. She started toward the tower where Celia's chamber lay.

Kayln followed Alice, her face showing none of her inner turmoil. She was hauntingly aware of an image of Hawkhurst's wicked grin looming at the back of her consciousness, but could not fathom why.

Only moments later, she entered Celia's room behind the nurse. Celia was not in the huge bed with its headboard carved in the shape of a heart.

Alice stopped short with a puzzled frown. "I do not understand. The draught I gave her should have kept my lamb in her bed."

Kayln walked over to the bedside and picked up the cup that lay on the table beside it. She frowned as her searching gaze halted on the puddle behind the table. "I think she has made fools of us once more.'' She spoke the words calmly, but her heart was thumping with worry and betrayal. All this time she had thought she knew Celia. She had raised the girl since their father died when Celia was only seven. The younger girl had always been one to wander about the demesne on her own. But Kayln had never considered that she might find a lover. A lover who would father a child on her.

Alice's eyes widened in concern and disbelief. ''But she lay down and went to sleep, my lady.''

''Obviously a pretext,'' Kayln answered with a heavy sigh. She sat down on the edge of the bed, her mind a mass of confusion. ''Why must she hurt me so?''

Alice shook her head. ''Methinks 'twas not done to hurt you, but because she hurts.''

''She hurts?'' Kayln gasped. ''What have I not given her?''

''Naught that can be bought with gold.'' Alice raised her head, her eyes sad. ''But of yourself, little. I understand your pain and that both your father and your husband wronged you. But your father has been dead these eight years and your husband nearly five. Celia needs your love. That is the one thing you need give her and the one thing that is most difficult for you.''

Kayln could not even reprimand the servant for speaking so freely. She glanced about with a heavy heart. The thick blue draperies exactly matched the color of Celia's eyes, and rich tapestries depicting scenes of love hung about the stone walls. Her extensive jewel coffer lay open on one chest, while lavish gowns tumbled from another.

Was it her own fault that Celia had first taken a lover and now run away? Kayln could not think, could not comprehend how to right such damage. What she did know was that they had to find Celia. She was a frail girl, and made more so by her condition. It was the fragile state of her health in the past weeks that had led to the discovery of her pregnancy. ''Where can she have gone?''

''I know not. Mayhap she is wandering the forests as is her wont. But we must find her,'' Alice said.

Thus the search began.

* * *

Kayln raised her hands to rub her tired eyes. During the long hours since they'd discovered Celia's disappearance she'd had the sense of being in a nightmare. That feeling had not lessened with time.

With deliberate patience she directed the serving woman who stood with her on the steps of the keep in passing out warmed wine to the tired men gathered there. Despite the late hour, the courtyard was alight from the many torches that burned from every possible spot. Kayln cursed her inability to join the search of the woods. But she must remain behind to organize the lookers. She must also be in the keep should word come of finding her sister. But that did nothing to ease the frustrated knot in her stomach.

It was as the servant turned to do as she was directed that a shout rose up from without the castle wall. With an expression that was a mixture of hope and dread, Kayln started across the courtyard.

A moment later a horse and rider came through the open portcullis.

For the length of a heartbeat she could not believe her eyes. Then realization dawned as Kayln saw that it was indeed Lord Hawkhurst. After the scene at Clamdon that very day he was the last man she would wish to see. But he was carrying Celia before him, and she knew she must be glad of that.

Rushing forward, Kayln reached out to touch Celia's hand where it lay limply in her lap. She looked up at Hawk in concern. "Is she all right?"

He nodded, pulling his horse to a smooth halt. "Aye, she is well. Though I think very tired. You see how she sleeps even now." He looked down at the top of her pale blond head with surprisingly gentle concern.

Kayln registered this only remotely. She held back the questions that tumbled in her mind, wanting above all to get Celia safely to her bed. "Come, we will take her in." Kayln motioned for one of the serfs who hovered close by.

Hawk ignored the man who hurried forward as he slipped to the ground with Celia in his strong arms. "I will take her." He kept his voice low.

Kayln did not care for the sight of her dear sister in the arrogant man's arms, but she turned and led the way without comment. They hurried through the hall and up the stairs to the lower floor of the tower. She wished to have Celia safely deposited in her chamber and Hawkhurst gone with all possible haste.

Just as Kayln opened the door to Celia's chamber, Alice called out behind them, "Oh, my dear girl, my dear girl." The nurse rushed forward to stop Hawk with a frail hand on his arm so she could see for herself that Celia was fine. "They told me she was come home, but I could not believe it. Where did you find her, sir?" Alice barely glanced at Hawk as she spoke.

Kayln looked at him expectantly.

Hawk shrugged carefully and glanced down at Celia, whispering, "I would speak with you of this and gladly, but I do not wish to waken the girl." He then turned to take Celia into the chamber, and laid her gently in the bed.

Alice hurried to pull the covers up over her.

Kayln moved toward the bed, reaching out to run a shaking hand over Celia's forehead. She'd been so worried and frightened for her sister, and now seeing her with Hawk was difficult. Celia would not be in this condition if it were not for his family.

Alice leaned over the girl, her relief clear in her pale face. Her gray eyes glistened with unshed tears as she said, "I feared to never see my dear girl again when we could find her nowhere about the demesne. I am most grateful to you, sir, most grateful."

Kayln focused her own gaze on the floor as she fought for control, knowing how accusing and hostile her glare could be. "When I returned here from Clamdon she was gone," she said to Hawkhurst. "We have been searching since."

He seemed oblivious to her feelings. "The child came to me with some tale of keeping Philip from trouble. For some reason she thought he would be punished. After assuring her that I would not punish him, I realized that I must return her here at once. You must have been beside yourselves with worry for her, off in the middle of the night like that."

Kayln's lips thinned. How very good of him to be concerned for Celia. Would that his brother had thought before disgracing her.

Alice spoke up from the bed, where she was tending Celia. "And for that we are truly thankful, my lord. You have done an old woman's heart good by bringing her this very night instead of waiting till morn."

Kayln stood, not understanding how Alice could sound so genuinely appreciative to this man when his family was at fault. Kayln's voice dripped sarcasm as she said, "Oh, yes, we are grateful, my lord. You have done entirely too much."

Hawk looked into her resentful eyes and blinked. Then his jaw tightened as he studied her.

Celia moaned in her sleep, drawing their gazes.

"Mayhap we should continue without." Hawk turned back to Kayln and motioned toward the door. "The poor child is exhausted and we should think of the babe."

Kayln looked from him to Celia. Alice's advice about showing more love toward the girl rang in her mind. She really should not argue with Hawkhurst here.

Alice seemed unaware of the tension in the room as she began to ready Celia for what remained of the night. "And we would not wish to neglect Lord Hawkhurst after the good he has done us." She beamed at the man.

Kayln was nearly beside herself at Alice's good grace toward the man. Had this one good deed blinded her to Hawk's true nature? It was likely that he had simply brought Celia home to keep from being bothered by her. With stiff shoulders, she led the way out into the hall.

Once there, she hardly knew where to begin, so chaotic were her thoughts. The night had been long and exhausting. She declared with heat, "I'll thank you to take your leave now, my lord."

When he replied, Hawk said none of the things she thought he would. "I see now why you were so angry when you arrived at Clamdon. Little Celia is indeed distressed. Though I must say that she seems overly concerned with Philip's well being and not enough with her own."

Kayln hardly knew what to say. She ran her hands over her cheeks. "Her heart seems well set on your brother. I can only think he is indeed as wonderful as she says or that he has cast some spell over her." As she looked up at Hawk, remembering the way he had kissed her that day and how she had responded, she could not help thinking it might indeed be the latter.

He shook his head. "Philip is no magician, simply a young man. And if this situation be as it appears, somewhat impulsive and heedless. But I think he may have made a good choice in your sister. She is only a slip of a thing, but definitely of strong mind. Else she would not have come to Philip's aid, no matter that it was a misguided notion."

"She is that," Kayln answered with a humorless laugh. She had not known just how strong minded until this very day. It must not have been easy for Celia to plan her trysts with the boy. She was well guarded and often complained of such.

"But there is something now that I do understand more clearly," Hawk went on. "When I first returned from France some months gone, Philip did visit me for a time. I was understandably occupied with becoming reacquainted with my duties as Lord of Clamdon. Philip was often gone fishing on his own. Celia tells me this is how they met, quite innocently. And from there they developed a more, shall we say, intimate relationship."

She could tell from the tone of his voice that Hawk was trying to be delicate, and this surprised her. It was a different attitude from the morning. In fact, his whole conversation seemed unreal. Why was he being so agreeable? Kayln could not think of anything he could hope to gain by that.

She peered up at him. There was only one taper burning in the hallway. With Celia found, the castle had quickly quieted for the night, and Kayln realized that for all intents and purposes they were alone.

As if reading her thoughts, Hawk said, "I can see how difficult this must be for you. I did not mean to be harsh with you this morn. I wished only to keep a clear head in the matter." He lifted his large hands, and she found her gaze following his long strong fingers. "You must see that I could not take every woman who might come to my door with such a story seriously."

In spite of the knowledge that he was trying to apologize, however arrogantly, she could not prevent herself from replying in kind. "And does that happen so very often, my Lord Hawkhurst?"

He paused, his brows rising, but he did not take the bait. "Never before, my lady."

She bit her lips, looking up at him as closely as she could in the dim light. It surprised her that he had not offered a retort, and she knew not how to take this calm reasonable Hawk. She was exhausted from both the lateness of the hour and relief at Celia being home safe. And for some reason the stone walls seemed to be drawing closer, pulling in around her and this man. It was as if they two were alone in all the world.

Looking up into the unreadable darkness of his eyes, she felt unaccountably vulnerable. He seemed so strong and solid and she was so very tired. Tired from all the years of looking after herself and Celia, from having to be the one who was strong no matter what happened.

Unconsciously, she leaned toward him.

He turned his head to the side, studying her with an intent but unreadable expression. His eyes were two dark pools that seemed to hold her captive. Kayln's breath quickened and she put her hand to her breast.

What was happening to her? She knew that she must think clearly, must consider what she knew of this man. This gentleness did not reflect what she had learned thus far. He was arrogant, hot tempered, and condescending. Yet none of that seemed to matter here with the night closing in on them.

He leaned closer over Kayln, his breath mingling with hers. "Can you feel it, Kayln?" He whispered the words so softly she barely heard them.

The rapid beating of her heart beneath her fingers told her she did indeed feel it. But she fought the sensations building inside her. As if saying the words aloud could make them true, she replied, "I know not what you mean, sir knight. I feel nothing."

"You lie, wench." He chuckled knowingly, his mouth so close to hers she could feel his breath on her lips. "You know precisely of what I speak."

She shook her head, trying desperately to force herself to move away from him, but she could not. A single word escaped her mouth. "Nay."

He placed one strong hand on her arm. She felt it burn her

through the velvet of her sleeve, and still she could not move. "Shall I show you, then?" he said.

There was no room for reply had she been able to form one. His lips closed the space between them and she felt her heart thud in response. His strong arms slipped around her, drawing Kayln to the heat of him with inescapable surety.

And she made no move to escape, but wriggled closer to his hard-muscled length. A delicious warmth grew in her belly, radiating in every direction. Her lower stomach quivered as her breasts grew heavy and firm against the wall of his chest.

Never before had she thought to be held and kissed so. The embrace of the morning had brought a mere shadow of the heat that rose up in her now.

His mouth left hers and she whimpered as his teeth found her ear and nipped delicately at the tender lobe. "God, how I want you, Kayln D'Arcy," Hawk whispered hoarsely. "You fire my blood."

Kayln groaned softly. She could not think past the whirl of rosy color in her head, the sweet singing in her veins.

Unexpectedly, through the mist of languor, she heard Hawk swear, and his arms released her.

Opening her eyes in confusion, Kayln was aware that the light in the hall seemed to have grown brighter. She followed the source to see Alice standing in the open doorway of Celia's chamber, her narrow face a study in surprise and speculation.

A wave of realization rushed over Kayln, nearly staggering her in its intensity, as she put her hands to her burning cheeks. Heaven help her, what had she done?

It was impossible to face Hawk after what had just gone between them. What must he think of her? She could barely tolerate this man, and here she was allowing him to make love to her in a darkened passage as if she was some light-skirted scullery maid.

But she knew it was not likely that he could think more ill of her than she herself did. Kayln did not know what to say to break the palpable tension in the air around them.

Alice saved her from having to do so. "My lady. I have seen to Celia's needs. I thought to make a chamber available to Lord Hawkhurst did he desire to abide with us this night.

'Tis late and 'twould likely be best for him to return home on the morrow."

Kayln had to stop herself from crying out nay. She had no desire to sleep under the same roof as Hawk. But she had no wish to admit that aloud for fear Hawkhurst would guess how thoroughly he had unsettled her. "I'm sure Lord Hawkhurst wishes to return to Clamdon with all possible haste."

Kayln did not look at the man who stood beside her, but she could feel his gaze on the back of her head. Please God that he would sense her need to be rid of him and go.

Alice frowned, looking from one to the other. Finally her approving eyes rested upon the man. "Forgive an old woman's forward ways, my lord, but I cannot allow it. You have brought Celia home to us at great inconvenience to yourself, and I will not send you out in the dead of night." She turned to her mistress. "Lady Kayln, you must help me to convince Lord Hawkhurst."

Could she allow him to remain here in her own keep? To sleep in one of her beds?

At last she found the fortitude to face him. His golden eyes were dark with challenge. It was as if he had divined her very thoughts and was amused by her confusion.

How dare he, she thought. Under no circumstances was she willing to let this knave believe he had gotten the best of her.

Squaring her shoulders, she schooled her features to impassivity. "My Lord Hawkhurst, you must indeed abide here for the night. I will not hear otherwise."

Kayln felt no pleasure when his own gaze became one of admiration. He continued to watch her closely as he nodded and replied, "How can I refuse such an offer of hospitality? To do other than accept would be nothing short of churlishness on my part."

Chagrined in spite of her resolve, Kayln swung back to Alice. Hawk was aware of her true feelings in the matter and chose to remain at Clamdon in spite of them.

This rankled even more.

Refusing to so much as glance toward him again, she moved to Celia's chamber door. "And now if you will show him to his appointed chamber, Alice, I wish to go in to my sister."

Without another word she went inside, shutting the portal

securely behind her. Leaning her forehead against the door, she took a deep breath to try to steady herself. Her fingers shook as she raised them to her breast.

What had she been doing, allowing Hawk to kiss her that way? All this talk of something special between them was not real. In her experience, men only paid attention to a woman when they wanted something from her. What could he possibly want from her? And then, as if someone had said the words aloud, Kayln knew. Hawkhurst desired to bed her. And she had done naught to discourage him from thinking he could do so.

Her face flamed with shame, for she had played right into his hands, responding to him without conscious thought.

He had just seemed too kind in those moments right before he had kissed her. Unlike any man she had yet known.

Her lips tightened. Obviously he had used the show of gentleness to persuade her to his desires. Hawkhurst, like all the other men in her life, simply wanted to use her, and Kayln would not be used or manipulated by any man. Even one who made her blood sing by simply looking at her.

When next she and James Hawkhurst met, she would be in total control of herself and her emotions.

Chapter Four

Kayln woke to the sound of an insistent voice at her chamber door. "My lady!"

With a groan she pushed the bedcovers back from her face, then blinked as the light from the windows assaulted her tired eyes.

Judging from the angle of the light that spilled across the oaken floor and the corner of eastern carpet, it was still quite early. It seemed only moments since she'd finally fallen into a restless sleep not long before dawn had begun to light the far horizon. Kayln had been so agitated by the way she had reacted to Hawkhurst's kiss that when she'd gone to her bed she'd not thought to close the heavy apricot silk hangings. And she'd long since sent her maid off to find her rest.

The voice came again. "Lady Kayln!" This time she recognized it as Alice's high reedy tone.

What could the nurse be thinking to wake her so early? In point of fact, why was Alice herself up at such an hour? She'd gone to bed no earlier than her mistress, and though Kayln doubted the nurse had lain awake with thoughts of Hawkhurst to plague her, Alice was getting on and did need her rest.

"Come," Kayln called out to her.

Alice entered the room in a flutter of her customary gray garments. Holding her thin hands folded before her, she approached the wide bed of polished walnut. Her nose narrowed as she sniffed. "He is here."

For a moment, Kayln frowned in confusion. Of course he was here. Alice had practically browbeaten her into having him. "And well I know that, for you did insist," Kayln replied, hoping Alice would not make any remark about the kiss she had most certainly witnessed. Kayln had no wish to, nor could she explain her behavior. "Is he up demanding that I dance attendance upon him already?"

But Alice shook her head quickly. "Nay, not that one. Lord Hawkhurst is still abed as he should be." She raised her narrow nose high. " 'Tis the other one."

"Other one?" Kayln muttered, pushing the heavy fall of her wheat-gold hair back from her forehead.

Then her brow cleared and she had to fight to restrain a sigh of irritation toward the nurse as understanding dawned. "Miles?"

"And who else is forever turning up where he isn't wanted?" Alice sniffed again as if some odor offended her greatly. "Especially today. One would think he'd some way of finding out when we least desire his presence."

Kayln could not allow that to pass. Miles had been Raymond's closest friend, and had proved to be the same to her after her husband's death. "You must not speak so disrespectfully. Miles is a most kind and personable knight. Wasn't it he who came to aid us in caring for Raymond when he lay dying of the plague? Wasn't it he who helped me to ward off unwanted suitors until I could gain control of the lands? He has no way of knowing that we were up half the night. Surely you can not blame him for that."

Alice said nothing.

Kayln shook her head in confusion. "You are forever telling me I should find another husband to care for me. Methinks Miles would be the answer to your prayers. And truth to tell, if I were inclined to marry again, I would most likely settle upon him." Miles understood how very much her independence meant to her.

Never would she contemplate tying herself to someone like . . . like Lord Hawkhurst. He was too strong, too virile, too sure of himself. He would expect a woman to completely subjugate herself to his wishes. Her lips tightened as she wondered what could have brought him to mind. Of course she would not consider such a man.

Alice was shaking her head. "There is something about Sir Miles that is not as it should be. He fawns and agrees with everything you say too readily for my liking."

Visibly stiffening, Kayln answered, "I have had enough of

men who treat a woman as a possession. If Miles seems a bit complacent, give me that over cruel and domineering."

Alice reached out to her mistress, then brought her hand back to her side when Kayln tensed. "I know it is not my place to say this, but someone must. Lord Raymond was no example of manhood. He was cold and never taught you the way it should be between a man and a woman. There was some fault in him that I cannot name. As for your father, I never knew him, my lady, but there is a wide gulf between brute and lackey. Many a good man resides in the middle. You have simply had no opportunity to see this. Mayhap until now, that is." She paused, then went on with a grin. "Lord Hawkhurst seems much more my idea of a man. And I did mark that you appeared to think so last eve."

Kayln sucked in a shocked breath. The nurse had gone too far. "Alice! You may not feel free to bring up such things." Kayln had no intention of discussing any of this—and most especially not Hawk.

Alice looked away with a reproachful expression. "He brought our girl home with no thought to his own comfort."

"And Miles would have done the like. He simply was not given the opportunity." She did not want to tell Alice that she felt Hawkhurst had had his own selfish reason for bringing Celia back so speedily. That he'd wanted to be rid of her.

Obviously Alice had chosen to favor Hawkhurst, and once her mind was set there was no changing it. Kayln could not make her feel the same toward Miles, though he was much more deserving of her regard.

What she could do was remind Alice to behave with civility toward Miles. There was no question in Kayln's mind that it was he she'd referred to as a lackey. "And furthermore, out of respect for Sir Miles's station, you will mind your manners. I would not have him insulted for your silly belief that 'something is not as it should be,' " Kayln added.

Alice lifted her slim nose high, hurt by the rebuff. She clutched at her skirt with her bony hands. "I am sure there will be no complaint from his lordship as to my manners. I have seen that he and his men were seated and made certain they were given refreshments. I hope this meets with my lady's approval." Alice dipped a curtsy, her voice quavering.

Closing her eyes, Kayln took a deep breath, willing herself to be calm. It had been an eventful day and night all around. She looked down at the nurse. "I know you would never intentionally offer insult to any guest, no matter your personal feelings. My worry over Celia has put me out of sorts."

Somewhat mollified, Alice sniffed. "I fear for her future."

As do I, Kayln thought. But aloud she replied with confidence, "All will be well."

Patting the older woman's slender shoulder, Kayln said, "I must go to Sir Miles now. It would not be seemly to keep him waiting any longer."

With a nod, Alice left the room, her wimple fluttering behind her.

Letting out a sigh, Kayln watched her go with regret. Alice was much more than a servant, and the older woman's feelings were growing more fragile with each passing year.

But Miles was waiting and there was no telling when Hawkhurst might arise. Quickly she leapt from the bed and took fresh garments from her chests. There was no time to call for assistance, and she donned a simple midnight-blue tunic and cotehardie of buttery yellow. She then braided her own hair, leaving it to hang down her back with no adornment but a blue ribbon that matched her tunic.

Without further ado, Kayln left her chamber and went down the stone steps of the tower. At the entrance to the hall she paused, seeing her home through new eyes. The one large hearth on the opposite wall burned cheerily. The trestle tables, which had been set up in anticipation of the morning meal, were pale from constant scrubbing. Along the wall were three window seats, and tapestries hung on the walls between the window recesses. Opposite this was the inner wall with several doors that led to the tower and various other storage and guest chambers. The serving women went about their work with smooth efficiency, completing a scene of comfort and warmth.

Kayln's expression showed her satisfaction. Aimsley might not match Hawk's castle for defensibility and strength. But here in her hall it was Clamdon that was found lacking.

Miles was seated at the high table with two of his men. The three of them had their heads bent close together and they were laughing softly as they studied something in the window embrasure. Lying between them on the table were several gold coins, what appeared to be a broach, and a well-wrought dagger.

At that moment, Miles looked up and saw Kayln approaching them. He raised his hand, beckoning her forward. "Lady Kayln, come and see our sport."

The other two men glanced toward her, then quickly fixed their attention on the window once more.

Kayln recognized only one of the men, Sir Louis. He was decidedly the most handsome of Miles's knights, though his darkly beautiful face had always left her cold.

Her father had been a beautiful man, tall and strong with a mane of dark golden hair and flashing green eyes. His good looks had not been a true indicator of the man. They had hidden a soul rife with blackest evil.

As Miles stood and came toward her with his hands outstretched, Kayln pushed the awful memory aside. Taking her hand, he motioned toward the other men. "Welcome, fair lady. You know Sir Louis. And this"—he indicated the other man—"is Sir Trevor. He has just come into my service."

The two men barely glanced up again as Sir Trevor was introduced. Miles laughed and shrugged slender shoulders encased in lush blue velvet. "You must forgive them. I fear my men have lost their manners in the heat of the moment."

Kayln frowned, both offended and puzzled.

By way of explanation Miles drew her toward the window. He pointed up into the corner. "Do you see that spider there?"

Looking up at the small creature, which was busily spinning the silvery strands of its web, Kayln nodded in confusion. "Yes, but what . . . ?"

Miles's eyes were bright with excitement. "We have a wager. Louis"—he pointed to the man—"has made a small rend in the web. If the tear is mended before the serving woman arrives with more wine, I win. If it is not, he wins."

Kayln studied the gossamer threads. The web looked very near completion to her. She watched while the tiny creature created a work of intricate grace and beauty. The spider wove its own world, a place of safety and order. Kayln admired such independence, and could readily identify with it.

With a smile, she turned to say as much to Miles.

She paused, taking note of the near fanatical gleam in Miles's eyes as he watched the spider's progress. She had always known that Miles loved to gamble. He had made countless wagers with Raymond, but this time for some indefinable reason, she felt uncomfortable with his single-minded intensity.

She glanced at Louis, who was now watching the door of the hall with unconcealed tension.

Her attention went back to the industrious spider. It secured the end of a silken thread, then dropped down upon its lead. Finished.

Miles gave a shout of triumph.

Kayln swung around to see Louis's reaction, just as the serving woman entered the hall. Seeing how close he had come to winning, Louis muttered an oath. Springing forward, he reached up and crushed the small creature in frustration. "You've the Devil's own luck, Miles," he cried as he stalked from the hall.

Kayln was horrified at the action. Not that she had any great love for the spider, but the act was done purely out of spite. Looking at the other two men, she saw that they appeared not to notice. They were chuckling as Miles busily gathered his spoils from the table.

He faced her with a smile. "Kayln, I am so glad you are come. I feared I might have to leave without having seen you." He took her chill hands in his. "The morning grows on and I must soon return to Harrow."

She spoke sharply. "That was uncalled for."

He looked at her with wide blue eyes, genuinely surprised by her disapproval. He bent to one knee in supplication. "To what do you refer, dear friend? But tell me and I will set all to rights."

Kayln looked down at him in consternation. Being so upset about the death of a spider suddenly seemed foolish in the face of his solicitude. But she couldn't just let the matter lie. Louis's behavior had left her feeling as if she'd stepped in something filthy. She tried to explain. "The way Sir Louis killed that spider. It was cruel . . . revolting. How could you have such a man in your employ? He behaves more as a willful child."

Miles rose to hold her hands against his chest. "Is that what has upset you? If you believe Sir Louis's character to be flawed, I will dismiss him. I would not have my men upsetting you."

Clearly, Miles had taken her distress to heart. "You are most considerate," Kayln said, attempting a more moderate tone. In dealing with her men, Kayln would not welcome interference from Miles. Thus she did not wish to offer such. "But you need not go so far. Whom you take into service is surely your own affair."

"Nay," he answered. "I have every need. Your opinion is of great import. You may consider him dismissed."

Kayln looked at Miles for a long moment, feeling oddly uncomfortable with his easy compliance. She only nodded, telling herself Alice had influenced her thinking. "As you will."

"And now, having seen that I have upset you, I will take myself and my men off from here for the moment."

Feeling that she had offered offense, Kayln attempted to make amends. "You are not able to break your fast with us then?"

His blue eyes focused on the outer door of the hall. "I fear not. I only came because we were hunting close by and I could not let pass the opportunity to share your sweet company. You know I always try to look to your safety and happiness. It is what Raymond would wish of me." He blinked as if fighting tears.

Kayln found herself wondering whether his grief could still be so fresh after all these years. And though she felt a certain amount of sympathy, she could not readily share his feelings. Her own clearest memories of Raymond were his silences. When he'd been displeased with her, he would completely withhold himself. Weeks often passed without them so much as exchanging a word.

As she looked at Miles, Kayln suddenly realized that his almost boyish good looks were not as attractive as she had previously thought. Not that he or any other man could come close to the incredible silver-blond beauty of her dead husband, but she had always thought Miles a handsome man. Now she found that there was something too feminine about the softness of his chin and the fullness of the lips smiling down at her. Even the hazelnut brown curls which lay across Miles's forehead looked as if they might have been carefully arranged there.

A firm jaw and strong countenance with black-lashed golden eyes came to mind. Hawk could not be called beautiful by any standards, yet there was something undeniably compelling about the ruggedness of his suntanned features, something that appealed to her senses in a very basic way.

Kayln checked herself, not wishing to think along such paths. Again she told herself that it was Alice who had influenced her thinking.

Yet Kayln had a sudden urge to keep Miles here. That way she would avoid being alone with Hawkhurst, though what her reluctance meant she refused to contemplate. She said quickly, "Surely you can delay for a short time. We have a guest with us whose companionship you might enjoy. You may even know Lord Hawkhurst."

Miles stiffened visibly, his eyes narrowing. "Lord Hawkhurst. Kayln, do you mean to tell me that that man is here in Raymond's keep?" His blue eyes registered shock and some darker emotion she could not begin to name. "That you allowed him to stay here with you, an unmarried woman, with no real chaperone? Why would you think to do such a thing?"

Surprised and irritated at his vehemence, Kayln drew herself up, her earlier sympathy forgotten. "Miles, I am most annoyed at your censure. You know I cannot allow you to speak so to me." She refused to contemplate the fleeting awareness that her agitation was sharper than it might have been if she did not find Hawk so overly fascinating.

He looked away, obviously working at composing himself. "Forgive me, dear lady. Obviously I have offended you for the second time this morn." He swallowed hard. "I am but concerned that you would allow that man to stay here. Raymond would not wish for you to entertain him unattended."

Despite her displeasure with Miles, the mist in his eyes at the mere mention of Raymond's name made her soften her tone. "Lord Hawkhurst only came to return—" She stopped herself. For some reason, Kayln did not wish to speak of Celia and her troubles. Even to Miles.

Miles seemed not to even notice her hesitation as she continued. "He arrived unexpectedly and only remained overnight as the hour was so late," she said. She stood then to indicate her desire to close the matter, for she could not allow him to question her further on this. She was feeling too confused and, if she was honest with herself, guilty for having let Hawkhurst kiss her and for responding to that kiss. Trying to convince herself that what she was saying was true, Kayln said, "Raymond would have no cause for concern. It was a matter of business."

Without another word, Miles rose, and his man with him. They moved through the hall to the great oaken door and outside with a last strained good-bye from Miles. The other man said nothing, leaving Kayln to stare after them with a frown.

It crossed her mind that she could try to make peace with her friend, but the notion was a fleeting one. Her nerves had been strained to the breaking point in the last twenty-four hours, and she must still face Hawkhurst at some point in the day.

She put a hand to her throbbing temple. She would speak to Miles when they were both calmer.

It was as she was nearly to the other end of the hall that something, some inner sense of awareness, made her look up. There stood Hawk in the door that led from the tower. His dark hair was damp as if just washed and his tanned face glowed with vitality. Unaccountably she was piqued that he appeared far more rested than she felt. Kayln was even further irritated by the mocking tilt of his brow.

How long, she wondered, had he been there? For some reason she could not explain, she hoped he had not seen what had happened only moments ago.

But from his opening remark as he came toward her, it was immediately apparent that he had. "Who, may I ask, was that?" He nodded toward the door through which Miles and his man had gone.

Though it was none of his business, she found herself replying, "My very dear friend Sir Miles Harrow and one of his knights."

"Those ill-mannered fools were knights of the realm?" he

said condescendingly. Then his expression changed as his eyes narrowed. "How dear a friend?"

She drew herself up stiffly. Had the world gone mad that she must suffer more prying male questions this day? "That, my lord, is none of your concern. And I'll thank you to mind that you are in my home where I may do as I will." She dared not add aloud that she felt it quite presumptuous of him to criticize the refinement of others.

He moved closer to her, stopping only an arm's length away, and she was aware of the stubble of black hair on his strong jaw. She was also mindful of the serving women who went about their work with ill-concealed curiosity.

Keeping his voice low as if aware of her thoughts, he said, "Aye, you may. I have no right to question you. But I did see the idiocy of their behavior and the way the good Sir Miles backed down from you like a licked cur."

"How dare you," she whispered, her eyes flashing her anger. "You know naught of Miles. He was simply sorry for having offended me. He is a kind and gentle knight, willing to admit when he has made an error." The implication that Hawk could not admit that hung in the air between them.

He stared back at her, his eyes dark gold with rising ire and something she might have thought was jealousy, had she not known better. Kayln knew the notion to be completely ridiculous. They could not be together for more than moments without conflict, as was evidenced by this latest discord.

Hawk's hands tightened at his sides and he took a deep breath. "You know nothing of me, madame, to imply such an insult. And for some unknown reason you seem to have taken the position that I am of ill character. Even so, it is beyond me that you would hold such a fool as that one up to me as an example. Is that your notion of a man, Kayln, that tearful toady who bows and scrapes at your command?"

Had she judged Hawk too quickly? But the question was immediately dismissed. He was all the things she thought of him, arrogant, powerful, and too sure of himself. The fact that he had taken it upon himself to kiss her twice in the course of her first day of acquaintance with him was proof of that. He certainly had no right to judge Miles and call him a toady. She faced him squarely. "You will not speak so of Miles again. You know nothing of him, nor do I believe you have any understanding of how a chivalrous man should behave."

A bright flash of vexation lit his golden eyes briefly. Then he smiled down at her suggestively. "Perhaps not, my lady, but I do have some understanding of what a woman desires."

She could not suppress a soft gasp of outrage. How dare he speak to her that way! The man surely was completely mad. She drew herself up, refusing to let him see how much the remark had affected her.

There would be no further familiarity between them and she would make that clear now. "I will thank you, my lord, to remember that what I do or do not consider to be manly virtues is not your affair. I do not seek, nor do I require, your opinion on the matter. As you are a virtual stranger to me, I will not allow you to insult my true friend. And I would also thank you to address me as Lady D'Arcy. I have given you no leave to be more familiar."

She paused, then in a more subdued tone brought up the problem that was uppermost in her own mind, the one that had kept her awake for nearly the whole of the night. "My lord, there is something else. I must tell you that I believe I have led you to misunderstand something. What happened last night was most unfortunate. I can only plead exhaustion for allowing you to take liberties which are unacceptable to me."

His lips tightened to a thin line, and she had to quell an urge to take a step backward. When he spoke he did not raise his voice, and for that much she was grateful, for they were already the object of much attention as the castle folk began to trickle in for the morning meal. But what he did say in that soft, deliberately controlled voice gave her pause. "Methinks I have heard quite enough of this. Salve your pride in whatever way you must, but spare me, dear lady. Make most certain, I shall be no more familiar than you are willing to allow."

With that he stalked away, leaving her to stare after him, wondering what he could possibly mean by such a statement. Salve her pride indeed!

But hers were not the only eyes that followed the knight from the room. And as soon as he was no longer visible many a surreptitious glance was cast her way.

Feeling the castle folk's gazes upon her, Kayln turned and with studied care made her way from the hall.

She took the tower steps to Celia's rooms slowly. Though she knew that her sister was likely still asleep, Kayln felt a need to be with her. Even though their relationship was strained because of the secrets Celia had kept about her meetings with Philip and her subsequent pregnancy, Kayln was drawn to her side. And not just for Celia's sake, but her own as well.

A serving woman sat sewing at the foot of the huge oaken bed. Kayln entered and motioned for her to leave. She did not wish to speak and waken her sister.

When the other woman had gone, Kayln bent over the girl's still form.

Celia's complexion was pale as ivory, and tiny blue veins showed through her lids. Her silver gilt hair fanned out over the pillows, its very thickness making the girl's face appear more fragile in contrast. Celia made her think of fairy stories, a child of earth, sky, and air.

Her sister was small, delicate, and lovely, everything Kayln was not. But Kayln felt no envy, just a deep well of love for Celia.

Kayln's gaze rose to study the chamber, the furnishings, the luxurious carpet, and the tapestries, which had been chosen specifically to please Celia. Her own thoughts of the night before came back to her. Perhaps she had been lax in her personal attention to the girl and had trusted in her many gifts to speak of her love for her young sister.

And she could not wholly put the blame on her busy life. True, it was no small feat for Kayln to keep abreast of her holdings, but the constraints on her time did not give sufficient excuse for neglecting Celia.

Nay, it was surely a lack within her. If Kayln had given more of herself, would Celia have been less apt to surrender her heart to a stranger? Had Celia lain in this large bed alone and looked at those hangings, which bore scenes of courtly love, and longed for someone to hold her?

Was Philip a decent boy who simply chanced along to fill that lonely void?

Or was he the despoiler of innocents that Kayln feared? She

knew she was no unbiased judge. Nothing in her life had given her cause to believe in men—much less a boy.

Kayln had only Hawk's faith in Philip to guide her. And heaven knew, the baron was at best a difficult and overbearing oaf. His parting remarks could not but give her an increasing sense of disquiet. What could he have meant when he said he would only be as familiar as she would allow?

Taking a deep breath, she urged herself to be calm. Surely he had meant nothing more than that he would abide by her wishes.

There would be no more familiarity, no more kisses to threaten her equilibrium.

And for that she was grateful—wasn't she?

Chapter Five

James Hawkhurst prodded his stallion, Mac, forward with impatience, though he knew it would do little good. Nothing could distract him, not the blue sky overhead nor the beauty of the lush English countryside. No matter where he went or how quickly, he could find no escape from his thoughts of Kayln D'Arcy.

In the days since he'd met her, he'd been driven to distraction by those thoughts. What was it about the fair young widow that kept him in her thrall? She was beautiful, that much was true. And he'd never known such an immediate awakening of desire as when he'd kissed her. He'd also felt her own responses to him and been further heated by them.

The problem lay in the fact that the fair lady seemed bent on denying both him and herself. He frowned, urging Mac to an even faster pace. Why did she pretend she had not responded to his advances? And why, when she rejected him, did he not simply put her from his mind?

It was not as if Hawk could not have another woman. Looking around his keep, he'd seen that there were females aplenty. And more than one had made it known that she would not reject her lord. The trouble was that Hawk could not arouse any real interest in them. It was a pair of wide gray eyes and a lush mouth that swam before the face of each, no matter how well favored they might be. It seemed that for some reason unknown to him, Kayln was the one he must have.

"Saints take me for a fool," he cried aloud, pulling his horse to a walk. The only thing he could do was bring the lady round to his way of thinking. No matter what she said about not wanting him, Hawk knew better. He'd lain with enough women to recognize passion when he saw it. Kayln D'Arcy was not as indifferent to him as she professed, though why she pretended otherwise he could not fathom.

Mayhap she simply played hard to get. 'Twas a pose some females adopted. Though it pleased him not, Hawk decided he would play along if it meant having her in the end. Never in his life had he felt such a deep and consuming desire to lay with a woman. Have her he must, and he would, so that he could get her out of his mind.

It was paramount that he get his life in order, settle down, and beget an heir. An ill-tempered, prickly dame like Kayln could have no part in the peaceful life he planned for himself. Not that Hawk expected to marry a simpering fool. His own mother had been quick to state her own opinions and act on them, but she had not been so very contrary, so ready to look for insult where none was intended. Beautiful, laughing, and loving Isabel. His heart ached at her loss even after all this time.

Hawk looked around him with a scowl of self-reproach. He had ridden out to talk with some of his farmers and lost track of where he was going. He had completely bypassed his destination and was headed down the road to Aimsley.

With a sigh of impatience he turned Mac back the way they had come. He had many problems to sort out that had no connection whatsoever to the Lady of Aimsley keep. They should be uppermost in his thinking. For the time being, at least, he must put her aside.

When he reached his first destination, Hawk pulled up his stallion and dismounted. He looked about the well-tended farmyard with approval. "Good day," he said, nodding to the yeoman, a tall, thin, lantern-jawed man with blackened teeth. His wife was short, plump, and pink-cheeked. Both of them were dressed in reasonably clean, coarsely woven garments.

The farmer bowed respectfully. "I am honored by your presence, my lord."

"Will you have a cool drink, my lord?" asked the woman hesitantly as if she were unsure of addressing her overlord directly.

Knowing he would please them by accepting, Hawk said, "Yes, with thanks." When the woman had gone into the house he turned back to the farmer. "How goes the harvest?"

The man smiled widely, obviously well pleased with himself and his efforts. "Very well, my lord, very well. Though not near so good as two years ago. That was a year to remember. Record harvest for all around and lovely fat livestock. Just enough rainfall and the right amount of sun to make the fields grow tall and the pasture grasses rich."

"Two years ago, you say?" Hawk asked, frowning.

"I could never forget because it followed a year when we all feared there would not be enough to eat." He grimaced at the memory. "Can't forget a year when God shows His goodness and bounty after such hardship." The man was smiling again.

Hawk massaged his forehead. He distinctly remembered mention in the ledgers of the lean year the farmer spoke of, but he could recall nothing to support the claim of a bumper year. He sighed heavily. It would take months to sort out the books, especially after his long absence.

He shrugged. No doubt the farmer was exaggerating his own success as some men were wont to do. Then, in all fairness to the farmer, he checked himself. The harvest might have seemed better than it actually was because of the severe deprivations they had suffered the year before.

The woman came out of the cottage. A child clung to her skirt as she approached, and was dubiously peeking out at the tall knight. Proudly the woman held out a drinking horn, and Hawk took it from her, making short work of the cool sweet water. "My thanks," he told her, handing back the cup.

"You honor us, lord." The woman bowed and stepped back.

"Why does the man have a sword?" the child lisped, pointing.

"Shh," his mother hissed, blushing. "Do not question Lord Hawkhurst."

"It is all right," Hawk said quickly. "I would not have the boy fearful of me." He turned to the little boy with a smile. "Come."

The boy hesitated for no more than a moment, then rushed toward the tall man. Hawk chuckled as he swung the child up in the air, making him laugh at being so high.

"I want to touch the horse," he stated, puffing out rounded pink cheeks importantly.

Hawk's expression grew serious as he looked down into the boy's small face, which resembled his mother's. "Mac is a war horse and you must never try to touch one of his ilk. He is trained to crush anything that comes under his feet."

The boy's eyes grew even rounder, and he looked at the stallion with new respect.

Setting the child back on his feet, the knight said, "Go to your mother now."

With that Hawk thanked the farmer for his time and rode on. The years since his parents' deaths had seen no Hawkhurst in charge of the lands. His steward, Harold, was capable, even if he did on occasion overstep himself by giving orders without first consulting his master. For too many years, the steward had had sole responsibility for what was Hawk's. It would take Harold some time to adjust to the proper order of things. But the clerk would soon learn that Hawk intended to familiarize himself with every detail concerning the estate. That was the way his father had held the lands, and Hawk would do the same.

Already some discrepancies had turned up betwixt what was told by the steward and what others had to say. Hawk wondered again about the information the farmer had just given him. Why would Harold lie about the harvests? Could it be that he had not managed the estates as well as he should? That would not be completely unforgivable. The man should just be honest. But if Harold was lying, and there was more to the matter than simple mismanagement, Hawk's retribution would be merciless. The only thing that moved Hawk to caution was the fact that his father had trusted the man. He would make no move against Harold without proof.

When he had left France several months ago, Hawk had looked forward to a more peaceful existence, his eagerness for war having drained from him with the blood he had seen shed on countless battlefields. He had readily volunteered to go with the entourage that would escort John II of France to Berkhamstead Castle after he was captured by Prince Edward of Woodstock at the Battle of Poitiers.

A dark frown creased his tanned brow. He'd had more than enough to occupy him before Philip had further complicated his problems by dallying with a young lady. For after meeting

Celia, Hawk was fairly certain that she was not telling a falsehood. The child was just too ingenuous. She had none of her older sister's cynicism and hostility.

Even such an uncomplimentary thought about Kayln D'Arcy brought a rush of wanting. His husky and self-deprecating laugh rang out as he kicked his stallion to a canter.

Some days later, Hawk and his brother Philip drew their mounts to a halt in the courtyard of Aimsley keep. Hawk took note with approval of the soldiers training on the practice field close by. It seemed that in this area Kayln D'Arcy showed common sense, even if she was no good judge of a man's character. It still rankled that she had chosen not only to reject Hawk's advances but to compare him, and unfavorably, to that cowering boy Harrow.

Hawk's jaw tightened with disdain. He was fairly certain that the fool was not Kayln's lover, though he had to admit to an uncomfortable moment of doubt when he first saw him with her. He would prove soon enough who was the better man.

He dismounted and turned to Philip, who had also dismounted. "We are arrived."

Philip swallowed hard and made no reply beyond a sharp nod, his expression hovering between eagerness at seeing the girl again and sorrow at what he had done. Setting aside his own preoccupation with Kayln, Hawk put a comforting hand to Philip's square-boned shoulder.

A burly dark-haired man, garbed in mail, came forward from the practice field. "My Lord Hawkhurst. I am Bertrand, my lady's master-at-arms. I accompanied her to Clamdon."

"Ah, yes, as I recall." Hawk inclined his head. "I am here to see your lady."

"She is expecting you?"

His expression was openly curious as he looked from the baron to his younger brother, but Hawk had no intention of satisfying that curiosity. "Yes, though she may be surprised at my speedy arrival."

Bertrand seemed less than satisfied with the reply, but he asked nothing further. "If you will come this way, I will see that my lady is informed and you are made comfortable."

"My thanks." Hawk nodded and motioned for Philip, who hesitated behind them, to follow him. They moved up the stone steps to the large oak portal.

Once inside the hall, Hawk looked around with interest. It was a wide, open room which had obviously been added fairly recently. The stone had not yet darkened except on the inner wall, which would have once been the outer surface. The old hall must have been divided into several chambers, as there were three doors leading inward. Velvet cushions were arranged invitingly in the window recesses, which narrowed to arrow slits as they should. But above them, just under the roofline, was a row of glass windows which let in the late summer sun. A narrow gallery ran alongside them where musicians might play.

Brightly hued tapestries lined the walls between the window recesses. Hawk knew they served the practical purpose of keeping out cold in winter, but they were also pleasing to the eye. Kayln D'Arcy had created a home of comfort and warmth that would make any man feel proud were it his.

Hawk realized he would welcome a few such comforts in his own life. He would certainly welcome a wife to care for such things. But an obedient and loving nature would be his first consideration, both of which qualities the Lady of Aimsley was sadly lacking.

Another man came forward, introducing himself as Lady D'Arcy's steward and saying she would be with them shortly.

Hawk smiled in anticipation. Kayln's was not the issue. Her very beddable form and passionate nature were. He only hoped that he did not have to play the waiting game too long.

Kayln paused as she reached the bottom of the steps from her tower room, and smoothed the fine fabric of her velvet skirts. She took a deep breath, but she could not dispel the nervous fluttering in her stomach at facing Hawk again. He'd unsettled her in a way no man ever had, leaving her feeling uncomfortably unsure of herself. And that she could not accept.

Only ten days had passed since she had ridden to Clamdon to tell him of Celia's pregnancy. If there be justice, they would have the matter of the child's parentage settled this very day. She assured herself that her nervousness at seeing Hawkhurst was due to her concern for Celia, not because of any interest in him.

Entering the hall, she sternly told herself that no man could be as disturbing as her memory of Hawk. She squared her shoulders and forced herself to cross the room slowly as she went toward the man and the boy who were settled in chairs before the fire. They were sitting with their backs to the room, but she would have known the wide set of Hawk's shoulders anywhere.

Something must have alerted Hawk to her presence, for he stood and turned to face her.

For the briefest moment, Kayln hesitated in her approach. She was more than a little startled to find that Hawk was even more attractive than she had remembered. There had been no way for her imagination to fully capture the overwhelming vitality surrounding him, the mobility of his hawklike features, which could display a whole host of expressions in a mere breath. His golden gaze slid slowly over the length of her, and she flushed like a silly milkmaid. Biting her lips in consternation, Kayln toughened her resolve to quell such reactions.

Kayln walked toward them one slow step at a time. Celia's happiness was at stake here.

"Lady D'Arcy." Hawk came forward and bowed over her hand. When his firm lips brushed the back of that hand, a shiver of tingling awareness raced up her arm.

She flinched, drawing her hand away, disgusted anew with herself and him. Her resolve clearly was as nothing when he touched her.

Hawk made no outward show that he had taken note of her reaction, and she told herself to be grateful for that much at least.

"Lord Hawkhurst," she answered stiffly. Kayln linked her still-tingling fingers together with those on her other hand as she willed herself to think about what must be discussed. She glanced at the boy without really seeing him. "I am so glad to see that you have indeed come quickly."

He shrugged, but his voice was deep and full of pride as he replied, "This is my brother Philip. When he learned of the child, there was no hesitation. I assured you that if he was the father of the child, he would not try to hide the fact.'' Hawk's eyes challenged her to recall her own doubt of his brother.

''So, he has admitted the child is his?'' Kayln chose to ignore the look, though she was gratified to learn that the boy was indeed of decent character.

''Philip admits that he did lie with your sister and she was a virgin when he took her,'' Hawk stated.

Kayln winced at having the matter put so bluntly. ''I am grateful for your brother's sense of honor,'' she answered sharply. Hawk spoke of these things with a forthrightness that made her uncomfortable. Her own inexperience in such matters made her feel foolishly naive.

What would it be like to be among those to whom love-making was no longer an oft-considered mystery? She pushed the unwelcome thought aside.

Kayln looked up at the tall man before her, realizing that Hawk was still talking about Philip and that she had not heard a word he said. When his lips curved in a smile, she could only remember their firm softness against hers. He raised his large hand to gesture toward his brother, and she wondered what it would feel like should he touch her.

It was hard for Kayln to think of anything in the devastating presence of this man. Every sense in her body seemed to come alive with some primeval awareness when he was near. Over the past few days she had done her utmost to convince herself that her initial reaction to Hawk had to have been exaggerated in her mind, that he was an insufferable madman who thought he could control everyone and everything. Clearly these attempts to deny her attraction, however distasteful it was to her, had been nothing short of self-delusion.

Without her being conscious of it, her tongue emerged to moisten her suddenly dry mouth.

As Hawk watched her, there was a hint of mocking humor reflected in the golden depths of his eyes. It was almost as if he knew what her response to him was.

His lids came down to hood his eyes, masking their expression, and his gaze moved lower to her lips. He smiled slowly, intimately. Kayln shivered, her heart beginning to pound with an irregular beat.

"Will I be allowed to see Celia?" asked a voice from behind Hawk as Philip unknowingly startled her back to reality.

Collecting herself, albeit with some difficulty, Kayln walked toward the boy, crossing her arms over her waist. Once more, she told herself she must give all her attention to the matter at hand. This was the boy who would wed her sister, and Kayln wanted to judge for herself if she thought him worthy of such an honor. She would overcome her reaction to Hawk.

As if he were aware of what she was thinking, Philip Hawkhurst squared his shoulders and waited silently while she studied him. Philip was a tall young man. Not quite as tall as his brother, but Kayln had to look up to see into his dark gray eyes. Surprisingly, his hair was not black like Hawk's, but a rich strawberry blond. He had none of the freckles that usually accompanied such hair, and Kayln thought it would probably darken to auburn as he grew older. His shoulders were square and large boned, promising to widen with maturity, even if they did make him look somewhat gangly at this stage in his growth. This impression was not lessened by his thinness, for the cloth of his dark green velvet tunic hung loosely about his waist and hips. When at last she raised her gaze to his face, she saw it was pleasant enough with large strong features. He stared back at Kayln openly, his gaze direct.

Yes. Kayln nodded thoughtfully. This one might do well enough. "Celia will be down shortly, I am sure," she answered him at last. "I told her she must make herself ready for the betrothal ceremony. I have sent for Father Julius, if that meets with your approval, so that he might draw up the marriage contract. Of course, the banns will have to be read as well." Kayln kept her eyes on Philip's face. She wanted to be certain the boy really understood the seriousness of the situation. He would know a betrothal was even more binding than the actual wedding in most cases.

Philip nodded gravely, and this made Kayln warm to him even more. At least he did not try to charm her into accepting him. And Kayln was sure this young man had a great deal of charm. Was he not Hawk's brother?

"I would like to arrange the wedding with all possible haste." Philip raised his chin, and she could see his Adam's apple move as he swallowed. "I want no scandal to touch Celia, can I prevent it."

"Perhaps you should have considered that before you made the babe," Kayln said, raising her brows, not willing to let him off too easily. If the boy was to be a husband and father, he must be made to understand that his actions had consequences.

Philip reddened and swallowed, his Adam's apple bobbing again. He lifted his shoulders even higher and said, "I know it is hard for you to believe this"—he looked down at Kayln with complete earnestness—"but I had not planned what happened between Celia and myself. When we met she was so sweet and gentle I fell in love with her. It is true, she is also as lovely as a spring morning, but the love I bear her goes much deeper than her beauty. What we did"—his blush deepened—"was out of that love."

"Philip!"

Kayln turned to see Celia standing in the doorway of the hall, her foot poised on the bottom step as she came from the tower. Beside Kayln, Philip caught his breath at the sight of Celia's loveliness.

For she was beautiful indeed. Her pale hair was unbound except for a transparent blue veil held in place by a circlet of finely wrought silver. Her slender frame was covered by a gown of white beneath a white tunic embroidered with bluebirds perched upon silver twigs.

Clearly Celia had heard what Philip said because her face shone with an inner light that was almost blinding as she held out a delicate slender hand. She had eyes only for her lover as she started toward him with a small cry of happiness.

Philip too seemed to glow with some inner fire. The two of them had clearly forgotten their siblings as they ran into one another's arms to share a kiss that made Kayln turn away from the depth of its intimacy.

Blinking back the tears that started to her eyes on witnessing the touching moment, Kayln looked at the floor. She did not want Hawk to see her weakness.

"Ahhhm." Hawk cleared his throat, drawing Kayln's gaze. "Might I hope that my brother has passed your inspection?"

When Kayln didn't reply, he motioned toward the embracing couple. "It is clear he meets with your sister's."

Kayln glanced toward Celia and Philip, who were still embracing, still oblivious to everything but each other. "There was never a question in my mind of that," Kayln said. She swung around to face him again, her back straight, her brows arched over eyes that held a hint of hauteur. "If it were otherwise, I would not have forced her into marriage with him, no matter what others might say."

Hawk watched her closely, one brow quirking upward. "Even the Church?" It surprised him that Kayln would be so sensitive to her sister's wishes. He would have thought she would want to observe the proprieties first and foremost.

He listened thoughtfully as she replied, "I would have found some way to seek retribution, but I could not have forced her into marriage. God would not want Celia to be tied to a man whom she did not love because of an afternoon's mistake." The way she looked at him with her chin set stubbornly told Hawk she meant what she said. He had to admit that no matter her faults, Kayln clearly loved her sister.

But that, he told himself, was none of his concern. He wanted nothing more from Kayln than to ease this aching desire he felt for her. Because in spite of her chafing remarks toward Philip, Hawk did still want her. His hands itched to mold that luscious form beneath them, to pull her close against him.

She looked up at him as he took a step closer to her. "You are an unexpectedly rare woman, Kayln D'Arcy. I shall enjoy delving into your most guarded mysteries." His voice and expression were seductive, chipping delicately at her innermost defenses.

"I—" Kayln began, then turned as she heard Celia call her name. She was glad of the interruption, for she did not have any idea what she should answer to Hawk's comment. Kayln was beginning to grow somewhat angry with herself. She was not some mewling maid, but a mature woman, perfectly capable of standing up to any man.

On the other hand, it was ridiculous for her to read too much into what he said. He'd made no move to touch her or take liberties as he had before. All he had told her was that he would enjoy getting to know her better, had he not?

His hot gaze seemed to say much more than that, but she had so little experience with men that she was not sure. Uncertainty furrowed her brow as she watched his face.

Because of her inner confusion, she could only manage a stiff smile when Celia ran forward to take her hands, breaking the silent communication. "Is he not wonderful?" Her ardent gaze moved back to Philip.

Kayln turned to see Philip poised, waiting for her to reply. There was a slight vulnerability in the way he hesitated to look at her directly, which made her realize how deeply he wished for her approval.

Not wishing to ruin Celia's happiness in this moment, she forced down her own sense of betrayal at what the boy had done. "I think you have chosen well," Kayln answered, gently squeezing Celia's fingers. "Your Philip seems a fine young man."

Celia swung around to beam at her lover. "Did I not tell you Kayln was the sweetest of sisters?"

"Enough of this talk," Kayln said, uncomfortable with her sister's praise. She released Celia's hands, aware of Hawk's gaze upon her. "We must get on with the matter at hand. There is the marriage contract to consider."

Hawk looked around them with raised brows. "Who will negotiate the terms of the contract?"

Kayln frowned, not understanding what he meant. "What say you, my lord?"

Hawk turned to her, his tone as if he were speaking to a dull-witted child. "The contract. Who will sit down with me and discuss terms and settlements?"

Grasping the significance of what he was saying, Kayln stiffened. "I will, my Lord Hawkhurst. Do you have some objection?"

Hawk stared at her. "Have you no male relative present to see to your interests?"

"I have no male relations."

"No one?"

"Nay. I was the sole heir of both my father and my husband."

He looked at the angry line of her mouth, unable to fathom what he had done to cause insult. He but wished to see her fairly done by. Mayhap they could not even continue without the consent of King Edward. "Then you are a ward of the king. We must gain his acceptance to go further."

Kayln drew herself up. " 'We' must not. I have paid a handsome fine to our dear king in order to control my own affairs. King Edward has much need of gold to fuel his war in France and was most happy to oblige me."

She went on, her jaw set in a hard line. "Do you have some objection to negotiating with a woman? Is it hard for you to imagine that I might be able to determine my own best interests?"

"We are not discussing my personal biases here, no matter what they might or might not be," Hawk persisted, planting his feet firmly apart. Hawk was not altogether certain how the conversation had deteriorated so quickly. In his own mind he had said nothing to cause insult to Kayln, who was behaving with the same unpleasant nature as a draft animal. He told himself he should not be surprised. She had already proved herself a most obstinate and unpleasant female. Once more he wondered what about her attracted him so fiercely. Surely he could learn to conquer such an unreasonable and imprudent attachment.

"But what *do* you think, my lord?" Kayln insisted.

Hawk sighed and decided that from this day hence he would avoid this woman if at all possible. Then his lips twisted in displeasure as he realized that once their families were joined, that might not prove so very practical. But he assured himself that he could keep himself from reacting to her. He could begin now by showing her that she could not rile him. In what he thought to be a placating tone, Hawk said, "I believe that with some assistance, a woman is perfectly capable of holding property. Of course, she would need advice on matters of security and such."

Kayln gasped. "With some assistance?"

His frown deepened. Why was she being so obtuse? "Am I to understand that you disagree?"

"You may," she answered coldly, defying him with her eyes. "I hold my lands by my own hand and need no man to direct me and know full well what I wish to do. Everything I possess will pass to Celia upon my death."

Hawk's brows rose in surprise. "You do not mean to stipulate that fact in the marriage contract?" In the event that she might someday marry and have children of her own, she must retain something for them. Hawk could not allow her to do this. He refused to acknowledge the tug of discomfort the thought of a future marriage brought, telling himself he cared only that he did not cheat her.

"I do intend to do just that." Kayln placed her hands on her gently rounded hips, seeming to have no clear understanding of what she was giving away.

"Please," Celia said, breaking in, putting her hand on Kayln's shoulder. It was obvious from her tone that she wished to forestall them from further antagonizing one another.

"Hawk," Philip added, "let us not forget why we are here. It is not our place to decide how Lady D'Arcy should dispose of her holdings."

"Philip, you must call me Kayln," Kayln told her future brother with a tight smile that obviously excluded Hawk. "*You* are part of my family now and I would not have you stand on ceremony."

"Now." She turned to Hawk. "Shall we continue, or will you persist in questioning me on a matter that, as Philip has so kindly pointed out, is none of your concern?"

Hawk only regarded her for another long moment before he grimaced and nodded. "As you wish," he said tightly. They were getting nowhere.

Kayln was startled by his sudden capitulation, and more than a little grateful. It would be most annoying to be the in-law of a man who felt he must question her on every detail of her life whenever they happened to meet.

She let out a relieved sigh, but kept her arms crossed defensively. Kayln wanted Hawk to fully understand that she was adamant in her determination to keep him from interfering in her decisions. She was sure it was something that would be hard for a man of his arrogant nature to accept. Just as she opened her mouth to speak, feeling enough time had elapsed to make her point, Hawk preempted her, his words stopping the sound in her throat.

"I will agree to this," he said, his tone gracious, his expression pleasant, "only if the contract states that all your properties pass to Celia only in the event that you should die without issue of your own.''

Kayln clenched her jaw, feeling her teeth grinding together. Why did this man feel the need to be so insufferably overbearing? Why must he make such an important point of this small thing? It could have no relevance to him. She did not care to go into her reasons for not wishing to marry. Even if she did marry Miles one day, she would never have children. Her own experiences had convinced her that they were better left unborn.

Unbidden, a scene came into her mind; herself and Hawk standing over a cradle. Gurgling up at them was a dark-haired babe with golden eyes. Kayln shook her head quickly to rid herself of the vision, her gaze flicking to Hawk, then away as she saw by his bland expression that he was completely unaware of her foolish thoughts. Whatever was the matter with her? Not in all her twenty-four years could she recall having so little control over her thoughts and emotions. Even with Raymond and her father, they might have held sway over her body, but never her mind. Such a domestic scene would not happen—especially not with Hawk.

She clenched her hands at her sides, wanting him gone from Aimsley, out of her sight and, she hoped, her mind.

If agreeing to his stipulation would achieve that end, then she would agree. What was the harm? Kayln would have no children. She ignored the flicker of unease that passed through her at giving in to Hawk. Doing as he asked just this one time meant little. She relinquished nothing of importance. Hawk held no power over her.

''Very well.'' Kayln motioned toward the high table in the center of the room. ''Let us be seated while we discuss the particulars.''

If Hawk was surprised by her agreement, he showed no sign of it as he nodded and turned to do as she bid.

Hours later, Kayln sat back with a sigh. It was incomprehensible to her that Hawk should be so aggressive in regard to what he wanted to see settled upon the young couple, when he refused to see her give them everything she owned. As it stood, Philip and Celia would receive Lindon, an extremely profitable property, upon Philip reaching the age of one and twenty. This, along with a substantial dowry of gold, made up a handsome marriage settlement.

Kayln looked over at the young lovers where they cuddled, whispering, in one of the window recesses. Now that Father Julius had gone to see that a clerk wrote copies of the document, which had been signed and witnessed, they had eyes only for each other.

"Kayln." Celia turned toward her sister, where she sat before the fire. "Might Philip and I go for a walk?"

Kayln's brow creased in a frown. "Is that wise?"

From the chair beside Kayln, Hawk gave a snort of amusement. "What harm can be done now, Kayln?"

She cringed at his familiar use of her name. Her gaze swung to him, and she had an intense urge to wipe the sardonic gleam from his golden eyes. "Indeed, what harm?" She placed her hands flat upon the arms of her chair, her fingers gripping the ends. "My sister is already with child. Surely she would not be harmed by the talk of all and sundry who might see them frolicking about the demesne."

"I would do nothing to harm Celia further." Philip leapt to his feet, making them look to him. "We wished only for a private moment in which to part, as I must return to Norwich without delay."

Kayln eyed him without blinking, then seeing that he was truly offended by her comment, nodded. "If that is your intent, you have my leave."

Without hesitating to offer thanks, the pair linked hands and went from the room, Philip shortening his long strides in deference to the small girl at his side.

Having had her attention focused upon Philip and Celia, Kayln was not attending to what Hawk was doing. This proved to be unwise for, as if from nowhere, he appeared directly in front of her. Looking up into his dark face above her, Kayln was amazed anew that one so large and heavily muscled as Hawk could move with such grace and speed.

Leaning over her, he placed his hands over her arms where they rested upon the chair, effectively caging them. His eyes were dark with barely suppressed anger. "You will cease baiting my brother."

Kayln flattened her spine against the back of the chair, an action that only served to call attention to her full breasts. She watched as his gaze came to rest there, his lids coming down to hood his eyes. Despite her irritation at his commanding tone, her breath came a little faster. As he continued to look at her she felt her nipples harden, all thoughts of answering him in kind flying from her mind.

Dark color stained Kayln's cheeks, and she felt a strange heaviness in her lower belly. Her own eyes moved over his wide chest and upward to where a vein pulsed in his heavily corded neck. Unexpectedly, she felt an overwhelming urge to place her lips there. Heaven help her, what was happening to her? It was as if nothing else mattered when he was near, and she could not think past the sensations he awakened in her.

He was the first man who had ever touched her in an intimate way. And in spite of the fact that she did not like him in the least, her body seemed to yearn for more. Oh, why, of all the men in England, had Hawk been the one to awaken her slumbering womanhood?

Knowing that she had little hope of rebuffing him if he did touch her—kiss her—Kayln was doubly grateful she had made him promise not to do so again. That was the way it had to be. He was too virile, sure of himself and his world.

She had to stop this—him—herself.

He raised one hand to place a finger upon her lower lip, but still she did not move. She was held immobile by her own reaction to him. He traced the full curve gently as he whispered, "Lovely."

Forcing her paralyzed throat to function, Kayln whispered hoarsely, "My lord, you have given your word not to press yourself upon me."

He smiled, the dark knowing in his eyes making her shiver. "I will not. You must choose. To kiss me, or nay."

She closed her eyes against the sheer pull of him. What was wrong with her? She knew nothing of this man to make her want him so.

At that moment a traitorous voice whispered inside her that this was not strictly true. Wasn't he here and now keeping his word? There was no one to prevent him from taking a kiss as he had that first time, but he was leaving her to decide. It was

Kayln who would choose to complete the contact—or not—as she desired.

A surge of self-awareness like none she had ever known raced through her blood. The feeling was heady as dark sweet wine, and completely irresistible.

Her lips parted and her lids were heavy as she looked up at him. Kayln leaned forward and placed her lips to his.

With a groan he pulled her up into his waiting arms. They enfolded her completely as his mouth claimed hers. As the contact deepened, Kayln realized she hadn't known what forces she was setting in motion. Their first kisses had been gentle and restrained. This one was neither. It was demanding, scorching, holding nothing back as the blood went rushing through her veins like floodwater. Her arms wound themselves around his neck as she strained toward him.

When Hawk lifted her by her bottom, she was made intimately aware of the hard aching need of him. Involuntarily, Kayln arched against him, shocked by the desire that sliced through her at this unbelievably sensual embrace.

"God help me, but you fire my blood," Hawk groaned as he dragged his mouth from hers. "If we are not more circumspect, it is you who will be talked of."

Kayln could not catch her breath, could not think clearly, as she leaned against him, her head on his chest. Never in all her wildest dreams had she believed she would feel such desire as this man stirred in her. Even though the baron was infuriatingly arrogant and commanding, she wanted him to carry her from the hall and ease this terrible, wonderful ache inside her.

"Has it been so long for you then?" he asked with a gentle smile. His voice had calmed, but the hand he raised to run through his black hair was unsteady, and she knew he had been as affected as she.

Because she was so befuddled by his kisses, it took a moment for his words to penetrate her mind. "So long?"

"You are so quick to respond that I can only guess you have not taken a lover for some time. Knowing that only makes it even harder for me to wait."

"Taken a lover?" she whispered, her body stiffening as she drew away from him.

"From the first moment I saw you I knew we would be together." He smiled confidently. "But I did not guess there would be such fire between us."

Kayln frowned, her lips thinning. Did this overbearing ass think she would fall into his bed so easily? She caught her breath on a sob. Had she not just given him cause to think that very thing?

She had responded like some crazed wanton to a man whom she barely knew and obviously disliked. Even he, as arrogant as he was, could not think she cared for him. Hawk clearly believed she was simply eager to bed him in spite of that. Though she was inexperienced, Kayln knew many women found a lover after they had once been married.

"I did not . . . I cannot . . ." she began, uncaring at this moment that she sounded nervous and uncertain. She must make him understand she had not meant to make him think she would go so far. How could she have believed for even one moment that she was in control of this sensual dance?

But he stopped her with a brush of his hand over her mouth. "I know, sweet. You would not have me now. It would be best left until all is settled and the young ones wed. Though I must tell you," he said, his golden eyes holding her own, "knowing how you welcome me will make the wait that much more painful." He drew her close again, seemingly blind to the rigidity of her body. Kayln felt him still firm and insistent against her belly.

For a moment, she could not reply, trying desperately to form the words to tell him she had made a terrible mistake in kissing him. How could she hope to make him hear her? Neither her father nor Raymond had ever cared for her wants or desires. Why would Hawk be any different?

Despair helped her find her tongue. Forcefully, she pushed at his chest until he released her. "How dare you. Do you imagine that I would just tumble into bed with you? Never would I allow you to touch me. Not even if you were the last man in Christendom."

Hawk stepped back, startled after her heated response to him. She had been the one to kiss him. Anger and frustration made his voice gruff with sarcasm. "I beg your pardon, my lady. I overstepped myself."

Kayln refused to acknowledge the irony. "Indeed you have. I'll ask you to remember that we have been brought together by our concern for Celia and Philip, nothing more." She took deep rapid breaths in agitation.

He studied her outraged face without speaking, fighting his own ire, not sure what he was searching for. Then he saw it as her gaze grazed his, a trace of sad longing in her light gray eyes.

Something had hurt Kayln. He was sure of it. And she used rage and implacability to hide that pain.

He reached toward her. "Kayln, what is it? What has been done to you?"

Obviously surprised at his frankness, she looked at him with uncertainty. For a moment he thought she might answer. Then it was gone and her eyes became shuttered. "Nothing that need concern you, my Lord Hawkhurst. I'll thank you to mind your own affairs and not mine."

Disappointment filled him, and Hawk bit back the questions that hovered on his lips. Devil take her, then. He had no need to involve himself with a woman who was so hot and cold.

Hawk had ever been one to protect and defend those in need. Kayln's vulnerability drew him as surely as the falcon is called by the night, but he was not about to put himself through hell trying to help her.

She had made it clear that she wanted no part of him. Hawk would do as she said and keep his distance. It was the best thing for both of them.

Chapter Six

The three weeks since Hawk brought Philip to Aimsley had passed in a blur of activity for Kayln. They had decided that the wedding should be performed with all haste, but it was to be both well arranged and well attended.

No expense had been spared on either the feast or Celia's new wardrobe. Eight women had been kept busy sewing an array of cotehardies and tunics for Celia. There was also a finely made pourpoint and cotehardie for Philip, as Celia's marriage gift to him. The pourpoint was a close-fitting quilted tunic, originally designed to be worn under armor, that had gained wide acceptance as it was highly comfortable, aside from being flattering.

The kitchens were filled with food in all stages of preparation. Pies, roasts, sauces, all manner of fowl, and other game were being readied for the wedding.

Even today, the very day the guests were set to start arriving, Kayln was working in the kitchen. It was a big open beamed room off the hall. A large wide fireplace dominated the chamber, and it burned so hot that sweat beaded on the foreheads of those working in the crowded room. Three tables took up most of the available floor space, two extras having been added to enlarge the work area. Even the wooden shelves that ran along each of the four walls and usually held silver and pewter, cups, trays, and pitchers, were cluttered with baked goods.

The spicy scent of cinnamon stung her nose pleasantly as she watched Mabel, the cook, sprinkle it carefully over the apples. It was not Kayln's usual custom to help with the cooking, but every pair of hands was needed now. A sigh escaped her lips, and she raised her hand to smooth back the damp hair on her forehead, leaving a streak of flour.

She went back to rolling the dough. Only two more days and the wedding would take place. Kayln could not wait until the whole affair was over.

The thought of having so many strangers in her home was unsettling. She had worked hard to bring order and quiet to her life, and resented any disruption.

Kayln had invited only Miles, but she had no idea if he was even coming, not having received any reply.

It was the Hawkhursts who had invited a great number of people to the festivities. Philip had even invited the Earl of Norwich, which meant the earl's household and retainers would arrive with him.

Kayln had also found that besides Hawk, there was another brother, Martin, and a sister, Jayne, who would be coming to the wedding.

All had to be accepted with forbearance. The wedding was the one last thing she could give Celia before she became her husband's property. Not that the girl was going away. It had been decided that Celia would continue to reside at Aimsley for a time. Philip was not able to take her to Norwich. He was only a squire, and so had no privileges that would allow him to keep a wife.

His training could be speeded up as much as possible, but it would still be at least a year before he received his spurs and was able to call himself a knight. Philip had not been pleased, and neither had Celia, but they really had little choice in the situation.

Never between Kayln and her husband, Raymond, had there been such intimacy. Her own marriage seemed all the more empty by comparison.

For a moment, she allowed herself the luxury of wondering what her life might have been like with some other man. Without warning Hawk's image popped into her mind.

Now there was a dangerous thought, she told herself in horror. He was the furthest thing from her idea of the perfect man. He was proud to the point of arrogance and had a daunting temper. She had suffered too much abuse at the hands of the other men in her life to disregard such rage.

Yet despite her misgivings, he awakened an awareness in her of herself as a woman, with long-buried needs and desires.

Every time Hawk was near, she seemed to go as soft as butter in sunshine. When Hawk looked at her in that way of his, as if every bit of his consciousness was centered upon her and her alone, Kayln's breathing quickened and an unknown heaviness settled in her lower belly.

She was not fool enough to try to convince herself that he was not aware of her attraction to him. That much had been made clear the last time she saw him.

Lord Hawkhurst seemed to think very highly of himself. And why should he not? she asked herself. If other women responded to him the way she did, he would be hard pressed not to see it. Her cheeks burned.

What she had to do was learn to control herself and all would be well. She only hoped following through with the decision would prove as simple as making it. It had not thus far.

With forced enthusiasm, she began to crimp the edges of the crust. When she was finished, Kayln pushed it aside and turned to the cook. "What now?"

Mabel put her hands on her wide hips. "I'll tell you what now! You must leave this hot kitchen and get some fresh air. You've worked harder than any of us. And truth to tell," she said, making a sweeping gesture about the room, "there's more than enough here to satisfy even the king's court." She patted her large bosom with her palm, a wide smile on her pink-cheeked face. Mabel was a strong, heavily boned woman, with broad shoulders and large hands, but not much spare fat.

"You are certain?" Kayln asked, her gray eyes expectant. She knew the guests were due to start arriving that very afternoon, and she would be overjoyed at a few moments to call her own. A few moments to ready herself for facing that man again.

"Would I be telling you a thing if it weren't gospel?" Mabel put her hand on Kayln's shoulder, turning her to face the door.

Kayln stiffened at the familiar contact, and Mabel slowly drew her hands away. Not since she was a child had she liked anyone to touch her. When Kayln raised her gaze to the cook's eyes, she could see the sympathetic expression in them. She took a step backward, uncomfortable with Mabel's pity. Kayln knew what the castle folk thought of her, that though they respected and honored her, they felt she was too remote and cool. She sometimes wished she understood how others managed it, allowing someone else to come close without fear of rejection or hurt. Kayln could not.

But she would never allow the cook or anyone else to see how very alone she felt. Kayln lifted her chin and said, "Should anyone have need of me, I will be in the orchard."

First she went to her tower room. A gentle breeze fluttered the apricot silk hangings of the bed, and sunlight gleamed off the hand-polished walnut posts. The rich carpet beneath her feet muffled her footsteps as Kayln crossed the threshold and removed one of her ledgers from the chest at the foot of the high wide bed.

She cast a long glance toward the new peach samite gown Alice had laid across the foot of the bed. Kayln couldn't resist running one hand over the fur that trimmed the edges of the white tunic she planned to wear with it.

She smoothed her flour-streaked skirt, frowning as she ran her hand over the simple braid she wore her hair in. What would Hawk think if he could see her now?

She groaned, reminding herself that she was foolish to care what he thought. By the True Cross, she despised the man and the way she'd behaved since meeting him.

With the ledger tucked under her arm, Kayln made her way out of the keep and into the orchard.

The trees were heavy with fruit, and she knew as soon as the guests left, she would need to see that the last of the apples and plums were gathered. From the reports of her bailiff, Luther, Kayln knew that her villains had been hard at work. The harvest would be completed soon, and her people would have an abundant supply of stores to see them through the winter ahead.

Kayln walked until she was nearly at the edge of the orchard, trying with all her might to enjoy the mildness of the late fall day. The air had a certain peaceful stillness about it, but it did little to soothe her spirits.

The trees were keeping their leaves later than usual this year, but the few lying upon the ground crackled under her feet. She halted automatically under a familiar apple tree with low-lying branches.

Reaching up, she tucked the book into the crook of a limb, then pulled herself up into the tree. Picking up her book, she held onto the trunk with her other arm and stepped over and up onto her special limb. The branch seemed to have been fashioned by nature just to suit her purpose. It was wide and flat, with a smaller branch growing out from the side to act as a backrest.

This was Kayln's private place, where she came when she wanted to escape the hustle and bustle of the busy life inside the keep.

The tangy sweet smell of ripe apples on the tree was a harmless temptation. She reached out to pick a big red one from the limb above her, then settled back on the branch and opened the book. Usually it gave her a deep sense of contentment to look at the numbers on the pages and know that all was in order.

Her ability to read and do sums was the one thing for which she was grateful to her father, though he had not had her taught out of the goodness of his heart. Edward Chilton had been an extremely thrifty man, and it had made perfect sense to him that his daughter be able to read and write so he would not have need to pay a scribe to do his business. After all, he had Kayln. What logic was there in feeding and clothing a daughter unless she was of some use to him?

Her mind veered away from thoughts of her sire. Down that path was only pain.

Determinedly, she bent over the figures. But today, Kayln could not quite concentrate on the columns. Before long, she found herself lying back against the limb, gazing off into space, agitatedly swinging her leg back and forth.

An unstoppable wave of uncertainty rushed through her as the hour of Hawk's arrival grew closer. She couldn't keep from remembering the searching sympathy in his eyes after they'd kissed.

What did it mean? She had no reason to trust such emotion in a man even though, inside herself where she was vulnerable and alone, she longed to.

It would be far wiser to remember the anger in Hawk's face

as they'd parted soon after. That glimpse of sympathy was more dangerous to her equilibrium than all the fury he could muster, for it made her want to think that Hawk might be different, and that was an indulgence she could not afford. Never would Kayln allow herself to be subservient to a man again, for that was what marriage made a woman. And any other liaison between herself and Hawk was forbidden by the Church and thus unthinkable. Was it not?

Oh, but how exciting it would be, a voice cried inside her, to give herself up to the desire she saw in his gaze, to yield herself to the mastery of his arms. She closed her eyes, feeling that strange honeyed warmth flow through her at the very thought. Was she to live out her life without knowing the sweet mystery of desire?

It was then that Kayln became aware of a sound that had been prodding at the edge of her consciousness. Someone was whistling. The tune was loud, reverberating through the trees, and what the whistler lacked in skill, he made up for in enthusiasm.

She leaned over the branch of the tree, peering out from between the leaves to catch a glimpse of the whistler. Kayln wondered who would have come this way through the orchard. Surely any arriving wedding guests would come to the front gate.

The sound stopped suddenly, and a deep male voice rose to swell in the air. The tune emerged in a pleasant baritone that revealed the singer's identity.

Hawk!

Horrified, Kayln looked down at her threadbare gown, which barely retained any of its green color. She reached up to smooth her untidy hair. In her haste to begin the day's tasks, she had secured the heavy braid with an old piece of string.

Kayln had no intention of meeting Hawk looking like this.

She drew up her legs and bundled the folds of her gown tightly in her lap so it would not hang down. Squinting her eyes shut, Kayln prayed that he would continue on without noticing her. She made herself lie still upon the branch.

Her hopes that Hawk would simply pass by were for naught. It was almost as if he had some inner knowledge she was there and wanted to torment her. She could hear him coming invariably closer, his voice growing in volume with his approach.

Saints in heaven, she thought desperately. He was going to pass right next to her tree. She held her breath, feeling as if her lungs might burst from the effort.

But instead of going on as she had hoped, Hawk drew his horse up under Kayln's hiding place and stopped, the sound of his voice dwindling away to silence.

She kept her eyes closed, afraid to look down from her perch. She kept praying all the while it was something other than herself which had made Hawk stop there and he would be on his way without much more ado.

"Good morrow, Lady D'Arcy." His voice was unexpectedly cheerful and rich with its own pleasantly rough undertone.

Kayln's heart sank to her toes. Screwing up her courage, she opened her lids slowly and looked down.

There was Hawk, directly below her, an equally unexpectedly cheery smile on his darkly tanned face. For a moment, Kayln detested that smile, for it made her heart beat faster, a reaction she was quick to dampen, for he was surely grinning at her expense. It would please the knave to catch her here this way.

A sharp retort sprang to her mind, as she wondered what he was doing here in her orchard. But Kayln stopped herself before the thought was uttered aloud. She was in no position to rile him.

The best course, she decided, was to pretend there were nothing at all unusual about her being in a tree. Kayln was determined to send him on his way without his having seen how humiliated she actually was.

"Good day, sir knight," Kayln answered, growing more confident when her voice did not betray her inner turmoil.

"It's a fine day for rabbit hunting," he told her pleasantly. He was riding bareback, but Kayln could see a bow and a quiver filled with arrows attached to a leather strap that fastened under the horse's belly. These hung from the left side of the horse's rump. On the right was a long rope from which several furry bodies had been strung. "I thought these hares might be of some use to you with so many mouths to feed."

"I thank you." Kayln nodded politely. "But you needn't have bothered. You have been most generous already," she said, thinking of the deer and sheep he had already provided. She had no wish to be more beholden to him.

"It was no bother." He grinned, his golden eyes sparkling as if he knew her thoughts, but his next words gave her pause to wonder if she was misreading him. "Hunting gave me fair reason for going off for a moment's peace. I felt the need to think, and I could not do so with Philip carrying on about Celia and the wedding." Hawk gave a husky chuckle, raising black brows conspiratorially. "I am happy for the boy, mind you, but one can find oneself at a loss for words."

Surprised at herself, Kayln felt the corners of her mouth curve upward in an answering smile. She could understand wholeheartedly what Hawk was saying. Celia had nearly driven her mad as well. "I understand much better than you might think," she told him.

Hawk took in her position above him with an understanding nod. "I see."

Suddenly, Kayln felt herself blushing. It was strange to be speaking of everyday things after all that had passed between them. It seemed as if she and Hawk had been locked in a contest of wills since the moment they met. And there was something very intimate about finding out they had something as personal as a need for privacy in common.

Feeling as if she must say something, Kayln held up her book. "I was going over the accounts."

"Most diligent of you," Hawk answered, with a troubled frown. "I oft find myself buried deep in like material of late." His intense look gave Kayln the feeling that there was more behind the words than he was saying. But his expression did not invite her to pry.

When he turned back, he looked up at Kayln as if he were genuinely interested in the answer to his next question. "Do you read as well?"

She took his lead. "Why, yes," Kayln said, lowering her book back to her lap. "Since I was a little girl."

"Did you know," he asked companionably, "that the library in the papal palace at Avignon has hundreds of books?"

"You have seen this library?" Kayln asked. The thought

of so many books was awe inspiring. Her gray eyes widened.

He shifted the reins from one hand to the other and leaned forward. ''King Edward is oft in communication with His Grace Innocent VI, though thus far his efforts have done little to end this war with France.''

''And you accompanied him to Avignon?''

He nodded as if even the memory was wonderful. ''There are no less than thirty-nine massive towers within the walls, and riches such as you cannot imagine. It is truly an amazing sight, though there are too many Frenchmen about for my taste. Innocent is too biased toward their cause, try as he might to hide it.''

Over the past years she had given little thought to the world outside Aimsley, other than what news Miles shared with her. Kayln had always felt she was safest and most secure right here on her lands, where she was the master of her own life. There was something about the way Hawk saw the world that renewed some of the wonder she had known as a child. Unconsciously she scowled, telling herself that it was a mistake to be lulled by his unexpectedly pleasant demeanor. They had not parted on the best of terms, and Kayln could only think that he was putting himself forward in order to avoid conflict with her during the wedding celebrations.

Hawk reached up and plucked a large red apple from the lower branches. He brought it to his mouth and sunk his teeth into the crisp white flesh.

Kayln found herself watching his mouth, fascinated by the shape of it. When she raised her gaze to meet his, she saw that he was watching her, as if he was trying to decide what to make of her. Kayln blushed and looked away.

Taking note of the long shadows of the trees, she realized afternoon had arrived. Kayln had not meant to stay out so long. ''I should return to the keep,'' she said. ''Our guests will be arriving at any time and I must make ready for them.'' She looked down at the ground, which seemed further away than it had any of the many times she had climbed this very tree.

Hawk must have seen the hesitation on her face, for he tossed his apple core aside. ''May I be of assistance?''

Kayln looked down at him curiously as he moved his large

chestnut stallion under her and held up his arms. Her teeth worried her lower lip as she tried to think of some way to tell him she could not possibly do what he was suggesting. Although they had just shared the most civil conversation of their acquaintance, she had no intention of going to him.

She was far too attracted to him, too aware of him as a man. Even the thought of Hawk putting those two strong arms around her was more than Kayln could bear. For him to actually touch her was unthinkable.

"I do not think—" she began to say.

"Come, Kayln, I would not feel myself a proper knight if I were to go away and leave a lady stranded in a tree."

"Oh, but I . . ." Kayln stopped, looking doubtfully down into his handsome face. Why could she not just tell him to go away? How did he always manage to make her feel so young and uncertain?

"Come," he insisted, reaching toward her. There was nothing in his tone to indicate that he was unsure of her acquiescence. His benign expression told her clearly that she was making much of nothing.

Unless she made herself appear an utter fool, there was nothing for Kayln to do but comply. Besides, she was already late in returning to the keep. Carefully she tucked the ledger in the crook of the tree limb.

When he saw her obvious capitulation, Hawk raised his arms. "Come, I will guide you down. Do not be afraid of Mac. He has been well trained to stand still for many hours. Sometimes before a battle it is necessary."

"Mac?" She frowned in question.

"I once knew a very large and wild Scotsman with hair the exact color of this beast's coat. It was he I thought of the moment I saw the horse." Hawk grinned up at her. "Now cease trying to divert me and come down."

Taking a deep breath for courage, she scooted herself to the edge of the branch and lowered her legs into the air. She told herself Hawk was just doing his duty as a knight by helping her from what he, mistakenly, saw as a perilous position.

If the hem of her cotehardie had not caught on a twig, all would have gone well. As Kayln felt her feet touch the back of Hawk's horse, she realized that she could also feel a cool breeze on the flesh of her legs. She looked down and saw that her gown had hiked up to her hips, completely exposing her legs and thighs.

Her lips pursed in mortification and irritation. Drat him for insisting on this idiocy! Frantically she groped behind her to discover the problem. When she wavered unpleasantly on top of her precarious perch, she looked to Hawk for assistance, but it was apparent that he was of no mind to help.

As Kayln began to slip down to him, Hawk's eyes came to rest on her long slender legs and stayed there. He wet his suddenly dry lips and realized that he was having some difficulty swallowing.

He heard her give what sounded like a gasp above his head, but Hawk couldn't raise his attention from her legs. They were the most beautiful he had ever seen, long, slender, and perfectly shaped, and he was no more than a hand's breadth from the smooth creamy skin.

The horse shifted beneath him, and Kayln cried out, grabbing for Hawk's head.

Just in time, Hawk reached up and caught her as she fell forward. At that same moment he heard the sound of rending cloth. He pulled her down facing him, her legs straddling his. There was such a look of dazed surprise on her lovely face, Hawk almost laughed aloud. But he stopped himself. All he had learned about Kayln told him she would not find this situation funny.

Any deviation from propriety seemed to disturb her greatly. For pity's sake, she appeared embarrassed and shamed by her own passion, even going so far as to deny it. Her antagonistic attitude had shown itself so plainly when last they'd met that he'd been determined to avoid any unnecessary contact with the fair widow.

It was a strange experience for Hawk to meet a woman who so obviously responded to him physically, as Kayln did, but seemed so reticent about those feelings. If Hawk had not known she was a widow, he might have thought her an innocent. But Kayln had been married for five years. No man with such a creature to grace his bed would fail to take advantage of the opportunity.

Even this very day when he'd realized she was up the tree,

he'd thought only to bait her, to see how she reacted to being in such a vulnerable position. But as they'd talked his attitude had changed, and he'd found himself speaking of things that surprised him. She'd seemed so different, almost eager to hear what he had to say.

Now here she sat, in his lap. Hawk's gaze followed the rise and fall of her full breasts as she panted to catch her breath. He tried to recall his resolve to quell his desire for her.

God, but she was delicious.

As if it were the most natural thing in the world, Hawk leaned forward and pressed his lips to hers. She sucked in her breath, and he put his hand to the back of her head to draw her even closer.

At first, Kayln's lips were hesitant and awkward under his. Then she moaned and opened her mouth to his questing tongue. His kiss was soft yet firm, giving yet demanding. She felt herself dissolving, melting into him. And her pulse throbbed in a rhythm with the pounding of his heart. Desire burned a honeyed path through her, settling in her lower belly. Kayln's breasts became full and heavy, straining toward him. She was lost in wanting him, yearning to give as she was receiving. Her own tongue slid over his.

Now it was Hawk's turn to groan in response, as she raised her arms to his shoulders, clinging to him as if he were her only source of life. The slow play of her tongue on his lit a fire that raged through his body. He reached out and connected with the soft warm flesh of her thigh, his fingers closing around her leg.

He drew back and looked down. Kayln was completely bared to his gaze, her gown still tangled about her hips. Free to touch her upper thighs without the restraint of clothing, he stroked the velvety flesh with consummate skill. He heard her moan and she began to tremble, her hands clutching at his shoulders.

When he brushed the tangled curls at the juncture of her thighs with the tips of his fingers, Kayln gasped, her breath hot against his shoulder. The muscles in her thighs tensed as if trying to capture his hand.

"Kayln," he breathed against the heated flesh of her throat, easing his hand forward, cradling the moist warmth of her. "I want you so much.'' He kissed her lips again, drawing on her passion. ''I know you want me too,'' he whispered, pushing his hand upward, his fingers brushing the dewy sweetness of her flesh.

''Hawk,'' Kayln cried out, opening her eyes and trying to sit up as she felt his touch on a part of her that had never known such intimacy. There was no way to prevent him had she any real desire to do so. She was utterly vulnerable to Hawk with his hard thighs between hers, and he was doing things to her that she had never imagined in her most exotic fantasies.

''Shh.'' He kissed her deeply, silencing her with his mouth.

From the moment Hawk's hand had come into contact with the sensitive flesh of her thigh, Kayln had been lost. She felt herself falling into a swirling haze of delight. The rough texture of his fingers sent a jolt of heat through her that made her body turn bonelessly weak.

Involuntarily, she arched her back, bringing Hawk's willing attention to the swelling fullness of her breasts. She bit her lip to keep from sobbing as he brought his free hand up to caress the tempting mounds, and her nipples hardened against the palm of his hand through the thin fabric of her cote.

Facing him as she was with her legs apart, Kayln was exposed to him completely. When one finger flicked out to brush against the swollen little nub at the center of her womanhood, she cried out, her legs opening wider to grant him further access to her.

The invitation of her body was not ignored as Hawk began to caress her there with a slow steady deliberation that was intoxicating. She knew a delight so unspeakably wondrous, her heart began to pound with a steady rhythm that became a hum inside her. Her pleasure escaped in little panting sighs that heated the air between them like sweet fragrant incense.

Her hips began to move in a rhythm to match the motion of his hand.

Kayln felt as though she couldn't breathe. It was too much, too incredible. Surely she would die if the ecstasy did not stop growing.

Just when Kayln thought she would scream with the glory

of it, she took flight, soaring into the clouds, rising with the sheer splendor of the light bursting inside her.

Moments later she was back in Hawk's arms and he was kissing her with tender care, his hand still cupping the small mound which pulsed against his callused palm. She was unable to move, her limbs weak with languor.

"Kayln, Kayln," he whispered, his voice husky with need. "I can wait no longer for you." He half lifted her as he tried to undo the belt that secured his drawers and hose.

Distantly, Kayln was aware of what he was trying to do and even what it meant. But she could not rouse herself to think clearly.

A loud insistent noise began to penetrate the thick haze that enveloped her. With a frown she realized that it was the horn being trumpeted from the keep. That horn was only to be sounded in time of trouble or, with the wedding approaching, when guests arrived.

It was this that brought Kayln to her senses. What in the world was she doing here with Hawkhurst on his horse? How could she have let this happen? Why, she barely even knew this man, and yet she had allowed him to touch her in a way her husband never had.

"Please," Kayln muttered, trying to pull away from Hawk, who was intent on trying to undo his clothes.

"Yes, love, I am trying," he groaned against her hair.

"No," she began to protest, but her voice was too soft, too breathless. She tried again. "No." This time she pushed at him with what little strength she could muster.

Hawk looked into her sea-gray eyes in surprise. "What is wrong, love?"

"We cannot do this. Can you not hear the horn? The guests are arriving at this very moment."

Hawk said nothing for a moment, then leaned his cheek against her soft hair. "You are right. When we come together it should be a time to remember, not a hurried coupling on the back of my stallion." He laughed, albeit shakily. "Though I must admit, if you were willing, I should be prepared to settle for that."

Kayln could voice no reply. She knew that by responding to Hawk as she had, she'd given him every reason to believe she would welcome more intimacy. She blushed as Mac moved restlessly beneath them. And it had happened on the back of a horse. Though, truth to tell, if the animal moved at all while Hawk was touching her, Kayln was not aware of it. She had been aware of nothing besides this man and the way he made her feel. Shame made her bow her golden head.

"Might we return to the keep?" she asked, her voice quavering. She would have to conceive of some way to tell Hawk what had just happened had been a dreadful mistake, but right now she wanted to be taken home. If she could just be alone to think, surely the words would come to her.

"I delight in fulfilling your every desire," he said, leaning toward her to thoroughly kiss her lips, which were full and swollen from his earlier attentions.

When he raised his head, Kayln felt a little dazed, surprised he could easily reawaken her desire so soon after what had just happened between them. She resented his power over her even more, and knew she couldn't let him continue. She pushed at his chest. "No more."

"You are right, we should not begin something more that can't be finished here." Putting one arm under her legs and the other around her back, Hawk lifted her easily, turning her around so she was facing forward.

Kayln flushed with outrage. But she said nothing, not wanting to delay their departure by arguing with him. She wished in fact never to speak to him again. But even as she let her resentment of Hawk rise to the fore, she knew in the back of her mind that the real reason she could think of nothing to say to him was that she had participated fully in what had just occurred.

The ride to Aimsley was a nightmare for Kayln. His arms circled her waist possessively even though she tried to sit as far forward as possible. If he noticed her withdrawal, he made no mention of it. She could only think that he was too preoccupied with his own thoughts of bedding her. At least Hawk did not try to speak. For that much she was grateful. Her mind screamed with the frustration of knowing he felt some form of privilege over her, as if she were his to do with as he would. This went against all Kayln wished for herself. She wanted no man to feel he owned her.

As they drew close to the gate, Hawk made an effort to pull the sides of her torn cote over her long legs. Kayln saw this as another sign of proprietorship, and drew the gown closed as best she could herself.

As they crossed under the portcullis and came into the view of the other people inside the courtyard, Kayln saw the way all and sundry stopped to stare at them. She raised her head high and refused to allow herself to blush. Kayln knew her people were all shocked to see her this way, bare-legged and sitting before a man, as if she were no more than a common serf.

So it was no wonder that her people, serf and villain alike, could only gape at the sight of their noble lady being brought into the keep in such a fashion.

Hawk rode directly across the courtyard to the stables. As they drew close, Kayln noticed there were a pair of strange horses. A very tall, slender man with auburn hair stepped from behind one of the horses.

''Hawk!'' he called, raising his hand in greeting.

Another figure emerged from inside the stables. This one was definitely female. Long coal-black hair, which tumbled in a riot of curls past her tiny waist, was covered by a gossamer-thin veil held in place by a silver circlet. Her cote was scarlet, and she wore a silver tunic trimmed with fur. The lady was tall and slim, Kayln thought, possibly as tall as herself, though she was not as full at hip and bosom. Everything about her was worthy of note, but it was her face which caught and held the eye, making one wonder if such loveliness could be real. Her skin was pale as milk, and God had seen fit to paint a flush of pink over her high cheekbones. Her lips were finely shaped, the top matched perfectly to the bottom, her nose narrow and aristocratic. And her eyes—her eyes were wide, a true deep blue and fringed with incredibly long black lashes.

But what bothered Kayln was that this lady was looking directly at Hawk, her expression filled with joy. With a cry, this lovely creature raced across the courtyard at the same moment as Hawk slid to the ground to meet her.

The Lady of Aimsley looked over at the tall auburn-haired man, thinking that he surely could not approve of his wife greeting another man with such enthusiasm. Kayln herself could not deny the spasm of envy that twisted in her belly as Hawk lifted the woman in the air, swung her around, then pulled her to him to place a loud kiss on her red lips.

"Hawk!" squealed the vision, grabbing at his enormous shoulders with her small hands.

Kayln's hands tightened upon her knees until her knuckles turned white.

Hawkhurst lowered the woman to her feet and hugged her tightly before he set her away to look at her with hungry eyes. "Oh, sweeting, I've missed you. You are more beautiful each time I see you. When are you going to leave this reprobate and come to live with me?"

Kayln sucked in a breath of shock at Hawk's blatant disregard of her husband's presence. And she was also more than slightly irritated that he could so easily spend the morning seducing her and then move to the next woman who caught his fancy. Not that Kayln would allow herself to care.

She was well rid of him.

The man spoke. "She looks after me very well and I have grown quite used to my comforts." He laughed, and there was something vaguely familiar about it. "I will not let you steal her."

Kayln gazed with astonishment at this man, who seemed so unconcerned about Hawk's attentions to his lady. He was definitely a handsome man with strong, noble features. She began to wonder who these people could be.

The man with red hair took a closer look at Kayln, his teeth flashing as he grinned widely. "I see you have been up to your usual pursuits," he said to Hawk.

Now the woman stepped back and also examined Kayln at her leisure. Her gaze took in Kayln's half-exposed legs and disheveled appearance with a certain amount of amusement. "My dear Hawk, I am surprised to find you so occupied. Such behavior is much more in keeping with Martin."

Kayln flinched, glaring at Hawk.

"I'm afraid you don't understand," Hawk said after a long moment in which he too studied Kayln sheepishly. And with something else Kayln couldn't help but see—possession.

"Oh, but I do," the other man said, raising his surprisingly dark brows, as his eyes narrowed sensuously. "Completely."

Kayln could bear it no longer. Lifting her head high, she slid from the back of the horse. "I am afraid you do not," Kayln said to him. "I am Kayln D'Arcy, chatelaine of this keep. It is my sister, Celia, whom Philip Hawkhurst will marry."

The man had the grace to look slightly askance, but she saw the way his gaze traveled over her finely shaped leg, which was exposed to her thigh by the long rent in her gown. Kayln's hands balled into fists at her sides. Just when she was about to give this rude man the rebuke he richly deserved, he smiled and held out his hand. "Then allow me to introduce myself"—he turned to Hawk, who was frowning at him—"as Hawk has failed in his duty to do so. I am Martin Hawkhurst. Philip and Hawk are my brothers."

Now it was Kayln's turn to be embarrassed. How obtuse of her! Of course she should have realized who the new arrivals were. What had occurred between her and Hawk in the orchard had obviously addled her wits.

Her appearance was certainly disgraceful. Thus she could hardly fault them for what they must be thinking. Kayln drew herself up, determined to dredge up some scrap of dignity, and turned to the dark beauty with a fixed smile. "You must be Lady Jayne."

Jayne Hawkhurst laughed huskily, and Kayln realized she should have seen the resemblance to Hawk immediately. While this woman was delicate, slender, and wholly feminine, there were similarities between them, such as her voice, her dark coloring, and the total confidence with which she held herself.

"It was not very good of Hawk to fail to introduce us," Jayne said, taking Kayln's arm and beginning to lead her toward the keep. She didn't seem to notice that Kayln stiffened at the touch before forcing herself to relax. "We shall have to decide whether or not we will forgive him for his lack of manners while you change."

Kayln was slightly taken aback. This woman was just come to Aimsley, and already she was organizing and smoothing over the awkward moments. Kayln answered stiffly, "I must tell you that things are not as they appear."

"I am sure they are not," Jayne agreed. "I have known my

brother long, and understand just how he can distort the most simple of things into the complicated.'' She smiled and nodded wisely. ''After all, he is only a man.''

Kayln was astounded that this oh-so-feminine woman would give voice to such rebellious attitudes. She glanced back toward the baron. Hawk certainly did not seem to approve, for he was frowning deeply, but to her surprise he had said nothing to this.

There was little time for her to consider this as they went on. Jayne continued to chat almost as if they were old acquaintances.

At the other woman's gentle encouragement, Kayln found herself telling Jayne how Hawk had insisted on helping her from the apple tree. Of course she did not share the more intimate moments of the encounter. But she felt much better when Jayne unashamedly laid all the blame for Kayln's torn cote at her brother's feet. She even went so far as to suggest that Kayln present him with the bill to purchase cloth for a new one.

When Kayln balked at this, Jayne simply laughed, telling Kayln it might make him think twice in the future before dragging a young woman out of a tree.

As the two women moved away, Martin let out a laugh of sheer devilment. ''I can see that warring is not your only talent, brother.''

Hawk turned to Martin with a frown. He had no wish to discuss Kayln. What had happened in the orchard was between the two of them alone. Even though their relationship was purely physical, Hawk felt a strange reticence to allow her to become the object of the younger man's speculations.

And there was another matter he wished to discuss with his brother, one that affected their family honor. He drew Martin to a quiet area of the stables.

As soon as Hawk began to speak, Martin sobered.

Hawk lost no time in informing his brother of the events that had occurred over the past weeks. Twice Hawk had almost lost his life. Once a piece of masonry had fallen from the battlements above him. The second incident had been more direct. He had fed a plate of cold meat that had been left in his room to one of his hounds. The animal had died. He went on to say that he believed the steward, Harold, was responsible. Hawk's investigation had uncovered the fact that large amounts of moneys and goods had been disappearing from the estate, and Harold was the only one who had unlimited access.

As Hawk spoke, Martin's green eyes widened with horror. "God's blood, Hawk. You must take him." He could only stare in amazement when Hawk shook his head.

"Nay, brother. I have come to realize that Harold must be in league with another. Only a landholder or merchant would be able to dispose of my gold, sheep, wheat, and countless other valuables without drawing attention."

"But what has that to do with not seeking to punish the steward now, before he can cause you harm?"

Hawk pounded his fist into his open palm. "I refuse to move against the steward until his accomplice is exposed. They have taken what belongs to me, and neither can be allowed to steal from the barony without retribution."

Chapter Seven

The folk of Aimsley lined the narrow track, and some threw flower petals for Celia's white mare to tread upon as she passed. There were smiles of pleasure and approval on the clean, scrubbed faces.

Celia was a vision of loveliness dressed in a cote of palest lilac. Over it she wore a tunic of deep mauve, lavishly trimmed in ermine. The sides of the tunic were not slashed as widely as fashion might dictate, in deference to Celia's pregnancy however slight the evidence.

Kayln knew the ermine trim on her own silver tunic, which was slashed wide to reveal her figure in a sapphire blue cote compared most favorably with that of the other ladies present.

Knowing that the other ladies, especially the earl's wife Lady Mary, often frequented the court, Kayln had feared she might feel at a disadvantage amongst them. But her fears had been for naught. Once she had met Philip's friends and family Kayln had discovered that they were not nearly so intimidating as she had feared.

She glanced over to where Jayne walked with the procession. Kayln had never had a friend of her own age, and she hoped to spend more time with the young woman, who was looking lovely in scarlet. After learning that Jayne was Hawk's sister, she found herself better able to accept the dark-haired woman's unusual beauty with good grace.

She had found no opportunity to speak with Hawk alone since that day in the orchard, and so had settled nothing between them. His attentions to her were becoming far too obvious; a brush of his hand on hers, an intimate glance. But unless she was willing to call more notice to his actions by openly rebuffing him, Kayln was forced to remain silent.

As the procession arrived at the church, they saw Philip waiting there, his two brothers flanking him.

It struck her what a handsome lot they were. Philip was a young man who would make any girl's heart beat just a little faster, with his bright hair and well-featured face. The tunic he wore was midnight blue and suited his tall slender form.

Martin, who she had learned was the middle brother, was dressed in forest green, the rich color highlighting the auburn of his hair and the dark pools of his eyes. He grinned wickedly at her as he took note of her gaze on him, and she couldn't repress the smile she returned. Martin Hawkhurst was a rouge of the worst kind. Any woman would need to guard her heart well should he decide to pursue her.

But it was on Hawk that her gaze rested longest and with the most intensity. He wore a shirt of sapphire blue, the same color as her cotehardie, and over it a tunic of black velvet. The lush fabric hugged lovingly close to the breadth of his wide shoulders. He was not much taller than his two brothers, all of them being big men, but the sheer power of him made them fade into the background. Hawk's golden eyes looked back at her with a hunger that was plain for any who wished to see. Kayln felt a shiver take her as she looked at him. The memory of the passion he had awakened in her was vivid, but she was determined to resist its lure.

She turned away abruptly, her gaze unknowingly wistful.

Kayln centered her attention on Philip as he helped Celia dismount from the white mare. He handled her with such delicate care that Kayln knew she had nothing to worry about in this marriage.

They moved to the doors of the church, and as a hush fell over the crowd of onlookers, the young couple exchanged their vows. Their voices rang out clear and strong in the crisp morning air, and all present were made deeply aware of their love for one another.

After the vows were exchanged, the priest led them into the church, where the marriage was blessed. The noble guests then made their way back to the keep, leaving the common people to attend a celebration outside.

Allowing her guests to seat themselves, Kayln stopped at

the kitchens to make sure all was going smoothly. Only the did she go to find her own place.

As guests of honor, Celia and Philip already sat in the hig seats, the earl and his wife flanking them. Approaching th high table, Kayln could see there was only one place vacan and that spot was next to Hawk.

When he looked up and smiled at her boldly, she was sur Hawk had deliberately arranged for her to sit beside him. Wit raised brows, Kayln stiffly settled herself beside him.

The Earl of Norwich, who sat on Hawk's other side, leane across him. "I believe I have rarely experienced warmer hospitality, Lady D'Arcy."

Kayln blushed with pleasure that her work had not gon unappreciated. "I thank you, sir, for your gracious words."

"Most prettily said, Walter," Hawk declared, turning so hi wide shoulders blocked her view of the earl. "I hope to experience the true depths of Lady Kayln's hospitality at th earliest opportunity." He grinned, making her aware that h spoke of something beyond her skills as a hostess.

Her lips tightened, and she folded her hands before her a she turned to Hawk with an expression of irritation. She wa beginning to grow quite tired of her own inability to put thi man in his place. Something inside her rose up to answer hin in kind. "I fear, sir knight, that I have no further hospitalit to offer you."

For a moment he seemed somewhat surprised and not a littl disappointed at this hostile reply. Then his eyes narrowe knowingly and he smiled. "From that which you have so generously displayed thus far, I would say you have much, muc more to offer." He lowered his voice and leaned forward s only she could hear his next remark. "And let me assure you my lady, that I myself mean to be equally generous with you.'

Kayln's face turned scarlet, and a wave of sheer swee honey flowed through her and settled in her lower stomach His words reminded her all too clearly of the pleasure she ha experienced in his arms. As she fought the feelings with al her being, she could only ask herself what madness could hav made him so bold in the face of her rebuke.

Angry with herself and him, Kayln raised her goblet an took a long drink of the heated wine. It trailed a warm pat down her throat, coursing outward through her veins. The sensation, she realized as she set down the cup, was not unlike the way she felt when Hawk looked at her just as he did now. It was growing harder and harder to recall precisely why she could not allow herself to respond to him.

Unable to wrest control of her wanton desires, Kayln tried to ignore the man beside her as the feast began with an official toast from the earl. He offered long life and much happiness to the newlyweds. Next came Martin, who offered the hope that Philip would have many fine sons, and daughters as beautiful as their mother.

Celia blushed prettily at this, and Philip put his arm around her shoulders as he whispered something in her ear which made her blush even more deeply.

And so they went around the room, with each man offering up a toast in keeping with the event. Some were very ribald, others were warmly sincere, but from all present there emanated a feeling of true goodwill.

Kayln could not help feeling surprised and secretly pleased by so much approbation. All these years she had thought of herself and Celia as apart from others.

Finally, it was Hawk's turn to toast. He rose, and Kayln saw the women in the room, even those who were happily married, gaze on him with appreciative eyes. He tapped his temple with his index finger. "Methinks that all the easy toasts have been used, which means I am obliged to come up with something inspired."

There was much laughter at this, and many admiring glances from the women, which he returned flirtatiously. Conceited oaf, Kayln told herself, looking away.

Then he raised his cup high, drawing her attention once again. "To Celia and Philip, may they have a life that is full—of birth, happiness, and sometimes sorrow. May they walk side by side and be true and loving partners."

For a moment there was silence as each person present thought about this unusual wish. Then as one, every glass was raised and all drank to the future.

How very unusual, Kayln thought. How very surprising. Never would she have thought that a man and woman could be "true and loving partners." Hawk had always given her the impression that he would very happily dominate any woman who came into his sphere of influence. Into her mind came the memory of how Jayne had spoken to him the day she arrived at Aimsley. He'd not even tried to rebuke her. Could it be that Hawk was not the devil he seemed?

Was that why she felt this overpowering attraction toward him? Had some part of her seen through his guise and found him a worthy object of her desire? Kayln did not know, and was too afraid to believe this possible. If it was true, what reason had she for fighting her feelings, for denying herself and him what they both so desired?

When Hawk sat down again, Kayln looked at him with searching eyes. Should she give him some opportunity to prove himself? The events of the last days, the camaraderie she had found in being with others, had made her wonder if she really needed to keep to herself so much. Mayhap she could at least try to know Hawk better.

Hawk turned to her with a questioning look and she smiled at him, a hesitant welcome in her eyes. So uncertain was her smile, Hawk could only stare at her for a moment, overcome.

This was not the cool aloof woman she showed the world. Here was the girl he glimpsed only on occasion; warm, alive, and just a little unsure of herself. It made him want her all the more, though why, he did not know, and he refused to question it.

Over the past two days he'd thought of little save bedding this woman. Though it was true that she had not appeared completely eager at his attention, neither had she rejected him. Hawk had saved her a place at table, hoping he would finally be able to press his suit more fully. He burned with a fire that would not be quenched until he had her.

Kayln had surprised him with her open rebuff, and he had felt his ire rise in response. But it had nearly disappeared as he realized that she must simply be playing her womanly games. Though he wished she would cease this and put them both out of their misery, he knew he must follow her lead.

And now, with her smiling at him that way, Hawk felt a heated response spear through his belly. She had a body made for love, this Kayln D'Arcy, with lush curves that beckoned a man's hands. The sensuality that fairly glowed in her was instinctual, a natural outpouring of the woman within.

Unaware of Hawk's thoughts, but uncomfortable with his intent gaze, Kayln felt her smile fade. He seemed to be looking right into her soul, searching for that place where she was most vulnerable. And Kayln wasn't at all sure she wanted him there. In fact she was most certain she did not. With a tremendous effort she forced her gaze from his. It was one thing to consider befriending this man, and quite another to think of allowing him access to the innermost parts of her. Her sense of self-preservation would not let her go so far.

Disguising her confusion with action, Kayln stood, thus drawing all eyes. "If some of the tables could be cleared away, we might begin the dancing. I have been able to hire the services of a troupe of players."

She took her place again, feeling strangely awkward as she continued to sense Hawk's fixed attention. Did she dare hope that he was different, that he would not hurt her as her father had—as her husband had? Surely she could not take such a risk.

Within minutes, a large space had been cleared in the middle of the room, only the head table remaining. From a small gallery above them, music began to play.

Philip led Celia out onto the floor, and they went through the steps together. Celia looked so tiny and delicate beside the large young man, Kayln felt a moment of regret that she would be a wife and a mother so young.

"He will care for her well."

She turned to Hawk. "Truly you must know that I hold no hatred for you brother. It is only that she seems so very young to me. She is barely more than a child herself."

"Not so much of a child, but a woman," Hawk reminded Kayln. "She must follow her own path, as you must yours."

As the musicians took up a new tune, he held out his large callused hand to her. "Come join me." The words were said in such a way that she knew they went deeper than a mere invitation to dance. For a long moment she hesitated, telling herself that she could be making a terrible mistake. But that voice of reason was not nearly as powerful as his golden gaze. She placed her hand in his.

Kayln was not at all surprised to find that, though he was

a big man, Hawk was a good dancer. He led her through the steps with practiced ease. And every time they met at the center of the circle of dancers, he smiled into her eyes, making Kayln feel she was indeed the only woman in the room.

She grew flushed from the top of her head to the tip of her toes, her whole being alive and tingling from the way Hawk took every opportunity to touch her hand or waist. Breathlessly, she asked him if they might stop for a moment. Obligingly, Hawk led her to a window recess, keeping her fingers firmly in place on his arm.

He was just seeing Kayln settled, when they were approached by a young man she knew as a member of the earl's entourage.

He bowed before Kayln. "Sir Jocelin, my lady. May I beg the favor of a dance?"

"The lady is tired," Hawk answered for her, patting her hand on his arm and drawing her closer to him.

Kayln stiffened, pulling away. His answering for her was like a blast of frigid wind. She told herself to remember that no matter how sweetly he behaved, Hawk was still Hawk.

Seeing her reaction, the young man smirked. "Can this lady not speak for herself?" His green eyes flashed as he brushed a lock of straight blond hair from his forehead.

"Listen, puppy . . ." Hawk began roughly, but his frowning attention was all for Kayln.

She interrupted him firmly. "I can speak for myself and I should be pleased to accept your invitation." Kayln cast Hawk a glance of warning as she moved away.

Jocelin turned out to be a more than adequate partner, and Kayln would have enjoyed their dance had she not felt the Baron of Clamdon watching them all the while. The young man was openly admiring, and Kayln could not help feeling somewhat flattered.

As the tune ended she felt a hand on her arm and stiffened, then relaxed as she heard a familiar voice. "Kayln." A voice that was not Hawk's.

"Miles," she said in greeting, attempting to be pleased that it was not the man who so troubled her. Kayln was secretly embarrassed at having been so preoccupied with Hawk that she had not even realized Miles was present. "Why have I not seen you before this moment? You were not at the church."

He looked gratified at her apparent happiness at seeing him. "I only arrived at Harrow a few short hours ago. I had been away. When I saw the invitation was for this very day, I immediately rushed to Aimsley."

Kayln should have known there was some reason for his lack of a reply. "Well, I am glad you are finally come."

With a nod toward Sir Jocelin, Miles said, "Excuse us, please. I must ask this lady to dance." Kayln barely noticed as the young man faded into the crowd of wedding guests.

Her pleasure at Miles's presence at the wedding soon evaporated as he began to speak, his voice slightly petulant. "Why, Kayln, did you not tell me that Celia was to be wed?"

She shrugged as they commenced the dance, hoping her tone would discourage further questions. "It was arranged quickly. You know how impatient the young can be."

"But Kayln, this seems somewhat extreme."

Her mouth thinned. "What are you implying, Miles?"

He blinked rapidly, obviously realizing he had gone too far. "Why, nothing. I only thought that you would know the matter would be of importance to me. With Celia settled you will be more free to concentrate on your own future."

Suddenly realizing where the conversation was headed, Kayln cautioned, "Now is not the time, Miles."

"And what better time could there be? Have I not waited patiently for you to get over your grief for Raymond?" His voice broke, but he went on. "It has been hard for both of us. But we must think of the future of Aimsley."

In all honesty, Kayln knew she had never experienced any true grief at Raymond's death, but she was sympathetic in the face of Miles's sadness and did not wish to hurt him. But she could not go so far as to give him false hope concerning his proposal. She had no wish to marry. Previously, Miles had accepted this fact with understanding. He must continue to do so. "I will not marry you, Miles," she stated simply.

His tone was unexpectedly sharp as he answered, "But should you not think of your duty to the lands? You must produce an heir."

Her jaw clenched as she bit back a retort. Surely if anyone should have worried about an heir, it should have been Raymond. And he had not shown the least concern. She did not know why Miles would pick this time, when she was already feeling so confused about her feelings for Hawk, to prod her when he never had before. Her voice held a warning. "You press too hard, Miles."

For a long moment, Miles did not look at her as he fought for composure. When he did, his eyes were dark with apology. "Forgive me. I don't know what came over me, Kayln. I think it must be the excitement of the day. I only wish the same joy for the two of us. You know I will wait however long it need be."

He was so contrite that Kayln would have been hard put to stay angry with him. Miles was the one man who had ever been her friend, who understood her need for independence.

But as they continued their dance, her gaze went to Hawk, who stood across the crowded hall with his brother Martin. He was not that kind of man. His pursuit of her could only be called relentless, and far from repelling her, he made her respond to him as if she had no more control than a mare. Did this mean there was some fault within her?

Miles was kind and patient and she felt nothing for him. She remembered Alice saying he was weak. What if it was true? Was that why she could not find it in her heart to say yes to his proposals?

Even though she assured herself this was not the case, Kayln excused herself as soon as the dance was finished, then went back to her place at the head table. She could hardly wait for this interminable evening to be over.

To her dismay, Hawk rejoined her there. Did he not understand that she wanted him to stay away?

"Why did you leave me for that *boy*?" He said the word as if it were a curse.

Her brows arched as she answered haughtily, "Lord Hawkhurst, I do not consider dancing with someone else having left you. And may I add that what I do is my own affair, not yours."

Hawk looked as if he were about to dispute the statement. Then he changed tactics. "Would I be overstepping myself if I were to tell you Jocelin is not a suitable companion?"

"Oh, I see." She nodded slowly, reaching to fill her cup. "And am I to understand that you are?"

"Of course." He looked at her in abject surprise that she would question such a thing. Then he grew serious. "Jocelin is in the care of the Earl of Norwich because of some trouble with a young girl a few months ago. The poor child was not of noble birth and so"—he shrugged, but his disgusted tone and raised brows told Kayln what he thought of this—"little was done. It was decided, though, that he should join the earl's household for a time. Walter is of such sterling character that it was felt Jocelin might learn by his example."

Kayln was silent for a moment, thinking of Jocelin and what a gentleman he had been as they danced. "Could this be your own possessiveness talking?" she asked, then covered her mouth with her hand, not knowing where she had gotten the courage to say such an outrageous thing.

Hawk leaned so close she could feel the warmth of his breath on her face. "You may be sure that I am indeed possessive of you. I want no other man to even touch you."

Kayln saw the burning hunger in his eyes, and could not control her body's response to the wave of sensual energy that flowed from his hand as he touched hers. She was suffocating, couldn't get enough air into her lungs, which felt tight and too small.

"I want you, Kayln." He leaned close to her, his breath hot on her cheek. "I can think of nothing beyond what happened in the orchard. I long to bury myself in the warmth of your body."

Her breath was coming faster from between her parted lips, and a rich golden warmth spread through her veins at the images his words conjured up. Heaven. But she must stop it, cried the voice of reason.

Yet Kayln was powerless to do so. Unwillingly she felt herself pulled into the net of his seduction. "Hawk . . . I . . ."

"Lady Kayln," said a voice beside her, forcing her to focus, to push those heady sensations away. Dragging her gaze from his, Kayln turned to see Alice standing there, her thin hands folded primly over her bosom. "It is time for the bedding ceremony, my lady."

Kayln blinked. For a moment she could not comprehend

what the older woman was talking about, so caught was she in the silvery web of sensuality Hawk had woven around her. "What?"

"The bedding ceremony." Alice nodded toward Celia and Philip, seated at the head of the table.

Kayln's eyes followed the nurse's gaze, "Oh, yes, of course," she murmured, collecting herself with difficulty. She wondered how much of what had just occurred had been witnessed by the nurse, but she soon realized there was little need for concern. Alice had her own preoccupations.

"It had best be done quickly, my lady," said the older woman, "or the boy will be carrying her away before us all." Alice's thin lips pulled down in a frown of disapproval.

Kayln forced her attention to what Alice was saying. Her gaze focused upon the young couple, and she could see what Alice said was true. Philip was nuzzling Celia's white throat, and her eyes were closed as she held the back of his head with her small hand.

Kayln heard a deep chuckle from the man at her side. She did not even look at him. He was despicable, she told herself, even though deep inside she knew that his open sensuality was what drew her to him.

"I will see to the matter at once," Kayln told the nurse. "Please make sure that all is in readiness in her room."

"Certainly, my lady." Alice nodded with a last disapproving glance at the newlyweds, before she turned and left them.

"It appears as if we Hawkhursts have no control where the women of your family are concerned." Hawk trailed the tips of his fingers over the back of her hand where it rested upon the table.

Not deigning to reply, Kayln pulled away. But she was completely incapable of stopping the shudder of pleasure that traveled up her arm.

"How could Celia be so silly as to make such a spectacle of herself?" she muttered as she rose. Though she knew she was more annoyed at herself than she would ever be at her sister.

"I see no one making a spectacle of themselves." Hawk wrapped his hand around her upper arm, successfully keeping Kayln at his side for the moment. "Look around you. No one else finds their hunger for one another out of place."

Glancing around the room, Kayln could see that what Hawk said appeared to be true. Most of the guests were still dancing, and the few who acted as if they noticed were laughing good-naturedly over the young couple's impetuousness.

"Their hunger for each other matters little," Kayln told him, motioning toward her sister and new husband with her free hand. "Celia is with child. Thus they will both have need to restrain themselves."

"Oh, ho." Hawk chuckled. "I see your husband was most mistaken in his thinking on the subject. If you believe one must call a halt to wedded relations just because a woman is breeding, mayhap that is why you have not had a child. Your husband would not have wished to forgo the pleasure of your body for such a time." He had begun with laughter, but by the time Hawk finished speaking, he looked as if he found his own words anything but amusing.

She wrenched her arm from his grasp, her face going scarlet as she turned from him and went to her sister. The pain of his comment was numbing, and she was unable to even feel shocked by his audacity. Hawk could not be further from the mark.

"Celia," Kayln said, more sharply than she had intended, making her sister look up at her in surprise. "It is time."

Lady Mary, Jayne, and two other ladies in the earl's party whom Kayln could not name also gathered with them as they went to Celia's room. With a will born of much practice, Kayln was able to block the misery of Hawk's words from her mind as she removed her sister's clothing. She was quick to stand between Celia and the others as her sister climbed into bed so none of them would see the gentle mound of her stomach.

But when Kayln turned to face the other women, she knew she had not been quick enough to hide the pregnancy from Jayne, who was standing closest to her. Hawk's sister smiled broadly, and moved forward to kiss Celia's cheek as she wished her a long and fruitful marriage.

Breathing a sigh of relief, Kayln stepped back, glad Jayne would not think ill of Celia.

It was only moments later when the assembled women

heard the approach of the men. Philip was carried into the room feet first, shouting to be put down. When they set him on his feet and he saw his little bride propped up in the bed waiting for him, he blushed brightly, looking slightly unsure of himself as he stood there with his hands hanging at his sides.

Kayln was reminded that the boy was only sixteen. As the men disrobed him, she kept her gaze on his face, and hurried the other revelers from the room as soon as Philip was tucked into the bed beside her sister.

Kayln could feel Hawk's attention on her as she led them from the room. She knew he would be amused by her eagerness to leave.

As they returned to the Great Hall, Kayln saw that many of her guests were obviously growing tired. Several had begun to stifle their yawns behind politely raised hands. The more hardy of the group went back to the tables to continue celebrating, while she went about seeing the others settled for the night.

By the time Kayln had an opportunity to seek her own chamber, she was exhausted. Or so she thought until she was actually lying in her big lonely bed.

Now that she was alone, Kayln tossed and turned, unable to forget the words Hawk had spoken in the hall. His belief that her husband had wanted her was completely false, and images of Raymond's many small rejections had been brought painfully to the fore.

Finally, drawing back the heavy hangings, Kayln rose from the bed to go to the window. It was a gentle autumn night, but she could smell the approach of cooler weather on the breeze that drifted through her window. She leaned her heated cheek on the cool stone of the sill. If only she had not met Hawk, had never known the heady rush of passion that warmed her blood and made her think only of him.

Even before she had realized Raymond didn't care for her, he had not made her feel this way. She had wanted her husband to come to her, yes, to make her feel as if she had some purpose. If he had put aside his aversion to her for even a short time, she might at least have a child to nurture and love.

The needs Hawk had awakened in her were so very different. In spite of her own sense of self-preservation, every fiber in her body screamed out to have him see her as a woman, a desirable woman. She wanted to be taken into his arms and experience again that wickedly splendid moment of bliss he had brought in the orchard.

It would be sweet torment to become involved with a man such as he. He would be able to rule her with the sensuality she found so very tempting.

For a few moments tonight, she had dared to let herself dream. After the toast Hawk had made at the banquet, she had thought he might be a man who would see a woman could be his partner and not his slave. But here in her room, without his presence to distract her, she realized Hawk would make her subservient without even trying. He was just too powerful, too magnetic, too sure of himself and his world.

Behind her, she heard the sound of the door opening, and she tensed. Without turning, Kayln knew who it was, and felt as if it might be her own need which had brought him to her. There was no sense in wondering how he came to be here. Hawk did as he chose. Yet she was hesitant to look around, aware that she must tell him to go and afraid she would not be able to. Kayln wasn't sure she had the power to deny herself the joy to be found in his embrace.

But she knew she must. She found her voice with the greatest of efforts, masking her vulnerability with anger. "You may not come into my chambers without my leave."

Silently, Hawk moved across the floor, willing her to meet his gaze, for the invitation he sought was not in her words nor the remoteness of her profile. There was no light in the room save that of the fire, and it basked everything it touched with a warm rosy glow. Kayln stood still beside the window, her full breasts outlined against the sheer fabric of her gown. Her heavy gold hair hung straight to her hips, obscuring his view of her other charms. His gaze moved upward again, seeing the way the moonlight silhouetted the beauty of her features. In spite of her continued lack of welcome, he felt a growing tightness in his lower belly. God, but he wanted her. Why did she not look at him? For he knew that only by seeing the expression in her lovely eyes would he know her true feelings about his being there.

As if in answer she turned to him, and to his amazement her eyes were unsure and vulnerable. He could also see that these emotions did not disguise her desire. Hawk hesitated, wondering, even as her need for him warmed him further, what circumstance had left such an alluring woman so very uncertain of herself.

He was unable to believe she had been ill used sexually. The very intensity of her responses to him told Hawk that Kayln was a woman who had been loved with a care that had opened her up to the delights of love. No woman who had been ill tutored would react to him as she did. Hawk hated the twinge of pain the thought of her with another man brought him. He had no right to be jealous of a husband who was long dead. But he couldn't help wishing, with some small part of himself, that he had been the man to teach Kayln the ways of loving.

Since that day in the orchard, he had relived over and over again the way she had responded to him without restraint, her soft cries of fulfillment heating his blood as he held her.

At the marriage feast he had no longer been able to hide his intentions toward him from others. He could not allow Jocelin to come close to her without stating his own claim to the woman he desired so thoroughly. And though Kayln had shown her resentment at this most clearly, he had not been fooled into thinking she did not want him. It was there in her eyes, in the way she started when he touched her hand. Her air of aloof reserve only made him want to break through to the passionate yielding woman beneath it. Seeing that Kayln's women lingered in the hall below, Hawk had grasped his opportunity to come to her, some inner sense telling him that she would welcome this opportunity for release from the passion that drove them.

Now Hawk moved toward her with the powerful grace that was so much a part of him, putting his finger to her lips as she started to speak again. He could not understand why Kayln felt compelled to deny what she so clearly wanted, but talk would only delay what they both knew must happen.

His other hand reached up under the heavy curtain of her hair to hold the back of her neck. For a moment she held back. Then, as she looked up at him, all her resistance seemed to dissolve. Her lids dipped down over eyes grown dark with a chasm of sensuality so deep it was all he could do to control the spear of desire that pierced his belly. But control it he did, drawing her toward him slowly, deliberately savoring the moment before he replaced his finger with his mouth.

The very moment his lips touched hers, Kayln raised her arms to put them around his neck and pulled him even closer, responding with a fire that was scorching in its heat. Her mouth opened under his, and she moaned as he took her lower lip between his teeth.

"Hawk," she groaned, pressing her soft body against him. Where her will to resist had gone she did not know, but in the deepest secret place inside her Kayln knew that this was what she truly desired. She wanted him as she had never imagined she could want a man. As shattering as her experience with Hawk in the orchard had been, she sensed there was more. And she knew Hawk could give her this—knew with an unshakable certainty he would know how to soothe her aching flesh.

Picking her up in his arms, Hawk carried Kayln to the bed. Now that Hawk was there with her it no longer seemed lonely, but intimate and inviting, and she knew there was no other place she wanted to be. Here Kayln would discover what it was to be a woman.

His hands went to her breasts, which strained against the gauze material of her nightrail. The nipples blossomed under his pleasantly roughened palm, begging for his attentions. With a husky chuckle, Hawk lowered his head and nuzzled first one nub and then the other through the gown. Thin as it was, the cloth was too thick a barrier between his mouth and her flesh. With one impatient motion, Hawk tore the flimsy garment from neck to hem.

Kayln arched her back as his lips found her bare breast. With nothing to hinder him, he circled one delicate nipple with his tongue before taking it fully into his mouth, creating an ache in Kayln that was dizzying. Then his mouth found her other breast, tasting with a connoisseur's delight of her silken skin. All the while his hands were busy seeking and finding the curves of her slender body, eliciting her willing response. The magic grew until she could not catch her breath from the tension overtaking her body and she reached out to pull him even closer, her insistent hands on his shoulders.

When his hand dipped lower and he touched the moist wetness of her, she could not control herself. She arched upward, offering herself to him without restraint. Hawk sat back to remove his robe, and her fingers flew to his chest to run over the corded muscles she found there with hungry delight.

"God, how I have wanted you." He moved to position himself over her. He had meant to make this last, to savor her for hours until she cried out with longing, but her need and his own were so great he could wait no more. Hawk was somewhat surprised when Kayln seemed slightly resistant as he parted her legs, but he did not want to think about that now. He was driven past rational thought.

When Kayln felt the hardness of him prodding at the entrance of her womanhood, she knew a moment of panic, and pushed herself away from him with her heels. But the gentle touch of his hands as he drew her back down to him made her doubts leave her mind. This was Hawk, the man who had been born to make her a woman. When he thrust into her, her instinct was to rise up to meet him.

Her eyes flew open in surprise as a fiery pain shot through her, and her gaze went to Hawk's face.

Nothing could have prepared her for the shock on the visage of the man above her. He clearly was torn between horror and the force of his need.

Intuitively understanding his dilemma, Kayln lifted her head and kissed his lips, arching toward him with longing as she urged him on. At that, the decision was made.

The passion that had been growing in Hawk in the weeks he had known Kayln rode hard on him. He began to move within her. His body was lost in her warmth, his hips thrusting down as she rose up to meet him.

Kayln could feel the heat beginning to build once again, as the pain ebbed away. She put her hands up to his wide shoulders, meeting him thrust for thrust, holding onto Hawk as he lifted her with him to the sky.

A white light of ecstasy exploded inside her and with a cry of joy, she was soaring high above herself, so far she thought she could never find her way back. But then Hawk was with her and his dark wings folded over her protectively, holding her as she drifted slowly back down to reality.

When Kayln opened her lids, she was staring into the golden eyes of the man above her. His gaze was confused and dark with some emotion she could not read as he put his hand up to smooth the tangled mass of hair from her sweat-dampened face. ''Why didn't you tell me?'' he whispered.

''I didn't know how.'' She had never felt so vulnerable in her life, and his reaction gave away so very little of what this might mean to him. Already doubt as to the wisdom of what she had just done was beginning to assail her.

Hawk rolled onto his side, taking Kayln with him to hold her against him. ''How could you be a virgin? You were married for several years.'' Still, his voice gave nothing away.

''I don't know where to begin,'' Kayln replied, covering her face with her hands. Her cheeks were hot with shame and her chest felt tight with the pain of remembering the unadulterated loneliness. Did she owe him an explanation?

As she hesitated, Kayln realized that she had just shared the most intimate experience of her life with this man. If he could not accept her as she was, then there was nothing for them. And she'd best know now. She lowered her hands. Taking a deep breath she began, her voice raspy and barely above a whisper.

''My father wanted sons. My mother wasn't able to give him even one, though I do not believe it was through any fault of hers. You see, he had many women and as far as we know, Celia and I are the only offspring he sired. He never forgave me for being a daughter. In all the fourteen years I lived in his home, he never once touched me except in rage. I hated him so, even while I loved him. Bertrand was the only one who ever showed me any kindness. My mother was too frightened to do so. I would pretend that Bertrand was my father. And then ask the Blessed Virgin for forgiveness out of guilt.'' A mirthless laugh escaped her.

''When I was fourteen, my father found Raymond. I didn't even so much as see him until the day of the wedding, but I had such hopes. I thought if only I could begin anew far away from my father, life would be different, that someone would care for me. When Raymond and I were first married, he treated me as if I were his little sister. At the time I was grateful, for I did not know him and coming to Aimsley was not as difficult for me as it might have been had he expected me to perform my wifely duties.'' Her face colored, and she was glad that Hawk could not see it in the darkness.

''I believe I must have been about sixteen when I began to wonder why Raymond did not come to me,'' she went on, a sob catching her voice. She forced down the tears that threatened to spill. ''It was then that I decided to try to make him . . . want me. Not that I knew what to do, but I had watched the serfs romancing one another and thought I had some idea. After a time Raymond became aware of my childish efforts to . . . seduce him. He must have taken pity on me, for he did come to my room one night. I was here in this very bed. Just the sight of him there in the doorway was terrifying. It was what I had wanted, but I knew so little of what would happen.'' Her body shook with the force of her agitation.

''Shhh . . . I . . . you . . .'' Hawk murmured awkwardly. For once he seemed unsure of what to say. ''You need not go on.''

But Kayln was unable to stop. It was as if she must purge herself of the memory. Even Hawk's presence seemed secondary to her need to speak of it. ''Raymond came inside and sat down on the bed. He talked to me for a very long time about duty and the getting of an heir and that sometimes one must make sacrifices to do what was right. Finally, he leaned over and put his arms around me. It wasn't a very long embrace, and I was so unsure of what should be done . . . well . . . one moment he was holding me and the next he had gone. He gave no explanation, only muttered that he could not continue and . . . left.'' Her voice broke and she took a deep breath, refusing to cry.

Hawk felt as if he should have somehow guessed. There had been so many clues. Knowing of Kayln's inexperience changed everything. It had been fine to think he was playing at love games with a woman who understood them. But now things were different.

Although he felt sympathy for her tighten his throat, he also knew that things could not go on as he had planned. The trouble was that he did not know if he could allow himself to become involved in anything more than a physical relationship with this woman. Knowing what had caused her to be so hostile and reserved did not change the fact that she was. This was not what he wanted in his life. Hawk was tired, tired of fighting, tired of being lonely. With Kayln there would always be a holding back, for he doubted she would ever allow anyone to become too close. She displayed that reserve with her own sister, not to mention others. He had seen the way she stiffened when touched. How could he put himself through that?

Hawk had no idea how much time had passed before Kayln spoke again. "He never touched me again in any way."

He was dragged out of his own reverie by shock. "You mean in all that time he only so much as put his arms around you the one time? It is hard for me to imagine that any man might have the privilege of loving you and not exercising that right. The man was mad." That he could say unequivocally. Hawk could never remember knowing such desire for a woman, nor such fulfillment. Just thinking of the way it had been with her drove all other thoughts from his mind even now.

"I do not think Raymond felt as you do," she answered, her voice low and matter-of-fact. "I did not appeal to him."

"You have near driven me mad for wanting you." His tone was husky and he reached for her, running a hand down her back to her bottom, pulling her against him.

She leaned over him, her eyes shining in the darkness as she ran an exploring hand over his chest and lower. "Do you want me now?"

Hawk knew he should say no, that he should end this right now, before it went any further. But her hand closed around him and he groaned, telling himself that she wanted him too. That she had given herself to him without coercion. Why should he deny her and himself because she'd been a virgin? He'd made no promises, nor had Kayln asked for any.

Putting his arms around her slender waist, he drew her up on top of him. He had just loved her, and already his desire was growing as if never slaked. Pushing all thoughts of tomorrow from his mind, Hawk pulled her against the hardness of him, bending to take her responsive lips in a fiery kiss.

Already she was learning the ways of love and passion with joy. She answered all he would give her equally, returning it to him in full measure. Mayhap they could come to some kind of understanding, find some ground where they would not have to forgo this unequaled pleasure. But the time for talk could come later.

Again he was taken over by the force of his desire for her.

Chapter Eight

When Kayln awoke the next morning, she stretched languidly, brushing against the pillow beside hers, then grew still. She bolted upright and saw the imprint of Hawk's head on the soft linen.

Dear God, what had she done?

Last night might have only been an unbelievable dream, but for that impression and the heavy languor in her limbs, all of which, coupled with the sweet ache between her thighs, convinced her that the previous night had been most confoundingly real.

Throwing back the covers, she got out of bed, blushing at the sight of her ruined gown on the floor where Hawk had tossed it. There was no going back now. The deed was done. Wrapping her arms protectively around herself, Kayln crossed to the narrow window. She raised her hands to brace them on either side of the window, and winced. A self-conscious grimace curved her lips as she remembered what had caused those stiffened muscles.

Kayln opened the window and looked out on a lovely October day, its very brightness belying the uncertainty inside her. The sky was blue and clear and there was a crisp chill in the air, making the air smell fresh and clean.

Laughter floated up to her, and she looked down to see a group of men assembled in the courtyard. Their collective breaths rose over them in a silvery vapor as they talked. From appearances she would judge that the party was going hunting. Each of the men carried a bow and quiver or a lance, and they were dressed in subtle forest colors.

It was not difficult to locate Hawk amongst the men. His dark head rose above the others, and she felt her insides quiver at the sight of him. What must he be thinking of her, of the way she had given herself to him so freely? How was she ever to face him in the unforgiving light of day?

Last night he had made her feel like a woman. That she could not deny. But at what cost? She'd told him far too much about herself and Raymond. Never would she have believed that she would open herself so completely to anyone. Least of all to an over-confident devil of a man like James Hawkhurst. Would he try to use that moment of weakness to control and dominate her? He'd never intimated at any time that he wanted anything of her but her body. And now that he'd taken that, would he reject her?

Her lonely heart cried out from inside her, telling her to put aside her doubts, to believe in someone, in Hawk. Hadn't he held her gently, told her she was beautiful? In those moments she'd felt safe as never before.

As Kayln looked down at Hawk, she tried to brush aside a lingering trace of anxiety. She wanted to believe Hawk was different from the other men in her life. Would it really be so very dangerous to try? The voice of reason cried aye.

As if he could feel her eyes upon him, Hawk raised his head and looked up to where she was standing. A slow smile came over his lips and his gaze shone with undisguised desire. Kayln felt herself flush with heat, and she knew that the night before had not dampened her desire for this fascinating man in any measure. If anything, the passion they had shared had heightened her awareness of him.

A loud boisterous laugh rang out, distracting her from her study of Hawk. Looking toward the sound, Kayln found that Martin too was enjoying the sight of her standing there with only her hair to cover her nakedness.

With a gasp, Kayln stepped back quickly and shut the window, calling for her maid to help her dress. She'd do well to remember who she was and that as mistress of this keep she must retain some measure of dignity. Her confused feelings toward Hawk could not change that.

When Kayln reached the hall, she was pleased to see the cook had made certain the guests had had sufficient food to break their fast. It relieved some of the guilt she felt at rising later than usual, but none of her mixed emotions over the reasons for that late rising.

Though most of the guests had already eaten, Jayne Hawkhurst was still at table. She offered Kayln a smile of welcome as she sat down.

Jayne had been speaking with another young woman with pleasant but unremarkable features, who excused herself with a hesitant smile, saying she must begin preparations for the journey home. Kayln looked after the retreating woman with a frown of concentration, and still could not identify her. Again she was struck by a sense of discomfort at having so many strangers in her home.

When Hawk's sister saw the puzzled expression on Kayln's face as she looked at the woman's retreating back, she laughed. "Lettice. Her husband is Sir Routon, our uncle."

"Oh, yes," Kayln answered, nodding, though she could not even recall being introduced to Sir Routon.

Jayne laughed again, patting her hand. "Do not worry. I ofttimes become confused myself. With so many relatives, one must do the best one can."

In spite of her preoccupation with her own jumbled emotions, Kayln found herself smiling back at the younger girl. She wished very much that she would have an opportunity to know Hawk's sister better.

As if divining Kayln's thoughts, Jayne said, "Now that we are family we should become friends, you and I. I shall set my mind to finding Martin a wife so he won't mind my coming to Clamdon more often. I have spoiled him dreadfully and he claims he cannot manage without me to look after his household."

"Could he not hire a steward?" Kayln leaned forward, helping herself to bread, cheese, and cold meat, even as Jayne's words went through her mind. They were now family. If Jayne felt this way, did Hawk as well? How would what had happened between them last night affect that relationship? She paused, realizing she would need to go carefully.

As if she were about to impart a secret, Jayne leaned forward, drawing Kayln's attention back to her. "Truth to tell, Martin is away much of the time and I am left free to do as I will."

In spite of everything, Kayln nearly laughed aloud. Now here was a woman to match her own heart. She couldn't help wondering what Hawk thought of his sister's independent nature.

Jayne's confident tone and posture were very familiar to the Lady of Aimsley. Kayln asked, "Has anyone ever told you how very much you are like your brother?"

"Which one?" Jayne quipped, leaning her elbows on the table and resting her chin on her hands. "I fear we are all an outspoken lot. We get it from our father, who never minced words. Of course, Mother could be very frank herself, even though she often pretended she was shocked at the things Father would say. But we could tell it was only for our benefit."

Kayln looked at the other girl for a long moment, wondering what it would be like to be brought up in a household where you were free to speak your own mind, even if you were a female. She envied Jayne, both for the way she had been raised, and for the love Kayln sensed between her and her siblings.

"Speaking of Hawk," Jayne said, changing the subject, leaning forward. "He certainly was full of good humor this morning."

If Jayne had been in the least unsure as to the cause for Hawk's cheerful demeanor that morning, Kayln was sure the fierce blush staining her throat and face would have changed that. Stiffly she turned her attention to her unfinished meal. "Was he?" she muttered, taking a bite of cheese to preclude having to say anything more.

"Oh, yes, of a certainty." Jayne's lips spread in a slow smile, and Kayln was again reminded of her brother.

Kayln knew she must guard her tongue well when speaking to this all-too-clever woman, for Jayne's curious eyes saw far too much. Kayln wasn't yet ready to share her feelings for Hawk.

Jayne's next words confirmed Kayln's suspicions. "Forgive me if I overstep myself, but I wish to tell you something of Hawk. Though he is a man of great strength, and some might even say he is too commanding, it is part of him and should be so in his role as lord over so many. He must be able to make decisions and enforce them." She gave Kayln a long glance. "But there is also gentleness in him. He loves his family without reservation and is loyal to a fault. When he does love it will be completely. Thus, of my brothers he is the one who can be hurt the most deeply."

Kayln looked at her hands. "Why are you telling me this?" When there was no reply, Kayln looked up to see the other woman watching her speculatively. But still she said nothing.

It was early afternoon when the men returned from hunting. Along with some of the other women, Kayln went out into the courtyard to welcome them back.

One of the men led a horse onto which a huge buck had been tied, its antlers stretched wide over the back of the horse. From the excited talk of the hunters, it was apparent that Hawk had been the man to fell the deer.

Hawk, who was one of the last of the mounted party to enter the courtyard, was deep in conversation with the Earl of Norwich, seemingly unaware of the way the other men were praising him. Laughing, he threw back his head, and Kayln felt her heart turn over at his sheer masculinity. She tried to quell the reaction, to remind herself that she should not allow herself to be ruled by her reactions to him.

Kayln couldn't help remembering what Jayne had said about her brother that morning. Was there enough gentleness within Hawk to overcome her fear and his powerful nature?

As he halted his mount, Hawk's gaze raked the crowd as if searching for someone. When it came to rest on Kayln, his obvious satisfaction at the sight of her made Kayln feel as if she were the only woman in the courtyard.

She could not repress the longing that came into her own gaze as his eyes darkened with hunger. A heaviness settled in her lower belly and her tongue flicked out to dampen dry lips.

Hawk seemed not to even see the young boy who took the reins from his hands as he dismounted. Without so much as a word to the earl, who watched with obvious amusement, Hawk strode across the space that separated him from Kayln, never taking his eyes from her. "Good morrow, fair lady." His husky voice sent a pleasant prickling sensation along her spine.

"Good morrow," Kayln answered softly. He was so powerful and alive, his dark head tall against the blue of the sky. Outside, Hawk was truly in his element, as no building could ever wholly contain his incredible energy.

Noticing the hush that had fallen, Kayln glanced around and saw that she and Hawk had become the center of attention.

Blushing, she stiffened and said, "Shall we go inside?" She had no wish to be the brunt of the speculations of others.

With a courtly bow that was surprisingly graceful for such a large man, Hawk held out his arm to Kayln.

She bit her lip, wishing she did not feel so very flustered. What was Hawk about? Did his open regard mean that he cared about her, that he wished others to know that he did? Kayln was not sure how she felt about that or him. She knew she should not care what others thought of her. Yet she was forced to admit that she did, and that was what made her realize she could not make a scene by refusing him. With a nod, Kayln placed her hand on his arm and they led the way into the hall.

Inside, he drew her to one of the window recesses. Still conscious of those who observed them, Kayln did not resist. "I trust you slept well," Hawk said.

"I . . ." Her eyes were held by the heat in his gaze. "Yes." She lowered her lids, her lashes fanning her flushed cheeks. "Most well." What did he want her to say, that what had happened between them had changed her for all time to come? Kayln would not admit that to him, not while she felt uncertain about him—and about her own feelings.

"I would see that all your nights were so . . . restful."

Kayln was more confused than ever in her life. In some ways she felt as though she had finally woken up after moving through these many years asleep. Her senses were alive as never before, and she breathed in the warm male scent of him beside her with heightened awareness. Her tongue tasted the soft, hard feel of his name as it escaped her lips. "Hawk . . ." But she stopped, not knowing what she wanted to say—to tell him to stop or to go on talking to her that way.

He put his hands on the wall behind her, enclosing her in the strength of his arms. She knew he was going to kiss her when his lips softened and parted slightly as he bent nearer. "Kayln."

The throbbing blood in her veins drowned out the soft voice of reason. Her eyes closed and she lifted her face to him. Even before all these people, she was completely at the mercy of the way he made her feel. What was between them was too powerful to hide, pushing all thought of dignity or propriety from her mind.

"Kayln."

From somewhere Kayln heard a voice that was not Hawk's say her name, but her senses were so deeply enmeshed in what she was feeling that the sound had a quality of unreality.

"Kayln."

Opening her eyes, she could see nothing but Hawk's face above her. He turned to find out who would have the temerity to interrupt them. The irritation on his dark face boded ill for whoever it was.

The realization of what she had almost done here, in the public view of anyone who might be interested, brought a hot flush to her face and neck. Mortified by her own behavior, Kayln peeked under Hawk's arm to see who was seeking her.

Miles was standing there and his eyes, as they took in the couple before him, were narrowed with annoyance.

Kayln jerked upright, which brought the full length of her body into contact with Hawk's. Even with Miles standing there, frowning with displeasure, Kayln could not stop the jolt of heat she felt at touching Hawk so intimately.

Slowly, Hawk stepped away from her, but not before his eyes told her he had felt her reaction and he was pleased by it.

Straightening her shoulders, Kayln took a deep breath and smoothed her hands over the dark green velvet of her skirt. She refused to meet Hawkhurst's gaze. The man was entirely too sure of himself, though in all honesty she knew she was partially to blame. Kayln realized she could not think about that and what she would do about it now, not with Miles staring at her with amazed hurt and disapproval.

"Miles." She extended her hand to him, trying to quell her vexation at his censure. How this must look to him she could not even hazard a guess. Surely it was not beyond her to spend a moment of her time making him welcome.

"Please join us," Kayln said, all the while remembering that Hawk's opinion of Miles was not a favorable one. Which made her all the more determined to treat him kindly. She motioned for Miles to sit down on the window seat, then settled herself next to him.

Miles did not take his eyes from Hawk. The fact that she

and Hawk were more than in-laws must be all too obvious. Naturally Miles would be hurt, especially after her repeated refusals of his proposals.

"Lord Hawkhurst, may I present Sir Miles Harrow." She introduced him with some trepidation, but managed to keep her voice even.

"Harrow." Hawk nodded politely, his gaze unreadable.

Surprised and pleased at his restraint, she turned to the other man. "Sir Miles, this is Lord Hawkhurst."

"Hawkhurst." Miles inclined his head fractionally and his eyes remained cool.

Hawk said with civility, "I believe we have met, but that was quite some time ago. Long before I went away to the war in France."

"Many years," Miles agreed curtly, turning to Kayln.

Kayln had the urge to tell Miles that his surliness did not flatter him, but she held her tongue. She watched as the knight reached up as if to run an agitated hand through his hair, but he checked himself and merely toyed carefully with the dark curls upon his forehead. A gesture which she found unexpectedly grating on her already raw senses.

Hawk didn't help by placing a possessive hand on her shoulder. Miles stared at that hand with a darkening frown. Though she did not wish to encourage the knight's unwanted possessiveness, neither did she wish to hurt him. And neither did she wish for Hawk to believe he might take liberties with her person. She refused to acknowledge the thought that he had certainly taken much greater liberties with her person and she had reveled in each and every moment.

Kayln cast a disapproving glance toward Hawk, who grinned and shrugged. Growing more irritated, she openly frowned at him, but Hawk only lifted his brows as if he did not understand what had displeased her.

Then, showing more tact than she had thought he possessed, Hawk looked out across the room. "Ah, I see Lord Walter. There are some matters we must discuss. If you will excuse me, Lady D'Arcy." He bowed over her hand and winked. "Harrow." He nodded vaguely in Miles's direction and withdrew.

She nearly gasped aloud at the impertinent wink. Scowling,

she watched him stride away. Then she turned back to Miles, intent on putting the knave from her mind.

Miles smiled thinly as he looked after the other man.

Turning to her, he wasted no time in letting her know of his displeasure. "That man will bring you naught but ill, Kayln. You must not let yourself be taken in by him. His kind think of women as nothing but chattel to bed and use as they will."

Kayln went rigid. The words were so similar to some of the very things she had told herself that they struck all the harder. A fact which made her reply all the more sharply. "You will not speak so to me, Miles."

Kayln was surprised by Miles's reaction. For instead of backing down immediately as was his usual reaction, he stiffened and fought visibly for control. "Kayln, I . . . I . . . Please, you cannot know how I worry that you are making a mistake with this man. He was about to kiss you before the whole assemblage. Hawkhurst is a near stranger to you and you allow this, when I have loved you year upon year with no sign of returned affection from you." He made no effort to hide the pain in his eyes.

Suddenly Kayln realized she might almost deserve some of his indignation. It was wrong to flaunt her feelings for Hawk—though she knew not yet what they were—in the face of his anguish. For anguished was the only way she could describe Miles's reaction, which surprised her no small amount. Friends they had always been, and he had asked for her hand on several occasions, but she'd had no idea Miles felt so deeply.

The idea that not one but two men might be interested in her was new, and she was not sure how to respond. Not that she allowed herself to even think that Hawk actually felt any deep emotion toward her. But even desire was new to Kayln.

Knowing Miles's feelings were involved made it harder for Kayln to dismiss him summarily as she was wont to do.

Kayln purposely kept her gaze from going to Hawk, determined to be fair to Miles. But she was completely aware of the other man where he stood across the room.

"Please, Miles." She placed her hand on his arm. She knew what she was about to say was misleading, and though it troubled her she went on. "Hawk is a member of my family now. I must show some courtesy."

"Courtesy?" His tone was rife with disbelief. "The whole keep is atwitter with talk about the two of you."

Even though she'd suspected as much, the words stung. Only she could stop it, and she would begin now. Giving him a level gaze, Kayln said, "I hope you would not heed gossip about me, Miles."

He frowned pensively. Then his eyes narrowed and he looked away. "Of course not. I was simply playing at dice when one of the men in the earl's party made mention of one brawny knight who would well love to further sample the hospitality of a certain widow." He shook his head. "I had my suspicions then, but I refused to accept the truth of his words, though they did put me off my game. It wasn't until I saw you enter the hall together that I gave credence to the gossip."

Kayln had had enough. Even though she knew she had brought this upon herself, she would not tolerate this berating. "Miles, you must cease with these accusations. I have never given you cause to think I would accept such censure from you or any other man." She rose to end the conversation. "I will await your apology."

As she turned to leave, she nearly collided with Sir Jocelin. It took her a moment to remember that he was the young man she had danced with the evening before.

She recalled how Hawk had warned her to stay away from him, and her eyes darkened with stubbornness. Hawk had as much as admitted that he spoke out of jealousy. Did these men think they could order her about as if she had no mind of her own? She was perfectly capable of deciding with whom she would and wouldn't associate. Resentment and the knowledge that Miles was looking on made Kayln greet Jocelin more warmly than she might.

Sir Jocelin smiled at her, his expression openly admiring. He seemed slightly surprised at her welcome.

"Sir Jocelin, may I present you to Sir Miles of Harrow," Kayln said.

Both men nodded, though annoyance still edged Miles's face. At Kayln's scowl of displeasure it faded noticeably.

Kayln stayed only a few moments more, trying to ignore

the hot glances that young Jocelin kept casting her way. She had not meant for him to take her warm greeting as encouragement. Heavens, now she was fending off the attentions of a third man. What juxtaposition of stars had brought about this unbelievable turn of events? It was beyond reason. At the first opportunity she left the two men, saying she must check on preparations for the midday repast.

She needed time to think. Hawk must be made to understand that she would not be the brunt of gossip and speculation.

Though he had moved about the room, speaking with different people, Hawk had never lost sight of Kayln.

Hawk watched her as she left the hall, not because he felt he had anything to fear in that ridiculous jackanapes Sir Miles, but because it pleased him to do so. Every movement of her slender body, every expression on her face were heated reminders of the previous night. He had never thought he would find such passion with any woman as he did Kayln D'Arcy.

And she had given herself to no man besides himself. A self-satisfied expression passed over his face as he remembered how willingly she had done so. It was as if she were made for his lovemaking, and he reveled in that fact.

His disdainful gaze swung to Jocelin and Miles. Neither looked pleased about Kayln's departure, but they conversed easily enough together. He smiled. The fools had reason for displeasure. Hawk intended to see that neither one came near her. Just what his feelings of possessiveness might mean he did not question. He only knew that he would not share even the smallest part of the desire she'd awakened until it had cooled. As Hawk knew it must, for they had naught else to bind them. But bind them it did, for this time at least, and with chains of sensuous delight that Hawk had no desire to shake off.

Soon the two men were bent over a pair of dice. Judging from the triumphant expression on Harrow's face, it appeared he was winning.

Hawk was irritated that Kayln was still being so warm with Jocelin. The boy was a blackguard. He did not feel it necessary to tell her the details of the serf girl's death at Jocelin's hands.

But Hawk would warn her again to stay clear of him, even though he did not think she would thank him for the warning. She was far too stubborn, which reminded Hawk anew of why he did not wish to become too deeply involved with her. Kayln would always have a need to question everything, to constantly make the man in her life prove his care for her. Everything she had told him the night before only made him more certain of that. The pain that had been wrought by the men in her life was no small obstacle to try to overcome. And he was not willing to do that. He wanted a woman who would trust and believe in him. Hawk had had enough of warring in France against his enemy. He would not have a war in his own house.

Yet he was not ready to give up the passion she awakened in him. The very thought of her warm and willing in his arms caused his lower belly to tighten.

Not that he wished to use Kayln simply for his own physical gratification. She too had seemed to enjoy their lovemaking. And she'd made no pretext at feeling any deep emotion toward him. Quite the opposite. She'd made it clear that she wanted nothing between them. But not even the strong-willed Kayln D'Arcy had been able to deny the depth of desire that existed between them.

The Earl of Norwich spoke, calling Hawk's attention back to their conversation. "I would like you to take a look at Lido's foreleg."

"I should be glad to," Hawk answered offhandedly. Now that Kayln was gone from the hall, he felt no great desire to linger there. He much preferred to be active. They had done too much sitting over the last few days.

They went out to the stable. After examining the horse's leg, Hawk told the earl he was certain his stable master could make a poultice to reduce the swelling.

"Good, then." Walter nodded, setting the hoof gently to the straw-covered stable floor. "I will stop at Clamdon on my way home. Lido is a favorite of mine and I would not like to have him put down."

The two men emerged from the stable in silence, Hawk occupied in wondering if Kayln had returned to the hall.

"She is very beautiful."

"What?" Hawk turned to face his companion, with a slight frown.

"The Lady D'Arcy." The earl chuckled, reaching up to pat the younger man's broad back.

"Yes, yes, she is," Hawk agreed, a frown marring his forehead as he wondered where this conversation was going.

"Will we be returning to Aimsley to celebrate that wedding?" Walter asked.

His unexpected question caused Hawk to pause, and the two men came to a halt beside the wall of the keep. Hawk looked down at the older man with raised brows. "I had not . . ."

"Hadn't you?" the earl said archly.

Hawk stole a quick glance around the corner of the building to see that they were truly alone. He heaved a heavy sigh as he turned back to his companion. "No. The truth of the matter," Hawk confided, "is that I'm not sure that would be a good idea. In point of fact, did I wish to make such an offer, I feel it would be thrown back in my face."

"Do you love her?"

There was a long silence. Then Hawk sighed. "Love her? Nay, I wouldst not call it love." He shook his head, leaning back against the cold stone wall.

The earl shrugged. "The lady does possess other assets which would make a match between you beneficial. Kayln D'Arcy is a very wealthy widow. First her father died without male issue, leaving her everything. Then her husband died and that whole lot came to her."

"I am aware of that," Hawk said with a trace of impatience. He did know well what Kayln's wealth was, having been involved in negotiations for Celia and Philip's marriage contract with her. He had even insisted that she make provision in the event that she had children of her own, though he was not sure why. Even now he did not care to question his motives. He went on. "I care for none of it. I need not choose a wife for those reasons." In fact he had no intention of doing so. The peace and happiness of his home meant too much to him. He wanted his children to grow up in the same loving environment that he had. Kayln was not likely to give them that.

"But her lands can only add to your prosperity," Walter said cheerily, unaware of the younger man's thoughts. "You would do well to make certain all her properties and moneys are taken into your care. It is not seemly for a woman to have so much power. It puts ideas into their heads.'' He shook a finger at the taller man for emphasis.

For a long moment, Hawk said nothing. The earl was a good and well-respected man among his peers, but Hawk's own thoughts on women did not completely coincide with his. Though Hawk did not think it wise for a woman to be so independent as Kayln, his own father had deferred to his mother in many instances. A female simply needed a man to protect and care for her, keep her from harm. A man could feel proud and worthy of honor when he fulfilled the role that was meant for him.

Walter went on. ''It is important to lead them to make the right decisions. I have learned this with my Mary as you will with your wife.''

Hawk shook his head, realizing he must clarify the situation. He had been too intent on his own thoughts and inadvertently had brought about this misunderstanding. His voice was harsher than he intended as he tried to explain. ''There will be no marriage between myself and the Lady D'Arcy. We are but enjoying one another's—''

But Walter had started for the keep, obviously believing the conversation was at an end.

Following him, Hawk started around the edge of the building. As he rounded the corner, what he saw made him stop in mid-stride.

Kayln was standing there, only a few feet from him. Her hand covered her mouth and her eyes were wide and filled with sorrow. Instantly, Hawk knew she must have overheard what he had said. He had not meant to sound so harsh.

''Kayln.'' He held out his hand to her. But she wouldn't allow him to touch her, backing away from him with a gasp of pain.

Hawk took another step toward her.

Hawkhurst's action cracked the frozen misery surrounding her and Kayln was able to make her stiff limbs move to turn and run. She didn't know where she was going, only aware of a need to escape. Hawk's words tore at her.

How could he have spoken about her that way, and to the

Earl of Norwich, a man whose respect she valued? Did he understand so little of her? Had all that had happened between them meant so little?

She ran on, tears blurring her vision, heedless of his cries for her to stop. A small building made from rough lumber loomed before her. Gratefully she recognized the pigsty as a refuge from her pursuer. Kayln quickly pulled the wooden peg from the strip of leather that held the narrow door secure, pushing inside. The warm sour scent of pig filled her nostrils, and she leaned back against the wall weakly, knowing Hawk would never think of looking for her here.

Hot tears scalded her eyes, and she moaned as she put her hands to her cheeks. How could she have been so dull-witted as to hope even for a moment Hawk would be any different from all the other men she had known? Not that she had allowed herself to even contemplate marriage to him. But to hear him put it so baldly, so coldly, telling the earl that he would not marry her when he and others had already gossiped about her—the man was evil incarnate. Kayln could tell him herself that she would not have him as a husband. She refused to even wonder why a sob caught her throat.

God rot James Hawkhurst's perfidious soul.

Before she could even catch her breath, she heard him, over the sound of her own sobs, calling her name. Then she heard the predatory tread of his footsteps through the thin walls of the shed.

Kayln jerked upright. Could the great lumbering beast not leave her alone?

She gathered her skirt in her hand and climbed gingerly over the low fence into one of the two pens, which were empty as the pigs were out in the open run. Her nose stinging at the stench, Kayln made her way to the back of the pen, being careful not to slip in the muck covering the floor. If Hawk were to look inside the sty, he might not see her back in the shadows.

Right now she had no wish to see him, to hear the lies that would come from the lips that had caressed her so thoroughly only the night before. Later when she had had more time to gain control of herself, she could face him with the disdain he deserved.

Closing her eyes, she prayed he would go away and leave her in peace. But her prayers went unanswered. The door of the shed swung open and she could see Hawk silhouetted against the light as he bent his head and stepped inside.

His breathing was slightly labored, and she could tell by the way he muttered under his breath that he was highly agitated.

This gave Kayln pause for thought. What right had Hawk to be upset with her? It was she who had been hurt and humiliated by him, not the other way around. He had used her, making her believe he cared at least something for her, encouraging her to give herself to him. And the worst of it was that Kayln had begun to question herself, to wonder if he might be someone in whom she could place her faith.

Rage as sharp as an arrow flared in her chest. It was an emotion she had not allowed herself to feel for many years. This depth of rage was something she had so deeply feared from her father that she had suppressed all such violent reactions in herself. Oh, she was quick enough to show irritation when aroused. But it was controlled, tight, and cold.

The stab in her chest grew to an ache that seemed to expand until it encompassed her whole body, making her shake with the fury of it. Her lips thinned and her chest heaved with the force of her breath as she clenched her hands into tight balls around the fabric of her skirt.

"Kayln." Hawk spoke her name as one would to a recalcitrant child.

"Leave me, Hawkhurst," she spat, unmoving.

"You will listen to me."

"I will listen to nothing you might say," she cried. "I want no more of your honeyed lies."

Hawk's entire body stiffened, and he said through clenched teeth, "Have we not previously discussed the honesty of the Hawkhursts and come to the conclusion that we do not lie?" He started toward her, slowly, deliberately, easily stepping over the low fence of the pen.

"Only at your own insistence." She advanced toward him a step, made incautious by her rage. "I have since learned that ofttimes a man who insists on his own honesty proves to be false."

Hawk growled, raising a fist to slam it into his open palm.

"You will cease with baiting me, woman, and listen to what I have to say." He stopped before Kayln, reaching out to grasp her arm.

Kayln neatly sidestepped him, keeping her eyes on her tormentor as she swung around and began backing toward the door of the shed. "What could you possibly tell me that would make you whole in my sight? You have behaved like the lowliest churl." She practically screamed the words at him. "You have used me, then bragged of your dastardly behavior." Abruptly Kayln was halted as she felt the low fence, which separated the pens, dig into the back of her hips.

Continuing to stalk her, Hawk did not stop until they were separated by only the length of Kayln's arm, which came out to ward him away. "You hurt yourself with these foolish accusations," he told her. "I can make you understand what you heard."

Kayln placed her hands on her hips, glaring up at him. "I am no green girl to be moved by you again. You have made your true self known, my lord."

Hawk leaned over her, so angry he wanted to grab her up and shake some sense into her stubborn head, and bellowed at the top of his lungs, "You are a foolish girl who guards her heart so jealously she looks for excuses to find fault with everyone."

Any other time Kayln might have been daunted, but she was too angry at him for having made a fool of her, and at herself for having allowed him to do so. She lifted her hand and shook her fist. "How dare you, you great hulking beast? You may not treat me as if I were one of your lackeys."

"Aye, lady. You listen to no one but yourself." He leaned even further over her, forcing her to bend backward over the fence.

She could feel his hot breath on her face, and her back ached with the effort to keep some small distance between them. "I detest you for the strutting rooster you are," she hurled at him. He was too big, too close, and Kayln could feel panic beginning to rise up to confuse her. She wanted to stand up to him, was determined to remain uncowed, and so used every ounce of her will to force down the feeling.

"You lie, madame." His voice was low, but even more

intimidating for its evenness. "You wanted me as much as I wanted you." His eyes on her mouth, he inched closer, until she thought her back would surely break with the strain to keep away. "You're angry because someone else knows about it and that makes you feel less independent."

Suddenly it was too much. She would not, could not let him touch her. If she did she would be lost. "No," she cried wildly, throwing her hands up to his chest, thinking of nothing save the fact that she must get away. With strength born of sheer panic, she shoved at him.

To her complete surprise, he gave way.

One moment Hawk was leaning menacingly over her, the next he was sitting, legs sprawled, in the vile slime that covered the floor. And the expression on his face was one of complete and utter shock, eyes round, mouth opening and closing like a fish out of water.

Kayln put her hand over her mouth in horror at what she had done. And yet in some small inner part of herself, she felt a blooming satisfaction to see the great Hawk bested by a woman. She felt an amusement, born of near-hysteria, tickling the back of her throat.

Hawk put his hand down on either side of himself and made to rise, though it was to no avail. His hands only slid to the sides, and he held them up to study the substance which oozed from between his fingers.

She could restrain herself no longer. A choking gasp of laughter, born of sheer nervousness, escaped from behind her hand. The sound caused Hawk to turn to her with the blackest frown she had ever seen.

But his voice was pleasant when he spoke, so it took a moment for the words to penetrate her amusement. "When I am able to extricate myself from this filth, I shall take great pleasure in spanking you until you beg for mercy." He smiled, but there was no light in his eyes. He moved then, managing to gain his knees.

Kayln needed no further warning. Swinging around, she climbed over the fence and was out the door without a backward glance.

Not that she was really frightened, she told herself. The devil wouldn't dare touch her in her own keep.

She would simply leave him to gain control of himself. After all, he had only gotten what he deserved.

Chapter Nine

Kayln went down to the evening meal with her head high. As she pointedly passed by Hawk without a word, she was the recipient of a few curious stares from the people who had seen them together in the courtyard early in the day. Let them look, she told herself. Soon enough they would see that she had no interest in Hawkhurst.

Looking neither right nor left, Kayln chose a seat as far from Hawk as possible. She barely glanced at him where he sat with his brother Martin, but she could feel his gaze upon her. She forced herself not to meet his eyes, not to care what he did.

It had been difficult to avoid Hawk since she had run from the pigsty that morning, but Kayln had been determined. She had no wish to face him, nor his accusations that she wanted him. For in truth, she might have wanted him at one time, but his disregard for her had changed that. Hadn't it?

Kayln could only assure herself that her attraction toward him was indeed dead. Complete indifference was what she sought. But she had to admit she'd known an ungracious sense of satisfaction when Alice had informed her that Hawk had ordered a very hot bath and had burned the clothing he'd been wearing. As was her custom, Alice had pried for information when she saw the way Kayln flushed at the news. But Kayln had refused to be drawn out. Not even Alice was to know to what extent Hawk had used her.

Her lips thinned in anger as she reached for her cup, her fingers clenching tight around the stem. How dare Hawk treat her so shabbily? His gentle ways with her during the last few days had been nothing but a planned method of seduction. And Kayln, fool that she was, had succumbed most readily. She shuddered in self-disgust, knowing she had been a very willing victim.

But no more. She lifted her cup, draining the contents.

Kayln would not allow herself to give in to the pain the decision brought. She had spent too many years with her feelings locked away to lose control now when her pride was at stake.

Hawk might believe what he would. Kayln was going to show him she could get on very well without him. If he thought to ever hold her in his sway again, he would do well to reconsider.

Kayln looked around the room, back straight, chin high.

"May I have the honor?" a voice beside her asked. Turning her head, Kayln saw Jocelin standing. She had been so engrossed in her own thoughts, she had not been aware of his approach. His young face was so open, his smile so ingenuous, that she found herself smiling back at him.

"It would give me great pleasure." Kayln nodded, indicating the vacant seat next to her.

Jocelin sat down and turned his admiring gaze upon her. "When you enter a room every other woman pales to insignificance beside you," he told her, resting his elbow on the table and leaning his chin on his hand.

Jocelin's adoration was flattering, boosting her flagging spirits. But Hawk's recent betrayal made her cautious. "Pretty words." She raised her brows.

"For a lovely lady." He put his hands to his heart.

Something made Kayln glance up. Across the room, Hawk leaned against the wall, studying her. Displeasure darkened his rugged face. He had warned her away from this young man.

It was difficult to keep from snickering aloud. How very ironic, she thought, for Hawk to be warning her against another man when he was the one who had set out to seduce her. What he had told her about Jocelin was probably nothing more than an attempt to keep her at a distance from other men so he might have the field cleared for himself.

When she met Hawk's troubled eyes, her expression was cool.

Her next action came more from a sense of revenge than she would have been willing to admit. The gaze she turned upon Jocelin was warm enough to melt ice on a cold winter day. "It is hard not to believe your words when they are declared so earnestly."

"Only because they come from the depths of my soul, dear lady," he insisted, emboldened by her answer.

Kayln settled back in her seat. Jocelin was an attractive young man, even if she did find him a trifle too immature for her taste, and made a pleasant companion. Best of all, he was no threat to her already wounded emotions. Kayln could spend time with him without feeling as if she were on a bolting horse with no way to stop.

Ignoring the growing anger she could feel Hawk directing toward them, Kayln ate and laughed and talked. Though she knew that after the meal she would not be able to remember what any of the dishes were, nor what had been funny, nor what she had said. No matter that she tried to hide it, her every sense was totally attuned to Hawk.

This made Kayln laugh all the more gaily, smile all the more widely, and accept Jocelin's compliments with extra warmth. She was determined to make Hawk see he had not broken her.

But such a performance was draining and could not be sustained indefinitely. When she could bear no more, Kayln found herself muttering an excuse about work that had to be seen to. After all, it was true that many of the wedding guests would be leaving on the morrow, and Kayln meant to see them off with sufficient food for their return journeys.

Jocelin, though he seemed reluctant to see her go, could only nod his understanding.

As soon as Kayln stood up to leave the table, Miles managed to place himself beside her. "Kayln?" His tone was hesitant and he seemed unsure of himself.

"Yes, Miles." She turned, feeling a stab of guilt at seeing him. He had tried to warn her of Hawkhurst's intentions and she had treated him abominably. Kayln smiled in welcome.

In spite of her obvious warmth, his tone was hesitant. "I just wanted to spend some time with you. I shall be leaving in the morning and I would not go away without being sure you were not angry with me over some of the things I said yesterday. You know I would never intentionally do anything to cause you upset."

Kayln put her hand on his arm, grateful that he was himself, her dear gentle Miles. "Even if I were angry with you, I could not stay that way. You and I have been friends for far too long to let a silly disagreement come betwixt us."

"You don't know how much that means to me." He took her hand in his. "I—"

"Do not say any more, Miles." Kayln looked at him with sympathy, putting up her hand to keep him from continuing. "It is not necessary."

Kayln turned to Sir Jocelin, who nodded to Miles. "You have met Sir Miles of Harrow?"

Jocelin grinned ruefully. "Oh, yes, my lady, you were kind enough to introduce us yesterday."

Kayln flushed. So much had happened since the day before, including her ill-fated tryst with Hawk, that she could hardly be faulted for forgetting such a thing. She recovered herself quickly. "You are right, Sir Jocelin. I fear there are so many people present that I can barely recall who *I've* been introduced to."

The two men laughed as they were meant to.

Feeling her neck prickle, Kayln looked up and saw Hawk staring at them. He spoke to the man beside him, then moved purposefully toward her.

"Miles," she said quickly, "will you walk with me? I have some things that must be attended to."

She barely waited for his nod of assent before she turned and started from the hall. She added, "If you will excuse us, Sir Jocelin?"

But once they were safely away from the hall and Hawkhurst, Kayln found she was aware of a certain awkwardness in Miles's presence. After all, she had just used him to escape the other man's attention, and that left her feeling decidedly guilty.

Drat Hawk for ruining her peace of mind.

Searching desperately for something, anything to say, Kayln asked, "What news have you about the war?" She knew this was a topic that Miles prided himself at being expert on.

She smiled with a great show of interest, which was no

small effort. Kayln cared for the small world around her. Generally speaking, what happened outside her lands was the concern of others. Her goal was to see her own environment safe and sound. Aimsley was always her first priority. More than her home, it was her refuge against the world and its deceits.

Miles seemed surprised by this request as he knew Kayln was not one to discuss politics, but he answered her readily enough. "The talk is mostly centered around what will be done now that King John has been taken to London. He resides in the Tower and is treated as an honored guest." Miles shook his head. "I do not understand how King Edward can be so accommodating to an enemy of England."

Only half listening, Kayln cast a backward glance over her shoulder. "Perhaps he grows tired of the war and seeks to make peace."

James Hawkhurst stood in the doorway of the hall behind them. As their eyes met, his lips curved in a slow knowing smile, which broadened as a pink flush stained her throat.

Miles followed her gaze with a displeased expression, but made no comment about the other man. He simply continued their conversation. "Methinks it more likely that King Edward believes the war will go on for some time."

Kayln frowned as they moved on, trying to concentrate on what he was saying. Though she knew that they were now out of Hawk's sight, she could still feel the press of his attention on her back. "Why do you say that?"

With a shrug, Miles said, "Edward announced himself King of France in 1337, when Philip the Sixth declared Gascony forfeit to the French crown, and set these wheels in motion. There is little chance that he will back away now. The French are too stubborn to retreat from their position no matter their losses."

Unable to dismiss the sensation of being watched, Kayln looked behind them. Hawk was not there. Irritation at her own silliness made her answer sharply. "War is a foolish game men play to outdo one another. Unless you are protecting your own lands, it is simply a waste of time and money."

Miles scowled. "You do not understand. Gascony belonged to England."

"Oh, I understand well enough." She put her hands on her

hips. "But what has it cost us to try to keep a holding in a foreign country? More than ever it was worth, and still the fighting continues. I must pay my own knight's fees, you know, and would be glad to see the end of it."

Miles's face reddened at her censure, and he swallowed audibly, fighting for control. "Excuse me, dear lady, I fear I have angered you yet again."

Kayln closed her eyes and took a deep breath. What had Miles done to deserve such a reaction? It was she who had broached the subject. "I beg pardon for my surliness. I do not know from whence it comes."

He was silent for a long moment, staring at the ground, then said, "I can only think you are overtired with arranging the wedding and so many guests to look after."

She sighed. "I fear you have hit near the mark, my friend." She had no intention of telling him that most of her irritation was directed at herself. And she had to admit that it was, for she was not able to follow her own resolve and ignore Hawkhurst no matter how she tried.

But despite his seeming understanding, Miles continued to look away from her, and Kayln knew all was not well. "Methinks I will speak with my men about making ready for our return to Harrow on the morrow."

What had once been an amicable relationship relatively free of conflict had deteriorated to this. And all because of James Hawkhurst. She had indeed allowed him to play her for a fool.

Distractedly Kayln nodded to Miles, grateful to draw the conversation to a close. She had had enough strife to last her quite some time. "Yes," she told him. "I have much to do also." And though it was difficult, she made an attempt at an apology. "When next we meet, I am certain to be feeling more myself."

Finally Miles looked at her, his eyes strangely assessing. At last he answered, "I will bid you farewell in the morning, then."

Kayln felt an odd sense of discomfort at the expression in his eyes. It was almost as if he was toying with her. But she quickly pushed the thought aside. She was only imagining things because of Hawk's devious actions.

Miles went without further ado, leaving Kayln thinking that

she must get herself and her life back in control. Hawk had no real power over her and she could not allow herself to be so affected by him. As soon as she had made certain of the readiness of the meals for her guests, Kayln went back to the hall.

Hawk was not in evidence, and she refused to acknowledge either a sense of relief or disappointment. A short time later, Kayln excused herself, saying she should retire early so she might be able to rise in time to see the first of her guests on their way.

Kayln paused as she made her way to the archway that led to the tower when she sensed Hawk enter the hall by the opposite door. One quick glance toward the spot gave proof to her feelings. He stood tall, his eyes searching out and finding her. She felt her pulse quicken with the heat of his gaze, and fought to control it. Turning away from the sheer force of him, his wide shoulders in black velvet, the tousled ebony of his hair, his liquid-gold eyes, Kayln reminded herself of how deeply he had hurt her.

Why then did she still find him so compelling?

Kayln kept her head lowered, her gaze forward. Ignoring the magnetic pull of his gaze as he willed her to stop and face him, Kayln quickened her steps. She was only able to let out a tired breath when she gained the relative safety of the stairs. Hawk was so strong, so completely sure of himself, that every time they matched wills she was left exhausted.

When she reached her room, Kayln closed the door behind herself, then bolted it. She leaned back against the oaken panel with a sigh. For once, the luxurious beauty of her chamber did not soothe her. Pushing herself away from the door, she crossed to the bed, climbing up to sit upon the soft silken coverlet.

All day she had been forcing herself to go on, to keep up the pretense that all was well. Now, alone in her chamber, she could finally allow herself to let the pain through. Kayln could feel the hot sting of tears behind her eyes and could hold them back no longer. They poured down her cheeks in rivulets, staining the bodice of her blue velvet tunic. She drew her knees up to wrap her arms around them and rocked back and forth, her misery so great it threatened to choke her.

Why, oh, why had she allowed herself to think Hawk might be different, that she might be able to trust in him? Even when living with Raymond, she had not felt the cold emptiness that now had taken the place of her heart. Never had she thought a man's betrayal would devastate her as Hawk's did.

Finally, exhausted, Kayln fell back to lie upon the bed, curling onto her side like a small child. Her swollen eyes grew heavy and her sobs subsided as she drifted into a troubled sleep.

Her dreams were cloudy and filled with formless faces that jeered at her mockingly. Disembodied arms grabbed at her as she ran . . . until the pounding of her heart grew so loud it thundered in her ears, banging against her ribs with terrible force.

Kayln opened her eyes to the realization that the pounding was coming from outside herself. There was someone knocking with determined insistence on her bolted door.

Slowly she rose, pushing her tangled hair, which had come loose from its braid as she slept, back over her shoulders. Groggily, she moved toward the door. It wasn't until she heard Hawk's voice call her name in a hoarse whisper that she remembered the events of the day.

Kayln halted in mid-motion as she reached down to draw back the bolt. She stood there silently, willing him to go away.

"Kayln, I know you are there," Hawk said. "I can feel you." With a start she jerked her hand back, puzzled by the fact that he had known she was on the other side of the door by mere intuition.

"Please, go away," she whispered, her voice catching on a sob.

"I must speak with you."

"No, I have nothing to say to you." She held her hands to her head. Then, thinking he had come to make good on his threat to punish her for pushing him into the pig filth, she added, "It was not my intention to push you down. I can only beg your forgiveness and trust the matter will be forgotten."

"It is already forgotten," he answered impatiently. "I did not come here to discuss that."

"Then leave me in peace." She closed her eyes and leaned

her forehead against the door. "You can have nothing else to say to me."

"I have to explain." He was nearly pleading, and if she hadn't known better, she would have believed he actually cared.

"I understand more than you think," she told him, forcing herself to speak coldly. "But let me make it clear to you I am no easy mark to fool a second time. I will not talk to you."

"Kayln." His tone became intimate, soothing, like a caress, and she felt her insides melting with the sweetness of it. "If you will let me in, I will make you see you have made a mistake about me. You will see that we can come to an understanding on this."

"No, my lord, it is you who have made a mistake about me." She tried to make her voice firm, but it was soft and breathless. She knew what he meant by an understanding. He wanted to make love to her again. And God help her, she knew she wanted it too in spite of everything. She was too vulnerable to him and the way he'd made her feel, with the night pressing close and dark around them.

It was clear to her that, under no circumstances, could she allow him to come into this room tonight. The memory of the passion they had shared the night before was so real she could almost hear their soft cries of release.

"Kayln."

Her body cried out, urging her to pull back the bolt. Was there anything to be gained by denying herself the pleasure he could give her?

But Kayln stopped herself, realizing she had actually put out her hand. She forced herself to remember the things he had done to hurt her. This was nothing more than an act he performed with consummate skill.

"Should I let you in so that you might boast to your friend on the morrow?" Her voice was filled with more bitterness than she had meant to expose.

She heard a thump on the other side of the door as if he had struck it with his fist. Hawk heaved a great sigh. When he spoke again, his voice was cold. "Very well, Kayln, believe what you will. There is nothing further I can do. It is your own fear that has put an end to what could have been between us. The passion we shared is rare and something that should not have been thrown away lightly."

She heard his footsteps as he turned away, then the clatter as he made his way down the steps, leaving her alone as she had asked. Turning back to her solitary bed, Kayln wondered why she was not more relieved at getting what she wanted.

All she felt was a deep aching void.

Chapter Ten

Hawk awakened early the next morning, his mood boding ill for anyone who might chance to cross his path. He could understand that Kayln had been hurt by what she had overheard, even though he'd not meant the words as they'd sounded. But God's blood, did she not owe him the courtesy of at least listening to his explanation? He'd made her no promises, had not thought she expected, or even desired, any. In point of fact Hawk had gotten the distinct impression that Kayln did not want to commit herself to any man, to him especially. He brushed aside the stab of disappointment he felt at the thought, telling himself there was no reason for it. He wanted no more from their liaison than she.

Yet he could understand how she could have become angered by what she had overheard. Even though he had not in any way meant to denigrate her, it must surely have seemed that way. That was why he had waited for an opportunity to try to speak with her all the previous day. And when he'd finally created his own chance, she'd turned him away without so much as a hearing. Her refusals to listen to him had only served to reinforce his opinion that any relationship with Kayln would only be filled with strife.

"Damn her," he muttered, throwing back the covers. He'd known nothing but strife from the moment they met. It was well he was returning to Clamdon this day, for surely he would strangle her in frustration did she keep rejecting him this way.

But even as he stalked out of the keep, Hawk knew he'd be back. The lovemaking they'd shared had only sharpened his desire for her, and he was not yet ready to acknowldge defeat.

All Kayln needed was time to admit that she too wanted him. In spite of her denials he had been able to hear it in her voice the previous night. Surely she would come to see that such a desire could not be denied.

As he was leading his horse from the stable, Hawk met Martin. He grimaced. He had no wish to speak with his brother alone. Since the day he'd told the younger man of his problems with the steward, Harold, Martin had been relentless in his efforts to bring Hawk to his "senses." He was sure Hawk was needlessly endangering his life by allowing the steward to live. But Hawk was determined to have the man's accomplice, for he was more and more sure that there was one. His goods had seemed to disappear into a void.

Thus Hawk was heartened to hear Walter of Norwich's cheery voice call out to them before Martin could begin anew. "Good morrow."

The brothers replied in unison, "Good morrow."

"I had thought to begin early this morning," the earl went on. "If we are to stop for a time at Clamdon, it would be best. That is"—he chortled, his gray eyes glistening knowingly—"if we can rouse your little brother from his marriage bed."

Martin let out a loud guffaw. "Philip is ever an easy one to goad," he said, his eyes sparkling with devilment. "With him along, it should relieve some of the tedium of the journey."

Martin and Jayne planned to accompany the earl's party as far as Norwich.

Hawk smiled in spite of himself, knowing Philip would receive more than his share of ribbing on the return to Norwich. The fact that Philip and Celia had not spared a moment for their guests would draw good-humored commentary. The newlyweds had even taken all their meals in her chamber.

Yet Hawk was sure Philip would not have given up one moment of the time he had to spend with his lovely bride to spare himself the teasing he would receive.

Hawk was not able to completely stifle the regret that only one of his nights had been spent in such pleasurable pursuits. Too much of his time with Kayln had been wasted in first waiting for her to see that they should become lovers, then trying to explain himself to her. With a heavy sigh, he began leading his mount from the stable, wondering how long it would be before he and the lady would be together again.

Outside, the keep was beginning to rouse. People were appearing, some of them yawning and rubbing their eyes, as they went about their duties—the women to the cooking sheds, laundry, and looms, the men to the armory, animal shelters, and tannery. All moved more slowly than usual, some holding stomachs that threatened to rebel at the abuse brought on by two days of celebrations.

A sensation of being watched drew Hawk's gaze upward. The window of Kayln's tower was open. He caught the glint of sunshine on dark gold hair and a flash of creamy skin. Then the space was empty. A knowing smile touched his sensuous lips and his eyes became hooded. Here was proof that the witch was not as indifferent to him as she claimed.

Hawk turned to Walter and Martin, speaking with more enthusiasm. "It is a fine morning, is it not?" Hawk looked up to see another slight movement at the window, and smiled.

The party left Aimsley with much ribald laughter on the part of the earl and Martin, Philip having finally appeared only after Hawk had gone to fetch him.

Everyone else was already mounted and waiting when Philip ran from the keep to climb atop his restless horse. He was flushed, and would not meet their eyes as they teased him.

Knowing how painful this was for the boy, Hawk refrained from adding any jibes of his own, though he did not intend to coddle Philip for long. The sooner his brother accepted that he must be separated from his wife, the happier he would be.

The route to Clamdon was a pleasant one at this time of year. And after the travelers had grown tired of teasing Philip, who would not answer any of their jibes, they settled into smaller groups to talk.

Looking back from where he was riding at the head of the procession beside the earl and Martin, Hawk saw Philip had fallen behind, his young face bleak. A brother-to-brother talk might be in order, he told himself.

"If you will excuse me?" He nodded without waiting for the other men to reply and dropped back.

When Philip was level with him, Hawk asked, "How goes it, boy?"

Philip raised his head, and Hawk could see his eyes were

shimmering with the pain of leaving his young wife. "I am not a boy." He drew himself up and stared ahead as he sought to control his tumultuous emotions. "I am a man."

Hawk grinned at his brother's outburst. He had not meant to insult, and realized he would need to be careful of his phrasing. "Of course."

His brother's expression of misery did not change in spite of the acknowledgment of his manhood.

"You will be home at Christmastide," Hawk said. "You will be surprised at how quickly the time passes. And besides, I have spoken with the earl and he believes if you apply yourself, you may be able to finish your training more quickly than is usual. His lordship says you have a ready mind for battle tactics and your skill with weapons improves apace."

Philip flushed with pride at this compliment from his overlord. It was well known what a skilled warrior Hawk was, and for the earl to have even voiced such opinions to Hawk would mean he felt Philip was indeed showing some aptitude. "I am most glad for my lord's praise," he answered, ducking his head.

Thinking to take his younger brother's mind from his troubles, Hawk challenged him, saying, "I will race you to where the old oak tree hangs over the road." Both of them knew the spot well.

A gleam appeared in Philip's eyes as he took in his brother's huge mount. Being larger and carrying as much weight as it was, the horse was not likely to be able to outrun his own more compact gray stallion. "Challenge accepted," Philip yelled, slapping his horse's rump with the reins. The smaller mount surged forward and Philip was off, getting the jump on his elder brother.

With a loud growl of mock outrage which clearly showed his opinion of Philip's sense of fair play, Hawk started after him. The line of riders before them gave way as the two galloped through.

Realizing what was happening, the others began to call out encouragement to the brothers. They spurred their mounts forward at a trot, anxious to see who indeed would be the winner of the race.

On rounding the sharp bend in the road just before coming

to the oak tree, Jayne grasped in shocked horror, as did everyone around her.

Hawk lay upon the ground, an arrow protruding from his chest.

Jayne urged her mount in front of the others. Her back bent low over the horse's neck, she reached her brother before the others had even recovered enough to act. She was on the ground and holding Hawk's dark head in her lap when Martin, who reached him next, leaped from his own stallion.

"Dear God, what has happened?" the earl asked as he halted beside them, dismounting clumsily in his haste.

"He has been shot," Martin said, though the words were not necessary. He went down on one knee beside his sister, his hands moving restlessly as he tried to think.

"Who . . . how?" Walter of Norwich asked.

"I do not know," Jayne answered as she worked to discover just how deeply the arrow was embedded. "I saw no one."

They heard the clatter of hooves coming toward them from the direction of Clamdon, and all eyes turned to face the sound. Philip came into view and his face became a mask of horror as he saw Hawk.

"What happened?" he cried as he leaped from his stallion before it could come to a full stop.

"We don't know," Martin told him while he helped Jayne to rip Hawk's clothing away from the wound. "When we rounded the corner, here he was."

"Give me your shirt, Martin," Jayne ordered.

Martin stood, stripped down to his bare chest, and handed the shirt to his sister. He shrugged back into his tunic, then knelt to help her pack the shirt around the wound, which was bleeding profusely.

"Did you see anyone, Philip?" Jayne asked without looking up.

"No, no one. Nothing. I thought Hawk was right behind me. I could hear him coming."

Just then, there was a rustling of brush nearby, causing the siblings to look up from their ministrations. Sir Jocelin came riding out of the forest to their left. He stared down at them with horror and what might also have been guilt.

With a growl of outrage, Martin leaped up and ran directly

to him, reaching up with both hands to drag him from his horse. "You bastard," he screamed. "If you've killed my brother, I'll see the flesh stripped from your hide one layer at a time."

"Hawk will not die," Jayne said reasonably, looking up from where she had been examining the wound. "The arrow has struck deep, but Hawk is a strong man and he will live." Her even tone and the certainty in her eyes must have reached her brother, for Martin loosed his stranglehold on the younger man.

Martin knew that when Jayne said a thing with such absolute surety, it would be so. "That only means your death will be slightly less painful than if you had killed him," Martin snarled into Jocelin's horrified face.

"I don't know what you are talking about," Jocelin protested, trying to pull away, but the tall auburn-haired knight had too sure a grip on him. "I have done nothing."

Martin's angry gaze held the other man as securely as his hands. "Then what, pray, were you doing in the forest? It seems oversuspicious to me that you should come riding out just moments after my brother has had an arrow shot at him."

"I was . . ." Jocelin looked around nervously. "That is . . . we . . ." He looked into the crowd around them as if searching for someone.

Martin followed the man's gaze until it came to rest on a young woman at the back of the group. He recognized her as one of the countess's women. Her face flushed and she brushed at the bits of grass that still clung to her skirt. Her full bosom was nearly spilling from the low neck of her gown, as if the garment had been hastily donned.

"I see." Martin turned back to Jocelin with less furor, but his eyes were still wary. "Did anyone see you leave together?"

"I did," Philip said, his voice unhappy. "They went off before Hawk had even come back to talk with me. There was no way for Jocelin to know Hawk would challenge me to a race."

Martin stared down at Jocelin for a long moment, his rage still evident in the flare of his nostrils and the restrained shaking of his hands. "Very well, then, weasel." Martin slowly set him on his feet. "But be warned that I will be watching you and should you ever look in the least suspicious, there is no power on earth or in Hell that will stop me from killing you."

"Who are you killing now, Martin?" Hawk's unmistakable deep voice broke the stillness that followed the pronouncement.

"Hawk!" Philip knelt at his brother's side.

"I had no idea you would go to such lengths to win a race, Philip," Hawk chided, nodding toward the arrow protruding from his shoulder.

"Hawk!" Philip was shocked. "How can you—" Then he stopped, his eyes going round as he realized his brother was teasing him, even wounded as he was. "What should we do?" he asked Hawk anxiously. "Do you want us to branch out into search parties and find the bastard who did this?"

With the hand on his uninjured side, Hawk grasped Martin's tunic and pulled him close. When he spoke it was in a voice only his brother would hear. "Ride for Clamdon. You must see to Harold's whereabouts." Out loud he said, "Go to Clamdon and organize my men. They can search the forests more readily than anyone, knowing it as they do."

The two men exchanged a knowing look. Then Martin mounted his horse and rode off.

"I'll tell you what we will do," Jayne ordered, taking control of the situation once again. "We will make a litter of some branches and get Hawk into bed where I can get this arrow out of his shoulder. We are not more than a half hour from Aimsley and if I treat him there, the danger of infection would be much less than if we go on to Clamdon."

"I need no litter," Hawk began, straining to rise from her lap. "Get my horse—"

Jayne pressed him down with her hand on his uninjured shoulder. "You will do no such thing," she told Philip, who had started up to do Hawk's bidding. "See the litter is made as I instructed."

Philip stood there for a moment, looking from one to the other in confusion.

"Instantly, Philip," Jayne commanded.

"It looks as though we have been outranked, Philip," Hawk

said with a scowl. But if the truth were told, he was not sorry to have the matter taken out of his hands. His shoulder was paining him fiercely, and he was beginning to feel a little light-headed from loss of blood.

When the stretcher was finished, the men lifted Hawk to place him on it. The motion sent a jarring shriek of agony through him. Mercifully he slipped into the void.

Chapter Eleven

Kayln did not come down from her chambers until well after Hawk and his party had left. She realized she might appear rude in not saying farewell to the others who rode with him, but she could not bring herself to face him. The memory of how she had so nearly given in to him last night, in spite of what he had done to her, was still fresh.

But she had not been able to keep herself away from the windows, yearning for a glimpse of the powerful baron even after telling herself she didn't care if she never saw him again. Her hands tightened into fists as she realized that lack of self-control might have given her away still further. For she feared Hawk had seen her there, no matter that she had darted out of sight upon seeing him raise his head toward her. Another quick peek had enhanced her suspicions. Kayln could think of no other reason for the smug grin that had creased his handsome face.

What a maddening devil he was. She told herself she certainly did hope that she never saw him, but the hollow sensation in her chest gave the lie to the words.

Determined to put Hawk from her mind, Kayln left her room in search of Miles. He had promised to bid her goodbye before returning to Harrow.

She was disappointed to learn that his party had been gone since before she had risen. Obviously he was still upset with her. Kayln was sorry to have pricked his feelings so deeply, but he would surely come around.

A short time later Kayln stood in the courtyard looking after the last of the departing wedding guests with relief. At last there would be some peace. She refused to acknowledge the silent voice that told her there would be no peace for her now that she had given herself to James Hawkhurst.

Unwittingly she sighed and turned to go into the keep, just as the sounds of a commotion drew her attention to the castle gate. Gathering the skirt of her gown in her hands, she hurried across the courtyard.

A frown of confusion creased her brow as she saw Jayne Hawkhurst enter the gate on her white palfrey. The mounted woman paid no attention to those in the courtyard, calling out instructions to someone behind her.

Two soldiers bearing a litter trod close on her heels.

Jayne wasted no time in formal greetings. "It's Hawk. He's been wounded. Direct the men to a chamber where he can be cared for."

At the first utterance, Kayln felt the blood drain from her face. In spite of everything the news was like a blow, but Kayln had no time to question why she would react so strongly to Hawk's being injured when she professed to hate him so thoroughly.

Dear God, only a short time ago she had seen him ride from the keep looking more powerful and hale than any man had a right to. Questions rushed from her trembling lips. "What? How badly?" An unexplainable fear for him paralyzed her and made it impossible to look directly at Hawk, though her mind supplied vivid details of a still-white face and clothing stained dark from lost blood.

"Please," Jayne asserted. "Might we see him settled before the matter is discussed?"

"Of course," Kayln answered, searching her mind for rational thought. But all she could think of was the fact that Hawk was injured. Hawk, the man who had taught her the physical pleasures of being a woman. "Follow me." She led them to the hall, then into the largest of the three guest rooms. A serving woman was still scouring the hearth, but the bed had been laid with fresh linens.

She hurried across the floor and pulled the covers down, then stepped back from the bed.

The men with the stretcher passed next to her, but she kept her eyes averted, still not able to look at the ravaged form. Only now, when she feared losing him to death's cold arms, could Kayln admit that she did feel bound in some way to Hawk, no matter that he had so sorely used her. He had spoken true when he said the desire they shared was too powerful to ignore. Even though she knew there was no hope of any future for the two of them, the thought of his death was devastating.

Jayne went to the bed and bent to examine her brother. A few moments later she began issuing orders for heated water, fresh linens, and sundry other items.

The servants bustled off to do her bidding.

And Kayln simply stood there bleakly, as still and cold as the castle wall. All the while she tried not to remember how empty, staid, and predictable her life had been before Hawk came into it, how devoid of passion.

Was this her fault? Hadn't she wished him out of her life forever countless times over the past two days? Had God heard her prayer and punished Kayln by granting her wish?

"Kayln."

She looked up to find Jayne looking at her with ill-disguised irritation. "Kayln."

Her answer felt as if it came from outside herself. "Yes."

"Would you attend Hawk for a moment? I must check for the herbs I require." Jayne motioned toward a nervous serving woman. "This girl does not understand what I am asking for."

"Of course," Kayln answered woodenly. She did not know what else to say.

She went to the side of the bed, her gaze rising no further than Hawk's darkly tanned, hard-muscled chest. A white scrap of linen covered his right shoulder. Jayne had her hand over it, but blood was slowly seeping up in a crimson stain.

"You must simply hold the bandage in place," she told Kayln, removing her hand, then pressing Kayln's fingers over the cloth. The bed was high and Kayln had to lean across Hawk's body to accomplish the task, but she did not look into his face, afraid she would see his approaching demise reflected there.

She was barely aware of Jayne's leaving.

At first Kayln just stood there as if carved from stone. But after a time, she noticed that his flesh felt surprisingly warm and alive under her fingers.

Just the way she remembered it from their lovemaking. Her heart lurched. Never again would she feel his hands upon her own flesh. Finally Kayln raise her gaze to his face, though she was still afraid of what she would see there. She simply had to look upon the face of her only lover this one last time.

She gasped on finding Hawk's eyes staring into hers with knowing amusement. His voice was husky with pain, but held every scrap of his usual self-confidence. "I did not think to find myself so near the same bed as you for quite some time. I must say, I am most gratified."

Kayln jerked back with a growl of outrage, her task forgotten. God rot him, he was very much alive. It was one thing to think of the passion they had shared with nostalgia when she thought Hawk lay dying, but now that she knew he was not, she could hate him again without guilt. "Filthy cur. Even now you think of nothing but your loins." Yet even as she spat the words at him, there was a distant thrill of relief inside her. It was immediately squelched.

He sobered, his expression mocking. "Forgive me for teasing. Though you know I but echoed the same thoughts that were running through your mind."

"I thought no—"

He raised a hand, then gingerly lowered it, with a grimace. "There is no use denying it. I sense your feelings when I am by. You cannot hide them from me."

Kayln blanched. Surely he was lying. It had been nothing more than a fortunate guess that she had been remembering them making love.

But Hawk continued. "What I really want to talk about is the fact that you were worried about me."

This she would not allow to pass even though it was true. "I was not."

"You were."

She raised her chin. "Not any more than I would be concerned about anyone. No more than a stray dog run down by a horse."

"Are you still so very angry with me?" Hawk asked softly.

Her answer was quick in coming. "Yes." Did he really think she could forget the way he had spoken about her to the earl, that he had openly admitted to having no care for her? The memory was deeply painful, and his injury did nothing to change her feelings about that.

He quirked a maddening brow, his lips parting to reply, just as Jayne came back into the room.

The raven-haired beauty looked from Kayln to the bandage, which was now completely red, with a frown of displeasure. "Kayln, did you not say you would hold the bandage? Look how the wound is bleeding again."

A retort hovered on the tip of Kayln's tongue as her cheeks flushed scarlet. This was her home and Kayln was not accustomed to being spoken to in such a tone.

How could she explain to Jayne that it was all Hawk's fault and that he was utterly impossible? It was he who had wronged her, not the other way around. But the woman thought very highly of her brother and would not accept criticism of him, especially under the circumstances. With great effort Kayln kept her peace.

To her utter surprise, Hawk said, "Have you forgotten that you are speaking to the lady of this keep, Jayne? She has offered us her hospitality and for that we should be grateful. Besides, it is entirely my fault Kayln left her post. I begged her to fetch me a drink of water. My throat is dry as French wine. So please, sister mine, apologize for scolding your hostess."

Kayln could only stare at him in amazement. But she refused to be grateful. It had been his fault.

Jayne cast Kayln no more than a glance as she apologized, although the words were said prettily enough. "I beg your pardon for my rudeness. I can only offer concern for my brother, though a poor excuse that is. It is kind of you to give us your hospitality. We were much closer to Aimsley when the accident occurred, and so came directly here rather than go on to Clamdon."

Jayne strode across the room to the round table next to the fireplace and poured water from the pitcher into a glass. She took it to Hawk without further comment, before turning her attention back to his wound. She seemed quite unabashed by the reprimand from her brother, and went on about her business as if naught had occurred.

What an imperturbable lot these Hawkhursts were.

Kayln risked a look at Hawk, and found him studying her with eyes that fairly glinted with amusement.

Raising her chin, she met his gaze levelly. Despite her dislike of him, she wished to know what had happened to Hawk and neither one of them had offered any information. She might as well take a turn at frankness herself. "Exactly what kind of accident occurred?"

Hawk spoke up quickly. "Just a poacher's arrow gone astray."

Kayln stiffened. "A poacher on my land? Did you capture him?"

"No," Jayne answered as she folded another scrap of linen over the wound. "But we did send men into the forest to look. Martin will be coming tonight to tell us how the search goes."

Kayln glanced toward Hawk as his sister spoke, and saw that his face was too bland. She had come to know him well enough to see that he was hiding something.

But what, and more importantly, why?

As the bedchamber door opened several mornings later, Hawk looked up with an unknowingly hopeful expression. When he saw Alice, he sighed with resignation before greeting her. "Good morrow, Alice."

"Your Lordship," the woman answered, coming across the room to deposit the things she carried at the foot of the bed. "How are you feeling this fine morning?"

He shrugged. "Well enough."

If truth were told he was not feeling quite right, but he put that down to disappointment at not seeing Kayln. When he had sent Jayne on to London with Martin the day after he was brought to Aimsley, Hawk had envisioned a quite different convalescence.

It had been no small task to convince Jayne to leave, though she knew he was in no danger from the wound. The arrow had not struck deep enough to do real lasting damage. Hawk had finally been left with no choice but to tell Jayne that though he loved his sister dearly, he wished to be alone with Kayln. He had not told Jayne that he was nearly burning with the desire to continue their liaison, but he did hope that once Kayln was alone with him she would give in to her own need.

Martin, who was present at the time, had given a great guffaw as Jayne took herself off to repack her belongings. "Don't concern yourself with Jayne's temper. Living with me has taught her a man has needs that must be seen to,'' Martin said sagely.

''Hmmm.'' Hawk scratched his head. ''Wasn't it you, Martin, who told me just last summer that Jayne did not allow you to even bring a woman into your own home? If I am remembering rightly, you were complaining about having to find other accommodations for your trysts.'' He eyed his reddening brother knowingly.

''You thrust deep, Hawk,'' Martin answered humbly. Then he looked at his brother with concern as his own comment reminded him of Hawk's possible danger from the steward, Harold. ''You must have a care, Hawk. Although Harold had not left Clamdon the day you were injured, he could have hired others to do his handiwork.''

Hawk sobered. ''If he did, then we will find him out. My men are questioning every man at Clamdon and round about for miles.'' He shrugged. ''The possibility does exist that it was only the stray arrow of some poacher.''

Martin gave him a hard stare. ''Yes, brother, but after the things that have happened thus far, I wouldst not count on that.''

Since Martin and Jayne had left Aimsley, Hawk had received several reports from his men, but they had discovered nothing new. They were no closer to finding the man responsible.

Even worse, Hawk's hope that in sending Jayne away he would force Kayln to attend him had come to naught. She had simply sent the nurse in her stead.

Kayln was still greatly angered with him. The Lady D'Arcy could teach most men about holding a grudge. He'd told himself repeatedly that were he wise he would set his desires elsewhere, but it was images of his night with Kayln that colored his dreams, and he knew he must have her again.

Alice briskly drew down the bed linens. She frowned as her hand came into contact with his skin, and Hawk shivered.

''Can you not warm your hands, woman?'' he grumbled.

There was no answering jest in Alice's gray eyes as she spoke. ''It is not my hands that are cold, my lord. It is you who burn too warm. Methinks you may be developing a fever.''

Hawk tried to deny the evidence of the achiness of his body. ''Nay, I am as strong as a team of oxen.'' He flexed a hard bicep for emphasis.

Alice smiled, though her face remained troubled. ''Strong you may be, my lord, but many a powerful man has fallen prey to sickness. It is not uncommon after an injury.''

Hawk scowled. ''I will be well.''

By afternoon Hawk had developed a high fever.

Kayln refused to see him herself, but she pressed the nurse for information about his progress every time Alice came from his chamber. In doing so, Kayln feared she gave away more of her feelings than she desired. But she did not trust herself to tend the loathsome man herself. He'd guessed too near the mark already, and Kayln was forced to admit, if only to herself, that having Hawk so near kept her from sleep each and every night.

She had no intention of going anywhere near him.

By evening, Kayln could see that Alice was exhausted. When Kayln suggested sending one of the serving women in to tend the sick man, Alice was appalled. ''And why would we do that, my lady? Lord Hawkhurst is a highborn guest. It is his due that we see him properly attended. I am most suited to nurse Lord Hawkhurst, since you will not see to him yourself as you should.''

Still, though Alice spoke true about Hawk's position as one of the king's own barons, there was more behind the nurse's concern than the dictates of propriety. Kayln could only think that the older woman had grown fond of the knave.

And how could she be surprised? Hadn't Kayln firsthand knowledge that Hawk could charm the fur off a rabbit?

Reluctantly, Kayln found herself agreeing to care for the sick man. She told herself she simply didn't want Alice making herself ill. Besides, Alice kept insisting it was the proper thing to do, and Kayln could hardly dispute the matter. She had learned all she knew of courtly behavior from the nurse.

Not for any reason was she willing to have the nurse guess at her real reason for not wishing to attend the man.

When Kayln followed Alice into the room, she crossed to the bed slowly, fighting her reluctance. Hawk was lying on his back, his breathing heavy. Gratefully, Kayln realized he was asleep. Her relief abated somewhat on finding out that it was not a normal sleep but fever induced. She began to wonder if Hawk's wound would indeed end in tragedy. The thought was oddly troublesome.

"Tend him this way," Alice said, taking a cloth from the bowl of water beside the bed. Gently, she smoothed the linen over his heated forehead.

Kayln took the cloth from the older woman with some confidence. She should have no problem in performing this simple task, even for Hawk. But when Alice pulled the bedclothes down and pointed to his massive chest, Kayln discovered that it was suddenly very difficult to breathe.

There was no way she could touch him so intimately.

But one look at Alice's tired face stiffened her resolve. After all, Hawk was sleeping. He wouldn't even know she was there. But it was the notion of having to fight her own reactions to his masculinity that disturbed her the most. She raised her chin, telling herself that she was made of sterner character than that. No man, including James Hawkhurst, could be allowed to have so much power over her.

And so it began.

Over the next two days, Kayln learned to distance herself from her feelings for Hawk as a man. She concentrated on the fact that he was ill and she was there to help him. Thus the task became easier, somewhat.

Finally, on the third morning after the fever began, she entered Hawk's room to find him sitting up in bed. On seeing a fully conscious Hawk give her a weak smile, Kayln felt her traitorous heart flutter in her breast. His chest was wide and deeply bronze against the pillows, making him appear more masculinely appealing than any patient she had ever attended. Every touch of her hand over that smooth flesh rushed into her mind with aching clarity. Flushing, Kayln muttered an excuse and made to back out of the room.

"Nay, please stay, Kayln," he rasped out.

She met Hawk's eyes with trepidation. But on seeing the exhaustion there, she realized there was no threat to her but her own thoughts. He had been too ill to be interested in her as a woman. "Good morrow, Lord Hawk," she answered.

"Yes," he answered simply.

Still, she had a hard time trying to find a place to rest her gaze. "I came to see how you fared. Have you a need for anything?" She realized her mistake as soon as the words were uttered. Even ill, the blackguard would find some way to turn them into a sexual taunt.

To her surprise, he only said. "Water. I have a great thirst."

She watched him for a brief moment, then moved to fulfill his request. Feeling somewhat foolish for even thinking Hawk would be interested in her when he had been so sick, she crossed to hand him the cup.

He took it and raised it to his mouth, draining the contents in one drink.

"It is good to see you so much improved," she said as she took the cup from him. "Would you care for more?"

He shook his head. "Nay, not right now." His unblinking eyes met hers, searching for she knew not what.

"Fine, then," she answered, unable to keep contact with his intense stare. The moment stretched tight as a newly strung bow, and she felt she had to do something or scream. Awkwardly she moved back, meaning to set the cup on the table.

But Hawk reached out to clasp her arm, preventing her. "Kayln?"

She stiffened, her gaze locking on his forehead. She reminded herself that she must remain calm and not upset him, though she did not like being held, especially by him. He had been a very sick man. "Yes."

She could feel him willing her to meet his eyes, and found herself giving in. The golden orbs were dark with determination. "I must explain what happened. The day after the wedding."

She gave a start and tried to pull away. Kayln stopped, startled to discover just how strong he was despite his illness. His long fingers held her firmly captive.

Her back became rigid. "I do not wish to discuss it."

"But I do," he growled, then softened his tone as she tried to pull away again. "Just hear me out. Then if you never wish to speak to me again, I will accept your decision."

She looked at him. "By your honor."

"By my honor."

"Then I will listen."

Slowly Hawk let go of her arm.

"What you overheard that day was not meant to hurt you, nor could it have come as any surprise. We know that there is no love between us, you and I. Both of us are too strong to give in to each other in that way. Can you say that you would want that from me?" He would not release her gaze.

She shook her head, answering, "Nay," even as somewhere inside her there was a fine point of pain that she could neither name nor explain. She told herself that he was right, that she would never trust her heart to a man like Hawk. He was a man who must dominate all around him, a man who was careful to withhold his own heart.

But the fact that he spoke truth about that mattered little. He did not, could not, understand that he had injured her on another level. He had wounded her pride. She continued. "But I cannot forget what happened because you did wrong me. You spoke to the earl as if I was nothing, as if it did not matter that he knew you used me without love."

"What matter what he thinks if we two know the truth of our situation?"

Stung by his remark, Kayln shook her head. "It is of grave import to me, Hawk. I must be respected for all that I am. I was beginning to believe you were the one man who could understand this. I have been treated with disdain and disrespect by the men I held most dear. My father abused me like an ill-favored hound, when all I wanted was his love. All my husband, Raymond, wanted of me was my wealth. He cared nothing for me." She clutched her clenched fist to her breast. "I might have been invisible for all that he saw of me—Kayln."

She took several deep breaths, fighting for control of her emotions. She had not meant to let him see so much of herself, had no idea why she was telling him these things. "But no more will I be ill used," she went on more calmly. "Any man who shares a part of me, even if it be no more than my bed, must treat me with honor."

"I would treat you with honor."

She looked into his eyes. "Would you feel as if I had shown you the honor that was your due if I spoke of you in that way to another woman, then made no effort to explain myself?"

He blanched, dropping his gaze. "But I am a man."

She turned away, stung, though she had already known how he would reply. "It is as I said. You do not hold me in the same regard." Unable to bear more at this moment, Kayln went to the door. She would send Alice to attend him. Her heart was too heavy right now.

"What does the future hold for us, then?" he asked.

"We are family now. We will always have Celia and Philip in common. We will forget we were ever more."

His black brows arched upward. "Do you really believe you can be content with nothing else?"

She did not look back as she opened the heavy oak door. "Not only do I say it, but you shall see that I mean just that."

Later that day, Kayln pulled her cloak more closely about her as she stood looking out over the battlements. There was a crisp chill in the pine-scented breeze that ruffled the tops of the trees in the forest the lay at the bottom of the hillside.

Winter would come soon, but before that Hawk would be gone from Aimsley. His fever breaking meant that he was clearly on the mend. For some unknown reason that made Kayln feel both relieved and bereft, and she did not know which emotion was the stronger. On the one hand, she was irritated by him for his overbearing ways and total self-confidence. On the other, she had to admit that he made her feel alive, more so than ever in her life. Even knowing he felt no deep emotion for her, nothing beyond a fierce physical desire which he openly admitted to, she was unable to deny that she still found him undeniably attractive.

The guard paid her little heed as she moved off around the other side of the tower, as it was often her custom to walk there. She sighed, her gaze running across the view before her, trying to ignore the ache of loneliness in her breast. But she knew that she had well become accustomed to the feeling. Hawk's betrayal had taught her that she had best keep herself safe. Never again would she try her faith with another man, nor would she allow one to get close enough to use her body no matter how much she wanted him in return.

Her gaze halted as she caught a stir of movement at the edge of the forest. Pushing her troubles to the back of her mind, she looked more closely. Two men emerged from the tree line. They sat there obviously conversing atop their horses, but from this distance she could not make out who they were.

She frowned. With Hawk lying wounded in her keep, Kayln was not about to allow this to go without notice as she might have at another time. Someone had shot him upon her lands, and she would take no chances with strangers, even though the two were probably nothing more than travelers taking a rest within sight of a castle to give themselves a sense of safety.

"Will," she called to the guard.

"Yes, my lady." He ran to her.

"Do you see those two mounted men at the edge of the forest? I wish Bertrand to go and find out what they are about."

"As you wish." He bowed and hurried down the steps around the outside of the tower.

Moments later she watched as Bertrand rode out and spoke with the two. When, to her surprise, he started back to the castle with one of them accompanying him, while the other turned and left, she went down to the courtyard to meet them.

Bertrand brought the man directly to her, and though he seemed familiar, it wasn't until her master-at-arms spoke that she recognized him. "It is Harold, my Lord Hawkhurst's steward, my lady. The other man was Lord Harrow."

Her brows rose in surprise. "Miles?" She turned to the steward. "Do you know Sir Miles?"

The steward simply looked at her for a long moment, then sputtered, "No . . . no, of course not, my lady." He waved a pale slender hand. "I came upon him in the wood. You see, Lord Hawkhurst sent for me and I became lost coming here. Lord Harrow was simply kind enough to show me the way. He bid me give you his greetings as he had other matters to attend to and could not come to the castle himself."

"I see." Kayln nodded. Obviously Miles had been unobtrusively checking about her lands to see that all was well. If only she could care for the knight. But she could think of little save that oaf Hawkhurst. Thus reminded of the still-recovering man in her keep, Kayln frowned at the steward. "Now what do you mean"—she folded her arms—"when you say you were sent for?" She had no intention of allowing Hawk to overtax himself and take another turn for the worse. Firmly she told herself that she had no wish to nurse him for longer than was absolutely necessary.

Harold waved again, drawing her attention to his hands. Almost against her will, her gaze followed those long bare fingers, as she tried to understand why they seemed odd to her. "You see," the steward said with more confidence, "Sir Martin came to Clamdon on his way back to court and said that my lord wanted to see me in a few days and that I was to bring the estate ledgers." He motioned toward his horse. "I have them with me."

She frowned. "But my Lord Hawkhurst is unwell at this time and should not exert himself."

"I am aware of the injury." The steward looked at the ground. "It is most unfortunate, but Sir Martin was terribly insistent." His hand fluttered again, and she suddenly realized what was bothering her. The steward's ring, his seal of office. It was missing, and most obviously so, for it had been of more note than the man.

Kayln looked at Harold closely. He hardly seemed distressed when he spoke of his master's injury. As when she had first met him, Kayln couldn't help thinking there was little liking for Hawk in his attitude.

But that she could do nothing about. Whom Hawk chose to keep under his protection had nothing to do with her. But she did have some say in what the foolish man did inside her walls. The baron was much too sick to be working, and she had no intention of allowing him to overtax himself.

It just might set him back and force him to stay at Aimsley that much longer. Yes, she told herself, it was her duty to make sure Hawk did not overdo.

This matter would take some consideration.

She motioned the steward toward his horse. "Get your ledgers and come this way."

* * *

Hawk frowned at Kayln. "I must speak with Harold." The wench had a nerve to come in here and tell him what she wanted him to do.

She held her ground, hands on her hips. "But you are unwell, my lord. I can hardly credit that you would have sent for him. Why, it was only this morning your fever broke."

His gaze passed over the ripe fullness of her figure, braced for battle. Kayln had no idea of how very enticing she was with her eyes alight like that.

Clearly she was expecting him to get angry and order her to do his will. But he had no intention of doing that. No matter that he had realized, however painfully, that she might be correct in that they should forget they had ever been lovers. He would treat her with respect. He was surprised at the depth of guilt he was experiencing over having hurt her. He told himself that it was only simple compassion that made him feel so. After all that she had told him about her previous relationships, he would be nothing short of a knave to feel otherwise.

With that in mind, the smile he directed at her was rife with every ounce of goodwill he possessed. "Dear lady, I beg your indulgence. I have been away from Clamdon for too long and there are details I must attend to. Please allow my steward entry to speak with me. I pledge to send him away as soon as the more pressing matters are seen to."

Kayln eyed him with speculation. He could see that his agreeable demeanor had taken her by surprise, and he nearly gave away his satisfaction.

"Very well." She nodded slowly. "I can understand that you would wish to speak with him. My own duties at Aimsley are something I take to heart." She turned to the door, then swung around. "But remember, I shall expect you to keep your word. You are to see to only the most immediate problems."

He placed a hand over his heart and raised the other, palm out. He felt a twinge of guilt at allowing her to believe his story of having urgent business to attend, but he quickly dismissed it. He must see the steward. What could be more pressing than discovering who was stealing from him? Not to mention attempting to kill him. How Harold reacted to him would tell Hawk if the man had had any hand in his near-fatal accident.

Kayln showed the steward in.

As soon as Harold hesitated at the entrance to the chamber, Hawk knew. If the steward had not been the one to let the arrow fly, he knew something about it.

Forcing himself to smile, Hawk motioned him forward. "Come."

The man moved toward the bed, but stopped several paces away. In his arms were some of the ledgers Hawk had asked for. His gray eyes darted about and his handsome face was stiff with tension.

Hawk could not fathom why this man would take to such intrigue. Clearly he had no heart for it.

Hawk gestured toward his lap. "Bring them here." He had no real need to see the ledgers. He had already discovered enough evidence to clearly implicate the steward. The books were simply his excuse for meeting the traitor face-to-face. But Harold did not know that, and his nervousness about giving the ledgers to Hawk was obvious. His long white fingers were gripped tightly around them.

"Of course, my lord," Harold said at last. He did not meet his master's gaze as he placed the stack of ledgers where Hawk had instructed. "I trust you are recovering from your mishap."

Mishap! Hawk nearly laughed aloud. But he confined his comments to a polite rejoinder. "Yes. A big to-do about naught. I am much improved."

Then, because he could not prevent himself, he prodded the steward by adding, "I shall finally have time to go over these books as I've been promising myself. There are ever more interesting tasks when one is up and about."

It seemed impossible, but the man became even stiffer. Hawk was certain that if a breeze were to strike the steward he would break.

"My . . . my lord. Are you sure you are able enough . . ." Harold reached forward as if to take up the ledgers again.

Hawk caught his arm in an iron grip. He would keep the ledgers, if only to make Harold squirm. "Nay, my good fellow. Have no concern. I want nothing so much as to get my house in order.'' Recalling that he did not wish Harold to know that he was suspicious, Hawk released the steward's arm and smiled.

He had to remind himself that this was a dangerous game he played. Hawk felt no real fear of Harold, just a deep-seated contempt. But he must have a care. Even a fool could triumph out of sheer persistence. Hawk would go slowly, for he was not ready to confront the steward yet. He still hoped the villain would lead him to his accomplice.

At that moment Kayln entered the chamber.

She looked from Hawk to the steward with a polite but stubborn expression. ''I thought surely you men must be finished by now. Hawk must rest if he is to be up and about soon.''

The relief on Harold's face was nearly comic in its intensity. ''Dear Lady D'Arcy, you have the right of it. I should be on my way. Lord Hawkhurst should get his rest. Besides, it is not wise for both of us to be away from Clamdon at the same time. Someone needs to be in charge.''

Hawk felt himself stiffen in spite of his resolve to hide his suspicions. ''Aye. And I do thank you, my lord steward, for looking to my holdings so conscientiously.''

In his haste to be gone, Harold seemed not to notice the mockery in Hawk's tone. ''Thank you, my lord.'' He took Kayln's hand briefly, then made his departure.

Hawk turned to Kayln as she moved toward the bed and gathered up the ledgers. ''You must sleep now,'' she told him. Despite his decision to accept her wishes and forget what had gone between them, Hawk was aroused by her nearness. The cote she wore was made of a fine amber cloth that hugged the supple fullness of her figure lovingly. He could not help recalling how sweetly her breasts had filled his hands, how she had risen up against him as her soft cries of ecstasy filled his ears.

He clenched his jaw in frustration. Why was he so set on a woman who had freely admitted that she did not want his love? Though he had said the same of her, he could not still a sense of disappointment. Hawk knew he would do well to set his sights on some damsel who could accept him and his heart completely.

But he could not help watching her as she took the books and laid them on the chair beside the fire. "Alice is having kittens," she said. "She was outraged that I would even allow the man in here." She came back to stand beside the bed, her arms folded over her bosom. His tortured gaze swept over the taut fabric. "I had to promise to send the steward away or she would have come and done so herself."

His lips tightened at her words. Here, then, was an outlet for the tensions building in him. "You had no right to send him away."

"I can bear no more of her nagging. Alice has an uncommon concern for your welfare."

"Harold came a great distance to speak with me, and you wouldst have it for naught."

She watched him silently for a long moment, then spoke quickly as if she could no longer hold the words back. "Why do you go on with this pretense, especially with me? There is something wrong betwixt you and the steward. I find it most strange that you profess to hold him in such esteem when your expression shows that you loathe him. And he has like feelings for you. Indeed, when you aren't watching, the steward looks at you as if he hates you. I cannot be convinced that you do not already know this, so do save yourself the effort of trying. Do you simply continue to employ him because your father did? If so, it would be better to send him to another position than to go on as you are."

While Hawk's mind was still reeling from this diatribe, Kayln paused for breath. If she had seen so much, could the steward also know that he suspected him? Before he could question her about it, she went on. "I noticed he no longer wears his seal of office. Have you taken it from him as some kind of punishment?"

Hawk's eyes widened as she mentioned the seal. By the Holy Cross, she was right. Harold had not been wearing his ring. The steward was quite fussy about his appearance and very proud of the seal of office. Until today, he had not been without it in Hawk's memory.

Hawk opened his mouth to reply, then closed it. The steward could not know his discovery or he would not have come. Kayln had simply observed more than he'd ever meant her to, though he didn't know why he was surprised. She was a very intelligent woman. And as he'd admitted to himself before, they shared an intense physical bond that gave them a heightened awareness of each other.

But he would not discuss this matter with the damsel. The more people who knew the situation, the less likely his efforts to find his thieves would remain secret. "I cannot explain, Kayln. I beg you to forget your suspicions. I have my own reasons for acting as I am."

She looked as if she would say more, but did not. Even now, when she was so very obviously battling her inclination to pry in his affairs, he found her lovely. Possibly even more so because of her sense of fairness and honor that would not allow her to ask him questions she would not wish to have asked of herself. Hawk did not examine why this might be. It could come to naught in the end anyway. She did not want him.

As he settled back into the bed, Hawk discovered that he was indeed tired, though he suspected more from fighting his attraction to Kayln than anything else. "Thank you for not prying, Kayln. You are a rare woman."

Her gaze flew to his, her gray eyes wide with wistfulness for a moment before they grew hard and distant. She swung away, leaving the chamber without a word. It was some time before he fell asleep.

The next evening Kayln was called once again to the sick man's chamber. She went reluctantly, having no wish to see Hawk. The way he looked at her, the things he said made her wish it was different between them. But Kayln knew the truth. Hawk had no real feelings for her. Nor she for him, she reminded herself firmly.

Kayln entered slowly to find Alice once again bathing him with cool water. The nurse turned and wiped a strand of gray hair from her tired eyes. At Kayln's expression of surprise she said, "Lord Hawkhurst has developed a fever again."

Forgetting her determination to remain aloof, Kayln hurried forward.

Hawk cast her a rueful glance, then scowled with mock

disapproval at Alice. "I am well enough that your concern is unnecessary."

Alice gave him an ill-mannered glare. "I'll be the judge of that, my fine lord. I'll grant you that the fever is not high, but we'll do what we can to prevent it from worsening. Now lie still."

Seeing how tired the older woman already was, Kayln took her by the shoulders and propelled her toward the door. Her voice brooked no argument. "There is a meal set up for you in the hall. After it is eaten, I want you to go up and rest for a time before you come back."

Alice ignored the authoritative tone. "But—"

Kayln halted her. "I will see to Lord Hawkhurst. You have no cause for worry." She smiled in spite of her own unhappiness. "I will coddle him as you would yourself."

Her grin broadened when there was a mutinous grumble from both patient and nurse. Hurrying to soothe the older woman, Kayln saw her to the door before going back to Hawk.

He was frowning, his black brows drawn together over his nose. He looked quite fierce, but Kayln was not worried. As she had learned in his first days of fever, the man became too weak to do more than lie there when ill. An ailing Hawk was no threat, either physically or emotionally.

As Kayln took up the cloth, he said, "She does not coddle me. I allow no one to coddle me. Not since infancy."

She merely sighed at the petulance in his tone. Did all men revert back to childhood when ill? Kayln smoothed the cool cloth over his heated brow. "Tell me about your mother," she said, both to distract him and out of true curiosity.

Kayln was unexpectedly moved when his eyes darkened with love and sadness as he began to speak. "Mother. She was, well, like Jayne but not dark. She was tall and slender with auburn hair and blue eyes. And she was clever, ever able to manage Father even when he was in a temper."

He smiled, the memories lighting his face. "You see, Father was quick tempered and, well . . . commanding. But she knew just how to calm him and make him see reason. She'd look at him with those big blue eyes and he'd just melt. Some people say I'm like him."

"I wonder," Kayln replied, eyes open wide in mock surprise. Commanding indeed. Overbearing was a more apt term.

If the sire was really so like his son, he must have driven his wife near to distraction, unless she was some unflawed paragon. But even as she told herself all this, Kayln was amazed and somehow uncomfortable with the fact that Hawk had opened up and told her so much about himself. Hearing of his family and the way they had been made it harder for her to reconcile her opinion of him as a despot and a user of women. Which only made her feel worse about his lack of care for her. This served to make her speak more sharply. "Did your mother never grow tired of his high-handedness?"

He frowned at the words and tone, but did not rise to her baiting. "Well, they disagreed at times, but they seldom fought. She just knew how to manage him."

"I see." Kayln scowled. "And you believe all women should behave thus. As if they had no right to raise their voices or disagree openly, but must play intricate games in order to have their say."

"I did not say that. Mother was not afraid to tell Father what she thought. But she would wait until he finished ranting and discuss the matter sensibly." His tone changed to one of incredible pride. "Between the two of them they left me a legacy to be proud of. The lands have been cared for so that generations of Hawkhursts may hold them. I was taught that I am only entrusted with what belongs to my son and his son after him, as long as there are Hawkhursts in England. I do not look upon my role as Baron of Clamdon as a duty, but as a privilege. I shall teach each of my own sons the same."

Kayln stood still, unable to take her gaze from the proud beauty of his face. A deep well of respect rose up within her. It was followed by a burning shame and regret that left her reeling. For clearly Hawk did not find her worthy of mothering those sons. She damped down her pain, determined to keep him from seeing her humiliation.

Oblivious to her reaction, Hawk went on. "I should not have stayed away. I loved them so much that when I learned of their deaths I could not face returning to Clamdon. Knowing they would be gone was more than I could bear. You see, I had not expected to hold the lands for many years. My father was a healthy and vibrant man. How could I have imagined his death at such an early age? But the plague cared naught for that. It took whom it would."

Hawk lay back then as he wrestled with his own demons, sweat beading on his upper lip and brow.

Kayln managed to cover her own sadness, telling herself that Hawk was only speaking of his family, that he had not meant any insult to her. Hawk was obviously seeking a love match, something she could not give him. Sweet Jesu, what was wrong with her to become so upset by such a thing? It was not as if she wanted to marry him and had made that clear to the baron. His words were not aimed at her. She concentrated with some success on his last words to her. She could hardly fathom such parental devotion. When her own father had died of drink, she had felt nothing beyond a very palpable relief.

Seeing the strain on his face, Kayln rewet the cloth and began to smooth it over his neck. She felt a desire to offer some comfort, but knew not how. She did not even know how to effectively relate to her own sister, let alone this all-too-compelling man.

Hawk lay unmoving beneath her hands as she drew the blanket down from his chest. At a loss to express her compassion verbally, Kayln tried to soothe him with her ministrations, being all the more gentle in her guilt over becoming perturbed with him over something that should have meant nothing to her.

His skin was warm and smooth to the touch.

After only a moment, Kayln began to know a growing awareness of him as a man. This surprised her for, as he had lain so very ill before, she had become able to care for him without discomfort of this kind. During most of her intimate care of him, Hawk had barely been conscious.

But now, as the firelight played on the bronze width of his chest, she felt a stirring within her. Despite her resolution that all was over between them, it was an obvious reawakening of the feelings he had previously engendered.

She glanced up. His eyes were closed as if he were not even aware of her, and she grew emboldened.

Why should she not touch him if it gave her pleasure? Even if she was not willing to love him and bear his sons, she could allow herself this small indulgence. It was a task she had performed for him repeatedly. Hawk had no way of knowing that this time was any different from the others. He could not read her very thoughts.

With slow gentle strokes she drew the cloth back and forth, then down the expanse of supple flesh and hard muscle. As she worked, her nipples tightened into tight little buds and her breathing sharpened.

God, was ever a man more beautiful to look upon?

She looked up, her eyes hungry for the taste of his face. She drew in a quick breath.

Hawk was watching her, his lids hooded over eyes darkened to molten gold. "Kayln."

"Hawk." Had she really believed he would not feel her desire? It was as tangible as the scent of lilacs and just as heady.

He reached out and drew her up onto his prone form.

She offered no resistance. Kayln was held captive by those eyes, those maddeningly sensuous eyes. For a long moment he simply watched her, then his gaze dipped to her mouth.

It was Kayln who closed the distance between them, slanting her lips to cover his. His hand caught at her hair covering. He drew it off, tossed it away, then buried his fingers in the luxurious curtain of gold.

He opened his mouth, and she accepted the invitation, dipping her tongue into the warmth of him. He moaned, holding her tighter.

She groaned, frustrated at having her hands caught between their bodies. She wanted to touch him, all her resolutions to stay apart from him forgotten in her need to feel his firm flesh under her hands. Kayln squirmed to free her aching fingers.

Hawk laughed, and putting his arm around her so as not to break contact with her lips, he rolled her to the side. Kayln sighed with pleasure. Now she could touch him as she desired.

Neither of them heard the door open, nor were they aware of anything save their passion, until there was a gasp of shock.

Kayln rose up to peek over Hawk's shoulder and saw Alice standing there, her mouth wide with amazement. Shame made her speak roughly. "What are you doing here?"

"I . . . forgive me, my lady, I but came to make sure that

the cool bath was helping Lord Hawkhurst's fever." She smiled knowingly. "I can see it did not. But perhaps the patient is not as ill as I had thought."

Leaping from the bed, Kayln heard Hawk's laugh, husky with frustration, as she ran from the room.

For the next few days, Kayln was careful to avoid any contact with the man who so plagued her. Whenever she felt her resolve weakening, she reminded herself anew of the sons Hawk so desired, that she had no intention of giving them to him. Kayln could not relinquish her independence even if he had wanted her to. Which he did not, and she told herself to be grateful for that, because if Hawk had really cared for her his pursuit would be undaunting. That much she knew about him.

Thus she left Alice to care for the baron as before. Yet even after all she had told herself, Kayln could not quite still a flash of disappointment when Alice told her only a few days after the mishap in his chamber that he would be returning to Clamdon.

She told herself to be grateful that he was at last leaving her in peace. Kayln had had little thought for anything else since Hawk's arrival at Aimsley, including Celia. And that was after Kayln had made a decision to try to be closer to her sister.

Aye, it was best he was going.

She did not approach him to say good-bye on the appointed day. But she could not keep herself from the tower window as his party was leaving the courtyard. She felt a momentary unease as the baron looked up toward her window, his expression unreadable over the distance that separated them. Quickly she tried to push nervousness aside, telling herself he could not have seen her. She'd been very careful to stay out of sight.

But somehow, she knew he'd sensed she was there.

Then, just as he was crossing under the portcullis, her suspicions were confirmed. For Hawk looked back, raising his hand in farewell before he was lost to her view.

Chapter Twelve

Some weeks later, Kayln was in the courtyard, speaking with the laundress, when she looked up to see Celia passing by. The girl was moving toward the open gateway and wearing a long woolen cloak.

Though she had been trying to become closer with her sister, Kayln was new to the skill, and hadn't met with much success. With this in mind, she smiled, calling out to the younger girl, "Whither do you go?"

Celia turned with a start, her blue eyes coming to rest on Kayln warily. "For a walk."

Kayln tried to retain her smile, though she felt a bit hurt at her sister's closed expression. "Might I go with you?"

Celia looked toward the waiting laundress, who was listening to the exchange with patience in her brown eyes, her worn hands folded across her middle. "You are busy," Celia said.

Shrugging, Kayln nodded at the other woman. "I am most certain Ester is capable of continuing without me. She would not mind my leaving her to her work."

Celia's surprised gaze flicked to Kayln's and away, before she shook her head. "Nay. I would rather be alone, if you don't mind." With that she turned and hurried from the keep before Kayln could say more.

Kayln looked after her with a sad sigh.

A few moments later, Kayln did indeed leave the laundress to her work, and made her way up the stone steps to the top of the keep. From atop the battlements, Kayln could see the road leading away from Aimsley for a long distance in both directions.

Almost against her will, her attention was drawn in the direction of Clamdon. Supporting her dejected stance, Kayln's elbows were propped on one of the merlons. With a heavy sigh, she bent forward and leaned her chin on her hands.

Six long weeks had passed since the day Hawk had ridden away from Aimsley. Kayln told herself to be glad of the fact he had not returned to plague her.

Another sigh escaped her lips, and she bit down on the bottom one in irritation. Most assuredly, she was well rid of James Hawkhurst. But what remained long after Hawk's departure was the sweet memory of his touch on her body. Kayln had thought herself cured of that memory until the night Alice had found them in his bed together.

Neither time nor her own constant reminders that she did not care for him, nor he for her, had lessened her desire for him. "God help me," she whispered, forcing herself to face the other direction, the one leading to Harrow. Why could she not accept Miles's proposals?

But it was not the thought of Miles which kept her pacing in her room long into the night, with only the red glow of the fire to light the darkness closing in on her. It was Hawk.

It was as if her chamber were haunted with the soft sensual sounds of their lovemaking. Even though he had been in her bed but one night, Hawk's presence lingered like the first taste of burgundy wine, rich and full.

Her gaze swung around toward Clamdon once more. Slowly she became aware of the fact that she could see a horse approaching in the distance.

Kayln stood straight peering down the roadway. There was something familiar about the rider mounted on a big horse with a chestnut coat. Her heart began to beat a little faster. Even from so far away, Kayln knew it was Hawk.

As was his wont, he rode without escort. The ridiculous man thought himself invincible, she told herself.

For a moment she just stood there, her hands clasped over her bosom, unclear as to how she should greet him. Finally, Kayln let out a sound of exasperation, startling the guard who had come to a halt beside her in his march around the battlements. She was not going to let Hawk upset her this way. He held no sway over her.

Kayln forced herself to go slowly to her tower room. If Hawk must wait for her to greet him, so be it. She told herself her desire to change had naught to do with him. She simply wished to be properly attired for a guest.

A short time later, Netta stepped back so her mistress could inspect the braids which the maid had threaded with sapphire ribbons and wound around her head. Just as Kayln turned to the polished metal that served as a mirror, the door opened and Alice entered the room.

The nurse opened her pale eyes wide as she took in her mistress's appearance. Kayln had never looked lovelier than she did in her gown of palest blue samite, embroidered around the hem and the ends of the wide sleeves with deep blue forget-me-nots and green leaves with connecting vines. Her tunic echoed the green of the leaves. "I see you know of Hawkhurst's arrival." Her brows rose and she sniffed, as she folded her thin hands before her. "You make yourself rather fine for a man you profess to hate."

"That will be all, Netta." After the maid had gone, Kayln turned to face the nurse. Languidly, she brushed an invisible speck of lint from her sleeve. "And who might that be?"

Alice's gaze went to the low scooped neckline of the gown, and a knowing smile lit her eyes. "You know that as well as I. I might be more apt to believe your indifference had I not seen the two of you in his bed together."

Kayln blushed. "I told you he forced himself upon me. I . . . I can only be grateful for your appearance. Anything might have occurred." She felt a sharp stab of guilt at the lie, but she could not give Alice cause for needling her. Besides, she was glad the nurse had arrived. She did not even wish to think about what would have happened had she given herself to Hawk again. 'Twas difficult enough to put their lovemaking behind her now.

"Aye, so you said."

Her chin rose. "Did Hawkhurst claim otherwise?"

The nurse chuckled, her tone full of admiration and affection. "Nay, he said nothing. He is a true knight."

In irritation, Kayln commented, "I understand little why you hold the blackguard in such high esteem."

Alice sighed. "Hawkhurst is a man, a real man, from the top of his head to the tips of his toes. He's not one to allow a woman to lead him around by the nose hairs. Not like that other one.''

Kayln felt heat rise in her cheeks, and turned to hide the blush. It was true she had first-hand knowledge of Hawk's manhood, but his skill in bed did not absolve him of his myriad other faults. Not the least of which was his already overblown ego. She was certainly glad he could not hear what Alice was saying. Kayln also chose not to remark on the jibe, which she knew had been directed at Miles.

Kayln changed the subject, not liking the way Alice was studying her. ''Have Celia informed that her brother-in-law is here.''

''She is not in the keep, my lady.''

''That I know,'' Kayln said, pushing thoughts of Hawk aside for the moment. ''I saw her as she was leaving.'' Kayln tried to still any hint of resentment toward her younger sister as she remembered how her overture of friendship had been rejected. It would simply take time for Celia to see that Kayln was trying to be closer. Right now, Celia could think of nothing beyond her misery in being without Philip.

Alice's voice was also full of disapproval, but held an undercurrent of worry. ''At least I was able to make sure she broke her fast well before she disappeared.''

Kayln shook her head, knowing neither she nor Alice could even take credit for this one positive change in Celia's behavior. They had been forced to write to Philip, asking him to plead with his wife to eat enough so the babe would grow strong and healthy. Since the day when Philip's letter had come, saying just what Kayln had requested, Celia had made every effort to take more nourishment. The improvement in her diet had meant Celia was not so gaunt looking, nor so weak, but she was still pale and listless, pining for her young husband without surcease.

''Celia is becoming harder to deal with as each day passes,'' Kayln stated. ''I hardly know which way to turn.''

''I have done my best,'' Alice said, her nose quivering.

Kayln's tone softened. ''Of course you have.'' The nurse was not young and shouldn't worry every waking moment. Kayln sighed, leading the way out. ''Send someone to look for her. She is most likely wandering beside the stream where she met Philip."

Kayln and Alice parted at the bottom of the stairs from the tower, Alice to find Celia, and Kayln to see Hawk again after so long a time. Taking a deep breath to calm her suddenly fluttering stomach, Kayln trod the last few steps down the stairs that would take her into the hall.

On first entering the room, Kayln could see no sign of the man who made her senses quicken even though she knew he would bring her nothing but ill. Her attention was drawn to a long leg extending from a chair that had been drawn close to the warmth of the fire. The foot was encased in a black boot that rose to the knee, upon which Hawk's hand rested negligently, his fingers closed around the base of a flagon. From the relaxed attitude proclaimed by his posture, Kayln felt Hawk could not be as nervous as she about their meeting. A twinge of self-derision made her pause.

Lifting her chin, Kayln forced herself to step forward briskly, at the same time wishing she had not troubled herself about her appearance. "Hawkhurst," she said, then stopped as she cursed herself for the breathless quality of her voice.

He rose, the motion swift and clean as everything about him was. Kayln doubted as she watched him come toward her that she would ever stop marveling that a man of his size and height could move with such easy grace.

"Kayln." He held out his hand, his tone gently mocking. "Dare I hope you are glad to see me?"

Fool, she chided herself, even while her heart skipped a beat. He was making sport of her. Her resentful gaze moved over his strong masculine features, taking in the curve of his lips, the angle of his nose, and above it, the magnetic pull of his eyes. Despite his maddening irony, as his fingers brushed hers, heat passed from his flesh to hers. She jerked away, stung by her body's immediate response to the simple contact.

Hawk's smile widened and his eyes took on a wicked gleam, but he said nothing.

Kayln looked down at her arms, which she had crossed in an unconscious gesture of self-protection. She felt awkward and unsure of herself. He was just too big, too male, too overpowering. Kayln had known it would be hard to face Hawk again after all that had passed between them, but she hadn't realized how difficult.

Only by reminding herself that Hawk would only use her weakness against her was she able to draw pride as a weapon in her own defense. She raised her chin and indicated the vacant chair with her hand. "Please, be seated."

"Only if you will join me beside the fire."

"Of course I will join you," Kayln said smoothly, coolly, motioning for a serf to bring another chair. The serving boy, Egbert, dragged the chair forward, placing it directly across from the one Hawk occupied.

"I am honored that you welcome me in your keep after what has gone between us."

Kayln sucked in a breath of shock that he would be so bold as to mention it. Then she forced herself to react calmly, rationally. He was only seeking to bait her and she could not allow him that. "The matter you refer to is forgotten. Do you think me such a poor hostess that I would turn you away? Why, I welcome all travelers who stop at Aimsley, no matter how greatly or lowly I value them." A deliberate smile touched her lips, but there was smoke in her gray eyes.

As his sardonic gaze pierced her, she knew he understood which category he numbered amongst. But he smiled in return, his golden eyes glowing as he answered affably, "I had not thought otherwise." Though the words were agreeable, Kayln had the distinct impression that he did not believe she had indeed forgotten what had occurred.

Kayln watched, chagrined, as he picked up his cup from the stone floor beside him and took a sip of the contents. He seemed relaxed and completely unaffected by her sarcasm.

Then he continued, and now there was just a hint of challenge in his tone. "I must admit, though, that I have enjoyed your hospitality more fully in the past." He raised his glass, taking a long pull of the liquid. Above it his lids were hooded to half cover his eyes, bringing to her mind a vision of him moving above her.

A flush of heat warmed her belly, and she felt herself quicken at the image. Kayln almost hated him for his easy command of her desires.

The only sensible course was to ignore his double-edged

remarks and by so doing convince him she was immune to his all-too-obvious charm. After what had passed between them that would be difficult, but she must try. "I shall try not to disappoint you," she answered, with a jibe of her own, "but 'tis the best that can be offered." Then she went on as if their remarks had been nothing more than the pleasantries they appeared to be. "I have had Celia sent for so you might see all is well with her. Would you like some more refreshments? It may be some time before anyone is able to locate her."

"What do you mean?" Hawk's expression became one of concern, their wordplay forgotten. "The girl is far gone with child now. She should be more carefully watched."

Kayln drew herself up. Did he think to instruct her in how to deal with Celia? Her lips thinned in a stubborn line. She would not explain to Hawk that Celia refused to allow Kayln to look after her more closely. After all the years of reserve between them, Kayln's efforts were being met with no small amount of resistance. A fact that made the criticism bite all the more. "Do you imply that I do not know how to look after my own sister?" She rose to her feet.

As soon as she was standing, Kayln realized this had been a mistake, as Hawk also came to his feet. He now towered above her.

"It is not only your sister whom you must keep from harm," he stated. "She carries my own brother's child, possibly his heir."

"How dare—" Kayln began to say.

"Hawk!" Celia's high clear voice interrupted their heated exchange. For a brief moment Kayln glared at him, a look which he returned in full measure. Over and over again he proved to her what an overbearing blackguard he was. How could she have ever been fool enough to give herself to him?

Swinging around, Kayln saw her sister hurrying across the hall. No longer were her steps light and springing. Already the weight of the child was becoming a burden for the girl's slight frame. At seven months gone, the swell of her belly was very obvious.

There was a pink glow of health in the fair cheeks. Kayln offered up a quick prayer of thanks that Celia had at least decided to listen to her husband and eat enough to provide the infant with the nourishment it needed. Yet Kayln couldn't help worrying as she saw the dull look of sorrow in the lovely blue eyes that brightened little, even as Celia met her guest with some degree of pleasure.

Hawk strode to the girl and took her outstretched hands. "The babe grows apace. Philip will be pleased when I tell him." He studied her more closely for a moment. "But what is this sadness I see in your eyes? That will not please him."

"You are going to see Philip?" Celia asked, her expression hungry with longing.

"There has been a problem with some of the tenants on one of my properties and I must go to settle the dispute," he told her. "Norwich is between here and Westvale, so I will be stopping there for a night." Kayln could see that Hawk had decided to follow Celia's lead in changing the subject, but the concern did not leave his face.

For some unexplainable reason, that raised her ire. She did not wish to think of Hawk as being sensitive enough to pick up on Celia's sadness. It made his ill treatment of *her* even harder to accept.

"Take me with you," Celia cried, drawing Kayln's gaze as she looked up into his face with yearning. "I would not be any trouble to you, I swear it."

Kayln bit her lower lip in consternation. Now Hawk had done it. Must he mention that he was going to see Philip and cause her upset when he must inevitably tell her she could not accompany him? It would be left to Kayln to soothe and calm her.

But Hawk answered, his tone gentle and reasoning, "I am sure you would be no trouble, pet. In fact, I should be glad of your company. But the trip will be a hard one. I go not for pleasure but to do my duty as the lord of my tenants."

"I care not." Celia's voice had risen in her excitement. "I could withstand any privation to see Philip again." She began to cry. Great tears fell from her eyes like wet pearls, spiking her long lashes and leaving damp trails as they slid down her cheeks.

Kayln took a step forward, preparing to help her sister to her room. She reached out to place a comforting hand on Celia's slight shoulder. "Come, you should lie down."

Celia shrank away. ''Oh, Kayln, you simply do not understand how it feels. I love and need him so very much.''

Hurt by the rejection and the unwitting pain caused by her sister's words, Kayln drew back. She did understand how Celia felt, more than the younger girl would ever know. Even though she could not say she loved Hawkhurst, the heated call of her blood was more powerful than anything she had thought to experience in her life. But she could not admit that to anyone, and so must hide her suffering with silence.

Before Kayln could form an idea of what to do next, Hawk had drawn Celia close into his strong arms. Picking her up as if she were a small child, he carried her to the fire and settled into his chair with Celia on his lap. Kayln could only watch in amazement as this powerful knight showed an amazingly tender side of himself that she had only glimpsed on occasion.

For a while he just held the girl, stroking her silver gilt hair as she sobbed. Then, acting on some unspoken signal that told him she was ready to listen, he raised her chin and looked into her wide blue eyes. ''Don't cry, little one. Philip will worry if I tell him you are so unhappy.''

Celia made no reply as she gulped back a hiccup, but Kayln could see the girl was listening. Why could it not be thus with her and Celia? Kayln would give much to be able to give comfort to her sister. Why was Hawk the one to cheer her? It seemed there was no justice in the world.

''You know it is difficult for Philip to be away from you also,'' Hawk continued, completely aware of Kayln listening close by with a frown marring her brow. ''But he does what he must for the sake of your child and that of any other you might have. His position as a knight will benefit both them and you.'' For the life of him he could not understand what he had done to displease the Lady of Aimsley this time.

She'd been anything but happy to see him since the moment he arrived. But that hadn't stopped his lower stomach from tightening with desire at the sight of her. God alone knew what it was about the prickly widow that drew him so irresistibly, but Hawk was powerless to overcome it. In the past weeks he'd thought of naught save bedding her again. Though he could see that there was little chance of that event occurring if Kayln was to have any say in it. And indeed she must, for he wanted her willing and eager as before.

"I don't care for myself," Celia whispered fiercely, drawing his thoughts back to her as she wiped at her tears with the back of her hand. "I would love Philip even if we should live in a hovel."

In spite of his annoyance over Kayln's ill will, Hawk had to force back a smile as he thought how naive this statement truly was. He knew that for a young girl raised in a home with all the comforts which could be provided, poverty would indeed prove most unbearable. He kept his opinion to himself as he said, "And this Philip knows well, for he feels the same of you. But you must remember the child. It would not be worth risking your babe's life for a meeting that will come soon enough." His tone was cool, brotherly, reasoning.

For a long time, Celia only sat there looking up at him. Then she gulped again and said, "It is so hard."

"I know, moppet." He pulled her close. "But not so difficult that you cannot do what you must. Philip has chosen well in you, little one. You will make him proud."

"I will be worthy of the love he bears me." Celia pushed herself away from Hawk and stood up, her back straight. Hawk could not resist a stray glance toward Kayln. He wondered how she would react to Celia's heated declarations of love. No doubt she found them naive. But she was watching them with a closed expression, and he could gauge nothing of her reaction. Once more he centered his attention on her sister.

"You are that and more." Hawk smiled at her. With Celia standing, their eyes were on the same level, and a look of understanding and affection passed between them. For a brief moment he allowed himself to wonder if Kayln had been more like Celia as a young girl. Would he have been more likely to give his heart to her then? He gave himself a mental shake, wondering where the thought had come from. There was no point in asking questions that had no answers. Kayln was not like Celia, as was evidenced by her disapproving scrutiny.

"When do you leave for Norwich?" Celia asked, wiping at a tear that still lingered on her cheek.

"On the morrow."

"Then you could take letters for me," she said eagerly.

"Yes, and gladly," Hawk said. "I am sure Philip will have some of his own for you when I come through Aimsley on my way home."

"You will be returning soon and will bring the letters directly to me?"

"Yes, within a fortnight." He had to stop himself from frowning. Now why had he said he would pass through Aimsley? He was only setting himself up for more of Kayln's open disdain.

He could feel the lady's continued attention on him as Celia left the hall. "You were gentle with her," she commented, though her voice gave nothing away.

Surprised at the words, Hawk turned to her and watched as her teeth worried her full lower lip, causing it to redden. To his utter disbelief he found himself wanting to kiss her. Ruefully he wondered what she would do if he were to transfer his thoughts to actions.

Looking down into her closed face, he decided to restrain himself. He knew Kayln would be outraged anew should he presume to kiss her here in the hall. He was relatively certain she had not forgiven him or herself for what had happened that day when she'd bathed him. Nor had she forgotten it no matter what she said.

He could not help needling her. "Was that praise for me, my lady? It gives me hope that we two might come to an understanding on some things."

She stiffened, eyeing him coolly. "I fear, Hawkhurst, that we two understand everything about one another that we have a need to."

Disappointment tightened his belly, even though he had expected her reaction. Hawk wondered if he had made a mistake in not kissing her as his instincts bid him. The woman could hardly object to him more than she did now. He had taken a step forward, meaning to put thought to deed, when there was the clatter of booted feet in the doorway.

Kayln's man, Bertrand, stood there, and he was breathing hard as if he had been running. Taking his helmet off, the soldier held it against his side. He lifted his free hand to wipe at the sweat that plastered his iron-gray hair to his forehead.

"What is it, Bertrand?" Kayln moved toward him quickly,

glad to have him barge in upon her and Hawk.

Hawk's sweetness toward Celia had produced an unexplainable yearning in her breast. But she had not liked the gleam of devilment she had seen rise in his eyes as he looked at her after her sister had departed.

"We have caught a poacher, Lady Kayln."

Now the soldier had her attention. Her gaze went to Hawk's. Could this be the man who had shot him? She was disappointed to find no answering suspicion in his eyes. "Why did you not bring him here to me?" She frowned with a trace of impatience.

Bertrand's tone was apologetic. "We were unable to bring him here because he is holed up in a tree. My men were prepared to have done with the fellow, when he begged us to listen to his story."

Hawk intruded. "You were wise not to bring him here, thus endangering your lady. What had he to say for himself?"

Kayln frowned at his interference, telling herself she should be grateful to him for reminding her of what an arrogant oaf he was. Undoubtedly his gentle treatment of Celia had only been an act to make her calm down. "I'll thank you, Lord Hawkhurst, to allow me to see to my own affairs."

Hawk scowled in return. "Clearly you will have need of assistance in this matter."

"I will not," she replied haughtily. Then, studiously ignoring Hawk's grunt of disbelief, she turned to Bertrand. "Would you be so good as to tell *me* what this man said?"

The soldier addressed only Kayln, standing tall under her gaze. "I thought that if my lady were to hear the tale from the man's own lips, she might be less biased by my own opinion."

"That was most wise," Kayln answered, still pointedly ignoring Hawk. "The situation intrigues me. You will take me to this man. Have my horse saddled."

"Yes, my lady." Bertrand bowed, then turned, hurrying to do her bidding.

Hawk moved to put a restraining hand upon her arm. "You don't seriously mean to go see this man yourself?"

Kayln swung around in irritation. "Of course I do. I have

seen to such problems many times. There has been no one else to do so."

He nodded to the door through which Bertrand had gone. "You seem to trust your man. Why not allow him to see to it, if you will not accept my help?"

Why must he continue to question her? This was the very reason she knew that becoming involved with him would be nothing but folly. Kayln's voice was cold as she replied, "I do trust Bertrand and with good reason. He was nothing more than my father's foot soldier when I first knew him. Even though he had naught to gain and all to lose, Bertrand stopped my father from continuing to beat me after he had just broken my arm when I was six. He was himself beaten and dismissed for his pains. But indeed, though I trust him with my life and more, he is not overlord of these lands. I am. All must see that I act by my own will and no other's if I am to retain their obedience and respect."

Hawk still did not seem to understand, for he said, "You do not have to be alone anymore, Kayln. I will help you." The sympathy in his voice did not soothe her. He had to come to grasp how much her independence meant to her.

"I do not desire your assistance," she told him, then looked down at his hand upon her. "Now, sir, if you will release me, I will change and fetch my cloak. I do not wish to keep my man waiting."

"You know what sort these poachers usually are," Hawk reminded her, taking his hand away, though his voice kept her immobile. "They are often the worst type of criminal, those who cannot find service with any lord. Only a man with nothing to lose would take to the kind of life that might see his hands removed from his arms."

"It seems to me that I have explained my position to you," Kayln told him. "I am mistress of these lands. I have dealt with such situations before, and will do so in the future, without your approval or any other man's." Her slender fingers rested on the rounded womanliness of her hips.

Clearly he did not approve, but thankfully he offered no further argument. He stated simply, "I will accompany you."

Kayln shrugged. "You may please yourself by riding wherever you will." Her eyes darkened and she drew her brows close. "Just remember that I hold what is mine. You will not interfere. Unless, of course, it proves he was involved in what happened to you."

His cryptic response satisfied her not in the least. "He was not."

"Do you know something I do not?" she asked.

Hawk said nothing.

She gave him a long speculative look, her lips tight. This was just another example of his believing he had a right to order her life when he felt no need to allow her into his. "You think yourself very clever, my Lord Hawkhurst, to hold so much back. And you have that right, so long as what you know concerns you alone. Just remember that should you learn something that might have a bearing upon me, or mine, I have a right to know it." She refused to believe her irritation with Hawk's mysterious ways had anything to do with worry for his safety.

"And now," Kayln said, "if you will say no more, I have business to attend to."

Hawk gave a black scowl as she left.

His fist came down to strike his open palm. The woman was too independent for her own good. Running the keep was one thing. Facing possibly dangerous criminals was another. Sometimes she went too far in protecting "her and hers."

Though she irked him beyond belief, Hawk could not bear to see any harm come to her. He told himself that it was simply because she was a widow with no man to protect her, but for some reason the words did not ring quite true even in his own ears.

In a relatively short time, Kayln and the two men drew their mounts to a halt beneath the towering fir tree. The men-at-arms Bertrand had left stationed underneath the poacher's perch moved aside for her. And though he made no comment, she was infinitely aware of Hawk where he waited a few feet behind her.

On peering up through the branches of the tree, Kayln could see the suspected poacher high above her. He shivered in the chill wind that blew through the tops of the trees.

"My master-at-arms informs me that you have a story to

tell,'' Kayln called up to him, her voice showing she was willing to listen. When there was only silence, she said more forcefully, ''Get to it, man, or accept your fate.''

Hawk looked to her in surprise, something telling him she did not threaten the poacher only for the sake of making the fellow talk. He was sure she would order the poacher killed if he did not defend himself instantly. His estimation of Kayln as a leader went up several notches. Although, for some reason, the realization made him uncomfortable.

''Bertrand,'' she shouted, drawing his attention.

''Lady, please,'' the poacher began, his teeth chattering so hard it was difficult to understand him.

''Go on.''

''I am not a poacher by choice. My family and I were tenants under Lord Nigel at Potterbrook. Lord Nigel took a liking to the daughter of our neighbor, who had long envied us the good land we farmed. His own fields were further from the river and not near so fertile. When Lord Nigel became interested in our neighbor's daughter, the man saw the opportunity to get my land.''

''And you were turned out,'' Kayln finished as the man hesitated to go on.

''Yes, and with nowhere to go.''

''You wish me to believe this is sufficient reason for you to poach upon my land? Why did you not come to the hall? All who seek entrance there are fed.'' Hawk felt an unwilling admiration for her astute questioning. Surely if any woman was capable of handling such matters, Kayln was that woman. But the knowledge still didn't set well with him. A beautiful woman shouldn't have to worry about such things. She should be raising children and trusting in her man to look after her safety. But, he reminded himself, Kayln had no man to do so, and wanted none. The irritation he felt at this made him grimace as he watched.

''My wife and one of our four youngsters have taken ill. They were too sick to be moved and must have something to eat to make them stronger.'' The man was sobbing now.

''Had he any weapons?'' Kayln said softly to Bertrand at her side, not taking her eyes from the poacher. All the while she could feel Hawk's attention heavy on her back. But she did not acknowledge him. He was only an observer here.

"None that we could find, my lady, and it is clear he has none up there with him, or he would surely have used them." Bertrand fingered the string of his bow.

"What is your name, fellow?" Kayln asked him.

"Samuel, late of Potterbrook, my lady."

"When came you here?"

"Only since the last full moon, my lady," he answered immediately.

Kayln bit her lip. If this was true, he could not have had anything to do with Hawk's becoming injured. And the ready way he gave the reply to her query made her think Hawk was right and the fellow must be innocent of that crime at least. No doubt Hawkhurst was gloating over being right at this very moment. But that only served to remind her that he knew something that he was not willing to share with her.

She pushed the thought aside as she told herself to concentrate on the matter at hand. "Send one of the men to Potterbrook and find out if his story can be confirmed," Kayln told Bertrand, shifting in the saddle to relieve the prickling sensation along her back.

"You must tell me where your wife and children are," Kayln called out to Samuel. She should have come without Hawkhurst, for he was distracting her and she did not wish to make a senseless error. The poacher's fate lay in her hands.

"Please, lady, I cannot do that. I fear too much for their safety." The man was shaking as if he were one of the needles covering the branches.

"You will tell me where your family is—now. They will come to no harm if what you have said is true, nor will you." When the fellow remained silent, Kayln turned to Bertrand. "Your bow."

As her glance raked Hawk, she saw his eyes widen with amazement when the master-at-arms handed her the longbow without hesitation. His expression irritated her further, but she had no time for him now.

She strung the bow and aimed carefully. The arrow flew straight and true, landing with a satisfying thwack mere inches from the poacher's head.

He cried out in fear, then gasped out the location of his family.

Kayln nodded to Bertrand, who dispatched two of the men to fetch them.

With one last look into the tree, she saw that Samuel had finally decided to join them on the ground, for he was climbing down. Obviously, telling them where to find his family had taken the resistance out of him.

She was uncommonly gratified, for Kayln had no desire to continue the interrogation here. Hawk's presence was too oppressive. Her men would learn soon enough if Samuel had spoken the truth. Kayln would deal with him then.

Quietly, she spoke to Bertrand. "When you have his family, see that they are fed. Even should Samuel's story prove false, we must see to the children."

As Bertrand nodded, she sighed. "I will return to the keep now."

"I will see you back," Bertrand told her, drawing up his reins in readiness.

"There is no need," Hawk said, speaking for the first time. "I will return your lady safely to the keep."

Not bothering to remark on how foolish she felt this discussion to be, Kayln turned her mare and nudged her forward. She needed no escort, least of all Hawk, and was quite capable of returning to the castle alone. She had gone only a short distance when Hawk drew Mac up beside her.

"Have you no care for your own safety?" he asked, slowing his stallion's pace to match that of her own horse.

His continued insistence on taking care of her was beginning to wear. "And why should I be concerned for my safety on my own lands?" She turned to face him, her brows raised high. "Who would harm me? You, my lord?"

A growl that was pure exasperation escaped him. "You know you need never fear me, madame. And I have just seen that you can be very resourceful in dealing with an irksome matter, but there are dangerous characters who might not allow you to use your clever tongue to best them."

She could not halt the flush of pleasure that stained her cheeks at the compliment, however cloaked in insults it might be. But she wouldn't allow him to know. "Such as?"

"Poachers, reavers, a disgruntled tenant. It would be far too easy to do away with you and leave your body here in the forest. By the time anyone looked for you, the villain would be far from the wrath of your men."

She raised her chin. "I am not so helpless as you assume."

He laughed ruefully. "So I have just seen. Where did you learn to shoot a bow that way? Or was the accuracy of the shot just good fortune?"

Kayln stiffened, outrage apparent in her tone. "Good fortune? Why, you knave. It is the law of the land that every man betwixt the ages of sixteen and sixty is required to own and practice with the longbow. Should I not at least have some knowledge of a skill known by the least of my vassals?"

Angrily she kicked her horse forward.

Without warning, Hawk reached out and drew her onto his own horse. "Release me," she demanded, pushing at his hands.

"Why should I?" His golden eyes gleamed down at her with mocking amusement and something else she dared not name.

"You think to make your point." Kayln leaned back as far as she could within the circle of his arms, her expression filled with bravado. "Your lesson is not valid. I have no fear of you, sir knight. You would not do anything I would not have you do."

He chuckled deeply, wickedly. "I have you completely in my power."

Far from frightening her, his words made her breath quicken with an emotion she had no wish to feel. She had to get away from him, from the way he made her pulse race. Desperately, Kayln kicked him with her booted foot, striking his thigh with the hard tip. Hawk gasped in surprise, his arms loosening just enough for her to push herself to the ground.

Kayln wasted no time taking to the dense undergrowth, where she knew he would not go with his stallion.

To her surprise she heard the sound of him crashing through the forest behind her. Thinking to outwit Hawk, Kayln turned in the direction of her men. He would assume she had run toward the keep.

She had taken only a few more steps when she almost ran

into the chestnut wall of the stallion. She looked up into Hawk's laughing face. "You devil," Kayln cried angrily. "How did you know which way I had come?"

"I simply asked myself what *you* would do," he answered easily. "Knowing what a contrary woman you are, I could only assume you would take the least logical of courses."

Surely he was evil incarnate, she told herself. "I hate you, Hawkhurst," she replied with the sweetest smile she could summon. Putting her hands on her hips, she turned her back on him and began to walk away. "Please leave me now. I have had enough of your company this day."

Hawk was of no mind to be dismissed so summarily.

As he watched Kayln stalk away, he asked himself why he continued to bother with her. Why did he not find some other girl who would be glad of his attentions and obedient? But he knew it was not possible at this moment. Kayln D'Arcy had managed to bring the level of his frustration to a finely sharpened point that left him feeling as if he would like to thrash someone.

He watched the gentle sway of her hips as if hypnotized. It was too much. His thoughts went from a desire to teach the maid a lesson, to a very real need to feel those hips writhing under his.

Without ceremony, Hawk prodded his horse forward until he was even with Kayln, and scooped her up onto his lap once more. Her gently rounded backside was sweet torment against his over-sensitive thighs.

"I no longer find this amusing." Kayln glared up at him, folding her arms across her chest. "Put me down." Then she grew still as she saw the look of hunger in his eyes. Her breath seemed to catch and her chest was so tight it ached. Or was the ache further down deep in her belly?

"No," she whispered as his dark head moved toward hers, blocking out the light. Kayln knew this was a mistake, but the tension that had been building in her the whole day would not be denied. She wanted him.

"Or what?" he asked, his face only inches from hers. "Call to your men. They will hear you."

But his warm breath was on her lips and she couldn't think,

couldn't move away from the promise of unutterable pleasure she read in his eyes.

His mouth touched hers, barely brushing. She felt her own lips soften, parting slightly as she lifted her head to make closer contact. He growled, and his hand came up to pull the hood of her mantle back. His fingers tangled in the silky fullness of her golden hair.

Kayln's arms twined around his neck to pull him to her. She gloried in the hardness of his chest and the firm muscles of his thighs beneath her.

Not breaking the contact of their mouths, Hawk put one arm under her legs, the other supporting her back, and they slipped to the ground. Slowly she slid down the length of his hard body until her feet were touching the earth. Their eyes held for a long moment, yearning and dark with desire, before she reached up and drew his head down to hers.

His kisses grew hungrier, and Kayln's mouth opened under the insistence of his. Hawk's tongue flicked out to taste the interior of her mouth. A warm sweet languor grew in Kayln and she pressed herself to him, feeling the way his manhood rose and pulsed against her belly.

Finally, Hawk held her away to look at her. Kayln's lips were swollen from his kisses, her lids heavy with passion.

Slowly, so very slowly, he raised his hand until it was poised just above her left breast. He paused, and Kayln looked up at him, questioning.

"Kayln?"

She knew what he was asking and couldn't answer. If she told him to go on, she was just as responsible for what they were doing as he. Though he had not touched her, Kayln could feel the heat of his large palm through the fabric of her gown, and felt her breast swell in answer. Kayln knew if she were to take a breath, she would brush against his hand. Her nipple hardened to a tight bud of anticipation, and she lost the battle with her own will.

She arched toward him, making the contact as she whispered, "Yes, yes." Hawk's hand closed around her aching flesh, and she gasped at the fire that coursed through her blood.

Then there was no time for thought as they tumbled to the moss-covered earth. Each of them worked impatiently to remove the other's clothing. Finally, Hawk ended by tearing her gown when the fastenings resisted his efforts to undo them, his hands running freely over the creamy flesh that was exposed to his heated gaze.

His own velvet tunic lay discarded on the ground as he bent over her to suckle the tips of her breasts. She twined her finger in the dark hair that touched the stark white color of his shirt, and groaned, "Take me now, my Hawk."

"I would savor every inch of you, Kayln, but my need drives me so I cannot wait another moment." He knelt between her legs, clad only in the white shirt, which he quickly removed, then paused glorious in his nakedness above her, his gaze scorching her with its heat.

Kayln stared, mesmerized by the upthrust shaft of his manhood. Then she closed her eyes and sobbed her pleasure as he plunged into the ready darkness of her body.

Higher she soared as her hips rose to meet his, yearning toward something that hovered just out of reach. But as she touched the clouds, feeling as though she would climb on forever, the ecstasy expanded within her. She cried out his name, clutching his wide shoulders beneath her hands as the spasms took her. Then, languorously, delicately, she fell from the heights of infinity.

Kayln opened her eyes slowly and saw his face above her. There was a tugging sensation in her chest. Care for him she did, though it galled her to know it was true. No matter that Hawk could not be the man she wanted. He had the power to bring her to this incredible joy and that could not be ignored.

Leaning back, Hawk put his hands on either side of her face and smiled into her mist-gray eyes. He bent forward and softly kissed the tip of her nose. "Do you know how beautiful you are when we make love?" he whispered.

"You watch me?" she asked, looking away. It was a little disconcerting to know he had seen her when she had lost all control over herself and her emotions. Already he held too much sway over her senses.

With his hands on her cheeks, he gently turned her face back to his, his golden eyes intent on hers as he spoke. "Watching you gives me more pleasure than you could imagine. I enjoy knowing I can make you forget yourself and respond without restraint."

She lifted her mouth to kiss him, not wanting to talk or think about what they had done.

After returning her kiss with a thoroughness that left Kayln breathless, Hawk leaned away from her. "You are such a stubborn woman. I had thought it would take much longer before you were willing to trust me once again."

Kayln felt her body go stiff as he spoke. Could he really believe she was so ready to dismiss all that was wrong between them and trust him? She drew her arms up to cross them in front of herself, rubbing her forearms as if that could diminish the chill that made her shiver beneath him.

"What is it, Kayln?" Hawk scowled, feeling the change in her.

She pushed at him, sliding away when he leaned back. She got to her feet with some difficulty as her legs were shaking terribly. Kayln bent to pick up her discarded gown, and turned her back to Hawk as she pulled it on.

"What is wrong?" Hawk asked again, rising to his feet, his hands clenched at his sides.

Kayln waited until she was dressed to turn back to face him. There was no way to repair her torn bodice, so she draped it over her shoulders as best she could. Without meeting his eyes, Kayln drew on her cape.

When she looked toward Hawk, she could see he had not used his time to clothe himself. He stood before her in all his naked splendor. He was big, wide shouldered, without a hint of fat, and solid as the walls of his castle. Just the sight of him reinforced Kayln's certainty that their coming together again had been a mistake. He was the epitome of strength and dominance.

But God help her, she wanted him still.

He braced his feet wide, his hands on muscular hips, as he looked down at her with tight lips and narrowed eyes.

Knowing he would not speak to her until she had answered the question he had already asked did not make it any easier for Kayln to say what she knew she must. "I . . ." She frowned over her own hesitancy, then raised her head higher as she forced herself to go on. "I am sorry if I have led you to believe that things have changed between us. I cannot place my trust in you.'' Her tongue moved out to moisten her dry lips, and she pulled her mantle close about her shoulders.

''So why, then, did you give yourself to me just now?'' Hawk asked evenly, coolly.

Kayln ran shaky fingers through her badly tangled hair. ''Who can say why what is between us exists? I only know that when you touch me I cannot think beyond that moment.'' It was a difficult admission for her, but Kayln wanted Hawk to know through her honesty that she meant what she said.

Hawk moved close, putting his hand under her chin and forcing her to look into his eyes. ''Are you telling me you feel nothing for me but lust?''

Kayln cringed, wanting to pull away from those golden eyes that sought the truth from the very depths of her being. But she made herself face him. A humorless laugh escaped her. ''What else have we? You share nothing of yourself with me. You have admitted that lust is what you want from me. Why should I be different simply because I am a woman?''

He looked decidedly more disturbed by her words than she would have thought possible. Though Kayln couldn't imagine why.

But Kayln could not allow herself to contemplate his odd reaction at the moment. There was something else she wished to say. ''I am also aware that you know more than you say about who shot you with that arrow, but you refuse to tell me anything of what is going on. You cannot trust me with even that much of yourself.''

He took a deep breath, turning his sharply chiseled profile to her. ''I can tell you nothing about it.''

''Why?''

''I cannot even say that much. No one may know. It is the only way.'' His jaw muscles flexed with tension as he spoke.

Kayln could not look at him any longer. She closed her eyes to the intensity in his, shutting him out. For in spite of everything, she still found him more beautiful than any man had a right to be, still wanted him.

Suddenly, Kayln knew what she would do, no matter how much it cost her in pride. Hawk had won. She would be his mistress.

Opening her eyes, Kayln looked at him, her gaze direct as she said, ''I will do what you want.''

He stared at her as if she was speaking in a foreign tongue. "What?"

"We shall be lovers. You may come to me here at Aimsley, and we will be together as today. I have admitted I feel desire for you. Why should we not do as you once said and take our pleasure from each other as we will?"

For a moment, the expression on Hawk's face was one of absolute shock. Kayln could not help feeling a sense of intense satisfaction that she had been able to shock the ever-imperturbable Hawk. Then slowly, his eyes began to smolder with anger that made the golden color swirl and darken. "You want me to play the stud to your mare?" he asked tightly, his jaw muscles flexing.

Kayln could not have been more surprised. Was he indeed mad? He was the one who had suggested the idea. But she would not back down. "If you will. Yes." Surely he must see that this was an answer for them. If Kayln could only quench the desire she felt for him, then mayhap she would be able to cease thinking of him to the near exclusion of all else.

Hawk's fingers tightened on her chin and he spoke very carefully. "I am no stud. I am a man. And you are a woman, Lady D'Arcy. Have you forgotten you were a virgin when you came to me?"

Flinching, she took a step backward, and he released her. There was no doubt in her mind now. The man was crazed. There was no other explanation for his complete change of attitude.

She could only watch in amazement as Hawk gathered up his clothing. Not bothering to pause to put it on, Hawk leaped atop his stallion without another word. He tore through the trees at a gallop, unheeding of the branches that clawed at his bare flesh.

The sting of his rejection was already being replaced by a blessed seeping numbness that dampened the anguish she knew would come later. Wrapping her arms around herself, Kayln looked after him, unmoving even after she could no longer hear the sound of his passage.

Never again, she told herself, would she allow James Hawkhurst to get close enough to hurt her. Oh, sweet Jesu, she thought, please let it be so.

Chapter Thirteen

All the way to Norwich Hawk tried to understand what could have gotten into him. He was surely mad to have refused Kayln's offer to share her bed. After all, it was exactly what he had wanted. But somehow the notion had suddenly begun to sound tawdry when he heard Kayln say it. Why this was he didn't know. It just seemed as if it was somehow wrong.

Mayhap it was because in beginning to know Kayln better, he had begun to understand how difficult it would be for her to agree to such an idea. She was a good and virtuous woman. Or had been until he appeared. She had in fact been a virgin in spite of having been a married woman. And the fault did not lie in any coldness on her part. His body tightened with tension just at the thought of the depth of her responses to him.

He told himself it didn't make any sense. But he couldn't go back and tell her that he had behaved like an imbecile and of course would love to share her bed. Mayhap it was because of the sadness he'd seen in her eyes when she said it. For some reason he did not wish to examine, it unsettled him to see the proud and beautiful Kayln agree to do something so clearly against her own principles. It was as if he had begun to respect her too much to see her do so. Had all Kayln's talk of respecting her as an equal changed his way of seeing her, his very way of thinking?

But that made no sense whatsoever. Kayln D'Arcy meant nothing special to him. She was a cold and distant woman who kept all her feelings bottled up inside her, giving nothing away to anyone around her, including her sister. What she did or did not do was surely her own problem, and Hawk had not forced her or any other woman to bed him. Nor would he.

But even as Hawk galloped on, he could not stop thinking

about some of the things she had told him about her husband that first night they'd made love. And this very day, she had shown him more when telling him of her trust in Bertrand. Could it be that Kayln was hiding behind a wall of reserve, that she was as soft and loving as her sister inside? There were times when he thought he saw a glimpse of yearning in the lovely gray eyes, such as when he had held Celia and comforted her. And that night before he had first made love to her, hadn't Kayln seemed warm and somehow softer? But the impressions were only fleeting, and Hawk was not sure of his perceptions. It could be that he wanted to see some sweetness in Kayln to help him explain the overwhelming sexual desire he had for her. It had seemed to be there when she told Bertrand to see the poacher's family was fed even if he was lying about his circumstances. But showing kindness to strangers seemed easier for her than showing it to those close to her.

Hawk groaned aloud. He was tired of thinking about the woman. Didn't this turmoil he was in prove that he should not become emotionally involved? He had enough troubles on his plate with trying to discover what had happened to his property and staying alive while doing it.

Surely the best thing for him to do was to stay away from Kayln D'Arcy. He would have done with her from this moment on. Yet even as the resolution was made, Hawk had the distinct feeling that the decision was easier made than carried out.

On arriving at Norwich, Hawk was surprised to learn from one of the earl's men that the earl himself was not in the castle but both Philip and Martin were.

Hawk first sought out Philip to tell him Celia was seeing to her own well-being and that of the child. After a grueling hour, in which Philip pressed Hawk for every detail as to what Celia had said or done during Hawk's visit to Aimsley, the elder brother simply handed him the packet of letters. Eagerly Philip took the pouch and departed to read them in private.

With a heavy sigh, Hawk went to search for Martin. He found his middle brother in the hall.

Martin greeted Hawk effusively. "God's truth, Hawk. I am glad to see you well."

Hawk's black brows winged upward. "And why would I

be otherwise? The whore's son Harold has grown more desperate, but I am on the alert. Just last week another one of my hounds died when he ate a piece of meat that had been left on a tray in my room."

A gasp of shock escaped Martin's lips. "God's teeth, Hawk. You are either mad or a fool." He shook his auburn head. "I wonder that you can place so little value on your own safety."

Hawk settled himself on a bench. "As I told you at Aimsley, Martin, I am always on watch." His lips tightened at the mere mention of Kayln's keep, but he forced himself to relax, to remember his decision to have done with her.

"Have you come any closer to finding out who is in league with Harold?" Martin asked, taking a seat beside him.

Hawk forced himself to attend to this conversation. After all, they were discussing the man he believed was trying to kill him. "Nay. I have questioned everyone between here and Clamdon. I can find no connection between the steward and any merchant or landholder I've spoken with. The knave has covered his tracks well."

"Then take him. You need have no more proof than you have. Let the rest go. Without Harold to supply your goods, the other will have no access to them."

Hawk hit the table with his fist. "I will not. I will see justice done. No man will take what belongs to our family without paying for that crime."

Martin opened his mouth to argue further, but Hawk stopped him with a thunderous glare. He was of no mind for conflict with his brother on top of his irritability over Kayln.

"At least have a care," his brother warned. "And remember, if you have need, call on me. I will be there."

A muscle worked in Hawk's lean cheek, but he forced himself to speak rationally. "You can do nothing. I would not be in this muddle if I had lived up to my responsibilities as I ought. It is my fault Harold grew bold and greedy. He is not of the blood. The lands mean nothing to him."

"Hawk, you do not have to see yourself killed to make up for your delay in coming home."

Hawk turned away. "I will not hear this." He had no intention of losing his life, but he did mean to carry out his responsibilities as his father would have done.

As if knowing he would only make his brother angry if he were to continue on this path, Martin remained silent.

Hawk made haste to change the subject. He would not be swayed on this. "What brings you to Norwich?" Hawk raised his arm and beckoned a serving woman to him, ordering wine.

"I go to France on the king's business," Martin answered when she had gone.

Hawk quirked a brow. "France?"

Martin shrugged. "I carry messages so secret that even I do not know their content, though I have reason to believe they involve King John's ransom."

Scowling, Hawk touched his brother's shoulder. "Have a care. Many would wish to keep from having any treat with our enemies. Especially those who hope for John's death."

"His Majesty must send someone he trusts," Martin answered. "Besides, Jayne is driving me to distraction with her cleaning and mothering. I do like her to see to my comfort, but sometimes she goes too far."

"It serves you well for allowing her too much license," Hawk told him. "It is your home." Hawk loved Jayne well, but she did at times drive one to distraction. One had little hope of ever winning an argument with her as nothing ever broke that cool self-confidence of hers. But she was also capable of great gentleness and warmth, two qualities which could make a man forgive much even when he knew he was being managed. Qualities that Hawk greatly desired in the woman he would take to wife.

Unbidden, a picture of Kayln as she told Bertrand to see that the poacher's family was fed crept into his mind. He pushed it aside, reminding himself anew that the fellow was not of her own inner circle.

Martin huffed, smiling too pleasantly as he folded his hands on the tabletop. "And you, with all your experience of women, could teach me to handle her, just as you handled the Lady D'Arcy."

Hawk flushed an angry red. "Pray, what are you trying to say, little brother?"

At that moment, the serving girl arrived with their wine. She bent low to display her full bosom to the two handsome men, her smile warmly suggestive.

Ignoring Hawk's question for the moment, Martin did not let this abundant display go unnoticed. His green eyes lingered with obvious appreciation on the wares before him.

Hawk noted that she was a pretty girl, but he felt no stirring of warmth when he looked at her. Damn Kayln, he swore silently.

When she had gone, Martin looked to his brother in amazement. "What is this, Hawk? First you overreact to an innocent jest on my part. Then you so rudely ignore the bounty that fair maid displayed for us."

When Hawk's face darkened, Martin knew he had struck his mark and made quick to press the point. It was not often that anyone caught Hawk at a disadvantage. "So the Hawk has finally been tamed to the glove."

"You know not of what you speak," Hawk growled, taking a long pull of his mulled wine.

"I know much more than you would have me know, good brother," Martin returned, lifting his cup high. "To the woman who has clipped the Hawk's wings."

Hawk caught his brother's hand. "No woman has or ever will 'clip my wings.' " He released Martin.

Martin cocked a brow, clearly unmoved by the show of temper. "Then why did you look through that lovely display of womanhood just now as if she had no more substance than air? In the old days 'The Hawk' would have taken her from this room and given her all she desired and more."

"What do you know of what I would do?" Hawk drained his glass and Martin poured him another. He drank this too, finding that the wine was beginning to take some of the edge off his frustration about Kayln.

"I was only a boy when you went to France seven years ago, but not so young that I didn't admire my older brother's prowess with women." Martin winked conspiratorially.

Hawk poured himself another glass of wine as he smiled fondly. "Mother would not have such goings-on in the hall. She was ever one to see that the proprieties were upheld."

Martin laughed. "Even though she and Father would disappear at all times of the day."

"They loved one another well." Hawk drained his cup and called for another pitcher as the last drop fell from the first one. "Though 'twas not done in the hall." If only he could find such happiness. But that was unlikely when all he could think about was a woman who drove him to new heights of frustration each time they met.

He listened through a slight haze as Martin laughed even harder at his remark.

Hawk did not feel like laughing. Speaking of his parents only dredged up feelings of guilt. "Would that I had been there at the end." Hawk's voice was rough with sadness. "By the time I heard of their deaths in France, it was too late."

Martin took a long drink from his own cup as if to ease the ache in his throat. "Don't . . ." He choked. "Don't feel guilty. Mother's last words were that we should all know her Hawk was with her in spirit if not in body." He shook his head. "She was exhausted from nursing Father. You wouldn't have believed how such a strong man could waste away so quickly. You know, you take after him more than any of us, but at the end he was no more than a shell. And Mother . . . well, none of us were really surprised when the fever came upon her too. On the very day Father died, she was taken to her bed. She just didn't want to be without him. I think her only regret was that she must leave us to be with him."

"I miss them," Hawk said simply, his voice gruff as he stared into his cup. "Clamdon is not the same without them." It made him all the more determined to find a woman who would give him the kind of loving relationship his parents had shared. A woman completely unlike Kayln D'Arcy.

Martin put his hand on his brother's arm.

Hawk was bone tired and could feel the wine seeping into his blood, lowering his guard. "Wanted me to play the stud for her," he murmured as he emptied another cup and refilled it, spilling a small amount of the liquid on the tabletop. Hawk only stared at the spreading pool as it ran toward the edge of the table, not bothering to try to do anything about it.

"What are you talking about?" Martin asked, obviously confused by the turn the conversation had taken.

"Kayln actually thought I would be willing to attend her at Aimsley whenever she felt the need of me," Hawk growled.

Martin's eyes grew round with amazement. "You cannot be in earnest? The lady wants nothing more of you than your, shall we say, physical attributes? What more could you ask for?''

''A pox on you, Martin. And a pox on her.'' Hawk took another long drink of his wine. But even as he said the words he knew Martin had just cause to be surprised. Indeed what more could he ask for?

Martin leaned back and looked at his brother closely. ''I find it hard to believe that you would not be willing to give the lady what she desires.'' He shook his head in disbelief. ''I, for one, would not hesitate. In fact, would that it were I she had taken a fancy to, for Kayln D'Arcy is a lovely piece of womanhood.''

To Martin's utter amazement, Hawk's fingers closed on the collar of his tunic with murderous intent. ''Don't you even think of touching her,'' he growled.

Martin pried his brother's fingers from his clothing so he could get enough air to speak. ''I meant no harm, Hawk. I but remarked on the stupidity of your having taken offense from such a thing.''

Hawk drew away slowly and picked up his cup to drain it. ''Forgive me, Martin. You cannot know how she haunts me.'' He was ashamed of himself, attacking his own brother that way.

Martin put his hand on Hawk's back. ''You, my friend, are in love.'' His tone was one of deep sympathy as he patted his brother's shoulder. ''You have my condolences. I myself plan never to be afflicted by that dread state.''

Hawk blinked at him as if his vision were unclear. ''You are mad.'' But even as he said the words his wine-befuddled mind tried to reconcile his position. He did not believe that what he felt for Kayln could be called love. He knew he wanted her, wanted to possess every part of her, but it was not love. Why, then, his besotted brain asked itself, did he bolt when she agreed to share her bed? With a groan of anger, Hawk raised his hand to call for another pitcher of wine. Mayhap in that way he would find surcease from the plaguing question of his feelings for Kayln D'Arcy.

Three weeks had passed since Kayln had told Hawk she would welcome him as her lover. And still she wondered what had come over her. Every time she remembered the way she had offered herself to the baron and been rejected so vehemently, her stomach rolled with nausea. Setting aside her own principles and fears of giving in to her desire for Hawk had not been easy for her.

Then, as she thought about what had happened that day in the forest, she began to change her thinking. It was true that Raymond had never shown any carnal need for her, but Hawk had made it abundantly clear that he did not feel the same way. He did want her, as she wanted him. Why, then, had he refused her acceptance of what he himself had proposed?

The only thing Kayln could think was that, Hawk being Hawk, he had had more enthusiasm for the game when he was in pursuit of a resistant prey. Understanding this made her all the more irritated with the man. Who was he to decide the sport was over simply because she'd agreed to participate? Well, Kayln was at the end of being used. She was not going to allow herself to be controlled by any man's whim, especially not James Hawkhurst's. For the first time in her life, Kayln meant to be the one with the upper hand in her dealings with a male. She would make him want her so much he would take her on her own terms. Her body was hers to give where and when she would, as her heart was hers to keep firmly locked away from harm.

The decision was a strangely exhilarating one, but not having much experience in these matters, Kayln was forced to rely on her own intuition. She could only hope that intuition would not fail her.

When Hawk returned to Aimsley, which she knew he would, because of his promise to Celia, Kayln would be ready for him. She didn't even allow herself to wonder why she was so certain of his honor in keeping his promise. That was not something she wished to think about. It was more important to center her thoughts on her proposed seduction of the scoundrel.

She had new gowns made of the richest, most becoming fabrics and cut in such a way that they showed off her female attributes to their best advantage. Jewels were purchased, and Kayln commissioned a new belt of delicate gold links to be worn low about her hips.

Even days later as her steward, Fredrick, sat across from her in the accounting chamber, Kayln could barely concentrate on his words. It seemed water had gotten into the hay one of her more affluent tenants had stored for the winter, and he had come to request that his lady issue him enough hay to feed his four cows until spring.

She startled Fredrick by telling him to borrow from the hay which had been laid aside for her own horses and livestock. The steward seemed surprised not by his mistress's generosity, but by the fact that she did not weigh every possible alternative before deciding. He looked upon her with ill-concealed curiosity.

Realizing he was watching her too closely, Kayln sent Fredrick to deliver the hay.

Damn Hawk. 'Twas he who had confused her and disrupted her life. It was her preoccupation with wondering when he would return and her uncertainty that she would have the courage to go through with her plans that had her so inattentive. Kayln was determined that once she had succeeded in seducing the baron, she would then be able to dismiss him from her life.

Even her relationship with Miles had changed irrevocably since Hawk had come into her life. The last time Miles had come to Aimsley there had been another unpleasant incident that Kayln couldn't remember without grimacing.

Miles had begun by telling Kayln in no uncertain terms that he did not like the fact that Hawk had become such a frequent visitor to Aimsley. He was certain the man had designs on Kayln.

Kayln had stiffened, though she tried to keep her tone even, as she was aware of how far Miles was from the mark. It was now she who had designs upon the baron. She'd answered, "He is Celia's brother and comes to see to her well-being."

He tilted his narrow nose high. "My dear lady, you can not be so blind."

Drat him for making her feel guilty. She had promised Miles nothing, but the sense of having betrayed him was there nonetheless. Thinking to distract him, she said, "You seemed to harbor much ill feeling toward him without ever stating your reasons. Mayhap I would better understand were you to tell me."

Turning away from her, Miles raised his foot so she could see it. "Let us just say that Hawkhurst has been a pebble in my shoe in many ways of late."

Looking down at his fashionably long-pointed shoe with a grimace, Kayln shook her head. "There you are again," she said, shrugging. "Can you not be more specific?"

He smiled narrowly, looking at her as if he knew some secret. "I fear I must leave it at that for the moment."

Raising her brows, she simply shook her head again. Miles had been deliberately mysterious. And it seemed just another attempt to hold her attention on himself. But she refused to be drawn in. Miles could go to the very devil if he continued to think he could decide with whom she could spend her time.

She came out of her reverie as she heard her name being called. "Lady Kayln."

She turned toward the sound. "Yes."

"Lady Kayln." The serf Rob stepped around the edge of the wide oak door. He was a short, thin man, but had a rounded belly and cheeks.

"What do you require?"

"A visitor has arrived."

Miles again. She sighed.

"Has someone seen that Sir Miles has refreshments while he waits?" she asked, remembering how little Alice cared for the man's comfort.

" 'Tis not Sir Miles," Rob told her, his round peasant's face pink. He seemed unable to meet her gaze.

"Then who—" Kayln began, but she didn't need to hear the next words to know. The embarrassment on Rob's face told her.

Kayln worked hard to control the color that rose to her own cheeks. How much of what had passed between her and Hawk was common knowledge amongst her people? But even that worry faded into insignificance at the thought of seeing him again. Heaven help her, would she have the courage to go through with her plans?

Kayln looked down at the mauve wool gown she wore. She knew a moment of intense longing as she thought of all the lovely new cotehardies and tunics folded away in the chest in her room. Was Hawk forever to catch her at her worst? There was no help for it now. She would just have to meet him as she was. She raised her chin.

On entering the Great Hall, Kayln saw that Celia was there with Hawk. Two chairs had been pulled close to the fire, and she could hear the sound of Celia's wistful giggle as it mingled with the deeper mirth of the man. She faltered for a moment, wondering if that husky laugh would ever sound so easily in her own presence. But she told herself not to even think about something so ridiculous. Hawk's humor was not what she wanted from him.

Celia called out when she turned and saw her sister. "Kayln."

Since the day when he had come to visit her and comforted her tears over Philip, Celia had spoken of Hawk with great affection, rattling on about her dear brother as if he were a saint. Kayln had refrained from telling her that Hawk was a scoundrel who used his charm to suit his purpose. If Hawk could help to keep Celia from her depressions, Kayln would not defame him.

"We have a guest," Celia was saying, her cheeks flushed with excitement. "He has brought letters from Philip, written only two days ago. Hawk stopped at Norwich on his return just to collect them. Isn't that wonderful, Kayln?"

But Kayln didn't answer, couldn't answer, her gaze going to the man who had been so much in her thoughts of late as he rose from his chair. How could it be that every time she saw him he seemed more handsome? Had she really thought his face was too rugged for true male beauty? She felt she must faint from the force of her reaction to him.

But his expression exposed nothing of his own feelings as he looked at her. Only the slight hoarseness of his voice as he said her name gave any hint that he might not be as indifferent to her as he appeared. "Kayln."

Kayln opened her mouth to reply, and found her throat was too dry. She closed her lips and swallowed before trying again. "Lord Hawkhurst."

Forcefully, Kayln reminded herself she was intent on luring Hawk to her bed. She realized she would have to behave much more cleverly than she was if she were ever to get Hawk to do anything he didn't want to. At this moment it was she who was wavering in her resolve.

Looking up from beneath her long lashes, Kayln asked softly, "How was your journey?"

Hawk's reply was nothing more than polite. "As well as can be expected. It took a few days longer than I had hoped to settle the problems on my estate."

This casual tone made her wonder if her quest might be impossible. Could Hawk's ardor have cooled so quickly? No, she told herself firmly, remembering the hoarseness in his voice when he said her name. Hawk wanted her too, and she could not start to doubt herself now before she had even begun.

If he desired small talk, then she would oblige him. "I too have been busy. Oh, by the way, my lord," she added as if it were an afterthought, "it seems that our little poacher was telling the truth about his circumstances."

Hawk nodded. "Would I be prying to ask what you have done with him?" His tone continued to be carefully neutral.

She turned away from him, answering as if it was of little importance, "He and his family have been given an empty cottage to live in." She did not wish him to think she was seeking praise for her actions.

He gave her a long, measuring look.

Uncomfortable with the way he was staring, Kayln searched for something else to say. "Have you been given refreshment?" she asked, even though she already knew the answer.

"Celia has been the perfect hostess." He smiled at the younger girl with genuine affection. Kayln could not completely stifle a strange sense of longing. What would she do if Hawk was to look at her that way, with that gentle tenderness? Hurriedly she told herself that she was fortunate that he did not. 'Twas difficult enough to deal with this intense physical attraction she felt. Aye, she was much better off not having to guard her heart against his considerable charm.

What she needed to do was get their relationship onto the proper footing.

Realizing she must make an opportunity to put her plan to seduce him into action, Kayln said, "If you would stay for the evening meal, we would be most honored, Lord Hawkhurst. My sister and I see too few visitors.'' She looked to Celia, who was beaming at the idea. ''It will also give Celia an opportunity to drive you to distraction with questions about Philip and what he is doing.''

Hawk's brows rose in surprise. He looked at her for a long indefinable moment, then nodded, his gaze never leaving hers. ''It is I who would be honored to accept your kind invitation.''

''How good of you,'' Kayln told him, trying to hide her elation. But she could not deny the shaft of heat that pierced her belly, nor did she wish to. Her voice was slightly breathless as she continued. ''And now, if you will excuse me, I will go to my chamber and make ready for the meal.''

''I shall await your return.'' He bowed again, his gaze still not leaving her face. From his puzzled expression Kayln knew Hawk was suspicious of her intentions.

Quickly Kayln turned to Celia to keep him from reading the triumph in her eyes. She could see her younger sister was looking from one to the other of them with a speculative expression. Suddenly, Celia smiled brightly at Kayln, then kissed Hawk on the cheek as she patted her enormous belly and said, ''I too must try to make myself presentable for the meal. Though 'tis near impossible now.''

''You are lovely.'' Hawk hugged her, his arms going around her easily.

''You are too kind to me.'' Celia laughed as she pushed away from him. ''But I do like the things you say.''

Again Kayln was assaulted by a sense of yearning, but she told herself that it was only because Celia was still somewhat reserved with her. And she realized something else. She must be careful not to give away her interest in Hawk in front of her sister. She did not wish the girl to read too much into the situation. What was between them was purely physical and once that desire was quenched, Kayln would be washing her hands of one James Hawkhurst.

As Hawk waited for Celia and Kayln, he returned to his chair before the hearth. The fire was warm and he was tired after so long a time in the saddle. He had only just returned to Clamdon, and might have delayed a visit to Aimsley for a few days, but he could not keep himself away. He had assured himself over and over that it was solely because of his promise to Celia.

Seeing Kayln again had made him doubt that certainty. She was as beautiful as he remembered, and more. And her ready welcome of him was more heady than any wine. But knowing her as he did, knowing how very obstinate she was and how badly they had parted, he could not help suspecting her motives.

Contemplating the flames that licked greedily at the logs in the hearth made him think of the way his desire burned for Kayln. After three weeks away, Hawk had almost been able to convince himself he would be able to see Kayln and manage to control his feelings for her. After all, he was a warrior. He should be able to face one small woman, no matter how strong willed.

But when he had turned to find her standing there, he had realized just how ridiculous this thought was. She was so lovely with her golden hair tumbling down her back and her cheeks aglow. He had wanted to take her in his arms then and there, unheeding of Celia's presence. But he could not. Something, some force he could not understand, kept him from giving in to his desire. For he knew that if he did, he would only be giving in to Kayln's proposal. And in spite of the fact that he knew it was madness, he could not do so. Though why, Hawk could not even hazard a guess.

He recalled again what Martin had said at Norwich. Did he love Kayln? It hardly seemed possible. She was none of the things he wished a wife to be. But even as the thought crossed his mind, another intruded. Was that completely true? Kayln did have many good qualities. She was intelligent and kind, and capable. He had seen for himself that she seemed to be trying to be closer to her sister, though it did not appear to be easy for her. But were her efforts to be more loving good enough reason to allow himself to love her?

So immersed was he in his own thoughts that Hawk was not disturbed from his place beside the fire as the trestle tables were set up for the meal. Unobtrusively, the servants saw he wanted for nothing. He felt catered to as he never did at Clamdon. At home Hawk was too busy to have a care for his personal comforts.

Would Kayln be willing to manage Clamdon with all the attentiveness she lavished upon Aimsley? He shook his head, unable to imagine her transferring her loyalties to his own home and people.

He turned from his contemplation of the fire as some inner sense told him Kayln had returned to the hall. She was standing just behind him, and his eyes took in the beauty of her in a forest-green samite cote, fitted so closely to her body that every luscious curve was exposed to his view through the wide-cut sides of the tunic of rose pink she wore over it. A pattern of dark green leaves ran up the sides and around the hem of the tunic. He knew it would have taken many hours to sew such an intricate pattern. She turned to the side, and he could see embroidered on the back of the tunic the design of a hawk, its wings spread and the talons protracted just as the bird appeared on his own standard.

He felt a surge of longing to gather her into his arms and carry her up to her tower, where he would make love to her until neither of them could move. Hawk gripped the arms of his chair tightly as he reminded himself of who and where they were. Of the obstacles that lay in the way of such an act of abandon.

''Hawk.'' Her voice was low and sweet and full of promise, as were her eyes.

He came to his feet. ''You are lovely, madame, and do me much honor in displaying my device.''

It was then that Hawk saw the expression of triumph in her light gray eyes. Need was replaced by confusion. Then realization dawned as an intense wave of fury shot through him like a jolt of lightning. In the past Kayln had never even once tried to lure him in any way. That was why her attempt to captivate him was so very obvious now.

Kayln was trying to seduce him, and he would not stand for it. If this woman thought she could manipulate him, she was in for a very unpleasant surprise.

Hawk was distracted as at that moment Celia came into the room behind her older sister. With a polite nod to Kayln, he went forward to take the younger girl's arm. He led Celia to the table and helped her into a seat. He then took the place on Celia's left, putting her between himself and Kayln.

Kayln stood absolutely still. Hawk could feel her eyes burning into his back, but he did not look around. He wanted her to understand that he knew her game.

Throughout the meal, Hawk was kind and attentive to Celia, but said little to Kayln. She neither by word nor action showed that she was in the least bit intimidated by his attitude. Even as he feasted on his outrage, Hawk could not help acknowledging the self-possession she displayed in the face of his disgruntlement.

Unwilling admiration rose up in him, and by the time supper was over and the tables had been cleared away, Hawk could no longer feel any anger toward Kayln. Her fiery spirit, which made her so determined to follow a course once she decided upon it, was one of the things he was growing to appreciate about her. If she were determined to make him bend to her will, he knew his show of reluctance toward her advances would not make her give up.

As if offering a challenge, his eyes met Kayln's when Celia left the hall after the meal to get her lute.

Kayln's expression was alight with suppressed rage. Her gray eyes flashed smoky fire and the color was high in her cheeks. So she was not so very self-assured as she appeared. For some reason, her ability to put a brave front on her uncertainty drew him to her even more. But he saw something else in her eyes, something that made his belly tighten in response—the heat of desire.

Hawk could not repress the throb that went through his own body. God, but she was lovely. She took a deep breath, her breasts spilling over the low bodice of her cotehardie, and his hands ached to be filled by them. Resting his elbows upon the table, Hawk leaned toward her, unable to look away.

She smiled slowly, and her eyes were knowing as they followed the path of his gaze.

"I know your purpose," he said, his tone raspy. "Do not do this."

She bent toward him, offering an unobstructed view of her bosom. "Of what do you speak?" Her tone was soft, beguiling.

Sweat beaded on his forehead, and he had to wonder that one so new to coquetry could play the game so well. She was so beautiful and sensuous, her eyes warm and dark with longing. Involuntarily, Hawk reached out toward her, touching the curve of her cheek. She closed her eyes and turned so her lips were pressed to the palm of his hand. A shock of pure undiluted desire gripped him, settling in his loins. His hand trailed down, over her neck, across her shoulder, and down her arm until he was holding her hand.

What a fool he was, he told himself, to deny them both the pleasure they could have. What matter why she came to him? He opened his mouth, ready to tell Kayln he wanted her on any terms she might name.

But he was saved from such folly, because at that instant Celia appeared at his side, her lute in hand. "What shall I play?" she asked, seemingly oblivious to what was happening between her sister and Hawk.

Kayln and Hawk broke apart. Hawk closed his eyes and swallowed to ease the dryness of his throat. "Whatever you will, little one," he managed to answer. At this moment he was less sure than he might have been about who would be the winner in this battle of wills.

Stealing a glance at Kayln to find her watching him with a knowing smile, he hardened his resolve. It would not be so easy to deny her as he had thought. But deny her he would. Hawk was determined not to be bested by this siren. For he was beginning to fear that should he capitulate, Kayln would end in having more power over him than he cared to contemplate.

Chapter Fourteen

And so it went for weeks.

Whenever Hawk came to Aimsley, he was polite and courteous toward Kayln but nothing more. She wore the gowns she had had made, each more lovely than the last, and had her hair arranged in new and intricate ways. And still, Hawk remained distant, focusing most of his attention on Celia.

As things went, Kayln might have completely lost hope for her plan to seduce the man, but in unguarded moments she would see the way he looked at her. James Hawkhurst was not as immune to her as he would wish to appear. Kayln could hardly revel in the fact, for he seemed determined to resist any attraction he might feel.

Early one snowy morning, when the sky loomed gray and heavy about the keep, Kayln arose to find that Celia was ill. Kayln went to her immediately. On seeing that Celia's eyes were overly bright and her cheeks too flushed, she questioned her sister further. Celia admitted that she felt hot all over and her throat was aching terribly.

Immediately Kayln called for Alice. Now, with her pregnancy so far advanced, Celia needed all of her strength.

For days, Kayln had little time to think of her lack of progress in making Hawk her lover. She worked beside Alice tirelessly, bathing her sister in a wash of herbs the old woman had made. When she began to see the signs of fatigue in the slump of Alice's narrow shoulders, Kayln ordered her from the room to rest.

The nurse did not go quietly, saying she must be present should Celia take a turn for the worse. Adamantly, Kayln refused to heed her, assuring her that the girl would have need of her in that event and that Alice must be rested.

Kayln watched her go with relief. Whatever would she do if they both became ill? Her experience with the Black Death had taught Kayln well how sickness could spread amongst the elderly and infirm.

By late on the fourth afternoon, Celia's fever had cooled and she was sleeping more easily. Kayln was just leaving Celia's room to go to her own for a much-needed rest when Alice appeared in front of her. "Lord Hawkhurst has come," she said without preamble.

"Saints in heaven!" Kayln put her hand to her forehead and leaned against the stone wall. She was of little mind to deal with his lordship this day. After nursing Celia for days, she knew that she was feeling vulnerable and overwhelmed by her responsibilities, wishing she did not have to face every crisis alone. Though what that had to do with Hawk she wasn't prepared to ask herself. She pulled herself upright and squared her shoulders. "How long has he been here?"

"For well over an hour, Lady Kayln," Alice answered.

"Have you told him of Celia's illness?"

"I have. He seemed very concerned for her well-being and wanted to see her, but I told him she was being seen to."

Kayln smoothed the front of her gown, which was stained from nursing her sister. "I should go to him now."

"No, you go up to your chamber and place yourself into the nice bath I've had readied for you." Alice patted the younger woman's arm. "I'll go and inform his lordship of how Celia is doing."

"But . . ." Kayln hesitated to keep Hawk waiting any longer. He was genuinely fond of the girl and must certainly be worried.

"There'll be no 'buts' about it. You do as I say and by the time you have finished, your dinner will be waiting."

Overcome at the care for her, Kayln placed her hand over Alice's. Suddenly she realized she was finally able to allow someone else to see to her, knowing as she did that it was taking nothing away from her ability to command respect and obedience. She said only, "Thank you, Alice. I don't know what I would ever do without you." Surely she would feel much more capable of dealing with Hawk after a hot bath.

"I but do my duties," Alice insisted gruffly, but Kayln

could tell that the older woman was pleased by the praise. She felt a momentary regret that she had not taken more opportunities to allow Alice to mother her in their years together. Kayln vowed to do so in the future.

As she made her way to her chamber, she realized that this was surely one time when she would not even try to appeal to Hawk. She would much rather he ended this visit with as little contact between them as possible. Her response to Alice showed that she was feeling vulnerable after Celia's illness. And while it might serve her well to be more vulnerable with those she loved, she could not risk exposing such weakness to Hawk.

When Kayln entered the hall the meal had already begun. It was her own fault she was late because she had lingered until the water grew cold in her bath. She was honest enough to admit, at least to herself, that she dreaded seeing Hawk on this day as she would not have dreaded a siege.

Just as she thought this, her eyes came to rest on the very man who was so much in her thoughts. He was not seated at the high table, but pacing back and forth in front of the blazing fire.

Forcing down her own self-doubt, Kayln went to him, feeling compassion for the worried frown that creased his brow. "Hawk," she said softly in deference to his obvious agitation.

He turned and took her hands in his. "How does she?" His golden eyes searched her face for any sign that might tell him how his little sister-by-marriage fared.

"The fever has broken, thankfully," Kayln told him.

"Thank God in His heaven." He closed his eyes, his shoulders slumping in relief. "The nurse, Alice, told me as much, but I needed to hear it from your own lips."

"Celia will recover," Kayln stated firmly as though she could make this true by will alone. But even as she did so, Kayln was moved by the obvious depth of his love for her sister. What would it feel like to be the recipient of Hawk's care and concern? It was not likely that she was ever to discover the answer to the question. But that, she reminded herself, was just the way she wanted things.

Hawk was silent for a such a long time that Kayln looked

at him nervously, fearing that he might be able to somehow read her thoughts. His question quieted her on that account. "What of the babe?"

She was able to smile with some confidence. "If the force of its movements are any gauge, then the child will be born hearty and whole. He never stopped in his thrashing even through the worst of it."

"Then we must be even more grateful to the Lord for His mercy." He stroked the back of her hand with gentle fingers, causing a tingle of awareness to travel up her arm.

Kayln could not draw her hand back. Letting him hold it felt so good, so intimate and reassuring. She swayed.

Quick to see her weakness, Hawk slid his arm along her shoulders and drew her to his side. "You are exhausted. You should not have come down."

" 'Tis only hunger." Kayln laughed shakily, putting her hand to her head. Determinedly she told herself the depth of her reaction was caused by fatigue, coupled with the fact that she had not eaten that day. "I fear I am starved enough to eat a whole roast boar."

"Then come at once," he insisted. He led her to her place at the table, not taking his supporting arm from her for a moment. Kayln could not explain even to herself why she was allowing him to take charge like this. She must be tired indeed.

Quickly, Hawk saw that her trencher was heaped high with venison in garlic sauce, savory stew, roast pigeon, and fresh-baked bread. "Eat!" he commanded.

With relish, Kayln did what he told her, though she knew she could never finish so much food in three days. Sometime later, she sat back, replete, and stared in surprise at the almost empty trencher before her.

"Aren't you going to finish?" Hawk asked with a frown of continued concern.

Still Kayln could not bring herself to tell him that she was perfectly capable of seeing to her own needs. She put her hand to her stomach, knowing that any discomfort there was caused more by her own inability to keep the lines between them clearly defined than by having eaten too much. But she said only, "I fear I am nigh unto bursting now. Never did I think I could consume so much."

Their eyes met and held, a jolt of awareness passing between them. Kayln found herself unable to keep from saying what was really in her thoughts. "What does this mean, Hawk? Why are you being so kind and considerate after the way you have been so cool these past weeks?"

Hawk only stared at her for a time, then said, "For now, until Celia is deemed completely well, I am willing to call a Pax Dei." He stopped as he saw the tension that thinned Kayln's lips, and wanted desperately to kiss it away. But he couldn't allow himself to do that. He knew he'd made her angry again by telling her this. But he was only being honest, wasn't he? He had instigated this peace with her because of her sister's illness.

It had nothing to do with the ache he'd felt in his chest at seeing how tired and lonely she appeared. Who better than he should know that Kayln really needed no one to look after her?

It was some time before she took a deep breath and nodded slowly, trying not to let herself feel the unexplained disappointment inside her. Of course he was acting out of their mutual worry for Celia. What other reason could he have for being so kind and gentle with her? "A sensible notion, for Celia's sake," she answered as matter-of-factly as possible.

"I am glad that we can come together over this situation if no other." He smiled down at her, his teeth white against his face, which was permanently tanned from exposure to the elements. As Kayln looked up at him, she could have sworn she saw something that looked like chagrin in his gaze, but she knew that could not be.

With as much enthusiasm as she could muster, Kayln returned his smile.

He pushed the remains of his own meal away with a tired sigh. After a moment he turned to her and said, "May I see my little sister now?"

"Of course," Kayln told him, rising when he did.

She led the way to her sister's chamber, very conscious of the man behind her. She wondered how long their truce would last.

Alice was with Celia, who was sitting up in bed. The nurse steadied a bowl which rested on the great mound of Celia's belly while she took some soup. Heartened by this sight, Kayln turned to Hawk. ''As I said, she is much improved.''

On seeing Hawk, Celia smiled wanly and held out her hand. The man went to stand at her other side. Hawk took the small white hand, which disappeared in his large one. Bending forward, he kissed her cheek. ''How are you, little one?''

''Much better,'' she told him with forced brightness. ''Have you a letter from Philip?''

''No, minx, not today. Has he not written to you?''

The light went out of her eyes at Hawk's words, and she leaned back among the pillows wearily. ''I miss him so very much. Do you not think that he might come to me?''

Sighing, Alice picked up the bowl and stepped back.

''Celia, you received a letter only two days ago,'' Kayln said, going to her sister's side and smoothing the fair hair back from her brow. ''Philip will be coming home at Christmas.'' She was aware of Hawk watching her and wondered at his intense scrutiny. She forced herself not to turn to him, but to continue smoothing her sister's brow.

''I cannot wait for three more weeks,'' Celia said. ''What if he is not here before the babe comes?'' She grabbed Kayln's hand. ''I am frightened. I do not want to go through this without him.''

''Now, don't get yourself into a fit,'' Alice instructed, shaking a long bony finger. ''There's been many a woman who has birthed her child without her man present. In fact, 'tis best. There's nothing to be done by him and he only frets.'' As Alice spoke, Kayln wondered how Hawk would react to the birth of his own child. Knowing how badly Hawk desired sons and how obstinate he could be when it suited him, she doubted he would absent himself at such a time. Surely his presence would be a comfort to the woman who loved him. She stopped herself then, wondering from whence such a mad thought had come. Hawk would drive the unfortunate woman to distraction. Quickly she dismissed such thoughts, centering her attention on Celia.

''Leave me be,'' Celia cried. ''I won't listen to your silly opinions. I want my husband.''

Alice crossed her arms in front of her. ''It is obvious how much my thoughts are valued in this keep.'' Her thin nose quivered as she fidgeted in agitation, making her wimple flutter about her head.

"You will apologize this instant," Kayln told her sister. "Alice has barely slept these past two days while you were ill and then you speak to her so cruelly." It was one thing for Celia to reject Kayln's every effort to comfort her, but the nurse had ever been close to her.

Kayln felt Alice's grateful hand on her shoulder, and reached up to pat it gently. Again she felt Hawk's careful attention on her, and wondered what she had done.

To her surprise she heard Hawk echoing her own sentiments. "Really, Celia," he told her gently but firmly, "you must have a care for those who love you. Both Alice and Kayln have driven themselves to exhaustion to see you well."

"I'm sorry, Kayln, Alice." Celia burst into tears. "It is just that I want Philip so desperately."

Still surprised and unaccountably moved at hearing Hawk defend her, Kayln watched as he reached out and turned Celia around so that she was leaning back against him as he settled himself on the edge of the bed. "Now, don't cry. The time will pass soon enough and then you'll wonder what all the fuss was about," he told Celia, clearly unaware of her sister's reaction. Kayln assured herself that he had only taken her part because of their truce, but the glow of pleasure did not fade.

Celia leaned against him and sobbed until she was limp.

Kayln felt a tightness in her stomach. This was her sister, and she was helpless to cheer her. Kayln felt more than a little sympathy for the young woman about to give birth to her first child with her husband so far from her. But it was Hawk who was able to comfort and soothe her. Kayln's gaze ran over his profile. He seemed so genuine in his attentions toward Celia. Would he be so gentle with her if she gave him an opportunity? The question was both appealing and terrifying, for how would she ever resist such a tender Hawk? But that, she reminded herself, was an eventuality that need not concern her. He'd never even hinted at having such feelings for her.

She shook her head. There was no way she could allow herself to even think such things. Kayln must remember that she wanted nothing of Hawk but his body. The threat of her completely losing herself in him was too great.

As if sensing her gaze on him, Hawk glanced up and said, "She has gone to sleep. The little mite was all worn out." His eyes were soft with care.

Almost against her will, Kayln continued to watch as Hawk laid the girl carefully back onto the pillows and rose. On first glance Hawk appeared to be a battle-hardened warrior, iron to the very core. But deep inside this huge imposing man was an astounding well of gentleness. And though it had never been directed toward her, Kayln could no longer keep herself from seeing its authenticity.

But the realization only galled her. Why was he so only with others? Kayln he treated as an adversary. Oh, he had offered his Pax Dei, but it was only that. Again she told herself it was best that Hawk did not turn that daunting tenderness upon her. Just thinking about it made strange feelings of longing rise up in her breast that could not be explained by the ever-constant smoldering of her desire for him.

Forcefully she reminded herself that she was simply tired and vulnerable because of her concern for Celia. Kayln tried not to remember how his defense of her to Celia had warmed her.

Clearly it would be well if Hawk were to be on his way. She gestured to Hawk, and he rose to follow as she left the chamber. She led him back to the hall. She was just trying to form a polite but firm dismissal in her mind when Alice joined them.

The nurse greeted Hawk effusively, causing Kayln to frown. Hawk viewed Kayln with a look of puzzlement in his eyes as if he sensed her resentment, but could not fathom its source.

Kayln stared back with undisguised vexation.

Drawing himself up, Hawk fetched her a mocking bow. "I am loath to end this pleasant evening, Lady D'Arcy, but I must return to Clamdon. The hour grows late."

"Traveling on this night might prove unwise," Alice said, causing them both to look at her as if they had forgotten she was there. She folded her hands in front of herself, watching them with speculation.

"How so?" Kayln asked.

"A blizzard has come up. A man would be doing well to see the neck of his horse in front of him." Alice smiled.

Kayln stared at her in consternation. "Surely the weather cannot have worsened so quickly." It was growing more and more important for her that Hawk leave Aimsley this night.

Hawk was scowling darkly. "You will not be offended if I look for myself." He inclined his head in a polite nod and strode from the hall without waiting for a reply.

In a very short time he returned to the waiting women. "Unfortunately," he said to Kayln with thin lips, "your woman speaks true. To ride out now would be foolish. It would be too easy for a man and his mount to be lost in such weather. I cannot put Mac to such risk."

Alice turned to Kayln. "I will have a room readied."

Kayln could only stare from one to the other of them for a moment, fighting a rising feeling of unexplained panic. Then, at the back of her mind, she knew what was causing the deep distress she felt at having Hawk sleep at Aimsley. Night was the hardest time for her. In the long darkness before dawn she most yearned for the touch of his body against hers. When she had thought of sharing her bed with Hawk, she had thought to keep it a physical matter, with no connection to her true inner self. That Kayln would hold safe within her.

But tonight she was tired, worn out with nursing Celia and trying to find ways to show she cared.

She had just seen Hawk with Celia, and knew how adept he was at offering comfort. Deep inside her, Kayln knew how vulnerable she was to his gentleness on this night, how she longed to allow herself the refuge of his strength.

She searched her mind desperately for an answer, a way out. Kayln wanted Hawk, yes, but not like this.

And she knew that if he should spend the night at Aimsley, he would come to her. It was there in the golden depths of his eyes in spite of the irritation he showed in answer to her near-rudeness. He would not resist such temptation.

But there was nothing to be done. She could not send him out now. Slowly, she bowed her head in agreement. "Aye, have a room readied."

Kayln did not notice when Alice left them. All her attention was focused on the man nearby. His mastery, his self-confidence, his incredible strength both physical and emotional drew her like the sun drew the wheat from the earth.

"I did not plan for this to happen," Hawk told her, taking a step closer to her. Against her own volition her gaze was pulled to his.

"I know," she whispered, unable to break the contact.

"It is divine intervention," he said with a touch of irony. "We are meant to be together." It seemed to be directed as much to himself as to her.

"Hawk." She held out her hand as if to keep him away when he took another step toward her.

"You desired this very thing," he reminded her. She could feel the heat of his body from where he stood. She caught his fresh-breeze scent, and knew a tightness in her chest that kept her from breathing.

"Not this night," she pleaded. "I ask you to stay away."

"We both know what will happen."

"No!" she cried, and ran from him to her tower, shutting herself inside with finality.

Hawk watched her go with a trace of unexpected sadness. When he'd come to Aimsley he'd neither expected nor even considered that he might feel as he did at this moment.

Over the last few weeks Kayln's attempts to entice him had weakened him to the point of breaking on more than one occasion. She was an incredibly beautiful and enticing woman. But he had refused to stay away because of it.

He was bound to make certain all was well with Celia for the sake of his brother and his own honor. Never again would he shirk a family duty as he had in staying away so long after his parents died.

And he had resisted her, though it took every ounce of his will to do so.

Yet it was tonight, when she looked exhausted and worn out from caring for her younger sister, when he felt drawn to her as never before. He'd seen her gentleness with Celia, watched as she allowed Alice to touch her without the usual signs of withdrawal. Clearly, somewhere along the way Kayln had changed, softened. But whether that change could include anyone other than her sister and the nurse, Hawk would not even hazard a guess.

He only knew that he ached for her with a new, even greater

intensity, longed to hold her in his arms. He could think of little save burying himself in her womanly softness, and did not believe that any power on earth could keep him from doing so this night. Only a rejection of him by Kayln could stop what he desired so intently.

Why, when she had openly admitted her intention of sharing her bed with him, did she make the pretense of telling him she did not want him now? It was especially confusing when he could see that she did still want him. In spite of what she had said moments ago, he knew she wished for him to come to her. And knowing that made it nearly impossible for him to stay away.

It was hopeless. Kayln could not go to sleep. She couldn't stop tossing and turning, so finally she abandoned the pretense and got up from the bed. The fire was the only light in the chamber, casting a warm glow on everything it touched.

Although she wore nothing but a sheer night rail, the room seemed too close and perspiration beaded on her brow. Thinking to cool herself, Kayln opened the window and leaned her head against the sill.

The snow was still falling, but not as heavily as it had been earlier. She put out her hand to capture one of the delicate flakes. As soon as it touched the warmth of her palm it melted away, just as her burgeoning trust in Hawk had gone on that day when she heard him speaking of her so deprecatingly to the earl. She was not a silly girl who did not understand that a man might make a mistake. In fact, she might have forgiven him that in time, but for the fact that he had not seemed to vary in his thinking toward her since. In spite of his clear ability to give affection, Hawk was still a man who would wish to control and dominate the woman in his life. Kayln could not accept that for herself. She must be respected as well as loved.

That was why she could not give in to this yearning inside her, this need to be held and cared for. Besides, she reminded herself, Hawk had never intimated that he did care for her. And without love to soften Hawk's obvious need to dominate, there could be no hope of a relationship that would make her feel whole and strong.

Surely he would heed her pleas to stay away.

Shaking her head with a sigh, Kayln moved away from the window, her feet taking her on an endless journey from one side of the room to the other and back. Stopping beside the fire, she stared into the flames as if she could find some answer to her problems.

And then, without knowing why, she turned. There, standing just inside the window, was Hawk. She did not know how he had come, but that place inside herself where she could not deny her innermost longings was filled with a joy so intense it rocked her.

The pounding of her heart was so loud that she could no longer hear or heed her own doubts. All she could do was feel. She knew she would not deny him or herself.

"How have you come?" she asked, her throat dry, aware that she did no more than prolong the moment of their coming together.

"I lowered a rope from the battlements," he answered softly. "I will stay."

Kayln could only look at the compelling features of his face, which seemed sharper in the flickering light from the fire. "You could have fallen to your death."

"Perhaps." He shrugged, then took a step into the room. "I knew I would not gain entrance though your door." Hawk held out his hand as he moved slowly toward her, stopping when he stood close enough to touch her. She knew he waited for her to make the next move.

Swallowing to moisten her dry mouth, Kayln put her hand in his, to be drawn into his strong arms. They enfolded her as her body quickened to the feel of his against her.

"You are so beautiful," he whispered. "I thought I would cry your loveliness to the world when I came through that window and saw you standing here with every perfect curve outlined against the flames."

Kayln blushed, burying her face in his chest, but she was not ashamed. His words flowed like honey over her heightened senses.

His hand closed around her chin and he lifted her face so that he could see her. "You are a disease in my blood, one for which I hope there is no cure. It eats at me until I can think only of you."

"Hawk." She reached out to touch his cheek.

His lips came down on hers in a kiss that was as fierce as the storm that had kept him there. She returned his passion in full measure.

Mere moments later they fell naked upon her bed. Kayln was aching with need, arching to him. It had been so long and her body cried out for fulfillment.

But Hawk would not have it that way. "Let me love you," he whispered, the words sweet from his tongue. His hands traced a pattern of delight over her heated flesh, and he cherished her breasts with his tender mouth.

She'd been so long alone, and very lonely.

Kayln felt herself falling, giving in to the empathy in his golden gaze. She had no will to resist the intensity with which he possessed her—his sheer commanding strength. Inside the soft womanly core of her a voice cried silently, "Take me."

When he entered her it was slowly, his eyes staring into hers, in the rosy glow of the firelight. Hawk quested for and found that place inside her that was all woman—all giving.

She had feared it would be like this between them, but she was powerless to stop the rush of emotions his tenderness drew from her. As he moved inside her, Kayln knew this was no mere joining of flesh. It was a joyful and absolute melding, on her part as well as his.

He wanted and elicited her complete surrender, drawing her very soul from hiding as she rose up to meet him.

He pleasured her, comforted her, filled her to the depths of her being, and she cried out with the force of her emotions as the tide broke inside her. As the ripples quieted and she settled into the safe haven of his embrace, she sobbed aloud at the release of her long-pent-up emotions. And he whispered soothing words as he smoothed his hands over the curves of her body.

If only for this moment, Kayln gave herself up to the potency of his embrace. She was unwilling to question the depth of safety and happiness she found there.

Tomorrow must answer for itself.

Chapter Fifteen

Kayln was awakened early by an insistent pounding.

She groaned, stretching, then stopped as her hand came into contact with warm solid flesh. She gasped in dismay.

Jerking upright in bed, Kayln pulled the covers close under her chin. Filtered sunlight was coming in the window through which Hawk had entered the previous night. The pounding came again.

Her gaze flew to the man at her side. He was awake and watching her, his golden eyes full of vexation. Obviously he was not happy about what they had done.

Kayln did her best to stifle the blush that stole over her cheeks, but could not. Last night she had given herself to him completely, holding back no part of herself, and his reaction devastated her. Was last night his revenge for her attempts to gain some physical power over him, to show her what could have been had he cared for her? To cover her humiliation Kayln spoke with more heat than she might have. ''Someone is knocking.''

Hawk's only reaction was a tight smile as he placed both hands behind his head, making himself more comfortable. He wasn't about to let her see how disappointed he was by her reaction at waking in the same bed as he. He told himself he should not be surprised at her displeasure, yet he could not quite suppress his annoyance after the way she had given herself to him so completely the night before. But what could he do? Kayln was Kayln and any unhappiness he was feeling was his own fault, for he had known that a relationship with her would be difficult at best.

''You must leave, now,'' she said.

''By the same method I entered?'' He looked to the window. ''It is full light and someone would surely see me.''

The fact that his point was well taken did nothing to dampen Kayln's desperation. "You cannot be found here," she cried.

"Would you have me hide under the bed?" His black brows rose in question, disappearing under the thatch of black hair on his forehead.

"Yes . . . no. I don't know." Her teeth worried her full lower lip.

Hawk pulled her down to him. "Every time you do that I want to kiss you," he murmured, and he proceeded to do just that.

Kayln struggled against him and he released her. Even though she knew he was simply demonstrating his mastery over her, his kiss darkened her eyes and made her breath come faster. But her own reaction only served to irritate her further.

"Oh, you are insufferable," she growled as she leaped from the bed, pulling the coverlet with her.

Hawk grimaced, but did not reply.

Kayln jumped at another thump on the door. "Dear Lord," Kayln hissed to the man who lounged so nonchalantly in the bed. "Do something."

"There is nothing I can do." He spread his large hands wide. "We are found out. You should have foreseen just such an eventuality when you decided we would be lovers, when you tormented me with your beauty time after time." There was no mistaking the resentment in his eyes, and she told herself she had guessed rightly in thinking he'd done this to repay her.

And she had fallen right into his plans, more fool she. But she did not have to let others know how silly she had been to think she could gain the upper hand with this enervating man.

"We are not found out," she said to herself. Kayln opened the door, being careful to block the opening. "Why have you awakened me at such an hour?"

Alice stood there. Kayln knew immediately when she saw the nurse was still wearing her bedrobe that something was wrong. Alice never went about the keep in such attire. Despite her growing unease, Kayln moved, effectively forcing Alice back into the solar. Quickly she closed the door behind herself.

"What is wrong?" Kayln asked the nurse, who was now wringing her hands.

"It's Celia. She is not in her chambers."

A *tisk* of irritation escaped from Kayln's lips. Of all mornings, must the girl pick this one to scare Alice this way? "She should not be out of bed so early after her illness," Kayln said, "but at least we can take this as a sign that she is much improved."

"You don't understand, Lady Kayln." Alice blinked back tears.

Thinking that she must get Alice out of her rooms so that Hawk could leave, Kayln took the nurse's arm. "We will search the keep for her."

"She is not in the keep."

"That ridiculous child," Kayln cried in frustration, finally realizing why Alice was so distraught. "Can she not tell that it is full winter outside?"

"Why was someone not set to watch her?" said a male voice from behind them. Hawk stood in the open bedroom door, black hair tousled, attired in nothing save his hose and tunic.

Alice's eyes swung to Hawk's face and her mouth dropped open in utter shock.

Kayln whirled around, her golden hair swirling about her, and stomped her feet. "Now you have done it."

"Don't be silly, Kayln. Your sister has wandered off before she can possibly be fully recovered from her illness and you worry about our causing a scandal. Alice here"—he motioned toward the woman who was still standing there as if struck dumb—"does not care a jot what we do. She is too much concerned for Celia. As we should be. Is that not right, Alice?"

Finally, Alice found her tongue. "Yes, my lord," she answered him. But Kayln could not mistake the fact that Alice was very much interested in what had occurred between herself and Hawk. The nurse's eyes nearly burned holes through her mistress.

Kayln knew she could not allow herself to care what Alice thought about this now. Reluctantly she found herself agreeing with Hawk. Celia was their real concern.

As if the matter were settled, Hawk turned to Kayln. "We must send someone to look in her usual haunts."

"I have already done that, my lord," Alice replied. "I sent two men." At her words Kayln began to experience a deeper feeling of dread. "Both returned without seeing any sign of the girl."

"Has anyone searched her room for a note?" Hawk asked.

"No," Alice replied. "I had not thought to."

"Do so now, and quickly," Hawk ordered.

"Wait." Kayln raised her hands to halt the woman. "We will not waste time on this. Searchers must be organized and sent out."

"Do as I said," Hawk insisted with the ring of absolute authority in his tone. Without another word to her mistress, Alice hurried to do as he had commanded.

Kayln moved to follow her, rage beginning to surge with in her at the way Hawk had countermanded her order. She would show him that what had happened between them last night did not give him any power over her. She meant to see that her instructions were carried out.

"Kayln." Hawk took her shoulders in his strong fingers. His thumb rubbed over the naked curve of her collar bone. "Would you go as you are?"

Kayln looked down at herself and let out a growl of frustration. She could not go to the hall with nothing to cover her but a blanket. She wrenched away from him to return to her bedchamber. Running to her chest, Kayln threw open the lid and pulled the top garment out. Without paying any heed to the fact that Hawk had followed her, she dropped the coverlet and pulled the cote over her head.

As she was searching for a tunic, Hawk drew on his cote and boots. "I can't help thinking," he said. "Yesternight your sister was very distressed, calling for Phillip and crying because he could not come to her."

For a moment, Kayln ignored him. She was too busy trying to dress herself so she could go downstairs and show this man who was really in charge at Aimsley. Then, slowly, the words began to penetrate.

Kayln swung around to face him, all thought of her own unhappiness banished from her mind. "You don't think she has tried to go to Norfolk?" Her face mirrored the horror that was growing in her heart. "That is two days' travel from here.

She would never make it alone in her condition."

"I believe that if you were to search the stables you would find a horse missing."

"Dear God." Her legs were shaking so badly, Kayln sank down on top of a chest to keep from falling.

"It is my hope that she has left a note," Hawk said. "It would make finding her much easier."

At that moment, Alice appeared in the doorway. In her hand was a roll of parchment. Kayln ran to her, and Alice put the missive in Kayln's outstretched hand.

With quivering fingers, Kayln smoothed out the roll so that it could be read. Hurriedly, her eyes scanned what was written. Then she turned to Hawk. "You were right. She has gone to Norwich. We must go after her."

"Have our horses saddled immediately," Kayln told Alice. "There is no time to lose." She would not remain behind. For Celia's sake Kayln could set aside her rage at Hawk. Their love for the girl was the one thing they had in common. So worried was Kayln that she barely felt the twinge of pain the thought brought.

Hawk made no comment about the fact that she would accompany him. He seemed to sense her need to help in locating Celia, for he only nodded. He was already focusing on what must be done. "We will send out several parties. She may not have taken the road, or might even have become lost."

"Yes, you are right," Kayln answered evenly, though her heart twisted at the thought of her sister lost and alone in the forest with all its dangers. "See that it is done." But Alice was already gone.

The snow was deep, and they were forced to pick their way carefully over the ground to keep from floundering in the drifts. Even the trees were completely blanketed in white.

Just when Kayln was beginning to think there was no hope, Hawk spotted something just inside the trees and went to investigate. It was a patch of cloth.

Kayln recognized the purple velvet immediately. It was torn from Celia's favorite cloak, the one with the sable lining.

They took to the trees.

When it started getting dark, Kayln could not stop the flow

of terrifying thoughts that went through her mind. With nothing to break the silence except the soft sound of the horses' hooves sliding through the thin crust that had formed on top of the snow, Kayln felt she would grow mad with her imaginings. Even her unhappiness at the way Hawk had again made a fool of her was as nothing compared to her terror at what might have befallen Celia.

Hawk rode on ahead of her, saying nothing, his shoulders set with determination.

"What are we to do if we cannot find her?" Kayln asked into the stillness. The crisp winter air clearly carried her words to Hawk.

"We will find her," he answered, turning slightly on his horse so Kayln was able to see the white vapor of his breath as he spoke. He sounded so very sure. She wished some of his confidence would fall on her.

She lifted her shoulders higher, determined that she would believe as Hawk did. This was one instance where she could lean on his strength. It was the only way to keep her sanity.

Only an hour later, they found the horse. The mare was lying on its side in the snow. Occasionally it thrashed about as if in pain.

Hawk drew up close to the horse and dismounted. After running experienced fingers over it, Hawk looked up to Kayln. "The mare has broken its leg."

In her fear for Celia, Kayln listened with horror. "Where could she be? How far can Celia go on foot? She is pregnant, has been ill, and may have been injured when her horse was."

"Evidently, Celia cannot be too seriously injured or she would not have been able to walk away," Hawk told her evenly. He went around to his saddle and drew his sword.

Kayln looked away as he approached the injured animal, and only turned back when Hawk spoke from atop his horse. "We will go on. Now that she is on foot, Celia may have left more signs for us to follow."

After a time, the hazy sky lowered until it was heavy around them and a light snow began to fall. This would make it even harder to see any tracks Celia might have left.

Kayln had no idea how far they had come or how late it might be. They had been traveling for hours in the dark, and her burning eyes told her that it was well past her usual hour of rest.

Finally Hawk dismounted and led his horse. "God's teeth," he cursed aloud, "if only the snow would stop. It is covering any traces she might have left."

"Do you think we are far behind her?" Kayln asked.

"I don't believe so," Hawk answered without turning around. He seemed completely indifferent to her, totally enmeshed in finding Celia. And that was as it should be, she told herself. "I am beginning to find deeper prints," he said. "We don't know when Celia left Aimsley last night, but we do know that she passed through this area sometime this afternoon, as it was snowing during the morning."

"She must be terribly frightened." Kayln peered around them. In the darkness the trees appeared threatening, offering cover for heaven knows what sort of menace. Realizing her back was aching terribly, she slipped from her own mare. With fingers that shook from the cold, she massaged her stiff backside.

She looked up as Hawk made a sound of triumph. One moment she could see the dark outline that told her he was ahead of her. The next he was gone.

Kayln blinked rapidly, thinking that her eyes were playing tricks on her. She reached down, took up a handful of snow and rubbed it over her eyes. When she opened them again he was still gone.

Then she heard, "Kayln."

The hair on the back of her neck prickled. His voice sounded as if it came from directly in front of her, yet she could see nothing. "Where have you gone?"

"I am just ahead of you. I have found her."

"Where?" she gasped, the word ringing with jubilation.

"I'll lean out so that you can see me," Hawk answered.

Squinting into the darkness, Kayln saw first the outline of Hawk's head. Then his shoulders emerged from the hillside.

"A cave," she cried, scrambling forward. A moment later, Kayln had passed through the opening. To her surprise the cave was quite large. There was room to enter standing if one bent forward, and more than adequate space to stand inside. It smelled old, like something long dead, but it was dry and protected from the elements. She did not know what sense of survival had brought Celia here, but Kayln felt that God must have indeed protected her as she had prayed for Him to.

From just inside the door, Kayln could hear the soft sound of her sister crying. She hurried toward the sound, nearly falling as she stumbled over what felt like the root of a tree in the dark.

"Celia," she said, as her hand inadvertently touched the solid shape of Hawk's shoulder. She drew it back quickly.

"I'm here, Kayln." The answer was followed by a groan of pain.

"Are you injured?" Kayln asked, dropping to her knees and feeling for her sister with her hands. She came into contact with the velvet of her sister's cloak, and Kayln hurriedly began to run her hands over Celia.

"Celia has not hurt herself," Hawk said, just as Kayln's questing led her fingers to Celia's swollen belly. It was hard to the touch and seemed to squeeze inward upon itself as Kayln's hands rested upon it.

"Dear heaven." Kayln looked to Hawk, though she could not see him in the dark.

"The child comes," he stated.

"It cannot be born here," Kayln cried.

"In this one matter I believe you have no control," Hawk told her, his voice full of wry amusement. "The babe does not care that this moment is inconvenient."

"What will we do?" Kayln could not take her hands away from her sister's stomach, even as she felt the contraction ease and heard Celia's moan of relief. She sat there as though paralyzed.

"I will get a fire going." Hawk stood. "At least then we will have some light."

Kayln could hear the scuffing of his feet as he left the cave, and she wanted to call him back. A wolf howled somewhere in the night, and Kayln gave a start. But when she felt Celia begin to tremble beside her, some of her own fear eased in her concern for her sister.

"I am so frightened," Celia said, sobbing softly.

Licking her lips to moisten their dryness, Kayln said, "There is no need. Everything will be fine. Hawk has gone to get some wood and soon we will have a nice cheery fire." To her surprise, her voice was confident enough to mask her own trepidation. She felt for Celia's hand in the darkness, and held the leaf-dry fingers in her own.

"I'm sorry, Kayln. This is all my fault. I promised Philip I would look after the baby and now I have put him in danger. I should have stayed at Aimsley, but I miss Philip so that I fear I shall die without him."

If the situation were not so serious, Kayln would have chuckled at the exaggeration of the statement. "You mustn't think of that now. You must put all your energy into making sure the babe is born hearty and hale. That is what Philip would want of you."

"Ohhh." Celia arched her back as another pain took her.

Kayln held tightly to her small hand and waited for the agony to pass. This contraction had come very quickly upon the last.

When Celia let out a breath and eased again, Kayln asked, "How long have the pains been coming?"

"Since early in the day," came the dread answer. "At first I thought 'twas nothing but a stomach ailment. This afternoon I wondered if it could be the child. Even then I thought I could get to Phillip before it arrived. It was when the horse broke its leg in a hole that I knew I would not get there. I could not go so far on foot."

Kayln had to suppress an urge to lecture. How could Celia have been so foolish as to put herself in such a position?

She was rewarded for her forbearance when Celia spoke. "I'm so glad you came, Kayln. I know that you will make it right."

Kayln said nothing, only held her sister's hand tightly as another pain came upon her. Hot tears stung Kayln's eyes. She loved Celia so dearly, though she wasn't sure she could fulfill her sister's faith in her.

It was so unfair. Celia was just a girl, forced to grow up too quickly. As Kayln had been. Was Celia up to the task of delivering a baby in a dark, dingy cave?

She heard a rustling at the entrance to the cave. "Hawk?" Her voice was laced with agitation.

"It's all right, Kayln. It is I," he answered soothingly.

"There is naught to worry about. Everything will be fine." She knew then that she could not do this without him, needed his strength to see them through. She refused to even allow herself to wonder what that might mean.

"Yes," she said aloud, patting Celia's hand as the grip loosened, "everything will be fine."

Turning to the mouth of the cave, Kayln could see the outline of the tall broad-shouldered man. His silhouette disappeared as he crouched down to build the fire, but she continued to take comfort from his presence.

In no time, a small blaze was going, though Hawk had to keep blowing on it because the wood was wet. Looking about in the dim, though welcome, light of the little blaze, Kayln could see what looked to be scraps of wood lying about the floor of the cave.

"I should help Hawk with the fire," she told Celia. "Will you be all right?"

Kayln could make out very little of her sister's face, but her blue eyes were wide and damp in the weak glow that illuminated the cavern. Celia nodded. "Go on, then. Don't worry about me. I will rest." She closed her eyes. The words would have been more believable had not another contraction caused the girl to suck in her breath and clench her hands into tight fists.

Quickly, Kayln moved to help Hawk. They needed to get the fire going, and he could not leave it or the feeble blaze would cease burning all together.

She wondered if possibly some of the roots on the floor might be loose enough to pull up. The first one Kayln grabbed proved to be stubbornly attached. Giving a vicious tug in frustration, Kayln found herself sitting on the ground with the root in her hand. She got up and began again. On closer inspection she found that some were old and dried, so they were not too difficult to remove.

Having gathered an armload, she took them to Hawk, who only muttered a hasty thanks. She watched as he placed them on the fire. With a little coaxing the flames began to lick at the wood, and it was soon burning more brightly.

When at last he felt that he could take his concentration from what he was doing, Hawk stood beside Kayln and grimaced. ''All will be well if we see this through, you and I.''

In spite of everything, Kayln blushed with pleasure that he was acknowledging her value, but made no reply. She told herself they must think of Celia and the babe.

Hawk had brought both saddlebags from their horses. She watched as he reached down and picked up the cooking pot that Alice had included in their supplies.

Kayln took the pot, which was already full of clean snow. ''The fact that water is needed in great abundance is one of the few things I know of birthing.'' She set the pot upon the fire, her optimism that all would be well fading as she heard her sister moan.

''What do we do next?'' she whispered, looking to Hawk with worried eyes.

''I have never delivered a child before.'' Hawk spoke in a low tone, but his manner was straightforward. ''But I have helped a mare to deliver a foal. In that case nature does most of the work and all that needs be done is stand by to take the glory.''

Kayln felt herself beginning to relax. No matter that they had their differences, no matter what sadness tomorrow might bring, she knew that in this instance Hawk's confidence would see them through. He loved Celia too well to see harm come to her.

Trusting in his judgment completely in this matter, Kayln nodded.

Chapter Sixteen

As it turned out, what Hawk had told her proved to be overly optimistic.

Kayln feared the night would never end. One scream after another tore from Celia's lips as she met each wave of pain. More than once Kayln stopped herself from taking out her own frustration on Hawk, who remained calm and steadfast through the whole ordeal. She held her tongue for Celia's sake as he repeatedly insisted that all was as it should be.

Both Hawk and Kayln held Celia's hands, bathed her damp forehead, and encouraged her, although Kayln felt far from certain of her own words. Then, in the early morning, just as dawn was beginning to spread its silver fingers over the sparkling snow, their nephew was finally born, screaming his protest at leaving his mother's womb.

Kayln held the slippery wet infant in her hands and cried for joy.

"A true Hawkhurst," Hawk shouted, "ready to make his opinions known." Hawk's eyes were suspiciously damp too, and he kissed his sister-in-law's cheek with a loud smack. Then he moved to Kayln and placed a hearty kiss on her full lips. So full of happiness was she that she did not even question the motive for that kiss, understanding that in spite of his earlier show of assurance Hawk was as overjoyed as she to see the babe's safe arrival.

"Is he well?" Celia asked before Kayln could even tell her the sex of the child.

"Don't you want to know if it is indeed a male?" Kayln laughed with giddy relief, all her fears having evaporated the moment he was born.

"I have given birth to a son," her sister insisted with utter conviction. Then she repeated, "Is he well?"

"He is perfect." Kayln held the baby up for her sister to inspect. "You have done beautifully. Now," she directed, wrapping her cloak around the squirming slip of humankind, "I want you to rest."

With a sigh of contentment, Celia lay back and closed her eyes. In only a moment, her breathing grew regular and she slept.

It was no wonder, Kayln thought, looking down at the red wrinkled face of the little boy in her arms. She could not help but be exhausted.

Kayln moved closer to the fire to help keep the little fellow warm. Hawk stood beside her. He too looked down at the bundle in her arms.

Recalling the difficulty with which this small being had been brought into the world, she peered up at Hawk with an arched brow. " 'Twas hardly as simple as you claimed it would be."

Hawk nodded. "It would seem that the process is slightly more complicated with a woman than a mare."

Despite his offhanded manner, Kayln saw the relieved glance he cast toward the sleeping Celia and decided not to press him further. Hawk had done well.

She looked down at the child, an expression of wonder on her face. "Isn't he the most beautiful babe you have ever seen?" she asked in awe.

"He looks like a wrinkled old man," he replied.

When Kayln gasped, he smiled. "But I would agree he is most handsome." Hawk reached out his finger and put it in the baby's small hand. To his surprise the small fingers closed around his. "The child has come a fortnight early and still he is strong." Hawk's expression was openly proud.

Kayln was suddenly glad this man would have a part in the babe's life. "Better he should be as the Hawkhursts than his Grandfather Chilton," Kayln said with a sigh.

Hawk clasped her shoulder, offering comfort, glad to see that she did not start away from him. "Not all men are of such evil get," he said softly. Mayhap in time Kayln would come to see that she need not guard herself so very closely. Perhaps then there could be some hope for them. Hawk didn't know what was happening to him, but his feelings toward her had changed over the course of the last few weeks. He was not yet sure what that meant, but instinct told him to go carefully with her now. Somehow he knew that his own well-being was involved.

Kayln gazed up at him, her eyes shining like water in a mountain stream. Hawk felt his heart swell with emotion. He wanted to take her in his arms and tell her that she was becoming very important to him. But something held him back, a knowledge that Kayln was not yet ready for that. She might never be.

Instead, he put his hand behind her head and leaned forward to place a gentle kiss upon her lips, tasting her mouth with sweet tenderness. When he pulled away, Kayln opened her eyes and stared up at him with unashamed desire, and more importantly, a hesitant happiness.

Swallowing hard, Hawk leaned his forehead against hers to block out the temptation she offered, forcing himself to remember the need to go slowly. "You require rest," he said with a sigh. "Go and lie down. I will look after the little one."

"What if he wakes and wants food?"

"I'm sure if this little man wakes and wants his dinner, no one will be sleeping through it." He flashed her a grin, holding out his arms. In matters concerning the child, at least, there was no discord between them. He was glad of that.

Kayln understood that Hawk was being so gentle and charming because of his joy in the baby, but that did not lessen his effect on her. She was fairly basking in the warmth of his approval and had no wish for this moment to end, even though she knew it must. None of this had changed anything between the two of them. Once they returned to their real lives things would go back to the way they had been. But she could not help wishing the time could be prolonged.

With only a slight hesitation, she relinquished the babe to his care. Kayln knew if she did not get some sleep, she would not be much help to either Celia or the baby. Taking the cloak Hawk handed to her, she lay down close to the fire and was aosleep before she knew it.

After what felt to her tired body like only minutes, Kayln was awakened by the screaming of the child.

Hawk was sitting across the fire and attempting to hush him. When Kayln got up to take the infant, he placed him in her arms with an expression of relief.

Kayln had to stifle a smile as she took the baby to Celia, who was trying to sit up. Hawk was, after all, a man for all his gentleness.

"What is wrong with him?" Celia wiped a weary hand across her forehead.

"I believe your son wants his first meal," Kayln answered, helping to prop her sister up so she could feed the boy. As soon as Celia brought him to her breast, he stopped screaming, kneading her milk-swollen flesh with his little fist as he opened his eyes and glared fiercely.

"Dear me, he's a little devil," Kayln said with a laugh, reaching up to push her tangled hair away from her face. She turned to Hawk. "You had best try to get some sleep yourself. It appears as though his lordship has begun as he means to go on."

Kayln's words proved truer that she could have imagined. It was almost impossible to believe that a tiny being could cause such an upheaval. She and Hawk took turns looking after him while Celia rested. She was still looking pale and exhausted, but they tried to put a cheerful face on their worries about her so she would not become frightened.

Finally, Hawk went out to see to the horses, and to try to get some food to supplement what was in their bags.

Thankfully, the baby settled down for a time. The three adults lay down and slept the sleep of utter exhaustion for a few short hours.

The next morning, after she had seen to the baby's needs and returned him to his mother for feeding, Kayln went to the fire to prepare the morning meal.

She was squatting down beside the fire when Hawk crouched next to her.

"We must leave this place today," he told her.

"Celia is still very weak," she answered. He had been out to see to the horses, and a sprinkling of snow dotted his dark hair. Kayln didn't question the impulse that made her reach up and brush it away. Only after all this was over and they had returned to reality would she force herself to behave as she knew she must in order to guard herself from hurt.

Hawk caught her hand in his and brought it to his lips to press a kiss to the sensitive palm. His eyes told her clearly how much he wanted to make love to her.

"Shouldn't we wait at least until tomorrow to leave?" Kayln asked quickly, to cover the fierce rush of desire she felt when his mouth touched her skin. In spite of her awareness that this interval with him was not ruled by the same laws as any other, she knew it was not the time for lovemaking.

Obviously Hawk felt the same, for his expression grew serious and he shook his head. "No, I think it would be best to get her and the child to Norwich where they can be properly cared for. I believe Celia has developed a fever again."

Kayln looked to her sister, and saw her cheeks were flushed and her eyes overly bright. Kayln had been so occupied with caring for the babe earlier that she had failed to see these signs. "Should we not return to Aimsley?"

"No, we have come so far that Norwich is closer. When she took to the forest, Celia somehow made straight for Philip." Hawk glanced over to where Celia lay.

"I'm sure she did not know what she did." Kayln's eyes followed his. "It is nothing short of a miracle that she found this shelter."

Shaking his dark head, Hawk stood up. "There I must agree with you. There are some things that cannot be explained any other way." He gave her an oddly assessing look that Kayln could not read before turning away with a resigned expression.

While Hawk prepared a litter that would hang between their horses, Kayln readied Celia and the baby for traveling.

It was almost dark when they stopped. Hawk knew it was only a few hours further to Norwich, but he could tell by Celia's extreme pallor that she could not tolerate any more travel that day.

He built a fire and settled the women and the babe under the shelter of a tree while he went to search for small game. He felt uneasy about leaving them alone, yet he knew he must find meat to help Celia regain her strength.

The wood was damp and the fire smoked a great deal, giving off a strong acrid scent that stung Kayln's nostrils. She was forced to move a few feet away from the fire, holding the baby close inside her cloak to keep him warm.

A wolf howled somewhere in the night.

"That sounded very close," Celia said from where she reclined against a fallen log.

"You know how sound carries when the air is so cold and still," Kayln reassured her, though she could not fully repress the shudder that passed though her as the howling came again. The noise did sound as if it were very close. Hunching her shoulders, she took a step nearer to the fire.

"Hasn't Hawk been gone a long time?" Celia asked. When Kayln swung around, she could see that Celia's eyes were wide with fright.

"He's only just gone," Kayln answered reassuringly. "Why don't you try to sleep? The baby is resting and you should take advantage of that fact."

"Will you be frightened?" Celia looked around them fearfully.

"No," Kayln told her with forced bravado. "Hawk will return shortly and I have your son for company." Her brave words must have convinced her sister, for with a tired sigh, Celia lay down and covered herself with her warm cloak.

As the minutes passed the howling came again and again. And Kayln realized that the sounds were growing closer. Kayln began to pace back and forth beside the fire, rocking and singing to the child in her arms.

Finally, it came to the point where Kayln knew that she could no longer hide the truth from herself. The wolf was moving toward them.

She told herself she had nothing to fear. The beast was probably stalking some deer. It was said that wolves very seldom approached people. And she did have the fire. But her eyes never ceased scanning the forest around her.

Just as she felt as if she would go mad with the fear of the unknown, she saw something. To the right of the small clearing where they had set up camp, a pair of eyes glowed with feral intelligence. Kayln clutched the baby close to her, thinking this could not be real. Surely the animal would not come close to the fire.

Then, as the large gray wolf stepped out of the trees, she knew she had real reason to fear. The foamy froth at the animal's mouth and the wild glint in its eyes told the tale.

The wolf was mad. His shadow loomed huge and threatening as he moved closer, the muscles in his shoulders bulky and sinewy at the same time.

Leaping toward the fire, Kayln yanked out a burning branch. She knew she would be at a disadvantage against this animal as she must hold onto the baby with her other hand. There was no time to give the child to his mother, and apart from this, Kayln was seized by an overwhelming instinct to protect the helpless being she held.

The wolf seemed to sense, in some way, that Kayln meant to fight, for he stopped for a moment as if sizing her up.

Kayln's breath was labored and she felt as if the tight band of fear around her chest would crush her. Where was Hawk and why did he not come? Kayln wanted to call out to him, but she knew she must not show any weakness or the animal would feel it.

And deep inside her she knew Hawk would not arrive in time.

The outcome was up to her and her alone. Kayln tightened her arm around the babe. Then suddenly something inside her broke.

All her life her strength had come from outside herself, born of a need to protect her battered heart. But now, for the first time in her memory, she felt it well from deep within, swelling out of her. It rose in a wave of desire to protect her sister and the baby. The sensation surged through her limbs, and Kayln lifted the branch to issue a warning.

As if accepting her unspoken challenge, the wolf sprang at her. Without pausing to think, Kayln struck out with the burning branch, knocking him away.

The wolf recovered quickly, but seemed to treat her more warily. It circled around her slowly, the froth dripping from its matted chin as it took her measure.

Just when Kayln thought her arm would drop from holding the heavy branch for so long, he sprang again. This time when Kayln hit him, he fell to his side. Acting solely on that river of courage inside her, Kayln struck again and again, until the large body lay still.

Unable at first to grasp that the danger was past, Kayln raised the stick high over her head, her arms shaking with fear and the excitement that raced through her veins. "Hawk!" she screamed, and the sound reverberated off the trees around her, causing snow to fall to the ground.

Finally, the fact that the wolf was actually dead reached her. Still Kayln stood there for a moment, quaking, before her hand fell to her side and the branch clattered to the ground. Sinking to her knees, she began to cry, hot tears of relief scalding her cold cheeks.

She felt a touch on her shoulder and turned to see Celia, standing there, swaying on her feet.

"You should not be up," Kayln sobbed.

"Oh, Kayln." Celia sank down beside her. "You saved our lives." She threw her arms around her sister's neck and cried with her. "No one has ever been more brave."

There was a crashing in the trees behind them, and Kayln jerked around with wide, terror-filled eyes.

To her abject relief, it was not another wolf. Hawk stood at the edge of the clearing, his chest heaving with the force of his breathing. On seeing the two of them kneeling on the ground, he dropped the brace of rabbits he had been carrying and ran to stand over the women.

"What has happened?" he asked, his tone sharp with anxiety. "Are you all right?"

Kayln could only point at the dead body of the wolf.

"God's blood," Hawk swore. He bent down and pulled them both into his arms.

"Kayln saved us," Celia cried. "I was so frightened that I could not even help her."

He could feel Kayln shaking, and knew that she was suffering shock from the ordeal. "Can you tend to the baby?" Hawk asked Celia, taking the infant out of Kayln's arms.

Celia nodded, but he saw how unstable she was on her feet, and briefly moved away from Kayln to help her to her makeshift bed. Hastily he settled her and the infant there, and went back to Kayln.

He pulled her into his arms and seated himself on a stump

close to the fire. "There, there," he whispered, smoothing her silky hair from her brow.

For a long while he just held her. Then, when he sensed that Kayln had calmed, he leaned back to look into her face, which seemed to be filled by the dark pools of her eyes. "Tell me what happened."

Kayln swallowed twice before she could get the words to come out. Then they poured from her as she told Hawk of the wolf and its attack.

"I hit it." Kayln pointed to the wolf, her gaze dark with hatred as she looked to the animal. "I hit it, and I hit it, until it just lay there. At first I couldn't believe that it was really over, but then I knew the wolf was really dead. That was when I screamed for you. It was only because of the body that I knew I hadn't dreamed the whole thing."

Hawk shook his head. "I have never heard of a wolf attacking anyone. It seems so strange. Never would I have gone off and left you alone if I had thought there was any real danger."

"The animal was clearly mad," she told him. "You could not have foreseen that."

Hawk held her close. "Celia was right. What you did was incredibly brave."

"I never thought I would be glad to have killed," Kayln said in confusion. "Yet I was almost disappointed when he stopped moving. But not because I was sorry. I hated the wolf so much that even its death did not seem to be enough."

"You were looking after those you love, my fierce warrior queen." Hawk pulled her head down to his wide shoulder. "I only wish I had come to help you."

"I don't know why," Kayln whispered, "but as it was happening, I was afraid that if I called to you it would know how weak and frightened I was." She forced herself to focus on what had happened, not allowing herself to feel too much pleasure in the fact that he was holding her, that he had called her his fierce warrior queen. Hawk was simply glad that she had been able to save their lives.

When he spoke, she could feel the rumble in his chest as he held her even more tightly. "You are many things, but weak does not number among them."

"I am so glad that I was able to stand on my own." She raised her head to look into his eyes, which were golden in the firelight. "Somehow I found the courage to be strong." She wanted, but didn't know how, to explain the feelings of courage that had welled within her when she needed them. If only he could comprehend this, then he might begin to see why it was so important for her to be accepted as an equal. She would wish to be a respected partner in any liaison. Words had never come easily to her, and now was no exception. But somehow he seemed to at least partially understand.

"You were that long before this night," Hawk told her. He did not try to stop the rush of admiration that rose inside him, but behind it lay a hint of a darker emotion that he could not name. He was beginning to understand just how strong she truly was. Mayhap he would have to change his way of thinking. All along he had believed that ultimately every woman needed a man to look after her, no matter how she might deny it.

But this was a woman who could stand on her own, as she had just reminded him. And while he admired her strength, he was fearful of it. As it became steadily more evident that Kayln could manage without him, it was equally clear he could not do the same without her. He was beginning to wish he could share those rare moments of sweetness with her as he had never wished for anything in his life.

He now knew that his unwillingness to become involved with Kayln had not been caused by a reluctance to be controlled, but because he was beginning to care. Yet he took no pleasure in this realization. His growing desire to break through to the warm loving woman within seemed less and less likely to ever be fulfilled.

Chapter Seventeen

When the small party arrived at the gates of Norwich the following day, the portcullis was opened instantly.

They found themselves inside the castle walls, which surrounded an enormous grounds. The keep sat back from the wall, with a high tower to guard its entrance. The courtyard was dotted with well-cared-for buildings, and soldiers wearing the earl's colors of red and gold swarmed about the area.

Kayln was gladdened to find her own men and Hawk's had already arrived at the castle. Soon after comforting her so attentively the previous night, Hawk had fallen into a heavy silence that she could not fathom the cause of. Perhaps she should not even try, she told herself.

She told herself to concentrate on Bertrand and the others, who were overjoyed to find their lady and her sister safe. And with a healthy baby to show for their experiences.

Her relief at seeing her men turned to dismay when she learned Miles was there as well. It seemed he had met Bertrand and his men in the forest and joined the search. Kayln felt an incredible reluctance to listen to his questions, which had grown more and more prying of late.

As Kayln dismounted, Miles tried to speak to her.

But before Kayln could think of a reply that might put him off, Hawk deliberately moved between them as if Miles was not even there. It was an overt snub that could not be ignored by the Lord of Harrow, and he bristled like a rooster.

But Kayln paid the two men little heed. She was not up to dealing with Miles's or Hawk's vanities at this moment. Too much had occurred in the past two days. Her feelings for Hawk had undergone a change that she was still very uncertain of. She knew that he had somehow found his way past her guard, but she did not yet know what that might mean. His distant demeanor after making love to her and now did not bode well.

Kayln pushed her uncertainties aside as Philip arrived and, after first being assured that Celia was well, made his joy at the birth of his son known to all. She watched with unconscious yearning as he bent forward and kissed his wife hungrily, then raised the child high in the air. "I have a son."

A cheer went up from the crowd, which was composed mostly of soldiers. They raised their arms high with jubilation, for Philip was well liked.

"I think we should find a place where Celia can be made comfortable," Hawk interjected. Thus prodded, Philip relinquished the infant to Kayln, lifted Celia in his arms, and led them into the keep.

Walter of Norwich met them as they entered the hall. He strode toward Hawk with a face filled with welcome. "I could hardly credit what your men told us of Celia's having disappeared when they arrived last night," he said as he looked at the ragtag group. "But as I can see, Philip's little bride has come through her mishap most well. And has brought him a gift." He beamed at the child in Kayln's arms.

He nodded to Kayln. "The Lady Mary has gone to prepare rooms for you. She knew you would have need of a rest."

"Thank you, my lord," Kayln answered gratefully. She needed some time away from Hawk's presence to think.

"Ah, here is my lady wife now," he exclaimed. All turned to watch as Lady Mary came toward them.

She held out a hand in welcome. "Lady D'Arcy and Lady Celia. It is good to see you again." She looked to Celia's flushed face where she lay in Philip's arms. "Though would that the circumstances had been more auspicious. Please come and I will show you to your chambers." With that the pleasantly rounded woman moved toward the other end of the hall with quick steps.

Philip fell in behind her, and Kayln followed after with the baby. She would be glad to see Celia and the infant settled.

"And now," she heard the earl say to Hawk as she walked away, "while my wife sees to the ladies' comfort, tell me of your adventures."

* * *

In the morning Kayln awoke to find herself in strange surroundings, and it was a few moments before she could realize where she was. The bed was large, with heavy gold brocade hangings, and Kayln pulled them back to view a spacious chamber with a high ceiling. The stone walls were bare, as was the floor. The room offered little in the way of beauty. But it was clean, and someone had come in while she slept and lit a fire in the hearth.

Kayln crept from the bed slowly. The shutters were closed, so it was impossible to tell the time of day, though she had the distinct feeling that it was no longer early.

Obviously she had fallen into a long and deep sleep, though she recalled having expected to lie awake for some time. Clearly exhaustion had taken over. She shivered in the thin material of her borrowed shift and moved closer to the fire, holding out her hands to its heat. Slowly, Kayln became aware of the thoughts that lurked at the corners of her mind.

Hawk.

During these past two days, Kayln had seen a side of him she had not dreamed of. They had shared experiences that had bound them as closely together as few people ever were. They had been through danger, triumph, worry over Celia, and the great joy that had accompanied the birth of their nephew.

But these thoughts only served to confuse her. She did not wish to feel this way about Hawk. In her life she had learned that caring for a man only brought hurt. As a little girl she had wanted nothing from her father beyond his love. Even the beatings would have been bearable had she felt cared for even the least bit. And as a young woman she had hoped for no more from her husband. But neither man had been able to give her any sign of affection.

Could growing to care for Hawk be just as deep a threat? If she came to love him, could he not hurt her battered heart beyond repair? His silence of the previous day weighed heavily on her. Kayln wrapped her arms around herself in a gesture of self-comfort.

She couldn't forget that he held himself back from her, not believing in her enough to share his own troubles. If he truly believed in her, wouldn't he tell her of his problems? He refused to even explain why he wouldn't tell her what he knew about his being shot with that arrow.

Kayln shook her head, feeling more confused than ever.

Suddenly she had an intense need to see the man who had so ably thrown her thoughts into confusion. Perhaps being with Hawk, looking into his eyes, would help her to know whether to trust in him or not. Her triumphs in the past days, helping Celia, killing the wolf, had taught her more than she had ever imagined about trusting her own instincts. She also suspected that it was knowing Hawk that had shaken her out of her complacency enough to discover these things.

Putting thought to action, Kayln went down to the Great Hall. She was surprised to discover that it was even later than she imagined. Only servants were in the hall, clearing away after the noon meal. Readily they supplied her with a simple repast of fresh bread, cheese, and wine.

As she rose from her meal, Kayln decided to go out into the courtyard. Knowing how Hawk enjoyed the outdoors, she thought it seemed a likely place to find him.

Halting a serving woman in the hallway, she begged the use of a mantle. In a very few minutes her own cape was delivered to her, dry and in surprisingly good condition after her adventures.

Amazingly after the recent storm, the sky was a clear azure blue, with only a few billowy clouds to dot its perfection. She took a deep breath, filling her lungs with crisp fresh air, and exhaled white vapor.

The courtyard around her was incredibly busy. Never had she seen so many people at one time. There were soldiers, plainly distinguishable in their red and gold colors. There were serfs, landholders, and the highborn, all seemingly oblivious to her presence as they went about their business. They had been forced to stay inactive during the storm, and now took advantage of the milder weather to see to things that might have been neglected.

But nowhere did Kayln see a sign of Hawk, or anyone else she knew, for that matter. She was just considering going back inside the keep, when she heard a familiar voice at her elbow.

"Kayln."

It was an effort to force back a sigh of resignation. "Miles." She turned to him with a fixed smile.

He stepped close. "I was worried about you when you did not come down to the hall for either meal."

"I am quite well. I assure you I was only tired after the experiences of the past days," she answered, folding her hands together under her cape.

She realized her mistake in mentioning her adventures as soon as Miles opened his mouth. "Yes." He nodded. "I'm quite sure you are." He frowned with slight disapproval. "I only wish that you had notified me of Celia's disappearance. Instead you confided your troubles to that dratted Hawkhurst. I had to find out from your man, Bertrand. Why, if I hadn't come upon him while I was out hunting, I would not have even known."

Kayln clenched her teeth as a wave of anger rushed over her. The recent ordeal had been difficult enough without the added irritation of Miles's possessiveness and his obvious disapproval of Hawk. She turned on him with narrowed eyes. "You would do well, my lord, to hold your tongue. It is most telling to me that you are more concerned with whom I have spent time with than Celia's well-being. Lord Hawkhurst was at Aimsley when we learned of my sister's disappearance. He was exceedingly kind to offer his assistance in locating her. I might add that it was through his efforts that she was found. And now, my lord, I hope you will understand if I feel the need for some solitude." With that, she drew her cloak close about her and stalked away.

She moved off across the courtyard, her rigid back effectively keeping him from following her.

Kayln knew this last skirmish with Miles had ended the closeness they had shared. For some time the once-comfortable friendship between them had grown steadily more strained, until there was no longer a common ground for her and the knight. What surprised her was that she felt so little at the loss. She now wondered if their friendship had ever been anything of real importance. Mayhap Miles had only behaved agreeably toward her as long as she had no one besides him in her life.

But she did not linger over this. Her current confusion over her relationship with Hawk was so overriding that she could concentrate on little else.

With no thought to where she was headed, Kayln moved off around the keep. The snow muffled her footsteps, and no one seemed to take any particular note of her.

And still she saw no sign of Hawk.

On arriving back at the front courtyard, Kayln realized she had completely circumvented the inner keep without having resolved anything in her mind. What she had managed to do was become quite cold.

She was just entering the Great Hall when she saw the knight Sir Jocelin coming toward her. He smiled widely as he stopped before her. "Dear lady, do come close to the fire. You look chilled to the bone."

Although Kayln was not pleased at the interruption to her thoughts, she went with him. They came to a halt before the huge hearth, where a cheery fire blazed.

As she raised her hands to its warmth, he said, "May I ask what took you out into the snow, my lady?"

"I felt the need of some fresh air," she answered stiffly. Then she forced herself to a more pleasant disposition. Jocelin could not know that she had no wish for company.

He seemed gratified to see her smile. "What an exciting time you have had, my lady. The whole castle is atwitter with talk of your heroics."

Kayln frowned. "Heroics?" Whatever was he talking about?

"Yes, my lady. There is not a soul who has not heard of your daring efforts to fell the mighty lupine."

Her eyes widened in surprise. "The wolf? But that was no great feat. It was simply a matter of defending myself and my family. Anyone would have done the same."

He bowed with courtly grace. "Ah, my lady, many would have attempted, but only a handful would have succeeded. Few women would have even had the determination to try. You, My Lady D'Arcy, are a rare and precious jewel. Would that I were the hawk who had won your favor." He ended with a knowing glance.

As he spoke of the wolf, Kayln could not still a flush of pleasure, though she knew the truth of what had happened in the forest. She had acted purely out of a need to survive, not bravery.

When he went on to mention Hawk, her blush turned to one of anger. She would not condone speculation on her private affairs. "Pray do not continue, sir." She turned from Jocelin, meaning the gesture as a dismissal.

He halted her. "Forgive me. I did not mean to cause offense. Please stay for a moment. I am lonely. I was not invited to join in the group that went with my Lords Norwich and Hawkhurst to ferret out the rest of the pack and find out if they are stricken with the same disease as the one that attacked your camp. I am hungry for your fair companionship."

Kayln swung around to face him, her irritation forgotten. "Lord Hawkhurst has gone after the other wolves?"

He appeared surprised by her worried demeanor. "But I thought you knew, my lady. The party left before dawn."

So that explained why she had not found Hawk. On thinking about the matter, she realized she need have no real concern for him. He was with a party of experienced knights. A pack of wolves would offer them little danger.

The heat from the fire was already beginning to warm her, and Kayln reached up to unclasp her mantle. "That is good. It will make the forest safer for other travelers."

Jocelin reached out to take the cape from her shoulders. "I cannot but agree, Lady D'Arcy. Though let us hope none will be undertaking such a dangerous journey as your sister. I'm sure you are most relieved to know that she will be staying on here at Norwich."

Kayln stilled in the act of smoothing her hair. "Staying on here at Norwich?"

Jocelin looked at her with genuine confusion. "But lady, I thought you would know, she being your sister. It is no secret. The matter was openly discussed over the morning meal. I was aware that you were not present, but I never imagined you were not privy to . . ."

Kayln did not linger to hear the end of his statement.

Celia was ensconced in a large comfortable chamber with a cheery fire. It was heartening to see that her fever had passed, for she was pale and wan but not unnaturally so. The baby was nursing, and she looked up with an expression of deep contentment as Kayln entered.

"You have just missed seeing Philip," Celia told her. "He had to deliver a message to one of the earl's retainers."

"So soon after your arrival?" Kayln asked, trying to hide her agitation. After the ordeal Celia had already been through, Kayln did not wish to upset her. But somehow she must discover if what she had been told was true. They had no right to make such a decision without consulting her. Celia was her own sister.

Slowly she took a deep calming breath and came forward to kiss her sister's cheek. She reached out to run a gentle hand over the babe's golden curls, and drew back quickly as she realized her hand was trembling.

"The earl offered to send another messenger, but it was a duty Philip had already been given and he does not wish to shirk." Celia smiled shyly and looked down at her son's head with complete adoration. "Philip does not want to make the earl think my presence will keep him from doing his duty."

Kayln turned away, blinking back tears. "Then what I have heard is true. You mean to stay on here." Kayln had known Celia would eventually go to her husband. But this was too sudden. She was just finally getting to know her sister.

After taking in Kayln's pale, set profile, Celia looked away. "Lady Mary has asked me if I would like to stay here at Norwich with Philip."

The lump of misery in her throat kept Kayln from making a reply.

"Please, Kayln, do not hold yourself from me as in the past," Celia begged, trying to make her sister see reason. "I was only to stay on at Aimsley until Philip was done with his knight's training. He tells me he's progressing so quickly that it may not even be a year. Then we would be going to live at Lindon, the property you settled upon me. We chose it because it is closer to Aimsley than the keep Philip inherited from his mother." She paused to take a long breath, then went on. "The night you killed the wolf I felt things had changed between us, that we had become friends. Can you not understand Philip is my husband and I need to be with him, as does his son? It does not mean that I do not love you."

Hearing what Celia said and knowing it was true did not make accepting it any easier. She had thought she would have more time with her sister, that she would come to know her nephew, help raise him. The night of the baby's birth, Kayln had felt that Celia was finally able to accept her overtures of affection and friendship for what they were.

Kayln closed her eyes on the tears that stung her eyes. Now she had no one.

Then unexpectedly, from that same inner core where she had found the courage to face the wolf, Kayln felt an outpouring of selfless love. For Celia's sake she must hide her disappointment and loneliness. She had no right to sully Celia's happiness.

Turning to face the younger girl with a smile despite her tears, Kayln kissed Celia on the cheek. "Of course your place is with Philip. I have no right to begrudge you. It is simply that the news came as such a shock that I didn't have time to grow accustomed to the idea." She met Celia's worried blue gaze. "All is well, though I shall miss you, you know."

Celia looked into her sister's face for a moment, then seemed satisfied that Kayln was truly not angry. "We did not think. I was so excited that I simply said yes when Lady Mary asked. It was last night when she came in to see the baby. You were sleeping, Kayln. I meant to tell you as soon as you came today, but someone has outpaced me."

Kayln smiled and nodded, hoping Celia would not see how miserable she was. Tenderly she leaned forward and hugged her sister. "I love you, Celia. I only wish I'd said it more."

Celia put her free arm around Kayln's neck. "I love you too. Thank you so much for understanding."

A short time later, Kayln left the chamber. She felt as if her whole world was falling apart around her. It seemed as if nothing was going as she had planned.

For her it was important to have a sense of control and some understanding of what would happen next. She felt as if she had been cast adrift, leaving her confused, frightened, and even less able to deal with her confusion over Hawk.

On her way to her own chamber, Kayln realized she had left her cloak in the hall. Hoping that Sir Jocelin would no longer be there, for she did not want him to see her unhappiness, she went to fetch it.

Upon entering the hall, Kayln saw that only the servants were present, setting up the tables for the evening meal. Her cloak was draped over a bench beside the hearth.

Quickly she crossed the rush-covered floor. As Kayln bent down to get the cloak, she noticed a scrap of parchment at the edge of the fire. This would not have been of any particular note to her, but the page lay face up and unmistakably bore the name of Hawkhurst.

As everything about the man was of interest to her, Kayln bent and picked up the charred remnant of parchment.

When her eyes focused on the rest of what was printed there, she gasped in horror. In flowing script it read:

Hawkhurst must die

Everything else had been burned away.

Kayln clutched it close to her bosom, then realized her strange behavior had drawn several glances. She knew she had to get away from prying eyes to think. The message could have been left by anyone. That person could be watching at this very moment. Kayln had to have time to consider how to act, for clearly Hawk was in danger.

Barely remembering to take the very object she had come for, Kayln grabbed up her cloak and hurried to her room.

Later that night, Kayln sat in a chair before her fire.

After careful contemplation, she had decided that she must show Hawk the note before going to anyone else. She had no idea who had written it or when they planned to strike.

On the chance that the attack could be this very night, Kayln had no choice but to await Hawk's return to the keep, no matter how late. At the evening meal, which she barely touched, Kayln had told one of the serving women to inform her the moment the hunting party arrived.

That had been several long hours ago.

Already emotionally exhausted after the scene with Celia, Kayln was nearly out of her mind with worry about who could be in on the plot to murder Hawk. Why she felt such a deep level of anxiety and near-panic, she could not even guess. She only knew that she must warn him. It was almost as if her own life depended on it.

Her eyes burned with a fierce intensity that made her head throb. Knowing she had stared overlong into the flames, Kayln sought to relieve the ache by closing her eyes. Only for a moment . . .

When she woke, Kayln knew a significant amount of time had passed. The fire in the hearth had burned low and the shadows were long in the still room.

Surely Hawk must have returned to the keep by now.

Kayln knew which chamber Hawk had been given after having asked a serf earlier in the evening. A deep-felt sense of dread, as real as an ice-cold hand on her shoulder, told her she must go there now.

Kayln could not shake the foreboding inside her. If Hawk was not there, she was determined to wait for him no matter how long it took.

When Kayln came to his door, she hesitated. What if he became angry at her intrusion, her fears? He'd certainly made it clear that he did not wish her to pry into whatever trouble he was experiencing, trouble that might have something to do with the note she had found. Yet Kayln's unease drove her on. Cautiously, she pushed the door open.

Shock and terror at what she found inside prevented her from making a sound.

In the glow from the fire Kayln saw the silhouette of a man. He was bending over the still form on the bed. And he was holding a knife, the blade long and deadly in the flickering light.

He could not kill Hawk. What would she do without him? Her heart gave her just a hint of the unbearable loneliness she would come to know if Hawk were to die.

In that moment, her mind hovered on the brink of madness, like a pebble at the edge of an abyss. But she forced herself back. She had to do something to stop him from murdering Hawk.

Spurred by desperation, Kayln reached for the clay pitcher on the table.

The murderer was so bent on his evil deed that he did not

even hear her until it was too late. Just before the pitcher came down on his head, he started to turn toward her. He never completed the movement.

Kayln hit him with all the force born of her fear for the man she loved. For love Hawk she did, against her will and with the certain knowledge that it could bring her nothing besides pain, but irrevocably.

The assailant fell backward, hitting his head against the stone wall. Then he crumpled to the floor like a discarded rag.

Kayln was only dimly aware of Hawk sitting up in bed, calling out in surprise. She dropped the pitcher from suddenly numb fingers and turned to him, her eyes dull. "He tried to hurt you."

Hawk was already kneeling beside the still figure of the other man. After a moment he stood and swung around to face her. "It is Sir Jocelin," he said.

"Is he . . . ?"

Hawk nodded slowly. "Aye, he is dead."

She felt nothing at the news.

Kayln's mind was too filled with chaos. Like a hive of bees caught under a bowl, her thoughts darted around her head, until they settled on one numbing fact. She had nearly lost Hawk.

It seemed as if her whole life had been a series of losses. Her trust in her father. Her hopes for a life with Raymond. Her plans for Celia's future. And just this very day she had learned that Celia would no longer be with her. Not that Kayln could hold Celia's staying at Norwich against her, but the message was clear. Eventually everyone she loved hurt or deserted her.

Hawk could only do the same.

Kayln knew she could not withstand the pain of it. Seeing him nearly murdered before her very eyes had taught her that. Even the realization that she had killed a man paled by comparison.

The knowledge that her own well-being depended on Hawk's continued existence was crushing in its intensity.

Hawk, not knowing all that was passing through Kayln's mind, was doing his best to completely grasp the situation.

Normally he was not such a deep sleeper. Staying alert was

what kept a soldier alive. But the events of the past days had left him exhausted. It was evident that Kayln had come in just in time to save him from a dire fate.

He knew he must discover how Kayln had known.

But first he had to find a safe place for the ring he had found upon the dead man's hand. Hawk had no idea how Jocelin had gotten his steward's seal, only that he had. Doing something about it must wait until he had time to fully reason out the implications. It was entirely possible that the ring had been used as payment for Hawk's murder.

With the ring safely tucked amongst his belongings, Hawk went to Kayln. Both thoughts and action had taken no more than a moment. Thus Hawk did not realize the depth of her distress until he took her unyielding body in his arms. "There, Kayln," he murmured, stroking his hand over her silky hair. "All is well."

She looked up at him, her gray eyes iron dark with shock. Dully, and without any coaxing, she told Hawk about finding the note, what it had said, and her plans to warn him.

As the true implications of the situation and her actions began to settle in, Hawk was filled with an intense and blinding sense of joy. "You do feel something for me."

Kayln stared at him for a long moment, then pushed backward out of his arms. "Nay, I have no wish to care for you." Never could she allow him to know how much she did indeed love him. No one must know. It was her only hope of ever being able to overcome the weakness. It had been one thing to realize she was starting to have some feelings for him, and quite another to know that he could completely devastate her with a disapproving glance. Why, she'd worried this whole day about his not speaking yesterday.

At her reply a bit of the edge was taken off Hawk's pleasure, but just a little. This revelation explained why Kayln had seemed less harsh with him over the last days, why she'd given herself to him so completely when they made love on the night Celia disappeared, why she'd wanted so desperately for him to go. After all she had been through, it would be frightening for her to feel as if she might be beginning to care for him. Hadn't he added to her distrust of men by hurting her in the beginning of their relationship? Understanding this softened his tone as he spoke. ''Nonetheless, you do feel something.''

With a cry that wrenched at his heart, she beat her fists against the hard wall of his chest. ''I've tried to stop it. It's wrong to allow myself to care for you. You give nothing of yourself to me, Hawkhurst, holding your pride and your secrets close to yourself.'' Then Kayln turned her fist against her own breast. ''But you want to get inside me and fill me up until there is nothing left of me—Kayln. You want to take everything I am and make it yours.''

Knowing why she kept her feelings so close to her, and knowing that she was not wrong in her accusations about him, Hawk was struck deep. Grief such as he had never known sliced through his guts like a dull spear.

It emerged as anger.

He grabbed her arm, pulling her up close against him, his pain oozing from him like molten lead. ''Little fool. Why must you fight me at every turn? I cannot deny that I have hurt you, however inadvertently. Or even that I would do so again. I am a man and therefore human. Who is to say you would not hurt me, have not already done so? If truth be told, I must admit that you do so now with your bitter tongue. But I would forgive you, did you allow me.'' He paused for a moment, loosening the tight hold on her arm as he realized that he might be causing her pain. That was not what he wanted to do now or ever. ''I know not what we have between us, but I wouldst be willing to find out.''

She jerked away from him, grasping the sides of her head with both hands as if trying to squeeze him out. Her voice rose. ''Nay! I want no part of this!'' With that she turned and ran from the room before he could prevent her.

Hawk called out after Kayln, running into the darkened hall. Other castle folk appeared at the doors to their chambers, obviously confused and curious at being awakened in the dead of night.

It was then that Hawk remembered what the two of them had forgotten in the midst of their argument. Jocelin's body. He realized he must see to that immediately. Besides, in Kayln's present state of mind, nothing could be solved between them.

He would do well to wait until the morrow to try talking to her again. Hawk had no wish to upset her further this night, and though it chaffed to force himself to wait, he knew neither of them was in any state to be making life-changing decisions. Kayln had admitted that she did feel some emotion toward him, and that had to mean something. Surely in the morning they would be able to mend this breach, for Hawk was beginning to understand that however difficult it might be to come to terms with the lady, not doing so could prove worse.

In the meantime, he must seek out Lord Walter and explain what had happened to Jocelin so Kayln would not be plagued with questions about his death. Certainly the thought of having killed someone had added to her distress.

He would ask Lady Mary to see to Kayln. Mayhap that gentle soul could be of some comfort to her.

Chapter Eighteen

Some weeks later, Kayln paused as she entered the kitchen at Aimsley to discuss stores with the cook. With a sigh, she raised her hand to stifle a yawn. She had been so tired of late, sleeping long hours but never seeming to feel rested.

Kayln would not even consider that her seemingly endless dreams of James Hawkhurst had any connection to that. As she did tens of times every hour of every day, she pushed him to the back of her mind.

Mabel, the cook, came toward her from where she had been basting a roast pig over the fire.

The greasy-sweet scent of roasting pork filled Kayln's nostrils as fat dripped onto the flames. Her stomach gave a sickening roll. Her eyes opened wide, and she covered her mouth and raced for the back entrance to the chamber.

Moments later, Kayln brushed the back of her hand over her mouth and straightened. This was not the first time she had become ill, and she doubted it would be the last.

She gave a start of surprise as she felt a hand on her back, and turned to see Mabel standing there. The cook held a clean, wet cloth. Gratefully, Kayln took it and wiped her sweat-dampened face.

Mabel stood by, her face creased with worry. "Is there aught I can do, my lady?"

A shaky laugh escaped her mistress as she looked down at the cloth in her hand. "I fear you cannot." She ended with a quiver in her voice. "No one can."

The cook was clearly unable to ignore the sadness in the other woman's tone. Even though Kayln had always rebuffed familiarity from her people, Mabel held out her strong arms.

To Kayln's complete surprise, she went into them. She had been so afraid of the knowledge growing inside her. But she could no longer deny it. She was to have Hawk's child, and soon all would know. The Lady of Aimsley realized that she now needed to be held and comforted, more than she needed to retain her pride. Mabel had always been a steadfast and kind woman. It seemed silly to hold herself away.

Even as these thoughts went through Kayln's mind, she knew an unbearable sadness. Hawk was much to be thanked for her new attitude. Loving him had helped her to see things in a fundamentally different way, softened her. But he could have no place in her life, for that softness made her vulnerable to his control. And control her he would, having never made any secret of his disapproval of a woman ruling her own life.

Unfortunately, it was his strength that drew her so irresistibly. Because it was that very quality that made it impossible for her not to love him, she had to stay away.

Later that day, Alice came to the tower where Kayln lay upon her bed. "Lady Kayln."

"Yes," Kayln said softly.

"I feel you have something to tell me."

"What do you mean?" Kayln asked, trying to feign innocence, but she could see Alice was not fooled. Obviously she had heard of Kayln's illness earlier.

"You know well what I mean," Alice stated. "Must I examine you as I did Celia?"

Kayln wrapped her arms around herself protectively. "No, there is no need. I know what ails me."

"Hawkhurst?"

"Yes. It is Hawkhurst's baby." One lone tear slipped down her pale cheek and her gaze went to the window, where the gray overcast sky matched her mood.

Alice came into the room and lowered herself onto the window seat. "Why have you refused to see him if you know you carry his child? Why, just yesterday you forbade him entrance to the keep."

Kayln refused to meet the other woman's eyes. "He is not to know of the child." After long thought Kayln had been forced to come to this decision. She knew that if Hawk became aware of the child, he would insist on being a father to it. She had seen the value he set by his name and family. Hawk would never be content to allow Kayln to raise her offspring as she saw fit. Determination hardened her tone. "I will never tell him."

"Pray why not?" Alice asked, holding up her hands in exasperation. "Lord Hawkhurst is a good man. He would look well upon you and his child."

"You know him not as I do," Kayln answered, clamping her lips together stubbornly. Since the night when she had killed Jocelin to save Hawk's life, Kayln had not allowed her mind to sway from her chosen path.

That very night she had donned her clothes, seeking out Bertrand and leaving Norwich with muttered excuses to Lady Mary.

"Then you are resolved to go through this alone, even knowing your child will be branded a bastard?" Alice asked.

Kayln winced at the word bastard, but she raised her chin. "I am. I do not wish to ever see Hawkhurst again."

The despairing tone of her voice was not lost on Alice, who rose slowly. "Very well, my lady," was all she said, but there was a determined gleam in her eyes.

Several days later, Alice found Kayln staring moodily out the window of her chamber. She had hardly emerged from her rooms since the day she had confessed that she was carrying Hawk's child.

"Kayln," Alice said.

Kayln looked around in surprise. It was not often that Alice forgot and called her lady by her given name. But since Celia had gone, the nurse seemed to need to be closer to Kayln. "Yes, Alice." Her tone was gentle.

"It is a fair day," Alice said, nodding toward the window. "Why do you not go out for a walk?"

Kayln sighed. "I am weary," she answered listlessly.

"The fresh air would do you good. We must think of the babe. All that we do is for its . . . well-being." Alice seemed unusually hesitant, and Kayln gave her a quizzical glance.

"I know," Kayln replied, realizing the nurse was just concerned for her child. "I would not wish to go on as Celia did." She moved from the window. "I will do as you say."

Alice turned to her with a wide-eyed smile. She went to the

trunk at the foot of Kayln's bed and removed the blue woolen cloak with the fur trim. "Wear this."

"That cloak is much too warm for today," Kayln told her. "I shall not be out for long."

"I wish for you to wear it," Alice insisted brightly. "I know that spring is fast approaching, but the days are still chill. Can you not humor an old woman?"

Remembering that the older woman was just feeling a need to mother, she took the cloak and fastened it around her shoulders. "Of a certainty," she answered.

As Kayln made her way from the room Alice spoke, not looking up from where she was tidying the clothes in the chest. "The orchard is a pleasant place to walk."

Kayln hesitated briefly, then continued on her way. She had no intention of walking in the orchard. That place had too many memories of Hawk. But she would not tell Alice this.

Once outside, she was glad of Alice's suggestion of a walk. It was a cool day, but the air smelled of spruce and pine. And the greening grass beneath her feet proclaimed the approach of spring.

Finally, when she began to grow tired, Kayln turned and started back for the keep. Having gone further than she had intended, Kayln was glad of the warmth of her heavy cloak.

She had just emerged from the denseness of the forest into the clearing which surrounded the keep when she took note of a lone rider on the greensward. He was turned away from her, but there was no mistaking the huge chestnut horse nor the wide-shouldered man atop his back.

Panic gripping her chest, Kayln stopped and backed slowly toward the cover of the woods behind her. She could only pray he hadn't heard her approach.

At that moment, Hawk turned in the saddle as if sensing her presence.

With nothing further to be gained by caution, she swung around and hurried into the woods. He was mounted and could move much more quickly, but Kayln knew the forest.

Yet, as if he had some divine assistance, Hawk was able to locate her in a matter of moments. He rode ahead of her and stopped the huge destrier, blocking her path. Looking up into his darkly handsome face, Kayln saw that he was far from pleased by her flight.

She put her hands on her hips and glared up at him. Why was it always he who acted as if she had done something to him? It was Hawk who so effectively made life difficult for Kayln. "What do you think you are about, my Lord Hawkhurst?"

"I will speak to you," he said, wiping with the back of his gauntleted hand the sweat that had beaded upon his forehead. "I had hoped that as time passed you would come to see things differently. That you might be willing to set aside some of your anger."

There was a strange note of sadness in his tone, but she wouldn't allow herself to be swayed. She must guard her independence at all costs. "I don't wish to see you," she answered, and tried to go by him.

He urged Mac forward to block the way. "I wish very much to talk with you."

She eyed him warily. "I have nothing to say to you. And I do not wish to hear anything you might say to me."

"I have missed you, Kayln," he told her softly, nudging Mac forward until he was even with the woman on the ground.

Kayln closed her eyes to the pain in his golden eyes. "It changes nothing."

"Can you say that you have not even thought of me—of us?" His voice was husky and sensuous, pulling her into the net of his seduction, reminding her of the complete mastery of his possession of her.

Kayln closed her eyes. It seemed so long since he'd touched her with that night-sweet magic only he could make. She swayed toward him, then something, some inner sense of self-preservation, made her pull back. Kayln couldn't allow herself to forget the agony she had known in the moment she had thought he would die. Nor could she forget her certain knowledge that Hawk would utterly dominate her. When she answered, it was haughtily to cover her inner turmoil. "And that changes even less than the fact that you say you have missed me. I will only tell you one more time that I do not now, nor do I ever, wish to speak with you on matters of a personal nature again. Truth to tell, I wish never to see you again."

His reply was quick in coming, and his eyes narrowed with anger. "Have you not something to tell me? Something that I have a right to know?"

Under the cover of her cloak, Kayln's hands went to the gentle mound of the child. Did he know? But he could not.

Kayln raised her chin. "Nothing," she said with deliberate finality. She turned to the forest, choosing to face the dense growth rather than continue the conversation.

Once more, Hawk nudged Mac forward, being careful not to allow the horse to actually touch Kayln, but effectively stopping her. "I cannot allow you to go, Kayln."

"You cannot allow . . ." She looked up at him with outraged disdain. "How dare you speak to me in this manner?" This, she told herself, was precisely why she could not give in to her feelings for Hawk. He cared only for his own will.

He held out his arms. "Come."

"Have you lost what little sense you once possessed, sir knight?" she exclaimed. Kayln pronounced each word distinctly, as if talking to a dullard. "I want nothing to do with you."

He leaned closer to her, his arms still outstretched.

Even now Kayln was not fearful. Overbearing and completely sure of himself Hawk might be, but he had never given her cause to think he would harm her. "This has gone too far, my lord. You must leave me in peace." She was growing tired of arguing with him, and wished for nothing so much as to end this confrontation.

"I cannot do that," he stated simply, placing his hands upon her shoulders and drawing her close to Mac's side. Then he simply put his arms around her and lifted her up before him.

Now Kayln began to know a sense of unease. "What are you doing?" she gasped. "You must let me down at once." She didn't know what Hawk was about, but she vowed to make him rue his ill treatment of her. Never again would he so much as set foot on her lands. She'd have a guard posted at every path along the way to keep him out.

He gave no answer, only set his mouth in a grim line and urged the horse forward. He did not go toward Aimsley when they emerged from the forest, but headed his mount in the other direction.

Suddenly she realized the truth. He was taking her to Clamdon.

Blind panic moved up to wrap its icy fingers around her throat, and Kayln could not even scream for the tightness of it. She took long labored breaths, trying to calm herself enough to reason with him. "Why are you doing this?"

He refused to reply. The only sign of his agitation was the white-knuckled grip of his hands on the reins.

"Hawk, what have I done to you that you would treat me so harshly?" When even this elicited no response, she began to struggle. Kayln knew she might suffer a bad tumble should she fall from the stallion, but anything would be preferable to being taken away against her will.

Hawk wrapped his arm more tightly around her lower chest as soon as she began to struggle. His other hand closed like a band of steel around her stomach, but he loosened it immediately, holding her gently but firmly.

As the significance of the action dawned, Kayln ceased struggling immediately. Hawk knew about the baby.

How, she had no clue, but know he did. The awareness left her empty and cold. It was an effort to form the words but she had to ask. "You know?"

"Aye," came the curt reply behind her.

"How? Who?" she cried, never having felt so betrayed. The information could only be given by someone close to her.

There was a long silence, and she thought he would not answer, but at long last he said, "Alice."

Kayln's eyes grew round with horror. "Alice," she whispered. The last being in all of England whom she had felt she could really trust. "Dear God."

Hawk seemed to sense the depth of her distress. "Please try not to harbor any anger against her. She did not want to see the babe born without a father." He laughed bitterly. "She was also of the mistaken impression that you cared for me and we could come to an understanding if only you would speak with me. In all honesty, I must tell you she does not know of my taking you to Clamdon. That sin is on my shoulders alone." He paused, then went on. "And possibly yours. If you had made the least effort to greet my suit with even civil consideration, I would not have followed this course."

Kayln held herself very still. "What course, Hawk? What are you going to do with me?"

But Hawk refused to answer even when she persisted, and Kayln knew he had had enough of questions. She would learn nothing further until he chose.

Exasperation and resignation kept Hawk silent. He had done everything he could to reason with Kayln, but she would have none of him. She left him with no choice but to take her to Clamdon.

Hawk had made many mistakes in his life, but he would not allow himself to make one now. He knew what had to be done, and would see it through no matter that Kayln might come to hate him more than she already did. The child was a Hawkhurst and must bear his father's name. There was no possible alternative.

On the morning after Jocelin died, Hawk had been devastated when he learned that Kayln had left Norwich. But he had held to his belief that she would eventually come to understand that they must be together.

The woman did have some care for him. She had admitted as much. If she allowed herself, she might even come to love him. And if she came to love him, might he then feel free to love her in return, for had he not seen the way her love for Celia and Alice had gentled her?

Hawk had waited, hoping for her to have a change of heart. Yet in these three months she had shown no sign of bending. Even the knowledge that she carried his babe meant nothing to her.

Well, it did to him. Hawk was not about to see his child born a bastard. The babe was a Hawkhurst. Kayln would not readily forgive him for what he was about to do, but there was no choice.

Other circumstances had pressed his hand.

Through the investigation of his steward, Hawk had come to look in the direction of Miles of Harrow. Harrow was known to be a constant gambler, yet he never lacked for gold. Hawk had also discovered that Miles's lands seemed to be much more productive than those around them, unbelievably so considering his many visits to court and the way he treated his holders. His agents were ever occupied with taking livestock and goods to market. As a landowner he would have had no problem in disposing of Hawkhurst goods and moneys along with his own. Finding Harold's ring upon Jocelin's hand had solidified Hawk's suspicions. Miles had become very friendly with Sir Jocelin at Philip's wedding, and was a very likely connection between the dead knight and Harold. Miles had also been at Norwich when Jocelin tried to kill him and he had discovered the ring.

Now Hawk only needed to catch Miles and Harold together. So far he had not met with success, but Hawk had the feeling that the unsuccessful attempt on his life had made the two men cautious for the moment.

He had no fear that he would fail. So sure was he of the truth that Hawk knew it was simply a matter of time now. What he was concerned about was Kayln's safety. If Miles became suspicious that Hawk knew the truth, he might act against Kayln. All but complete fools could see that they were lovers, and from the way Miles had questioned him about their relationship at Norwich, he could see that the knight was not the *complete* fool he pretended to be.

Hawk reasoned that if Kayln was safely at Clamdon, Miles would have no access to her. He refused to think that he was doing anything so rash out of anything but unselfish reasons.

Unconsciously his arms tightened around Kayln. He closed his eyes and breathed deeply of the clean scent of her silky hair. Even with her sitting so remotely before him, she felt good in his arms. Surely he had not done this because he wanted, needed to be near her.

The line of her back continued to be unrelentingly rigid. As if sensing his thoughts, she tried to pull away from him, but he held her firmly, drawing her back until she was molded safely against his strength. She did not struggle, but Hawk could feel the tension and hatred within her.

Cut to the quick, Hawk sighed and left it at that. Surely time would see her forgive him. If for no other reason than the sake of their child, she must. He refused to contemplate what would happen if she did not.

When they arrived at Clamdon, Hawk was careful to keep a tight hold on Kayln, though he did not really think she would try to escape him here, surrounded by his people.

He couldn't repress a sense of satisfaction at her regal stance as he led her into the keep. Kayln had pride. Even in a situation like this, she refused to yield.

Kayln did not look at Hawk as he led her directly to his chamber. It was a simply furnished room with little thought having been given to beauty. There was a high wide bed, a table, a large chest, and two chairs. One of the chairs had been pulled up close to the fire. She took it without waiting for an invitation.

Now Kayln's gray eyes pierced his. "Well, Hawkhurst, explain your witless action in bringing me here."

Hawk took a deep breath, raising black brows high as he considered his answer. Why, he wondered, was he having such a difficult time telling her if his plan made as much sense as he was convinced it did? He told himself that it was only his reluctance to make her more furious that made him hesitate. She would eventually come to see that he had had no choice. He prayed that it did not take too long a time. Hawk took another breath. "I mean to marry you."

For a moment Kayln could not credit what she had heard. "Surely you jest, my lord. I will not marry you. Even your indomitable will is not strong enough to make me say the words." She folded her arms over her chest and glared her anger and disbelief.

He watched her with an unhappy frown for a long moment, as if in indecision, then inexplicably changed the subject. "Would you care for something to drink?" Hawk crossed to a small table upon which a tray laden with cups, a pitcher, and a plate with cheese and bread had been set.

Feeling as if it might ease the terrible ache in her throat, Kayln nodded. "Yes."

Bringing the cup forward, Hawk handed it to her. "Forgive me, Kayln."

This last statement gave her pause to hope Hawk had changed his mind. Mayhap he was coming to his senses. But Kayln made no reply. She wasn't about to pretend she could just forgive him for abducting her. His actions only enhanced her certainty that she could not abide with him.

Kayln eyed him over the rim of her cup, taking a cooling

draught of the liquid, which was soothing and sweet. It settled in her belly and radiated outward with a pleasant warmth.

Hawk continued to watch her, and there was an unmistakable hint of sadness in his golden eyes. Kayln did have some feeling for his pain. She knew how much having sons of his own meant to him. But her instincts for self-preservation would not allow her to show that sympathy.

He quirked a brow and held out his hand. "May I get you more wine?"

Kayln licked her bottom lip. The wine had been refreshing, and she had been without sustenance since early that morning. She nodded and handed him the cup, then settled back to stare into the flames. She felt exhausted. Kayln was not looking forward to the ride back to Aimsley, but she had no wish to remain under Hawkhurst's roof for even one night.

Her unknowingly wistful gaze went to Hawk's wide-shouldered back. She assured herself that her reluctance had nothing to do with the fact she still found him so undeniably compelling, despite what had come between them.

Hawk brought the cup back and stood over her, his face showing concern. "I can see that you are indeed fatigued," he told her. "Would you care to lie down?"

"No, I am fine." Kayln straightened with an effort, took the drink, and brought it to her lips. For the first time she noted Hawk's empty hands. "Are you not going to have some yourself?"

Unexpectedly, he gave what she could only describe as a guilty start. "Not at this moment."

She looked down at the half-empty cup. Like an uncoiling snake, a painful suspicion was beginning to grow inside her. No wonder her limbs felt so heavy. "You have drugged me!"

A dark flush stained his face as he met her gaze with unwavering determination. "I had no alternative. You would not even consider a marriage between us. Can you not see that I must protect the child—our child? Possibly the heir to all that I hold in trust. I have a responsibility to continue the line as have all the Hawkhursts before me."

Kayln laughed bitterly. "What about me? What about the things I hold dear, my independence, my desire to raise the child as I see fit? You will take him from me and make him yours.'' She found her inclination to hold back dissolving within her. ''Am I to have nothing of my own in this whole life? I want my child to know that he is wanted, that he is free to be what *he* will. And what if the child be female? My father wanted sons. He never forgave me for being a daughter, never understood that I was a thinking, reasoning being. In the fourteen years that I lived beneath his roof, he did not once touch me except in anger. I hated him so, even while I loved him. I will not allow you do that to my child.''

Her impassioned speech affected him deeply. ''I would not use a child so merely because it was not male. I would love all our children.'' Hawk swallowed, visibly fighting for control, realizing that it was true and that he wanted to have many children with Kayln. He had watched her learn to show her love to Celia, and knew she would be a firm but loving mother.

''I have not seen the evidence of that in your treatment of me,'' she cried.

He took her hand, but she jerked away and he grimaced. ''Kayln, I say again what I do is for your own good and that of our child.''

From somewhere inside herself she found the strength to ignore the desperation in his golden gaze. ''Spare your breath, my lord betrayer. I know what you are about.''

He started as if she had struck him.

Unable to bear the despondency in his eyes, Kayln stood. The action brought her a hairsbreadth from the hard expanse of his chest. ''I will not marry you. No priest will force me against my will.'' She swayed and put her hand to her forehead as a strange dizziness overtook her. ''Mayhap you have poisoned me with this drug.'' She peered up at him.

He reached out to clasp her to him. ''Have no fear, Kayln. I have been assured on pain of death that this drug will not harm you or the child. But it will quite effectively diminish your ability to resist.''

Kayln was weak, and felt as if she was hearing him from a distance, but she was unwilling to succumb to the sensations. ''I will resist you with every . . . breath in my . . . body.''

''You cannot,'' he replied. Was she crazed or did he actually sound as if he was sorry? But even if it was so, she refused to allow herself to care. Nothing had given him the right to do this.

He went on. "Even now the potion affects you." Hawk leaned over her to brush her silky wheat-gold hair back from her forehead.

Her eyes would not focus as she looked up into his darkly handsome face. "I . . . hate you for this . . . Hawkhurst."

His jaw set with resolution. "I have also done this to protect you, Kayln."

"Pro . . . tect me?" The words were slurred.

"Aye, to protect you. It is why I was not able to tell you of my suspicions concerning the man who shot me. You see, I knew it was my steward, Harold, and that he had an accomplice. But I did not know who that accomplice might be. I could not risk your knowing, for your own safety. As the game plays out, I find I was right to withhold the information. It seems that your friend Miles Harrow may be at the very heart of it."

"Miles?" Her eyes widened in shock as her mind tried to absorb what he had said through the fog of the drug she'd been given. She'd never so much as heard Miles mention the other man, had never seen them together. . . . With a gasp, Kayln put her hand to her head. There had been that once when she had seen them come out of the forest at Aimsley. But Miles had only been helping the steward find his way. "This is insane," she whispered.

Briefly Hawk told her about his suspicions of Miles and his unaccountable wealth. He went on to say how he had found Harold's ring on Jocelin's finger the night he attempted to murder him, and that he believed Miles was implicated in that attempt on his life.

Kayln lifted a heavy hand to rub her forehead. What was he saying? That Miles had tried to have him killed? But that was ridiculous. Miles might have become overly possessive of her, and he might gamble too much, and he might even be more than a little jealous of Hawk. She had refused to even allow him access to her keep since the scene at Norwich. But murder? It was impossible. She'd known him all these years, and could not believe he'd be capable of such a thing.

It was just too hard to think right now. She couldn't even form a defense, her mind was so muddled.

When he saw that Kayln was unable to completely grasp what he was trying to tell her, Hawk decided to wait before trying to convince her. For now he had other plans to carry out.

Hawk looked to the chamber door and called out, "Come!"

At his command several women came into the room, each with their arms full. They stepped aside as a huge wooden tub was brought into the chamber and set close to the fire.

"No," Kayln moaned, her voice barely audible as one of the women moved to her side. "Do not do this to me."

Gently, Hawk lowered her to the chair, his voice husky with concern. "Kayln."

One of the women came forward to draw him away from Kayln. "This silly girl would have your child born a bastard, my lord. Once you are well wed, she will surely come to her senses."

He cast one more glance toward Kayln, who lolled in her seat, and his fists clenched at his sides with strain. But he forced himself to turn from her. He would not let her slip away from him again. In time Kayln would come to see that he had done the right thing, for both of them.

Guilt nearly made Hawk stop the proceedings, but deep inside him, in the place where he was most vulnerable, a voice cried nay. Then, as she signed the marriage contract he'd had transcribed by the priest, Hawk felt himself hesitating again. But he could not end it. The marriage would bind her to him at least in some way, even if Kayln continued to fight him.

After the wedding in the castle chapel, the women brought her to his room. They began to disrobe her, but Hawk stopped them. For them to expose the dazed Kayln as if this were any other bedding ceremony seemed yet another betrayal.

He dismissed the women and performed the service himself. Tenderly he tucked her into his bed, then removed his own clothing and got in beside her.

Hawk drew her into his arms, curling his body around hers protectively. This was where he had dreamed of her, and now she was beside him. He closed his eyes and breathed in the clean fresh scent of her golden hair. Reverently he spread his hand over her gently rounded belly, awed and humbled by the knowledge that their child grew there inside her.

But even as he felt this, Hawk acknowledged that he had used the child's existence for his own purpose. In this moment he could no longer deny the truth to himself.

It was Kayln he wanted, needed more than life, cared for more than even his lands or heritage. Suddenly he knew that he loved her, though he knew not when his feelings had turned to love. If only Kayln would forgive him and accept his love, they could try to find their way together.

He could only pray that it would be so. But whatever tomorrow might bring, though she might continue to hate him, no one, not even God, could take this night from him.

Kayln woke slowly to the knowledge that she was not in her own bed. She lay still, her gaze moving over the dark blue bed hangings that had been pulled open to let in the warmth of the glowing fire.

Behind her in the deep recesses of the bed, she could hear deep even breathing.

Hawk.

He had rolled away from her, but one hand rested possessively on her bare stomach. Foggy images of herself being bathed and gowned, of having her hair combed and left to hang down her back, passed through her mind. Then her eyes opened wide as Kayln remembered the drugged wine, where she was, and why.

Why could she not have resisted? Hawk had said the potion would take away her will to do so. Was that why Kayln had nodded quietly in response to the questions put to her?

But somewhere inside her a voice was crying nay. Was this truly not what she wanted in her deepest heart of hearts, to belong to this man, to share her life with him? It was true that in her conscious mind she had fought against her feelings for Hawk, but she could not drive him out of that innermost core of her being.

As soon as the thought entered her mind, Kayln was overwhelmed by a sense of panic. She had to get away.

Carefully, praying that she would not wake him, Kayln slid

to the side of the bed and then onto the floor. She crouched there listening, but the rhythm of Hawk's breathing remained the same.

Crossing the room with swift silent steps, Kayln saw the clothing tossed over the back of the chair beside the fire. She did not bother with anything but the cotehardie, simply pulling it over her head and slipping into leather shoes. Her blue woolen cloak lay upon the chest against the wall, and she drew this around her shoulders.

Knowing speed was her only ally, Kayln made for the door, but paused as she took note of the roll of parchment on the table. Dimly she remembered signing something the night before. Acting on pure instinct, Kayln shoved the roll into her sleeve, then left the chamber.

She passed through the hall with held breath. Only when she had traversed the length of the room without waking any of the sleeping servants did she expel it.

Once outside, she headed directly for the stable.

Dawn was just spreading its pink light across the horizon as she crossed the courtyard. The air was crisp and helped her to calm down and reason more clearly. As she entered the stable, Kayln recalled something Hawk had said the previous night, something about Miles having been involved in a plot to kill him.

Was the man addled? It was incomprehensible that Miles would do such a thing. What could he possibly have to gain by such an act? What connection could there be between Miles and Hawk's missing goods, the attempts on his life?

But how was Hawk served by making up such a tale? Was it out of jealousy? He did not know she had broken off her association with the Lord of Harrow.

She paused, wishing she could better remember what Hawk had said. She knew that some details might be lost in haziness of her memory.

Should she go back to the castle and allow Hawk to explain more clearly even though what he said seemed impossible? It would mean giving up her chance for freedom, mayhap for nothing. Kayln bit her lip with indecision.

Then something occurred to her, something Miles had said the last time he came to Aimsley—something about Hawk being a pebble in his shoe. Was it possible that the words had meant more than she had thought? And that time when she had watched Miles and Harold come out of the forest together. Why had they lingered there so very long if Miles was only giving the steward directions? At the time she had not questioned, had been too occupied with worrying that Hawk might overtax himself with the work the steward had brought.

Putting her hands to her cheeks, she took a deep breath, uncertain as to what to do.

It was then that she became aware of a soft scuffling behind her. But before Kayln could turn to see the source of the noise, she felt a sharp flash of pain in her head.

Then nothing.

Chapter Nineteen

When Kayln opened her eyes, it was Miles's face she saw above her.

Though she had only been to the keep on a handful of occasions, Kayln recognized enough about the room behind him to know she was at Harrow. Shifting her position, she felt cold stone beneath her and realized she lay upon the floor. Confusion creased her brow.

Miles grinned. "You are awake at last."

Kayln was even more confused and surprised when he made no attempt to help her rise.

Miles turned to someone behind him. "You were very foolish to have hit her so hard, Harold. The babe must live if I am to see my ambitions fully realized."

Another face appeared above her. Kayln gasped in shock. It was the steward, Harold, here at Harrow. Hawk had been right.

Miles put a companionable arm around the other's shoulders, and leaned close to his ear. "I fear, my friend, that you have bungled for the last time. You have clearly become more of a liability than an asset." Just as Harold opened his mouth to protest, he gave a grunt of pain.

Kayln looked down to see Miles's knife protruding from Harold's belly. A man who seemed somehow familiar came forward to catch the steward's body when he fell backward. Harold was carried away. With shock, Kayln realized the man with the familiar face was Louis, the same one Miles had said he would dismiss so many months ago. Clearly he had not done so.

With dawning dread, Kayln tried to sit up, but the throbbing in her head forced her to lie still. Her mind worked furiously to grasp the significance of what was happening. "But why,

Miles? Why have you brought me here? Hawk tried to tell me something about you and his steward plotting against him and I wouldn't believe him. Obviously it must have been true, but why? What could you possibly hope to gain?"

He shrugged. "That should be most obvious. You."

She raised a weak hand to her forehead. "Me? Harming Hawk will not gain you me."

"Oh, but it will, my dear." He stared down at her with contempt, as if she were some insect he wished to crush. "Please, don't misunderstand. There are other reasons. Hawkhurst could not be allowed to come between me and his steward. I simply couldn't allow it. Harold had not paid me nearly enough of the money he owed me."

"You see, my dear Kayln, the steward did have a lust for gambling. Unfortunately, luck rarely smiled upon him. When Hawkhurst was away in France playing the hero for king and country, this was not a problem. Harold was ever able to pay his debts. When the baron returned . . ." Miles shrugged.

"But—"

He held up a hand. "No more questions now. I have other things to attend to first. We must make certain that your dear husband knows you are here." Miles swung away from her, obviously having said all he would at the moment. "Take her to my chambers."

Two men came forward, grasped her arms, and pulled her to her feet. Kayln cried out as a white-hot shaft of agony pierced her skull.

Kayln awakened some time later.

Immediately, she realized that at least she was lying upon a bed this time. Slowly, being careful not to jar her head, she sat up. Kayln was forced to hold very still until the pain eased somewhat, taking a deep breath to steady herself. She would have to think. It was her only hope of escaping this situation.

First she must try to determine how bad her head injury might be. Gingerly raising a hand to feel the back of her head, Kayln heard the rustle of parchment.

It was the document she had taken from Hawk's room.

Kayln removed it from her sleeve, but before she could

unroll it, the door opened. Hastily she lay back, tucking it into her cloak, which lay beneath her.

Miles strolled into the room. He came toward the bed and smiled when he saw she was awake. "Ahh, good, you are awake. How is your head?"

She answered hesitantly. "Better."

"Good, good. I had feared that fool might have caused you permanent injury, or at the very least injured the child." He studied her as if with genuine concern. "All is well in that respect?"

Kayln put a protective hand over her belly. "Yes, I believe so." Doubt assailed her, but she pushed it aside. Surely there would be some sign if something were wrong with the babe. Her lips firmed in determination. She would not allow anything to happen to the child.

Kayln turned to Miles with raised brows, some of her old self-assurance returning. "Why have you done this, Miles?"

His expression was pleasant. "I told you, Kayln. You."

She took a deep breath. "I am Hawk's wife."

His smile widened. "That I know, and that you carry his child. I will have you both."

"Hawk will come for us." She knew that Hawk would not rest with his child in jeopardy.

"Oh, most assuredly. And I am eager to welcome him. I shall have Hawkhurst completely within my power."

"How do you hope to attain that goal?" She was certain that Miles was underestimating his enemy. Hawk would not be so easily overcome.

"Your Hawk will never attack this keep with you inside. He would not risk injury to you and the little fledgling." Miles fussed with the curls on his forehead, laughing at the pun.

What he said was true. Hawk would not endanger his child. Anger and growing fear that Miles might actually prevail made her incautious. "You have no right."

Miles answered her rage in kind. "I have every right. You tried to take from me what was mine. Because you attempted to give my rightful belongings to Hawkhurst, it is only fair that I should have his. I did not ask you to marry him, Kayln. In fact, I did my utmost to prevent it. You are the one who has made Hawk's death a necessity."

She could only stare at him in astonishment. "How has my marrying him taken anything that is yours?"

In control again, Miles settled into a chair, his tone casually reasoning. "All that you hold is mine, and I cannot allow you to take what is mine to any other man."

"You speak in riddles. I do not understand."

He faced her directly, and to her surprise Kayln thought she saw a glimmer of tears in his eyes. "Raymond! If you would but open your eyes you would see, woman. Raymond is the link. You must pass on what was his to me. Because this world does not understand a love such as ours was, I may only have what is rightfully mine through you."

In a bright flash of insight, things suddenly became very clear to Kayln. How could she have been so blind?

But Miles seemed not to notice or even care that she had realized what he was trying to tell her. It was as if once he had begun to speak the words he'd held back for so long, they could not be halted.

"The first time I saw him he was sitting atop a horse. It was a bright autumn day and he was laughing. I was seventeen and Raymond twenty-five and so full of life. I never thought he would notice me. But he did, and for ten wonderful years we had as near to a marriage as this cruel world is wont to give.

"But then came you, my dear Kayln. Raymond had reached the age of thirty-five and knew he must produce an heir. He met your father, I know not how, and a deal was struck." Miles smiled coldly. "Oh, what a demon he was, your father. He knew what Raymond was, and seemed to gain great amusement from giving you to him. Raymond did feel sympathy for you, and he tried to be a husband to you. He once told me that if you had been other than what you are, he might have been able to do what he must and get you with child. But he could not, you see. You, Kayln, are all that is womanly, with your full breasts and flaring hips. Raymond could not but feel repulsed by you.

"He had to come back to me. We"—he hit his chest with a clenched fist—"Raymond and I had the true marriage. You were nothing more than a duty. If the world was a just place, I should be the one to have all that was my love's. It is what he wished for. Why should Hawkhurst ride across Raymond's lands, hold Raymond's belongings in his hands? They are nothing to him, and all to me.'' Miles's face was a mask of misery. ''When Raymond died, I thought I would too. He was my life.'' He sobbed aloud. ''I shall care for his lands as he would.''

Despite all that he had done, Kayln wanted to reach out to Miles. She understood now what it was to truly love another. Before she could speak to offer comfort, to convince him that what he was doing now would solve nothing, he went on.

''With Hawkhurst dead and you married to me, I could avenge his very presumption. I would hold not only Raymond's lands, I would also become the guardian of the heir to the Hawkhurst possessions.'' He raised his hands to emphasize the logic of his thinking. ''In that way I am doubly recompensed for all the years of waiting. I will be vindicated for all the times I swallowed my pride and accepted your verbal slights, for all the insults to my manhood.''

Kayln's sympathy drained from her like wine from an overturned cup. She felt sickened to know that Miles could carry out such evil. It also hurt to know he had pretended to be her friend. Only a few short months ago she would have trusted him with her very life.

What a complete and utter fool she had been concerning the knight. Realizing that drove her thoughts in another direction. If her perceptions about Miles had been wrong, then could not the same be true of Hawk?

Mayhap she had been wrong to fear loving him?

It was true that he had kidnapped her and married her against her will. But she had refused his every effort to speak to her. She knew how much his child meant to him, how seriously he viewed the duties of being a father. What right had she to rob him of that? And he had been correct about Miles and Harold. Hawk had been trying to protect her, and had finally told her what was going on there. She realized that this was a clear sign that he was beginning to understand that she could be trusted to know what was happening. Mayhap he had done wrong in their relationship, but she was not entirely blameless either.

Was it possible that they could have worked out their differences, that she could have made him understand how much her need for self-government meant to her if she had tried? He had said he was not like her father. In myriad ways she had seen the evidence that he spoke true.

Others saw that he was a good man: Celia, Alice, the Earl of Norwich. He was loved and respected by many. Only she had seen the ignoble in him. Oh, she was not trying to convince herself he was perfect. Hawk was arrogant and domineering and impatient. But he was also intelligent, loving, kind, and loyal to a fault.

Quite unlike the treacherous Miles.

Running away from Hawk had solved nothing. She had endangered not only herself and her child, but also the man she loved. She was jolted out of her self-recrimination by a pounding upon the door.

A man called out. "My lord, he is arrived."

Miles's eyes took on a gleam of satisfaction. "Your lord husband must have already been on his way. There has been no time for my message to reach him. At long last I will attain what is rightfully mine."

Kayln started up from the bed. "No, Miles, please. The marriage can be annulled. I would wed you willingly if only to save my lord's life." Ordinarily, Kayln would not fear for Hawk in a contest of strength against Miles. But her husband was walking into a trap, and Miles had admitted he would use her and the babe to spring that trap.

"The time for such action is past. I will have all now." He took her by the arm and pulled her to her feet. "Let us commence the game."

As he drew her through the courtyard, Kayln saw that Harrow had been made ready as if for a siege.

Miles's soldiers, many in mail and helmet, stood about the grounds and along the battlements. Spears, bows, and swords stood at the ready. Huge vats of hot pitch, which could be poured on the army below, sat over slow-burning fires. No animals, women, or children could be seen.

From the battlements, Kayln studied Hawk's army below, an unmistakable sense of pride mingled with her concern for him. Her husband's strength, which had been such a source of irritation, was also one of his greatest assets.

His silver armor shone bright in the early morning light. His men ranged out behind him, mounted knights grouped closely about, hundreds of foot soldiers with spears, bows, maces, and shields surrounding them. All were ready to follow their lord with unquestioning loyalty. Even to rescue his recalcitrant bride.

But Kayln knew Hawk's very sense of power could be his undoing this day. If he had been other than what he was, he might have come at Miles with subterfuge and therefore beaten the man at his own game. Hawk was not capable of serpentine thinking.

As she looked down at her husband, Kayln knew she would not have him any other way. Other than when he had kidnapped her, which she now realized he had only done out of the direst need, Hawk had always been straightforward and honest even when he made mistakes. He'd never pretended to love her when he did not. And though the knowledge that he didn't care for her as she did him hurt, she loved him for his honesty. Loved him with all her heart.

Miles pushed Kayln to the fore. Her heart throbbed as Hawk rose up in the saddle to shake a threatening fist. "Death is sitting upon your cowardly shoulders, Harrow. And he's smiling."

Miles yawned, resting a nonchalant hand on his hip. "Would you care to wager all you hold dear upon that thought, my Lord Hawkhurst?"

Hawk gave a growl of rage. "You have already done that for me, my lord charlatan. Had I the choice, I would decline. I prefer to game against men of honor."

Kayln noted that Miles's jaw tightened momentarily at the remark, but he soon regained his composure. With a swift and unexpected motion, he reached for Kayln, taking his knife from his belt. He brought the weapon to her throat, his other hand catching in her hair and pulling back her head to expose the soft white flesh.

Surprise and pain wrested a cry from her.

"I will not hesitate to kill her," Miles screamed.

"Bastard!" Hawk roared.

A volley of arrows from the ground accompanied the curse.

Miles held Kayln before him, using her body as a shield. "Call them off, Hawkhurst."

Hawk swung around. "Hold, you fools. I will personally kill the man who harms her."

Kayln wanted to tell Hawk that Miles had no intention of killing her, but his hold was too firm and her head was tilted too far back to allow her to form intelligible sounds.

Miles's next words showed that he had grown impatient. "I want *you,* Hawkhurst. You will give yourself up without a struggle. Your men will not interfere. If you do not follow my instructions, Kayln dies." The knife pricked, and Kayln felt a trickle of wetness run down her throat.

Hawk made no verbal reply. Slowly, he spurred his horse toward the keep. The counterweight dropped as the guard at the gate tripped the cog and the drawbridge lowered to admit the horse and rider.

A few short moments later, Kayln had been dragged from the top of the tower to stand in the courtyard as an uncooperative Hawk was pulled from his horse and bound. Miles kept his hold on her until Hawk was safely secured.

As soon as Miles loosened his arm, Kayln rushed toward the silent Hawk.

Miles reached out and caught her. "Halt."

But he could not stop her from speaking. "Hawk, he would not have harmed me. He means to marry me and through the child to have your lands as well as mine."

Hawk looked at her then, his golden eyes narrow with betrayal. "Congratulations to you both. It seems I have been duped. I thank you, madame, for telling me, as now I will die without fearing for your safety."

It took Kayln a moment to understand why he seemed angered at her. Then comprehension dawned.

Hawk believed she was in league with Miles. For a moment she felt a shaft of white-hot rage. But it was gone just as quickly, to be replaced by guilt. How could she blame Hawk for thinking such a thing? Hadn't she given him cause?

Miles laughed, pulling Kayln close against his side, obviously enjoying the idea of making Hawk believe she had betrayed him. "I am sorry, my lord, but would you expect otherwise? Kayln and I have been close for a very long time.

Of course her first allegiance would be to me."

Hawk strained against his bonds, groaning in an agony of fury.

Kayln knew she had to do something. Miles would not give her an opportunity to explain the true situation, even though he meant to kill Hawk regardless.

Her hand brushed against the knife in Miles's belt, and without stopping to consider, Kayln wrenched it free. Quickly she pulled away from him at the same time.

As Miles started for her, she held the knife to her own breast. "I will kill myself. I will. Don't doubt it. And if I do, all will be lost to you. You shall not get Clamdon and neither will you have Aimsley. For even if you lied and said we had been wed, the properties would go to Celia. It is part of her marriage settlement that anything of mine goes to her in the event that I die without issue. You are to tell Hawk the truth and release him. If you do that, I will marry you, and only if you do that."

The Lord of Harrow frowned in annoyance. "Now, Kayln, don't be ridiculous. Give me that knife."

She backed away from him, being careful to make sure that no one surprised her from behind. "Tell him the truth."

Sighing, Miles shrugged. "I yield. But I see nothing to be gained by it. These heroics will not prevent me from having what I want." He turned to Hawk. "What the lady says is true. She knew nothing of what I was doing. Your steward brought her here against her will."

Trying to pass her still-scowling husband a message with her eyes, Kayln moved closer to him, the knife held to her chest. She knew she had to act to regain his trust, to redeem herself for getting them into this situation.

But all of Hawk's attention was centered on the other man, his eyes chilled with frost. "And where is Harold? He will pay for plotting against me and mine."

Miles grinned. "I regret that you will not be able to carry out that threat. I have been forced to kill Harold. You see, he had been careless in his treatment of Kayln. Besides, the man had quite outlived his usefulness."

As if only just realizing that Kayln was edging closer to her husband, Miles swung around to glare at her. "That is quite close enough, my dear."

Kayln faced him without blinking. "Mayhap you are correct. It would be best if one of your men cut his ropes. That way I will not be distracted while doing it myself. You see, I want Hawk released now." She shrugged when Miles's brows rose with skepticism. "Methinks you do not believe I will really harm myself. You do not understand that I do not care for my life if my husband should die. It has no value for me." She met his challenging gaze without flinching.

Hawk broke in, his voice edged with command. "No, Kayln. I will see to my own release. You will do nothing."

She didn't even look at him, but at Miles, who had taken an unconscious step backward at the power of Hawk's order. She said, "I think you both know that I will not do as I am told. Now release him."

There was a long moment in which the silence bound the whole assemblage in one tight knot of anxiety. Finally, Miles nodded to one of his soldiers. The man hesitated, then moved forward to cut Hawk's bonds.

Hawk brought his hands to the front, flexing his stiffened shoulders. The heavy armor did not seem to encumber him as he studied his adversary.

Miles turned slightly, seeming uncomfortable with the scrutiny. Loudly he issued another order. "Set him out the side passage, so it will not be necessary to lower the drawbridge."

Just as the man took a step toward him, Hawk acted. He fell upon Miles before anyone could even think to prevent him.

Kayln stood there stunned for a moment as soldiers came running from every direction, though they knew not what to do. They did not wish to harm their master, who grappled with his attacker. Who would have thought Hawk would behave so brazenly, surrounded as he was by Miles's men? His armor precluded free motion, but it also deflected blows.

If only Hawk had the support of his own soldiers, Kayln thought desperately.

It was then that Kayln knew what she had to do. It was their only chance. She would have to rely upon Hawk's strength to see him through until she could get help.

Intent on trying to get a clear opportunity at Hawk without harming Miles, the men failed to notice Kayln as she raced across the courtyard. Going to a vat of pitch that had been prepared for the siege, Kayln grabbed up one of the arrows which rested close by. It was indeed the type she needed. A ball containing pitch rimmed the sharp head. Catching up a longbow, she touched the arrow to the fire burning beneath the vat of pitch, then fitted it to the bow. She drew the string back and took careful aim on the rope that bore the counterweight for the drawbridge, held her breath, then let fly. Her heart ceased to beat as it sailed through air.

The arrow struck true.

By this time someone had taken note of her intent. Strong hands grasped her shoulders. But it was too late. The hot pitch was doing its work. The rope was visibly fraying.

An exultant cry went up from without the castle walls as the rope parted and the drawbridge came down.

Gasping in triumph, Kayln swung around anxiously to see if she had acted quickly enough to save her husband's life. Before she could focus on the spot where Hawk and Miles had been, a stinging blow landed upon her cheek, knocking her head backward.

As she righted herself, she felt like sobbing her despair aloud to see Miles before her. "You whore! Look what you've done!" He looked down at her, his eyes burning bright with hatred. "Take her to the hall and hold her!"

Then he turned and called out, "To arms!" though the words were superfluous, as his men were already engaged in defending the keep.

Hawk's soldiers had poured into the grounds, and the battle had been set upon so hard that she could hardly tell one army from the other. Everywhere about the courtyard, men grappled with swords, morning stars, and other weapons.

The man who clasped her arms gave a vicious tug as he drew her across the courtyard. Kayln resisted him, trying to find Hawk amongst the fracas. But her strength was no match for the burly soldier, and he simply picked her up and slung her over his shoulder.

The wait was interminable. Kayln suffered a thousand deaths in not knowing whether Hawk lived.

When Miles finally appeared again, she almost felt a sense of relief. At least now she might learn something of Hawk. She hurried forward as Miles came up to them, running a hand through his filth-caked hair. She noted that there were several rends in his velvet tunic and many patches of dried blood. "Does he live?" she asked.

"I pray not, my lady slattern. Though I am beginning to believe that the Devil does indeed see to his own, and that would give your husband considerable advantage."

Hope surged inside her at knowing this much at least. At least Hawk had not died in his struggle with Miles.

He grabbed Kayln by the arm. "The battle is lost. You and I will not be staying for the end, and so may not know of my Lord Hawkhurst's much-desired demise."

She struggled against him. "No." Surely if there was a God in heaven, he would not let Miles take her now.

Beyond Miles's shoulder, she heard a beloved voice call out, "Take your hands from my wife."

Relief washed over her like a cool, sweet rain. Alive. Oh, Blessed Savior, Hawk was alive.

She strained around Miles, trying to see him, needing to know he was all right. Hawk still wore his armor, but it was no longer shining. It was caked with dirt, blood, and sweat. Yet other than a narrow gash on his forehead, her beloved seemed to have suffered nothing ill. He passed his sword from his left hand to his right as he moved across the room. No one tried to halt him.

Looking into his eyes, Kayln knew why. The golden orbs were fixed on Miles with a hatred so intense that it made her shiver.

Miles pushed Kayln away from him, drawing his own sword as he made ready for his opponent. "You, Hawkhurst, have brought me nothing but calamity from the moment you returned to England. Now is the time to even the score."

Hawk didn't deign to reply. With a growl of rage he raised his sword and brought it down. Miles would have lost his life in that very moment had he not jumped to defend himself.

As the two men fought, Kayln backed to the wall.

From the beginning there was little doubt of the outcome. Hawk gave no quarter, not even when Miles's eyes grew round with fear as he strove desperately to save himself.

Hawk simply waited for his opponent to make a mistake, then struck. His sword bit deeply, and Miles crumpled to his knees. Hawk jerked his weapon free and stepped back.

Just as Miles toppled forward, he reached out one hand and murmured, "Raymond." Then he lay still.

For a moment no one moved.

As if released from invisible bonds, Kayln rushed forward. She leapt into the arms Hawk opened wide for her, his sword clattering upon the floor, forgotten.

He held her so tightly she felt as if her bones might break, but Kayln only sought to burrow even closer. His armor precluded the kind of nearness she desired and needed, so she raised her lips to press joyful kisses to his chin.

Hawk pushed her away, his gaze raking her face. "All is well with you? You are not hurt?"

"No," she answered. "And you?"

"Fine, now that I have seen you safe." Hawk held her face in his hands, his golden eyes filled with overwhelming relief and tenderness.

Kayln gazed up at him. At long last she would be able to tell him all that was in her heart. That she was willing to be a wife to him.

But what Hawk did next halted her before the words were spoken.

Gently and with obvious regret, he set her from him. "I have something that I must say to you, though it breaks my heart to do so. Kayln, I have wronged you. In thought and deed I have not shown you the respect you deserved. This very day you acted with bravery and intelligence to save not only my life and yours, but the life of our child. I had no right to marry you against your will, and now know that I must release you. I told myself that I was acting out of a desire to protect and defend you, but I was not. I took you because I could not bear being without you. And that was wrong. More wrong than I can say."

Kayln shook her head. She was gladdened to hear these things, but she had to make Hawk see she understood and that she wanted him now. "Please," she said. "I must tell you that I do not wish to be released. I want to be with you."

Hawk gazed down at her in surprise. Then slowly, he shook his head, his face growing sad. "You have read the marriage contract. A few short days ago I would have been ready to settle for this. But not anymore. Ironically, the very qualities I best love about you are the ones that most frightened me. I now know that I must have all of you, your spirit, your courage, and your self-reliance. If you cannot come to me with a whole heart, then it will only bring us each more pain."

Marriage contract? She didn't know what he was talking about. But she didn't want to worry about that now. Heavens above, he'd just said he loved her. What could be as important as that? She needed to tell him how much that meant to her and that she truly loved him. Her mind stumbled, searching for the correct phrases.

She did not know what to say. For too long Kayln's feelings had been bottled up inside her. Now, when it was so important to make Hawk understand that she wanted to give him all, her little-used tongue would not cooperate. She knew not how to express the words that would make him understand that she was ready to believe in him—in them.

Before she knew what was happening, Hawk stepped back from her. He motioned to a group of heavily armed soldiers who stood in the doorway of the hall. "You will please escort my lady to Aimsley and without delay."

With that he turned and walked away. Only the emptiness in his eyes gave away how he felt.

Kayln could only stand there in stunned silence. Once again she had not been able to give of herself, had been held back by the many years of protecting herself from possible hurt. All of her thoughts and feelings regarding Hawk had remained unspoken and thus unknown.

As the men moved to flank her, one of them said, "We have a horse ready in the courtyard, my lady."

Kayln looked up at him in confusion, rubbing her chill arms. "I . . . yes, of course. But I must fetch my cloak."

The soldier insisted on accompanying her for her safety. It wasn't until Kayln picked up the cloak and the roll of parchment fell to the floor that she remembered what Hawk had said about the marriage contract.

Completely disregarding the other's presence, Kayln read

the document. As she did so, she sank down on the bed.

Never before had she heard of such a thing. Not only had Hawk left her lands in her name, but she was to have sole say in the disposal of those lands. Kayln and Kayln alone was to have the right to decide even the smallest matter on her properties.

She stood. "I must see Lord Hawkhurst."

The man cleared his throat, his cheeks reddening beneath the battle dirt. "Forgive me, my lady. But we are to see you safe at Aimsley and without delay. My Lord Hawkhurst has said we would be dismissed if we deviate in any way from his orders."

"I see." She raised her chin high. Kayln would not argue further. She needed to think, and Aimsley would be the best place to do that.

As the five heavily laden wagons entered the gates of Clamdon, people came out of their homes and workplaces to stare. The conveyances easily held enough goods for an entire household. A number of serfs and men-at-arms walked or rode alongside.

At the head of the column, Kayln sat atop a snow-white mare. She was attired in the gown she had once worn for Hawk, the one that displayed his hawk device so very beautifully. Over the course of the past six days, while she had arranged for her household goods to be packed and loaded for transport to Clamdon, she'd thought only of her husband and her need to make him see that she did love him.

Only now did she begin to feel unsure as she looked about her at the gathering throng. But there was nothing in Kayln's outward appearance to mark the dread of Hawk's possible rejection that made her heart race and her throat burn.

The crowd around them thickened, the expressions on the people's faces not wholly welcoming. It seemed the good folk of Clamdon knew of the troubles between Kayln and their master, though they likely did not fully understand them.

Despite their cautious expressions, Kayln held her head high. What she did this day could very well mark her entire future for good or ill.

By the time they reached the inner gates of the castle, Kayln felt as if she would surely be sick. Her hands on the reins were cold and damp, but she forced herself to go on, refusing to give in to the fear inside her.

Even if Hawk rejected her now, Kayln would know she had indeed done all she could to make him see how much she loved him.

When her mount came to a halt, Kayln looked up in surprise. She had been so intent on her thoughts, she hadn't noticed the size of the crowd in the courtyard outside the inner keep was such that she could go no further. She looked up to see Hawk at the fore. It was near her undoing to see him standing there, sunlight shining on his ebony hair, looking tall and powerful in his black velvet cote. There was no way to gauge his thoughts, for his face was devoid of any expression as he watched her.

What would she do if he turned her away? Panic nearly kept Kayln on her horse.

But she closed her eyes and took a deep breath to calm herself. Kayln had considered her actions this day as none before in her life, and knew them to be right. Somehow, loving Hawk had helped her to open a pathway to her inner strength, and she meant to use it to make her life whole.

She would make Hawk see that she was now ready to trust in him, completely and irrevocably. Peace settled on her like a warm cloak. Slowly, but deliberately, Kayln dismounted.

Hawk moved toward her, his face now clouded with confusion and uncertainty. She wanted to run into his arms, but stopped herself. This must be done properly.

When Hawk halted before her, Kayln removed the marriage contract from her sleeve. Holding it high so that all could see, she looked into her husband's eyes. Deliberately, she tore it in half and dropped the pieces to the ground.

Then, before Hawk could speak, she sank to the dense carpet of sweet-smelling grass in a formal curtsy, holding one hand toward him in supplication, her voice ringing clear and true as she spoke. "My dear and most beloved lord, do you but want me, my hand, my heart, and all that I possess are yours, now and for all the days that I shall walk upon this earth."

She did not know what she had thought Hawk would do,

but when he sank down on his knees before her, Kayln's heart knew a rising song of joy. He clasped her hand in his two strong ones. "Do I but want you? My love, I want nothing else."

He frowned, his gaze searching as he spoke for her ears alone. "But are you sure that this is what you want, Kayln? I can only be myself. Though I am sorry for having married you against your will and would not do so again, I cannot promise that I will never give orders without thinking or that I will never do any other thing that might anger you. You see, I have come to understand that love is not hearts and pretty verses. Love is an ache inside you that is agony one moment and joy beyond heaven the next. It is an all-consuming need to give yourself to another and an equal need to take from that other. It does not, unfortunately, cleanse one of all faults, or I should have become perfect from the day I fell in love with you. You must accept the truth of this if we are ever to know any happiness, Kayln. I ask again, is this truly what you desire for yourself?"

She returned his gaze without wavering. Over the course of the last few months, she'd come to understand herself and others as never before. For the first time in her life she did know what she wanted, who she wanted, had found the strength to give of herself and her heart freely. No matter his imperfections, Hawk was a man on whom she could depend, and she now felt secure enough to do so.

With all the love that filled her breast shining in her eyes, Kayln held out her arms. "Yes, my Hawk, yes."

With that he drew her into his arms, holding Kayln close to his wildly beating heart as if he would never let her go.

Around them a cry of exaltation went up. The lovers looked up to see men and women alike wiping from their eyes tears of happiness.

"I love you," Hawk told her as he stood, drawing her up with him. He surprised her by placing one arm behind her back and the other beneath her knees in order to lift her high against his chest.

"And I you," she cried, her gaze lustrous with the depth of her joy.

Then, as Hawk moved with her across the courtyard, his

eyes took on a gleam of amusement. He whispered softly, the words for her alone, ''That was a very pretty gesture with the marriage contract.'' He bent closer, his lips touching her ear and sending hot shivers of desire through Kayln. ''I just want you to know that there is a copy.''

She pushed away from him with a frown. ''But I meant it, Hawk. I have no fear of you now.''

He hushed her with his lips. ''And I have no fear of you. I do not wish to bind you to me with contracts and oaths. Unless my lady's love and loyalty are freely given in the years ahead, they mean nothing.''

As he carried her to his chamber and his bed, she kissed him. ''They are freely given—will always be.''

And they were. For she was *his* lady.